THE
XENO
SOLUTION

THE
XENO
SOLUTION

NELSON
ERLICK

FORGE®

A TOM DOHERTY ASSOCIATES BOOK
NEW YORK

This is a work of fiction. All the characters and events portrayed in this book are either products of the author's imagination or are used fictitiously.

THE XENO SOLUTION

A Forge Book
Published by Tom Doherty Associates, LLC
175 Fifth Avenue
New York, NY 10010

www.tor.com

Forge® is a registered trademark of Tom Doherty Associates, LLC.

ISBN 0-765-34971-X
EAN 978-0-765-34971-2

First edition: October 2005

Printed in the United States of America

0 9 8 7 6 5 4 3 2 1

For my father, Milton,
Silver Star and Bronze Star recipient who never
allowed the loss of his arm to hamper his abilities
and
For my mother, Estelle,
who served with strength and love as both a mother
and father for these many years since his death

ACKNOWLEDGMENTS

My unending gratitude for *The Xeno Solution* extends to:

My editor, Natalia Aponte, who continues to exhibit patience and provide needed insights; to my assistant editor, Paul Stevens, who has always cheerfully answered my often frantic questions; and to Tom Doherty, for his continued confidence in me.

My agent, Susan Crawford, who continues to encourage, support, and guide me through this often arduous process that is the modern world of publishing.

My number one editor, my wife Cheryl, without whose editing skills my works would probably wind up filed in an old banker box beneath the basement stairs.

My children, Rayna and Melissa, for their understanding and relinquishing time with me that can never be replaced.

My in-laws, Solomon and Elaine, for their support over twenty years.

The researchers and scientists whose published works provided the scientific foundation for *The Xeno Solution*.

Anyone who, willingly or not, provided any bit of knowledge or insight for this novel.

And to Rachel, who so graciously shared her thoughts, her experiences, her fears, and her strengths—far beyond the clinical symptoms—about multiple sclerosis.

ONE

How could she be dead? She was perfectly healthy, Dr. Scott Merritt wondered, gazing at the woman laying on the operating room table and covered with crisp blue surgical drapes. The scalpel handle with number ten surgical blade resting comfortably between the thumb and forefinger of his surgical-gloved hand was fresh, gleaming, and had obviously never been used. *I haven't even touched her!* Yet, unmistakably, there lay his patient, her gray hair tucked neatly beneath a flowered surgical cap, her late sixtyish softly wrinkled face, clay-like, her dark brown eyes staring lifelessly. "Dan, what just happened to my patient?" Scott called out through his surgical mask to the anesthesiologist.

Traces of his voice bouncing off the O.R.'s tiled walls answered him.

"Dan?" Dr. Merritt looked up from the woman's face to the anesthesiology station behind the head of the table. The anesthesia machine was there—turned off and with no anesthesiologist. Had Dan abandoned his post—an unforgivable breach of protocol, the kind that make malpractice attorneys salivate?

His long surgical gown swishing, Dr. Merritt stepped around the supine woman, and banged his thigh into the corner of a low, long green-draped table that jingled with the impact.

"Oww! Nurse, move that instrument table! It doesn't belong there!" He surveyed the table's wide array of neatly-laid surgical instruments: there were dozens of differently sized and shaped forceps, hemostats, hand-held and self-retaining retractors, various Metzenbaum and operating scissors, needle holders, and blade handles. But there were also at least forty other instruments that Dr. Merritt hadn't ordered; some he didn't recognize. He did not see the ball and shaft prosthetic shaped like a cockeyed ice cream cone that was supposed to be soaking in a basin of sterile solution, ready for the hip implantation. Dr. Merritt scrutinized the contents of the table, using his finger as a laser-pointer. *Where's my bone cutters and rongeurs: My bone curettes? My osteotomes, chisels and bone mallets? My bone files and rasps?* "Nurse, what is this? It sure as hell isn't an orthopedic tray! And where is Mrs. Thornton's implant? We were supposed to do a hip replacement this morning!"

Dr. Merritt looked up from the instrument table. There was no nurse attending it. Something flickered just in the corner of his right eye.

He whirled around: alongside the patient was a separate, braced metal table, with IV poles on two corners. On top of the metal table, a compact box hummed. Two long, ribbed plastic tubes extruded from the box. Dr. Merritt immediately recognized it, though as a general orthopedic surgeon, he'd never needed one: a pump-oxygenator, more commonly known as a heart-lung bypass machine. Used to temporarily take the place of the heart during open heart surgeries or transplants, it replaced the heart's pumping action and transferred critically needed oxygen to the lungs.

Am I in the wrong surgical suite? No, that machine wasn't here a moment ago. And where's the tech who's supposed to monitor it? Gazing around the O.R. *For that matter, where is everybody?*

Surgical Suite #7 was deserted, except for the patient. The room itself felt—altered: a bit more spacious, the green tiling slightly brighter, the suction outlet on the wall to the right side of the anesthesia machine instead of the left. He glanced behind him toward the sign of O.R. #7 over the doorway. It wasn't there.

Scott wanted to turn and leave, but his eyes fell on the pair of tubes that led from the heart-lung bypass machine onto the surgical table and into a square opening in the blue drapes over the patient's chest. That wasn't there before. How could this possibly be his patient? Tasting sweat dripping from his upper lip under his mask, he shuffled forward, following the tubes to the skin, rustic brown from the mixing of iodophor scrub and incidental blood, peeking through the blue drapes. Crinkling his nose to make certain his mask was secure, he peered into the surgical well, a clean-bordered cavity in the patient's chest.

The cavity was empty. The patient's heart was gone, neatly excised, except for the back walls of the heart's upper chambers. The tubes, one draining blue, spent blood from the patient and the other, returning red oxygenated blood, continued working flawlessly on the corpse. It was as if the surgical team had excised her heart, but had decided not to transplant the replacement. *Unbelievable, unconscionable to leave a patient like this!*

"This is Dr. Merritt. Somebody get in here! And I mean *right now!*"

No one came. Unwilling to leave a patient alone—even a dead one—under such abhorrent circumstances, Scott would not leave. He glanced at the woman's lifeless eyes. They were dull green now, her face far smoother, and her mouth and nose more petite. She wasn't his patient. He didn't recognize her.

Behind him, something dropped onto the floor. He jumped.

After a long deep semi-calming breath, Dr. Merritt slowly turned around. Behind him was an sturdy, plastic transport chest, its latches undone. Guessing but uncertain of the contents, he squatted down and gently lifted the lid. Waves of cold, pungent fog made his skin blanch, his nose crinkle, his eyes water. The cold vapor veil dissipated, revealing the contents of a small clear container surrounded by dry ice: a perfectly preserved heart maintained with cold solution, and still pulsing. *Why didn't they transplant it? The donor heart looks viable and*, glancing at the heart-lung machine, *that's still working. Why did they stop?* Condensation around the plastic storage container cleared. The heart inside looked functional enough, but odd—not like any drawing in *Gray's Anatomy* or any patient he'd seen.

He closed the lid.

On the floor beside him lay a scrub nurse. A moment ago, she had not been there. He knelt and checked her carotid pulse. Even through surgeon's gloves, she was cold to the touch. Young, attractive, with a pleasantly-angular face, she'd apparently died in agony. As he stood, the rest of the surgical team appeared—the anesthesiologist, surgical and scrub nurses, techs, residents—none of whom he recognized—laying on the floor, curled in fetal positions.

He moved from victim to victim, screaming in between for help. All were dead.

He ran out of the O.R., and stopped. Doctors, nurses, support staff—none of their faces familiar—lay curled in balls on the surgicenter floor, except for one elderly doctor hanging over a scrub basin, water pouring into his open, lifeless mouth. He checked two of the dozens fallen: dead like the others.

Scott tried to slow his breathing, to slow his perception of time so he could act rationally, responsibly. He strode through the surgicenter, keeping himself gowned, gloved, and masked, fearful that it was all that kept him alive. The double doors opened.

Bodies on gurneys, in wheelchairs, and slumped on floors

filled the corridor. Fighting dizziness, he listened for faint groans, shallow breaths, looked for any movement as he tread slowly over the unburied dead. He found none.

He ducked into a stairwell, taking the stairs down two at a time. Four flights down, he tumbled over a man who'd died with his arm locked around the railing. Bruised, his paper surgical gown torn, he ripped it away, and continued rushing down the stairs.

The grand hospital lobby was a morgue, congested by people who'd streamed in, desperately seeking help. He could not reach the entrance without stepping on twisted torsos.

Collections of dead drivers, their cars smashed or hopelessly snarled, filled city streets stretching to every horizon. Weaving his way between them, sometimes sliding over their hoods, he ran toward his house, his wife and children miles away.

His feet no longer touched the ground. He could see the hospital, the entire street from the air. Higher, higher—he was flying. Looking back, he could see the entire city, dead. The world spun below him. He could see the cities of Europe, south Asia, the orient, their lights fading—their peoples dead.

"Doctor, are you all right?"

Scott blinked. A gowned and gloved surgical nurse stood to his left. Below him, his patient, Mrs. Thornton, lay on the operating room table, the surgical site on her hip prepped and ready. Another nurse wiped his perspiring forehead. He nodded slowly to the surgical nurse who placed a scalpel handle with shining number ten blade neatly between his thumb and forefinger.

His head pounded. He started seeing double. The side of his face began to burn. The room blurred. Numbness consumed his legs. Feeling weak, he braced himself on the table. His scalpel fell to the floor. His right eye went blind.

FOUR YEARS LATER

If the thunder is not loud, the peasant forgets to cross himself.

—A PROVERB

TUESDAY, FEBRUARY 1

TWO

TUESDAY, FEBRUARY 1

Cranbury, New Jersey   9:03 P.M.

Evelyn Cruz tried to immerse herself in his kiss. She needed his excited tongue in her mouth to dissolve the guilt of her terrible blunder—a blunder that had killed the only man she'd ever loved. Part of her envied her dead lover: he was now free of the festering secret. How many had died before their time? They might have succumbed anyway, but if she remained silent, how many more might follow? Evelyn wanted it to stop, but she also wanted to live. The only way to do both depended on the man beside her in the backseat of the car.

His hand reached beneath her cashmere sweater, beneath her bra. By pale streetlight, she gazed at him: dark gray suit, silk tie, ginger hair, gleaming white teeth. His fingers began drawing smooth, concentric circles around her nipples. He released a deep, longing breath. Moist air condensed on the car's rear passenger window. Entombed within fogged glass, she glanced at horizontal rain battering the windows of his black coupe. Wind-driven droplets merged into rivulets descending into the car door's rubber weather-stripping. Slowly, his hand reached down, delving deep beneath her skirt.

Head tilting against the damp glass, she permitted herself just an instant of pleasure: *he* had so often touched her that perfect way. "That's right. Ye—ess, Jim!"

He withdrew his hand. "I'm *Dylan*, not Jim. I'm sorry Evelyn—but James Todd is dead."

She huddled against the car door, her arms clasped across her double-breasted overcoat, her face toward the window. The face that stared back was caramel-complexioned with high sloping cheeks and wide tawny eyes with long, thick lashes, framed by shoulder-length cinnamon hair. Long, diamond-drop earrings flashed with the same sparkle as when she'd taken them from the gift-wrapped box in Jim's hand, held them to her ears, and gazed at their reflection in the window of his Maserati—except that she had been five years younger and mascara tears weren't flowing down her cheeks. It had been a mistake to accept such an expensive gift from a married man. Her last mistake had cost him far more than a pair of diamond earrings.

Dylan Rogers stroked her hair. "I know it's been over between you two for some time, but his death was still a terrible shock."

She closed her eyes, trying to erase an image of Jim slumped over the wheel of his Maserati, quietly choking on fumes. She placed a finger over Dylan's lips. "Take me home."

"Can't convince you to come back to my place in Philly?" As she started to scowl, he kissed her cheek, climbed over the emergency brake, plopped into the front seat, and started the engine. "You cold?"

"I could use some warmth."

Peering through narrow swaths cut by wiper blades creaking across the windshield, Dylan drove three miles through unlit back roads. Hard rain changed to mist. Fog enclosed them.

"Are you seeing Merritt tomorrow?" she asked.

"I've a meeting with him in the afternoon. Why?"

"No reason." She added, "I'm flying to Boston in the morning."

"The Piggy Bank give you time off?"

"You know how it irks me when you use that term."

Yellow street lamps amplified the fog. He nearly overshot the right turn at the second stop sign. "Evelyn, I was thinking. I have a few personal days—"

"It'll be awkward enough with just me at the funeral—me being the *other* woman."

The car crept down a row of three-story colonial-style brick townhouses and pulled in front of the large one on the end. Dylan got out, walked behind the trunk, and opened the rear door for her. Evelyn glanced at her front walk and gasped, pointing at garbage scattered around slashed, green trash bags. "Someone's been here."

He inspected the bags, gingerly shifting them with his foot. "Looks like a raccoon ripped them," he said, pointing to slits in the plastic with his shoe.

"Leave the trash. I'll take care of it in the morning," Evelyn said. She shivered as he escorted her up the walk. At the front entrance, she quickly punched in seven digits on the security keypad and unlocked the door. "Would you mind checking out the place?"

The foyer opened into the living room dominated by a sofa and love seat surrounding an olive Oriental carpet on three sides. A mahogany-inlaid breakfront featuring Wedgwood serving dishes, soup tureens, and commemorative plates filled the far wall. "No one's here," he said. Pointing to a sky blue punch bowl ringed by white Grecian relief, "New?"

"Yes, Dylan. It's expensive."

He looked down. "That's not what I asked."

She kissed his cheek, took his coat, then reached into the umbrella stand and handed him a poker with a duck head handle. "Just in case."

"Of what?"

"Take it."

He shrugged. Gripping the poker like a five-iron, he disappeared into the kitchen and den beyond the breakfront wall. "Nothing here," he called.

"Check the basement."

Quickly, she opened the closet door behind her, reached blindly into a recess in the top shelf, and removed a four-by-five-by-one inch tightly stapled manila package.

"Nothing down here," he called.

"Now the upstairs, please."

Waiting until he entered one of the bedrooms, she scribbled on the package and stuffed it beneath a leather glove in his right coat pocket.

Dylan emerged from the near side of the room, twirling the poker like a high school majorette. "Safe and sound." The smile on his face dissolved as Evelyn handed him his coat. "I really am not staying?"

"I'm taking an early flight." Gazing at his downcast eyes, "Dylan, it's not a brush off. I have vacation time coming. A nice week in the Caribbean would do us both good. *My* treat."

His eyes brightened. "Sounds great." He presented her the poker. "Your sword."

"I keep its mate under my bed." She sheathed it in an umbrella stand and kissed him good night. "Thanks for trying to make this time—bearable."

She closed the door behind him, locked both bolts, and reset the alarm. After removing her coat and boots, she trudged up the stairs. In her study, the first room on the right, she noticed that the computer tower light was on, but the monitor was off. *Careless,* she thought, walking into the room. The tower light was flashing—apparently a program was running. She turned on the monitor. File folders fluttered across the screen as individual files rapidly appeared, were replicated, then disappeared. Along the screen's bottom, a blue bar jerked toward the 100% marker at the right edge. Files were being written onto her CD. By the far corner of the room, she spotted a newly exposed section of carpet, which had been covered by furniture, in front of the locked attic door. The bookcase stood three feet farther away from the wall than usual. "Oh my God!"

The attic door exploded open. A bulky shadow smashed through the bookcase.

Screaming, she dashed into the bedroom. The powerful intruder tackled her from behind. She crashed into the floor. Eyes watering, head pinned to the floor, she reached under her bed.

"Stay still," the man rasped, driving his knees deep into her spine.

Her groping fingers touched the duck-headed poker beneath the bed. Straining, she grabbed it and tried to swing it at the assailant on her back.

"Owww! Fuckin' bitch!"

He yanked the poker out of her hand and flung it across the room. It stuck in the far wall like a dart in cork. The man dragged her to her knees.

"No, pl—"

He grabbed her head, wound it slowly left, then wrenched it three-quarters to the right. Evelyn's cervical cartilage crackled in his fingertips. Her body crumpled to the floor.

The man massaged his throbbing arm, then took a wireless phone from his coat pocket and punched in a preset code. "We've got a problem." He paused, running a gloved hand through his hair. "No, I haven't done inventory yet, but I will. Don't—" click "—worry."

A car door slammed just outside the house. The man crept to the window and peered through the lace curtains. Dylan gazed from the dark townhouse to the package in his hands, then slowly started up the front walk.

Trust, but verify.
(Dover-jay, nuh prover-jay)
—A PROVERB

WEDNESDAY, FEBRUARY 2

THREE

"Happy Groundhog Day, Dr. Merritt."

Scott Skylar Merritt nodded at the receptionist in the glass booth. "Morning, Val."

"It's cloudy over the whole East coast. Punxsutawney Phil's not gonna see his shadow this morning." The crow's feet at the edges of her chestnut eyes crinkled. "That means early spring." Before Scott could pull the oversized brass handle on the front entrance heavy glass door, she added, "Sorry but everyone has to use security cards this morning."

"Everyone?" he asked.

She folded her arms.

Just turned forty-five, Scott's appearance had changed over the last four years. His once thick shock of Norweigan-Scottish sandy hair had thinned, sporting patches of gray. Flecks of red had infiltrated once pure lagoon blue eyes. His full beard, still dense and tight to his jawline, had lost its original bronze shading, replaced by a mélange of nut brown, russet, and gray, while hiding sunken cheeks on a face growing insidiously sallow. Broad wire-rimmed frames held glasses so thick that they extruded around the edges and his optometrist would no longer guarantee their integrity. Despite general emaciation and signs of chronic fatigue, remnants of his once athletic physique were still visible in muscular forearms that controlled long, pianist-like fingers—hands that he'd kept in training, just in case by some miracle, he could return to surgery. "How come?"

She leaned close to the hole in the glass. "Government people, or something or other."

Scott opened his worn leather briefcase, rummaged through outdated notes and spreadsheets, removed a magnetic card from the upper pocket and swiped it through an access slot beside the door. The green light twinkled. He gave the receptionist a worn, fragile smile before he opened the heavy door. Fourteen-inch gold and black lettering relief dominated the wall dead ahead:

VERITY HEALTHCARE CONSULTANTS
SERVING INDUSTRY AND GOVERNMENT TO BUILD A HEALTHY FUTURE

He strode across the floor, inlaid with a smartly-fashioned caduceus and computer balanced on scales, to the elevator and rode up alone to the fourth floor. The hallway had not yet filled with cliques lounging around the mini-kitchen or employees sprinting between offices. He stopped at the third office on the left, and as customary, realigned the blue slate nameplate marked SCOTT SKYLAR MERRITT, MD, MS—SENIOR CONSULTANT.

His office was plain: a semi-messy workstation of pressed-wood veneer, ergonomically-designed executive chair, two steel file cabinets guarding a wastebasket, and atop a waist-high bookcase in front of a window, a mini-coffeemaker and cigar humidor, which he opened. Though the humidor was empty, and had been for years, every morning he deeply inhaled from it, drawing in memories of rich aroma, re-tasting the full-bodied flavor from the long-gone Dominican cigars. Reluctantly, he'd acceded to Candice's insistence that he give them up, forever. As both physician and patient, he knew he could not risk further compromising his condition.

He poured himself a cup of strong Colombian coffee from the timed coffeemaker, and stared out the window at Northern Delaware. Headlights streamed between barren trees lining Interstate 95 as the road wound into a shrouded horizon. Dock lights of the Port of Wilmington to his left and street lamps from the city to his right shone through the gray overcast. Barely perceptible, tucked away in the right-hand corner of his peripheral vision, created by his mind's eye, he could see a stopwatch ticking. *Stop that! Stop that!* He yanked his wire frame glasses from his face. One hand wiped them with a chamois from his coat pocket while the other vigorously rubbed his eyes. The vista degenerated into an indistinguishable blur. When he put back on his glasses, the clock was gone.

A red light flashed on Scott's phone; the LCD displayed "1 New Message." He hit the message button and entered his PIN. A familiar, throaty voice began:

"Hey Scott, Ryan here. Should've called you Monday, but didn't get the chance. Well, even with the points, you lost on the Super Bowl. That makes eighteen losses in twenty weeks. You owe me big bucks, but since like always, Janine doesn't approve of my gambling, we'll settle for an expensive dinner, on you. Next time you wonder whether you've got a magic window on the future, remember that every team you bet on tanks. We'll settle up in a few weeks. Till then, may the boomerang be with you."

"Yeah, yeah, don't rub it in," he mumbled as he checked his mail bin: two journals, a copy of a newspaper article, and a travel folder. He leafed through *The Institute Update* quarterly publication, then tossed it into the out bin. "Demagogue."

Beneath that was a photostat of a February 1 *Boston Globe* article with the initials **FYI—Vince.** scribbled at the header. He read:

NOTED TRANSPLANT SURGEON AND FAMILY FOUND DEAD

Cambridge—Dr. James Todd, 57, an internationally renowned transplant surgeon, died early this morning in his home on 1787 Franklin Way, along with wife Laura, 44, and children Jamie, 16, and Steven, 13. Detectives report that one car in the garage had been running during the night and preliminary findings are consistent with carbon monoxide poisoning. The house was equipped with a carbon monoxide detector, but the battery had expired. Dr. Todd was an innovator in *xenotransplantation*, the process of transplanting animal organs into human beings. Dr. Todd revolutionized the field of xenotransplantation by successfully transplanting a pig kidney into a young women dying of kidney disease. Today, thousands of patients with end-stage kidney disease are spared dialysis because of pig xenotransplantation techniques developed by Dr. Todd. A founder of the Institute for the Research of Animal Compatible Transplantations, Chief of Xenotransplantation at Harding Medical Center, author of more than 300 scientific arti—

Scott crumpled the paper and threw it across the room at the corner wastebasket.

Inside the travel folder, he found a reservation number for the Washington Grand Hyatt, a map of the District, a preliminary schedule of the Senate subcommittee hearing, and a small cash advance against expenses.

The phone sounded long single rings, indicating an outside call. The LCD flashed his home number: undoubtedly Candice, his wife, checking up on him, as she always did the first three days after treatment. He picked it up on the fourth ring. "As I was saying, you're my mistress and I love you, but you've got to stop calling here before my wife finds out."

"I hate caller ID. And if by some chance she's real, you won't be for long," Candice shot back. Her voice softened. "How are you feeling?"

Monday, the day following the weekly Sunday night injection, was always the worst: the sweats, the fever, the aching joints—like a cross between a bad flu and going cold turkey off heroin. "Much better."

"Rest as much as you can, dear."

"I'm not an invalid," he said. *Yet.*

"I'm worried about you," she said. "You've been working at the condo almost a week. You've taken on way too much."

Visualizing his wife's pursed lips, and alluring, but narrowing eyes, "Just a few more days to finish the packing. There's piles and piles of photo—"

"Box it all up tonight, we'll ship it to storage tomorrow, and sort through it later. Tonight's your last there."

He shut his eyes and exhaled into the receiver. "Candice, I'm the best judge—"

"Your mother's gone. The condo's been sold. It's time to move on."

"You don't understand."

"Of course I do, sweetheart. You're a wonderful husband and father and a good provider. Even with all that's happened, taking on so many extra hours at the office, selling your mother's condo *by yourself,* finding a new house for us, largely *by yourself,* trying to sell our old house *by yourself* after the realtor flopped. I—"

"I'm running out of time, Candice."

"No, love. You're *making* yourself run out of time." She stifled a sniffle. "Are you traveling this weekend?"

"No, but I have to be in D.C. on Monday night."

"Meet me for lunch, this Friday, one o'clock, at *Tout a Vous* in the Bourse building."

Smiling, he pulled at his beard. "Oh, I think I can manage to get away from the office for a few hours."

"Afterward, we're taking a weekend in Annapolis. Mother will watch the kids. I've reserved a suite for us at the Robert Johnson House. It's quiet, a place we can talk."

"Maybe more than talk?"

Hearing her smile over the phone, "I love you. Don't be late."

Scott removed his thick glasses, folded it, and tossed it on the cluttered desk. The physical world blurred. The astigmatism in his eyes that had prevented him from wearing contact lenses and had greatly worsened over the last four years had also stopped him from producing tears. He hadn't cried in years, though the urge often seemed too strong.

His head suddenly felt light, dizzy. His mouth felt intensely dry, as if stuffed with cotton balls and sand. His stomach growled, growing steadily more queasy. *Damn it. Not again!*

Norlake Xenotransplant Center (Clinic)
Norlake Hospital
Cleveland, Ohio

Twenty-five years of enjoyable practice had enabled Carlton Emery, MD, PhD to wield his six-foot-six, 260-pound frame like a broadsword. Counting loudly to five, he peered down at the wispy thin resident, blocking her view of the nurse's station, tasting the fear in the young woman's eyes. "Well?"

Dr. Sarah Novia swallowed. Petite, a full sixteen inches shorter than Emery and mousy-looking with straight fine hair, she had difficulty making eye contact with the attending surgeon towering over her. "Serologies for hepatitis B and C, Epstein-Barr, cytomegalovirus, varicella-zoster, and RPR for syphilis. Oh, and HIV and PPD for tuberculosis."

Emery glanced at the other two residents. Though much of the muscle he'd had as a starting center on the Ohio State football team for three straight years had turned to fat, accumulating in a semi-Santa potbelly, he retained his massive frame. When teaching, he always spoke from the diaphragm so that power resonated with his every word, like that of a trained broadcaster. "Gentlemen, is that the standard preop infectious profile workup for a kidney xenograft?"

Both men in short white coats nodded.

Emery snorted, scratched his trim black beard, and glanced around the hospital wing. The monitors surrounding the circular nurses' station, the high-powered integrated equipment humming, the nurses, techs, and support personnel scurrying, even the delicate potpourri scent set against pastel pink walls—everything in the intermediate care stepdown unit had been built to his specifications. Carlton Emery *was* the Norlake Xenotransplant Center. As Norlake Hospital's largest single revenue generator, he directly or indirectly accounted for a quarter of hospital resource utilization. A gifted abdominal and organ transplant surgeon with quick, soft hands and majestic-proportioned self-esteem, he had brought prestige to Norlake, establishing the Cleveland hospital as Ohio's mecca for animal-to-human transplantation. "What about endogenous donor retroviruses," turning on the blond male resident with wimpy moustache, "Dr. Collins?"

"Excuse me, sir?" Collins asked.

"Before transplanting a pig's kidney into one of our patients, shouldn't we also screen the organ to make certain that it isn't harboring porcine retroviruses that could infect our patient?" As Collins timidly nodded, "Then why don't we perform that routinely here?"

Collins glanced at the nursing station, as if the answer were posted on one of the monitors.

"Dr. Putenkin," glancing at the third resident with the black beard, "do you know?"

The man avoided Emery's eyes. "No, sir."

"Because every porcine organ used for transplantation into a patient comes from a genetically-engineered pig that does not carry dangerous viruses," Sarah answered for him. "Every porcine organ is screened at the Sacrifice Center, *before* being shipped here for grafting—as mandated by the FDA."

"Exactly." Emery scowled at the other residents. "I'd better see you gentlemen at grand rounds this evening."

Soon it would be time to decide which of these third-year surgical residents would be lucky enough to receive his lone fellowship in xenotransplant surgery. Had any of them truly appreciated the privilege of working in the world's finest xenotransplant facility? Each had gained their position through favor: Collins for a Paradigm board member, Putenkin for an enigmatic prime investor, and Novia for his old colleague, Dr. Theodore Salsbury. Emery remembered his last discussion with Salsbury, on this very spot, before accepting her. *'Yeah, Theo, I am a hard-ass. That's what it takes to prepare them for this brave new branch of medicine you and I forged. I do not haze my residents—I do educate them under fire. So if she's not up to it, pushing her on me won't do anybody any good.* Two and a half years later, Dr. Sarah Novia, brilliant, altruistic, the niece and heir apparent to the Institute's only other surviving co-founder, posed a grave threat.

"Speaking of which, I've read your proposed paper." Emery leaned down and whispered in her ear, "You and I have a great deal to discuss, young lady." He pretended not to notice her half-step retreat. An orderly cleared a gurney from their path. A pair of nurses smiled submissively at Caesar on his rounds.

Institute for the Research of Animal Compatible Transplantations (IRACT)

Princeton Junction, New Jersey

Edward Barbieri, MD, Chief Operating Officer of the Institute for the Research of Animal Compatible Transplantations, shuffled by his secretary, Amanda, and slowly closed the door to his inner office. Awards, both meritorious and solicited, decorated with gold seals and bold lettering, covered mahogany-paneled walls. His head still pounding from last night's party, he collapsed into the embrace of his high-back, winged, burgundy leather executive chair with brass studs, pivoted away from the stack of documents on his marble-top desk, and stared out the back window at misty suburban Princeton. Doubtless he had a full day ahead of him, but he needed a moment to wipe away the hangover and replace it with the endearing smile of his public persona that had salvaged the last phase of his otherwise dismal career, now approaching retirement age. With his distinguished, gentlemanly face of a stately knight with ruddy nose, grandfatherly crows feet around naturally festive emerald eyes, and a creased mouth shaped by perpetual smiling, Barbieri exuded a conviviality that served him perfectly at social gatherings as both intent listener and enthusiastic, if not effervescent, storyteller. A scraggly island tuft of gray hair in front that had survived an otherwise bald head added a comical charm to his appearance— though he hated that chunk of hair like hell and wanted to shave it off.

He closed the door to the inner office. Awards, both meritorious and solicited, decorated with gold seals and bold lettering, covered mahogany-paneled walls. Stacks of documents lay on marble-top desk near the back window. Behind the desk was a high-back, burgundy leather executive chair with wings, hand-finished brass studs, and a wooden swivel base. He collapsed into the chair's soft embrace, pivoted away from the door, and stared out the window at a misty suburban Princeton. He closed his eyes a moment.

He turned back and found Amanda standing over him with a note pad. "You're late for a full facilities tour with Patrick Corliss of the *Journal*. He's waiting in the Main Conference Room. Evelyn Cruz was supposed to accompany you, but she's not here and hasn't called in."

He squeezed the bridge of his nose for stimulation. "Wonderful. So I go it alone?"

"Loretta Lockhart of Americans for Transplant Organ Progress is in the building."

"You said *full* facilities. Lockhart isn't cleared for the lower levels."

"I could have her meet you at IT."

"Good idea. Next?"

"Speaking of IT, the network's been down for hours. You might want to have a talk with the geek squad."

"As if it would make a difference. Next."

She hesitated, glancing around the room. "Dr. Stone is here."

"Shit! How long?"

"Hours."

"Has 'The Great One' commanded my presence yet?"

"Not that I've heard."

Barbieri sighed. "I'll take that as a small miracle—for now."

"I've been doing some research on Dr. Stone and—"

"We've been through this before. I made it quite clear. Let it lay!"

She stepped behind him. "I can be discrete."

He reached up and squeezed her arm. "I mean it. You can't imagine what Stone is capable of."

FOUR

Verity Healthcare Consultants
North Wilmington, Delaware
Sometimes, the images would come to Scott preceded by a
warning aura—dizziness, dry mouth, cold sweat—like that
before a *grand mal* epilepsy seizure. Other times, the images
would come silently, as if crossing beneath an archway to an
altered state of consciousness. Rarely, they'd explode on his
consciousness, like a bomb, wiping clean his senses to the
surrounding world. But always triggered by some subcon-
scious stimulus, be it an errant thought, or subtle sensory
cue: a sight, a sound, especially an odor. More than dreams;
less than hallucinations. Not premonition, not ESP. Closer to
hunches aided by vivid imagination—neither impossible nor
real. They'd been growing stronger in the past four years, in
concert with the affliction silently stalking him.

Scott felt himself floating above a dreamy, distorted
view of an intensive care unit—the generic central nurses'
stations with its array of staffers and integrated computer-
ized monitoring equipment; a frazzled woman in a worn

blue coat waiting outside a room; the cadre of faceless white-coated doctors walking in slow motion through double doors at the far end of the hall, one doctor always wearing a bright red embroidery stitched on his coat, sharpening as he approached. Scott could just see the loops in the fancy stitch.

Someone rapped on Scott's office doorjamb.

Scott exhaled, sweat pouring down his forehead. At least it wasn't the haunting horror of unburied millions. Patting away his perspiration with a pair of tissues, he put on his glasses. His research assistant stood politely waiting. "Come in, Dylan."

Institute for the Research of Animal Compatible Transplantations (IRACT)
Princeton Junction, New Jersey

Barbieri straightened his tie and smoothed down a pesky tuft of his hair as he entered the Main Conference Room. The room was dominated by a great semi-circular table with several rows of chairs fixed to the floor—a half-scale version of the United Nations Security Council. The wall with the main entrance was floor-to-ceiling glass. The other three walls were decorated with the $300,000 Great Seal of the Institute—the rear view of a man and woman looking at a sunrise inset against the Institution's name—and several portraits, including the three co-founders. Barbieri extended his hand to a man in a three-piece gray who was standing at the apex of the conference table. "Mr. Corliss, I'm Edward Barbieri, Chief Operating Officer of the Institute for the Research of Animal Compatible Transplantations. It's a pleasure to have a senior reporter for the *Wall Street Journal,* though I must tell you, as a non-profit organization, we're not for sale."

Patrick Corliss woodenly smiled. Trim, with square shoulders, graying at his temples, and wearing round, horn-rimmed glasses, Corliss looked more like investment banker than reporter. "Our readers are interested in the continued development of animal transplantation technology. Naturally, anything relating to Paradigm Transplant Solutions captures the attention of both portfolio manager and small investor alike."

"We're an independent research organization. We are not affiliated with PTS."

Corliss changed his smile to polite and sardonic. "I did not imply that you were. Simply that the history of the Institute and PTS intertwines."

Barbieri rested his hands on the table. "Mr. Corliss, we're at a critical junction in the Institute's development. Next week, I'll be testifying before the Senate Subcommittee of Health and Human Services—"

"After which the Institute will become the National Xenotransplant Registry as the FDA's database is decommissioned," flashing a subdued smile, "assuming all goes well."

"Any hint of impropriety could table years of work."

"I wouldn't want to see that," Corliss said, his smile affected.

What does he want? Barbieri thought. *Is he tied in with Stone? It can't be coincidence that they're both here at the same time. And what the hell does Stone want anyway?*

Corliss took out a notebook. As his eyes glanced up over Barbieri's shoulder, the polite smile grew into a gaping grin. Following the reporter's eyes, Barbieri turned around and looked up. A large photograph of a pig hung on the wall. The animal's eyes slyly gazed back from its haughtily-cocked head, a half-smile gracing the jaw beneath its snout. Against a pastoral backdrop, it was reminiscent of the Mona Lisa.

"That's Wally," Barbieri declared, straight-faced. "His actual name was porcine strain SPF-4912-alpha-sub-zero. '*SPF*' standing for *specific pathogen-free*. Wally was the progenitor, the first of his line. Today, there are nearly half a million clones of him."

"How quaint—having a portrait of the original hanging in this reception area," Corliss said facetiously. "A very special pig,"

"Was. And you can quote me on that," Barbieri said. "Xenotransplantation, a.k.a. xenografting, is the transplantation of tissue or an organ from a donor in one species to a recipient in another species. Before Wally, xenotransplantation was an abject failure. The first known verifiable attempt was in Russia, 1682, when a Russian nobleman had a piece of dog skull grafted onto his own. Things didn't fare much better in the twentieth century. In 1963, chimpanzee kidneys were transplanted into humans. In 1964, researchers tried it with baboons—which were, by the way, the last attempts at kidney xenografting before Wally. In 1984, in probably the most famous case of the last century, Leonard Bailey grafted a baboon heart into a newborn—Baby Fae."

"A failure, wasn't it?"

Barbieri nodded, probing the reporter's impassive face, his hopes of a fluff piece quickly fading. "The baby died within three weeks. There was quite an outcry after that. But early experimentation continued right up through the end of the century, much of it with animal livers, because patients in need of those organs often have only hours to live." He cleared his throat. "The human immune system, the very system that protects us from infection, invariably disintegrates animal organs within days, sometimes within hours after transplantation."

Corliss crossed his arms. "Your point being that no patient survived more than a handful of weeks?"

"Until Wally. Before porcine strain SPF-4912, transplant surgeons spent their time trying to make the human body accept animal organs, mostly through chemicals that depressed people's immune systems. The drugs would work for a time, but often lead to life-threatening infections." Barbieri pointed at the portrait. "Wally was a fundamental shift in 'paradigm'—excuse the pun. Porcine strain SPF-4912, developed by Paradigm Transplant Solutions, Incorporated, is the product of the most extensive genetic engineering program ever conducted."

"I thought it was PPL Therapeutics that really shifted the paradigm," Corliss countered. "Back in Christmas of 2001, they produced five cloned piglets that all lacked some key gene—"

"The gene in those piglets coded for an enzyme which produces a sugar that the human immune system recognizes as foreign, thereby causing organ rejection," Barbieri interjected. "But that was just one gene—there's many more than that needed for proper transplantation. Paradigm Transplant Solutions eventually acquired the patent from PPL Therapeutics—along with developing and perfecting many other genetic alterations—so that its donor pigs could provide life-giving organs that aren't rejected by human hosts. And by the way, the only one to have more patents on an animal than Paradigm Transplant Solutions is God."

Corliss chuckled. *"That* I'll quote."

Barbieri tried to hide a sigh. *Damn, I can't keep my mouth shut.* No doubt that sound bite would lead to some backlash from the far right. *But some of them will be needing organs, too.*

"How exactly have these pigs been altered?" Corliss resumed.

"Pigs have certain chemicals, sugars to be exact, that reside on blood vessels throughout its body. After transplantation into a human body, the human immune system recognizes the sugars on transplanted organ vessels as foreign and attacks the organ. Wally and all his cloned SPF-4912 descendants have had these genes on their DNA that coded for these sugars knocked-out—that is, removed from their genetic structure. The animals are incapable of producing chemicals that irritate the human immune system. Not only that, the SPF-4912 strain has also had a slew of human genes incorporated into its own DNA."

"Transgenic animals. A multi-billion dollar industry. But with so many human genes, aren't these pigs, well, part human?"

Barbieri administered a well-practiced smile to Corliss which the reporter did not return. *Is that his angle?* "The transferred genes are just to make pig biochemical processes more compatible with our own. I assure you, Mr. Corliss, not one xenotransplant patient has ever started growing a snout."

"Some people worry that these transplants might accidentally introduce a pig virus into people—one that could turn deadly and spread, like AIDS."

That was it! Good, the grand tour should squash most of that nonsense. "It's called *xenosis*—transmission of an infective organism from one species to another via xenotransplantation. An exceedingly small risk, but one we take very seriously here."

"Do you?"

Barbieri beamed. The reporter himself must be a skeptic—otherwise he would have asked 'how'. "I'm glad you asked. First of all, SPF-4912 was the most intensely scrutinized biological product/device in the history of the Food and Drug Administration. Twelve years of rigorous testing revealed no evidence whatsoever of xenosis. Second, PTS constantly checks its SPF-4912 stock to be certain that the animals are free of potential viruses and infections. Third, strain SPF-4912 has had all endogenous viruses knocked out of its genetic structure, just like those chemicals I mentioned a moment ago, so it simply isn't possible for a retrovirus to hide in the pig's genetic structure. And fourth, but not least, here at the Institute, we check the blood and tissue samples from every patient, every consenting family member, and every hospital worker that routinely comes into contact with patients for possible viruses. We have yet to find one single pig retrovirus in a human being. Mr. Corliss, statistically, you have an infinitely better chance of getting a salmonella infection from *your next door neighbor* eating bacon than developing an infection from pig donor organs."

"Not according to your critics." Corliss glanced at the wall to Barbieri's right: three portraits hung beneath a giant caduceus. The portrait on the left, that of a square-jawed man with rough-hewn features and thin moustache, was draped with a black cloth. He pointed at the draped portrait. "Some sources have indicated that Dr. James Todd, one of your founders, was beginning to have doubts himself. His suicide certainly was unfortunate."

You working for the Journal *or the* National Enquirer? With a placating smile, Barbieri pointed at the thick-necked man in the center portrait, "Ask our other co-founders. Dr. Carlton Emery, the Institute's President, currently in Cleveland running the country's most successful xenotransplant clinic. A premier researcher to boot. Or," pointing at the portrait of an elderly man with a thick, white handlebar moustache and sparkling blue eyes, "Dr. Theodore Salsbury, now retired and living happily in Richmond, Virginia."

"I intend to."

Barbieri stood. "Why don't we first start by showing you where we keep the possibility of hell frozen over."

Norlake Xenotransplant Center
Cleveland, Ohio

Dr. Emery stopped outside of Room 353. Resident doctors Sarah Novia and Robert Collins nearly bumped into him. "Survival statistics for renal grafting, Dr. Collins. Allotransplantation."

The young man cleared his throat. "About 91% of patients who receive a matching kidney from a living donor, usually a family member, survive five years. But around 25% will, at some point, need re-transplantation with another kidney. The rates are lower using human cadaver donors, around 81% survival with about 40% requiring re-transplantation."

"And porcine xenotransplants?" Emery asked.

"Patients fare better with donor pig kidneys than with those from human cadavers, around an 88% five-year survival rate with a third requiring re-transplantation—according to the In-

stitute for the Research of Animal Compatible Transplantations, which sir, I believe you have some passing acquaintance
with."

Emery chuckled, his residents respectfully joining him.
This was more like it. Perhaps they were beginning to appreciate the blessings available to this next generations of transplant surgeons. *See, I'm not such a ball-buster when you come
prepared.* "Those rates aren't quite as good as with donor kidneys from living relatives." He turned directly to Dr.
Putenkin. "So why on Earth would any patient with end-stage
renal disease ever choose to have a pig's kidney inserted into
his body when he could have a human kidney instead?"

"Donor relatives with HLA-matching kidneys are hard to
find," the Russian replied. "Many possible donors are
afraid, too."

"Dr. Collins, anything else?"

Collins, caught off-guard, hesitated before answering. "It
can save the patient a two-year wait or more for a human cadaver donor, with survival and transplant rates that aren't as
good."

"What Dr. Collins is trying to say, Dr. Novia," turning his
gaze on Sarah, "is that a pig's kidney grafted onto a patient
with end-stage renal disease will save that patient from being hooked up to a dialysis machine." Leaning closer, "Perhaps you're a little young to have had much experience with
dialysis. They're brutal machines. Patients are hooked in via
a tube protruding from their abdomen. The machine filters
their bodily fluid in lieu of functioning kidneys—three to
five times a week, in some cases every night, accompanied
by an endless parade of catheter infections. Dialysis retards
bodily deterioration; it doesn't stop it. Xenografting with
porcine kidneys eliminates the slow torture of the body poisoning itself."

"Dr. Emery, I understand about—"

"Keep that in mind when we discuss your paper, tomorrow," Emery said.

"Would you like Mrs. Folcroft's chart, Dr. Emery?" a nurse asked, holding a thick silver binder.

Nurse Christina Forman had jade green eyes, high cheekbones accentuating flawless skin and a rear end that reminded Emery of his wife Grace's thirty years ago. Wordless, he took the chart from her as she walked back to the central monitoring station, his eyes focused on her rear sliding seductively beneath her white skirt. When she turned the corner, he shoved the chart into Putenkin's stomach like a quarterback executing a handoff. "Our patient?" Before Putenkin could open the binder, "Without the chart, doctor."

"Constance Folcroft, sixty-two-year-old white female with history of chronic glomerulonephritis leading to endstage renal disease," Putenkin answered with his thick accent. "Underwent kidney xenotransplantation a week ago, but has had episodic high fevers since surgery."

"Is that normal?"

"No. Patients are normally up and around in several days. Discharged in seven to ten."

"Dr. Novia, name the short-term possible complications following renal xenografting?"

"The most common is urine leakage, usually at the ureterovesical junction or through a ruptured calyx, secondary to the surgical procedure. Others include infection, acute rejection of the graft, bleeding, obstruction or stenosis of the ureter, and swelling of the lymphatic system around the kidney vasculature," she answered.

"Wonderful, gentlemen and lady. Now that we've spat back textbook responses, let's try being real doctors. What's happening to Mrs. Folcroft, Putenkin?"

The resident thoughtfully massaged his beard. "Graft failure, I think."

"So the kidney we gave Mrs. Folcroft is failing? What do you recommend?"

"We order urinalysis to check for red blood cells in urine,

certain sign of kidney failure. Also check electrolytes, BUN, and levels of anti-rejection drugs."

Emery folded his arms. "What if those tests prove unremarkable?"

"Then transplant ultrasound, I think, followed by kidney biopsy."

Emery rolled his eyes. "Check the serum creatinine levels."

"Sir?"

"You know, creatinine, the muscle waste product. Check her latest level. How far is it above her baseline?"

Putenkin scoured the lab section of the chart. "Up 40% from pre-transplant levels."

"Pretty damn good, considering 20% or less defines a transplant failure. Which makes you wrong, Putenkin. You'd have subjected her to a needless invasive procedure and risked compromising her new organ's integrity." To Collins, "So what is happening?"

"Organ rejection," Collins answered, carefully avoiding Emery's eyes.

"So you're telling me that Mrs. Folcroft's immune system has tagged her porcine kidney transplant as 'foreign' and is now attacking it, like an infection."

Collins nodded.

"What kind of rejection? Hyperacute, acute, chronic?"

"Umm, hyperacute."

"Collins, haven't you learned anything since you've been here? In a hyperacute rejection, the host's immune system overwhelms the transplanted organ. Turns it black within hours. You can literally see it destroy the organ before your eyes." Shaking his head, "There's never been a single case of hyperacute rejection to *any* porcine strain SPF-4912 organ. Never."

Collins looked down. "I meant *acute* rejection."

"You're still off-base. The more specific T- and B-cell immune reactions are still rare, although less than 2% with SPF-4912 organs. But if it were, the symptoms would be more severe—graft swelling, pain, tenderness, profound hypertension. You've missed the obvious." Pivoting around, "Which perpetually brings us to you, Novia. Care to share your learned opinion with us?"

Sarah looked up at him. "Infection."

"Somehow I knew *you* would suggest that," Emery said. "Such as?"

"During the first month post-op most infections are related to surgery itself, primarily *E. coli* from a urinary tract infection, *Staph aureus* and *Staph viridans* arise either from the lines, drains, or wound in the patient. Pneumonia's a problem, too. Within the first six months, cytomegalovirus and opportunistic organisms. And after six months . . ."

Emery glared at her. *Are you going to say it here, now, in the open?*

". . . Epstein-Barr virus, and hepatitis B and C."

He masked a sigh. *At least she had sense enough to keep her mouth shut—for now.* "Let's just concern ourselves with the likely present. Have you run a C and S?"

"Yes, doctor. The infection is bacterial, specifically *Staph aureus,* susceptible to standard broad-spectrum antibiotics. We should be able to knock it out without having to take the patient off her immunosuppressant drugs." Novia hesitated, then quietly added, "That is, assuming the bacterial infection isn't secondary to a viral one."

Emery rolled his eyes. "What did you say, young lady?"

"Mrs. Folcroft's bacterial infection could just be opportunistic—bacteria taking advantage of her weakened state." Sarah clenched her jaw and gazed up at the clinic's director. "She could have an underlying viral infection."

"Don't you think it's more important that we concentrate on the problem at hand rather than chasing down nonexistent viruses?"

She glanced at her two silent colleagues, then pursed her lips. "Shouldn't we at least consider the possibility that Mrs. Folcroft has a viral infection? It could—"

"As physicians, we make decisions based on knowledge, experience, and intuition. We don't have the resources and our patients don't have the time for us to pursue every half-baked possibility." He prepared to open the patient's door. "By the way, Dr. Novia, you did inspect the incision site, didn't you?"

"No sir, I did not."

"That's probably where the infection originated, and the first thing any competent doctor would have checked."

FIVE

Verity Healthcare Consultants
North Wilmington

"You wanted to see me, Dr. Merritt?" Dylan Rogers asked.

Scott pointed to a chair across from his desk. Dylan glanced around the room, then focused on a placard behind Scott's right ear. " 'Avert indecision through calm, poise, and balance,' " he read. "Interesting—who said it?"

"My wife found it in a fortune cookie." The smile on Scott's face dissipated. "Dylan, your performance has been slipping over the last three weeks." Scott watched his subordinate's hands fumble. "I don't know how else to put it, but there are rumors about you and Evelyn Cruz, the Database Administrator over at IRACT. You were supposed to liaise with her during the xeno kidney audit." Scott took a deep breath. "Did you more than liaise?" Dylan gazed past him. "You've been an excellent assistant. I want to help you. But you have—"

"It's not what you think. I'm afraid, not for me, but for her."

"Care to run that by me?"

"Evelyn had a long-standing affair with James Todd, one of the Institute's founders. In fact, Todd set up the Institute's computer system. He was Evelyn's mentor, brought her in, trained her, put her in charge of the databases."

"Todd's dead. I just read his obituary."

"Uh-huh. And Evelyn's afraid."

"With Todd gone, her job's probably on the line."

"No-no, I mean terrified." He fumbled with his jacket, then handed Scott a stapled rectangular package. "Last night, I found *that* stuffed in my pocket."

"'To be opened only by Dr. Scott Skyler Merritt.' Hmmm—misspelled my middle name." He shook it. "Must be sealed in bubble paper. What is it?"

"Maybe a CD—I don't know. I found it stuffed in my coat pocket after I left. When I went back to the house, Evelyn didn't answer. I stood outside yelling for half an hour until a neighbor threatened to call the cops."

"If it's additional patient records from IRACT, she's too late. The audit's closed. I'm testifying on Tuesday." He tossed the package onto his additional work pile on a chair by the window.

"Sir, I'd like to postpone our meeting this afternoon—and take a couple of personal days. Evelyn's gone to Boston for Todd's funeral. I thought maybe I could—"

"Oh, go on. Be with her. This can wait till next week."

"Thank you." Dylan headed for the doorway, then stopped and looked back. "Evelyn's not the type to play cloak and dagger."

IRACT

Instead of heading down the bustling hallway lined by offices and cubicles, Barbieri turned left. Corliss, a half-step behind and not expecting the turn, nearly tripped over Barbieri's back heel. "We're now entering a restricted area," the COO. said over his shoulder as he led Corliss down a long, deserted white, doorless, featureless corridor. A quick turn right, and he stopped just short of the corridor's abrupt dead-end. "We have to wait here for clearance."

"I don't see anything," Corliss said, two steps behind him.

Barbieri snickered. "The latest and best in security—"

"That money can buy," the reporter finished. "Speaking of which, several highly-placed sources have expressed growing concerns about your Institute's finances."

"We're not a front for Paradigm Transplant Solutions."

Corliss said quietly, "A number of very influential sources allege that you are."

Barbieri inwardly beamed. *Great! He's probably just here investigating the financial end. I was worried about nothing!* "Yes, our history is undeniably tied to Paradigm Transplant Solutions. PTS pioneered pig strain SPF-4912 technology. PTS developed the practical cure for juvenile and insulin-dependent diabetes—Diabend, the biodegradable polymer-covered SPF-4912 pancreas islet cells that diabetics inject twice a year and that ultimately replaced daily insulin. PTS also developed Tremulate, biodegradable polymer-covered SPF-4912 brain cells, which is the practical cure for Parkinson's disease. On those two products, virtual cures for diabetes and Parkinson's, PTS quickly became a pharmaceutical giant."

"Yes, yes, I know. After which PTS conceived, developed, and created your Institute to—"

"You have it backward. Doctors Salsbury, Todd, and Emery, all leading transplant surgeons, approached PTS after the successes of Diabend and Tremulate. *They* solicited the company to endow an *independent* institute that would research and monitor SPF-4912's next frontier—whole organ xenotransplantation. Flush with cash, PTS donated $150 million the first year and another $100 million the second." Barbieri hardened his jaw. "Since then, other major pharma houses have contributed to position themselves to capture market share when the PTS patents expire. It's in their best interests to have a strong, independent institution."

"What did PTS's quarter billion dollars buy, besides congressional influence?"

A red light emanating from a peephole in the wall scanned the retina of Barbieri's right eye.

"Dr. Edward Barbieri recognized," a female automated voice sounded.

"Visitor, Patrick Corliss, cleared for entry this time only," Barbieri announced. The red light swung toward Corliss. Instinctively, he backed away. "Hold still so our expensive security system can scan you."

Corliss complied. The red light passed by his eyes.

"Visitor Patrick Corliss recognized," the automated voice sounded.

The wall quickly rolled away to their right, exposing a closet-sized room. Corliss hesitated, then followed Barbieri into the enclosure. The wall slammed closed behind them. The floor seemed to drop away. Corliss fell back against a corner.

"High-speed elevator," Barbieri said nonchalantly. "Don't worry, the brakes are expensive, too."

The elevator opened onto a long, sparkling white corridor that smelled of spring fresh aerosol and caustic antiseptic. Barbieri motioned Corliss into one of a series of tiny trams lined along one side. With a single touch on the ignition button, the electric tram slowly proceeded down the corridor along invisible tracks in the floor.

"Where are we?" Corliss asked.

"Five hundred feet below ground."

The tram car turned a corner and stopped beside sealed double doors. Barbieri hopped out of the car and placed his palm on a wall panel. The doors opened into a huge chamber whose walls teemed with glass-encased, one-foot cube freezer units, each beneath a coded electronic display attached to tiny modular monitoring cryostatic-control systems with independently flashing green lights. Barbieri watched Corliss' eyes follow those flashing green lights as they stretched down the length of the chamber leading into infinity.

Barbieri wiped away a circle from a nearby container's murky white frosted glass exterior, exposing a small, encased rod. "Tissue specimens from every patient who's undergone xenotransplantation. More than a quarter million, and increasing between 2% and 3% weekly. We also store serum, which are blood-derived samples, from all of these individuals, but they're in another area of the facility because they don't require this level of cryogenic preservation."

"How does that compare with the FDA's?"

"Back in 1997, the Public Health Service Agencies, which includes the FDA, were supposed to initiate a National Xenotransplant Registry of databases that should have included tissue and serum specimens from every patient undergoing xenotransplantation, *and* every close family member, *and* every hospital worker coming in close contact with these patients. Specimens were supposed to be preserved for a minimum of fifty years so that, God forbid, if a xenozoonotic infection spread, we'd have a historical tissue bank to help us to pinpoint critical information about the virus. We fulfilled that mandate flawlessly." Shaking his head, "FDA, on the other hand, has less than a few thousand specimens."

Corliss crossed his arms. "Why should that be the case? FDA has more resources—"

"And the Federal bureaucracy to go with it. Not so in the private sector."

"But with a greater potential for abuse—if the bottom line is threatened."

Barbieri snickered at the *Journal* reporter. "You sound dangerously like a Democrat." With two fingers, he motioned Corliss out of the chamber and back into the tram. The car started immediately after Corliss climbed in, hummed down the corridor, made a sharp left, and deposited them beside a ten-by-sixty-foot viewing window. On the other side of the glass, an assembly line of robotic arms picked up tiny, virtually invisible tissue fractions and lifted them into cylindrical processing containers. At another area along the assembly line, bluish-black, semi-translucent screens appeared with patterns of ghostly lines, each flashing rapidly before being scanned by laser light. Hardware systems positioned at junctures in the assembly line integrated the scanning processes and collected the data.

"Every specimen is run through a battery of tests," Barbieri said. "Due to the crushing load of specimens, we've had to automate. What you're looking at right here is automatic processing of Western immunoblot assays for the detection of possible antibodies to porcine endogenous retroviruses. Thirteen other tests for possible pig viruses are being performed further down the assembly line."

"This is where the quarter billion dollars went?"

"Cynicism aside, Mr. Corliss, we are the nation's first line of defense. No matter how careful, there is always the possibility that a pig virus could be transmitted via xenotransplantation to a human host. Retroviruses, even ancient viruses, dormant in pig genetic structure for millions of years, could suddenly emerge."

"Earlier, you said that *all* pig retroviruses had been removed from SPF-4912's genetic code?"

"Of course they have." Barbieri hesitated, then started up the tram. "I was merely speaking *theoretically*. Please make sure I'm quoted correctly on that. PERVs, porcine endogenous retroviruses as they're called, have been removed. But other pig viral contaminants might exist and could potentially be transmitted to human hosts, despite the pigs being raised in the world's most excruciatingly sterile environment. Viruses such as swine parainfluenza-1 and influenza viruses. The porcine adenovirus, cytomegalovirus, rotavirus, endogenous and exogenous retroviruses. Aujeszky's disease, Japanese encephalitis, vesicular stomatitis, encephalomyocarditis virus, rabies. Even prions, a protein 'virus' that led

to Mad Cow Disease back at the first years of this century."
Smiling, "Still, I can't deny the slight *possibility*—but I trust
that it won't be unduly emphasized in your article, will it?
Frankly, with all the tests we perform, I'd feel safer getting a
donor kidney from a SPF-4912 swine than from my brother."

"Then with all the *potential* risk from pigs, why not use
primates—like monkeys, chimpanzees, or even baboons?"

"Economics for one. There's only a limited number of
monkeys and baboons but a virtually unlimited supply of
pigs. Baboons yield one or two offspring beginning at three
to five years of age. Pigs produce a litter when they're less
than a year old. Baboons take nine years to develop to matu-
rity. For pigs, it's six months. There's physiologic reasons,
too. Baboon organs aren't sufficiently large to meet the
physiologic demands of most human bodies."

"But with pigs you're risking—"

"Monkeys and baboons have a much greater risk of xenozoonotic infection *because* they are so fundamentally similar to human beings. Their DNA is far more likely than a
pig's to harbor retroviruses that would find a comfy fit in
human DNA. Don't forget, it was the simian immunodefi-
cient virus, SIV, that crossed over into human beings and became the human immunovirus, HIV." Lightly touching
Corliss' arm to enhance his attention, "Baboons, gorillas,
and chimpanzees are like our cousins. Sacrificing them
brings out a kind of instinctual revulsion at an ugly
concept—cannibalism."

The tram turned another corner.

"How do you coordinate all this data?" Corliss asked.

"Supercomputer. With frequent backups. Release in quarterly reports and periodicals by the publishing department
upstairs. Our next stop."

Corliss leaned away from the edge of the slow-moving
tram. "Isn't there a—statistical risk with automation?
Couldn't some viruses be slipping through, undetected?"

The tram stopped beside another large picture window.

Beyond the glass, fourteen technicians in biohazard suits worked in compartmentalized laboratories.

"We have teams of very capable pathologists and virologists down here, twenty-four/seven for any conceivable viral threat, randomly testing and re-testing specimens and findings that the automated processors spit out."

As Corliss jotted notes, Barbieri glanced down at his pager. Dr. Stone had been in the building for hours. And still no message.

". . . out of control?"

Barbieri looked up. "Pardon?"

"I said, 'What if something gets out of control down here?' "

"We use CDC preferred guidelines for specimen storage. Guidelines, I would add, that FDA hasn't itself implemented."

"Dr. Barbieri, have you ever wondered whether the risks of xenotransplantation outweigh the benefits?"

Barbieri gazed at the reporter with cold eyes. "Why don't you ask the hundred thousand people who won't spend their lives hooked up to a dialysis machine this year? Or the twenty thousand who will survive with a pig liver? Or the two million diabetics who continue to enjoy being cured?"

Norlake Xenotransplant Center
Room 353

His face awash with light, Emery entered the patient's room, his three residents following him like ducklings.

Constance Folcroft tried to sit up in bed: intravenous drips, wires connecting electrodes to monitors, and the catheter between her legs hampering her movements. Her face, gaunt with prominent cheekbones, had liberally applied rouge that accentuated her ashen pallor. Emery sandwiched her hand between his palms. "How's my favorite patient from Fredericktown?"

"I'm your only patient from Fredericktown," Constance said weakly.

"I hope you don't feel like you're wearing out your welcome."

Constance coughed, then spit into a plastic dish by the side of her bed. "I almost wish I hadn't gone through with it."

"I bought you a gift." Emery's eyes never wavering from his patient as she propped up her head. He held out his right arm, palm up. Putenkin placed a thick, black book on it—which he presented to Constance. He smiled as she gazed at the cover: *Hawaii* by James A. Michener. "He tells a complete story."

"Thank you," closing her eyes, "but I don't feel well enough to read."

"Mrs. Folcroft, you know what makes life interesting, and ironic?" he whispered. "Choices. You've been on dialysis for two months. Not a very pleasant way to live, is it, hooked up to a machine four to six hours a day, half of your life? The infections, the slow wasting of your body."

"You're right about that."

"And because you had no living relative with a matching kidney who could serve as donor, you would have had to go on the waiting list for *three years*, assuming you survived that long." Lowering his voice, "Some people would prefer to die rather than live a life enslaved to a dialysis machine. Stop their treatments. Go on with their lives—until the toxins accumulating in their body killed them."

She turned away. "Such as?"

"The author of this book," he said, tapping it. "Mrs. Folcroft, you had a choice that, only a few short years ago, one of the world's greatest writers never had. Would he have chosen xenotransplantation with a pig kidney over dialysis or death? We'll never know, but the thousands who've made this decision are living normal, fruitful lives. In time, so will you."

"I suppose so."

"Even if you had received a human kidney from a dead stranger instead of a genetically-engineered pig, you'd probably be feeling physically exactly as you are now, if not worse."

"I'm so—afraid." Constance started tearing. "Is my body—rejecting the kidney?"

Emery squeezed her hands. "There's no evidence of that."

"But it might."

"That could happen with any graft, whether from a relative, a deceased human donor, or an animal source. The difference is that if your body rejects this kidney, we can have another here in hours. If it was a human donor, you'd go back on dialysis and wait years."

Her hands shaking in his, "Then what is happening to me?"

"You have an infection. They're common posteroperatively—nothing to be unduly worried about." Emery leaned forward. "Now, we're going to change your dressing, check your incision, probably insert a drain, put you on antibiotics, and after you're feeling better, send you home."

Constance nodded weakly, then looked away.

To Sarah, "Dr. Novia, you do the honors." Then whispering in her ear, "Since you should have done it anyway."

Sarah went to the small, clean room area tucked off a corner of the room and returned with a mask, gloves, drapes, and plastic-sealed kit that included sterilized gauze, tubing drain, and suture scissors. She had Constance rotate on her side to expose the incision along the flank. The kidney graft had been placed in an abdominal flap. Without removing the bandage, Sarah inspected the site and, with her stethoscope, listened for abnormal murmurs that might indicate narrowing or obstruction of the key renal artery. "No bruits or signs of arteriovenous malformation, doctor," she said. "Edema appears within normal limits. No outward signs of acute rejection, renal vein occlusion, outflow obstruction, or pyelonephritis."

"Remove the dressing."

She placed the surgical mask over her mouth and nose, gloved herself, and began to remove the adhesive overlaying the bandage. Slowly she peeled back the gauze. The incision, maintained by sutures and steri-strips, was red, angry-looking, swollen. Dry yellowish exudate stained the dressing's interior. Not good, but not severe either.

"Putenkin, check the patient's history. Any mention of 'Hanoi Flu?'" Emery asked.

The resident fumbled through the chart. "No history, sir."

"Mrs. Folcroft, there was a real bad flu running around a few winters ago. By any chance, do you remember whether you had it?" Emery asked.

Constance turned toward him and squinted one eye. "Come to think of it, I did. Headaches, fever, throwing up. I was out from work for almost two weeks."

Emery edged Sarah away from the side of the bed. "I'll take it from here, Dr. Novia."

The resident brushed his shoulder. "Dr. Emery, I'm perfectly capable—"

"I said I'll take over!"

Sarah furrowed her brows and stepped away from the bed. Emery took a mask and gloves from the clean area, and quickly began removing a few of the tiny steri-strips from the center of the incision line. A few drops of faintly yellow purulent liquid oozed from the site. "No sign of significant bleeding. We'll fix this right up." He copiously flushed the area with sterile saline and broad spectrum antibiotic, inserted a plastic tubing, and partially closed the incision, allowing room for the tubing to slowly drain off any residual fluid. As was his custom, he applied a topical antibiotic, more for his own comfort level than the patient's, and a fresh dressing over the area. "This gets changed tomorrow," he told Sarah. "Start her on a drip of an IV fluoroquinolone antibiotic or whatever the organism's sensitive to." He gathered the used dressing and gauze and placed it in the center of the disposable, absorbent drape. "Remind me, Novia. What is Mrs. Folcroft's immunosuppression therapy?"

"Currently she's on combination therapy to prevent organ rejection—fifty milligrams daily of a class two sphingosine 1-phosphate receptor agonist to redirect white cells away from the new organ, and five daily of antisense-GSMab715 immunosuppressant to counteract the cells that don't. She's scheduled to remain on the former for another four days and the latter for at least six to eight weeks."

"Discontinue them both."

"Yes doctor. What other agents should I start her on?"

Emery folded the corners of the drape together. "Nothing."

"But Dr. Emery—"

"We can't very well fight off Mrs. Folcroft's infection if we have her on immunosuppressant drugs that are hampering her immune system, now can we?" He stood, drape and disposables in hand. "There's no immediate danger of acute rejection." *You're too bright for your own good. Don't you think I know that stopping immunosuppressants is risky? But it's riskier keeping her on it.* He said, "Those are my orders."

"Yes, sir."

Emery took the folded drape and its contents to the clean area behind a screen.

"Oh doctor, there's something I've been meaning to ask you," Constance called. "It may sound stupid."

Emery stood over the biohazard container. "There are no stupid questions."

"I've heard about—cellular memory. Is it possible that my pig kidney—"

"That's a myth, Mrs. Folcroft." He peeked around the corner of the clean area at his patient. "The new kidney we transplanted doesn't know that it came from an animal, and in time, neither will your body." Eyes on his patient, still gloved, he tossed the bundled drape back across the clean room into the biohazard container. It struck the back rim and opened. The contents of the drape emptied into the waste container—all except for one square of gauze from the worn, stained dressing.

An hour after Emery's entourage left, Nurse Christina Forman carefully checked the patient-controlled analgesic pump to make certain that it was infusing her patient, Constance Folcroft, with sufficient medication to stop the pain. Maintaining sterility with latex gloves, she inspected the incision site that Emery had redressed earlier. The incision was dry: no overt hemorrhaging, no exudate stain beyond the inserted drainage tube. Semi-conscious, the patient turned uneasily in her bed and accidentally knocked her copy of *Hawaii* off the nightstand. Christina knelt, placed the copy back on the table, covered the patient, and proceeded to the adjoining clean area by the biohazard container.

"How am I doing?" Christina heard her weakly call from the bed.

"Mrs. Folcroft, in a few days, you'll be lifting three hundred pounds," she said, removing her gloves before tossing them into the biohazard container.

"I'd be happy just to stop the pain. I keep pressing the button, but the medicine doesn't help."

"There's a lock-out on your pain med pump," Christina said. As she washed her hands, the water irritated a deep paper cut she'd suffered while writing notes an hour earlier. "It's an opioid, so it's not safe to take too much at a time. Makes you giddy. Then you'd really try lifting weights."

"Can't you do something? Please, I'm in—agony."

Christina dried her hands, threw the paper towel toward the wastebasket, and returned to her patient's side. Again, she checked the PCA pump. All the controls appeared to be functioning properly. Mrs. Folcroft had received a bolus of forty micrograms of morphine per kilogram of her body weight, followed by a maximum of 240 micrograms per kilogram of body weight per hour, with a ten-minute lockout—high dosing, but not a ceiling. "I'll let the doctor know. We'll see what we can do."

As Christina started to leave, she noticed the crumpled paper towel she'd used in the clean area was on the floor by the biowaste container. If Emery came by and noticed it—she'd seen him berate staffers for far more minor transgressions. Annoyed, she reached under the sink and picked up the moist towel. She crumpled it again, but it felt unexpectedly sticky, adhering to her right forefinger, the one with a paper cut, before slam-dunking it in the wastebasket.

SIX

Verity Healthcare Consultants

Scott picked up the phone ringing on his desk. "Hi Vince. Can I help you?"

The voice hesitated. "Did you get the FYI that I left for you?" It was Vincent Ingenito, Verity's Junior Vice President and Scott's direct supervisor.

"You mean Todd's obituary? Yes, but what—"

"We don't have much time, so listen. Gavin just left my office and he's headed toward yours. The roof's ready to cave in, so don't—"

"What're you talking—"

"Shut up and listen! Play it straight. Play it smart. Make them believe you don't know."

"Know? Know what?"

Ingenito paused. "You really don't know, do you? Christ, I guess why the hell should you? Even I don't know the whole damn convoluted thing."

"Vince, will you please tell me what you're talking about?"

"I'm sorry Scott. I've told you as much as I can at this point. See you later on seven." Click.

IRACT

"Our publications division," Barbieri said, waving his hand as he and Corliss walked through a small collection of corrals and conference rooms at the back end of the second floor. Overall, we've produced more than thirty-five monographs, many accessible online. Those in addition to our four periodicals, including *The Xeno News Forum,* a monthly patient-oriented newsletter; *The Institute Update,* a quarterly describing Institute news, protocol, and upcoming seminars; *The Institute Compendium of Xeno Research,* a physician-oriented quarterly, with recent abstracts, articles, and letters from leading researchers; and *The Journal of Xenotransplant Investigations,* giving firsthand preliminary reports of Institute research."

"Your subscription department?" Corliss asked, pointing to several rows of primarily women wearing headsets at the far end of the suite.

Barbieri shook his head. "Highly skilled nurses manning our free information hotlines, open to patients, and physicians. Available 24/7 by phone, fax, or e-mail. There's never a shortage of legitimate questions, myths that need dispelling, and occasionally irate ranting from those who're more concerned with animals than people. We available online either directly through the Institute's website, www.iract.org, or the xenotransplantation information center we maintain at www.xeno-solution.org." He pointed toward the elevator and steered his guest through a series of interlocking corrals. "We also have the largest online database of xenotransplantation technology publications in the world, larger even than the National Library of Medicine. Physicians, hospitals, consumer organizations, institutions, patients, anyone who subscribes has instant access to any xenotransplantation article published anywhere in the world."

"Effectively managing information is quintessential to

any successful operation, wouldn't you say Dr. Barbieri?" Corliss asked.

Just what the hell does he know? That reminds me of a more serious problem. "Please excuse me a moment," Barbieri said. He turned his back, whipped out his wireless, punched a preset code, and whispered, "Amanda, is our *other* VIP still here?"

"Yes," he heard her reply. "But not a word. I'll let you know the second I hear."

"What about Cruz? Has she come in yet?"

"No. And no one knows where she is."

"Where's Lockhart now?"

"Waiting for you at IT."

He disconnected. The elevator doors opened onto a sea of cubicles and corrals. CPUs blazing, the great room hummed with discordant chatter of operators on headsets as personnel scurried along the four-foot high divider maze. "Our pathology facilities underground may seem more exciting, but this is where it all happens. You see, there are never enough human donor organs to meet demands. Desperately ill people are placed on lists where they wait years if they're lucky enough to survive. To manage the chronic shortage, the Organ Procurement and Transplant Network, OPTN, managed by the United Network for Organ Sharing, UNOS, was established to make certain that organs were distributed in a fair manner. Organ Procurement Organizations, OPOs, sprang up to coordinate human organ retrieval and distribution. Though these OPOs were non-profits, their fees went unregulated." Barbieri lowered his voice. "And there were a number of situations in which some OPOs distributed organs in a questionable fashion. I still remember a case in which a state governor in need of a heart and lung was immediately moved to the head of a list. With an exact-match donor accidentally dying in the same city." Barbieri winked.

Corliss stared impassively at the COO.

He's not here for background info. That's for sure. Will I have to turn him over to Stone? "We make it possible for anyone who needs an organ to get one, on demand. We don't shuffle people through waiting lists. Or contact physicians in ICU facilities, waiting for declarations of brain death and family consent. Or force physicians to choose between a damaged organ or none at all. With us, everyone has the chance to live. After receiving a physician's request with specs, we contact PTS's Sacrifice Center, relay the case requirements, then coordinate transportation and delivery of the appropriate source organ. Our fee is less than 10% of that charged by a standard OPO—all paid directly by PTS."

"PTS won't always monopolize animal organs. What happens to this Institute then?"

He's probably just looking at the financial implications of PTS's expansion—nothing more! He smiled, masking a sigh of relief. "Our immediate challenge is finding additional working space and qualified personnel for the upcoming expansion."

Corliss looked up from his notepad. "Expansion?"

And that confirms it—just the financial end. There's no way he walked in here without knowing PTS's basic expansion plans! Peak this irritant's intellect, then get him the hell out of here! Barbieri said, "First of all, the FDA's recent approval of SPF-4912 liver organs for transplantation. We anticipate an additional twenty thousand transplantations next year alone. But that's relatively minor. Overall, PTS is ramping up source organ production. One of their goals is to provide sufficient source kidneys to reduce the number of dialysis patients to five percent of current levels."

"Ambitious, considering the hefty cost of animal transplantation. And in the face of growing annoyance within the beltway at PTS's monopoly status."

"PTS officials tell us that they have cost-effectiveness analyses to substantiate their claim. They're going to move that all health insurers be mandated to cover xenotransplantation as an option to dialysis."

"An uphill battle against the insurance lobby to be sure."

Barbieri shrugged and smiled. "Over the years, I've learned that PTS always finds a way. But then, that's only a small element of the expansion."

Corliss' eyes widened. "Then there is validity to rumors that PTS is entering the European market."

Barbieri nodded. "That's still unofficial, although PTS officials have informed us that they've passed through final review at the European version of the FDA, the EMEA, and anticipate an approval package within sixty days, indicating that PTS will be permitted to market SPF-4912 organs in Europe. However, the agreement stipulates that PTS must construct a Sacrifice Center *on the Continent* so that European regulatory agencies can more easily monitor production of SPF-4912 animals. That could potentially double the projected demand on Institute organ procurement activities. And it doesn't end there. PTS is working with the World Health Organization and the US State and Commerce Departments to make xenotransplantation more affordable in Third World countries."

"Because of black market organ activity in countries like India, where the poor often sell their kidneys to feed their families? Like on *60 Minutes*?"

"From a humanitarian standpoint, yes, of course," Barbieri said. "But more important, it's in our own best interests that we make xenotransplantation a viable option in other areas of the world. PTS has spent billions to produce specific pathogen-free animals for transplantation—animals devoid of harmful viruses. Resource-poor Third World surgeons may try to cut corners by using slaughterhouse pigs filled with God-knows-what kind of diseases."

Corliss took a moment to finish jotting his notes. He looked to Barbieri. "What do you have to say to your detractors who call this place the 'Piggy Bank?'"

Barbieri stared at Corliss. "They should thank God we're here."

On the next floor, they stopped at a computer center, an enclosure behind reinforced glass and steel security doors.

"This is information technology—IT," Barbieri said. "Behind those doors are—." He stopped and peered through the window: six workers were idly milling around their terminals. With the network down, they should have been frantically running around, but they looked bored. *What's going on?* Barbieri mouthed to the nearest technician.

The systems operator shrugged and pointed at the ceiling.

A well-groomed woman with ocher-colored hair in French braids appeared at Barbieri's side. She clutched a jade-colored pamphlet.

"Mr. Corliss, this is Loretta Lockhart, President of ATOP, Americans for Transplant Organ Progress. Also, one of the Institute's most ardent supporters."

They walked to a set of glass-enclosed offices. Nine data entry clerks had their feet propped on desks or were huddled in the kitchenette by the coffee machine. One clerk noticed Barbieri, standing arms akimbo, and promptly nudged two coworkers. The clique dispersed. Along the back wall, the door marked **Database Administrator—Evelyn Cruz** lay wide open. He peeked at the empty office a moment, shook his head, then continued, "Mr. Corliss, our Data Management Center. All data obtained from the laboratories below ground are coordinated with information submitted by participating hospitals and xenotransplantation sites around the country. In excess of two hundred thousand records all total, with continuous updating." He turned to Lockhart who handed him a jade-green booklet. "A sample initial report. Each xenotransplant center is required to submit one for each patient. With full approval for liver grafting, we're starting to color-code them by transplant type." He flipped through the pages. "They're quite extensive, including critical information on disease type, stage, general medical history, previous treatments, severity, patient response, recovery condition, laboratory reports, even cross-referencing to the patient's surgical team, as well as recovery and step-down nursing care personnel. More than four hundred entries on this initial report alone. Every patient requires periodic updating with the most comprehensive, xenotransplantation case report forms in the world. Our database has five times the depth of the FDA's."

"And centers can submit their reports electronically?" asked Corliss.

"Absolutely, but we still keep hard copies, including receipt acknowledgements and sign-offs by submitting doctors, and the usual array of security features. Evelyn Cruz, our Database Administrator, would be the best one to ask. Hopefully," turning toward her office, "she'll be in soon."

"How do you keep track of all that incoming data?"

"The thousands of patient reports coming into the Institute, whether mailed, our direct Electronic Data Interface which we call EDI, or via internet, are entered into the master SAS database. That's the Statistical Analysis System, latest version. The same one as the FDA and regulatory agencies around the world mandate for pharmaceutical, biotech, and medical device manufacturers. These patient records are entered as patient listings for a particular date. Unlike databases used for pharmaceutical clinical trials, ours never lock—meaning that they never close. Improperly managed, we'd have chaos. So, when our data management staff completes a series of new entries, that information is bundled in carefully coded listings files within SAS and is then made available for researchers, staff, and auditors. It's the only way to keep records in our massive databases straight so that they can be properly statistically analyzed. On the modern medical frontier, statistical analyses are more crucial than ever."

"So is the ability to manipulate them. What safeguards do you have to prevent that?"

Barbieri noticed that the data entry clerks were still idle. *Is the network still down? Why so long?* He approached one of the clerks and angrily pointed at the computer. The woman shrugged and pointed upstairs—just like the sysops in IT. *Who?* Barbieri mouthed.

The woman looked over at her desk, picked up a geode paperweight, and pointed emphatically at it.

"Oh shit!" Barbieri said, "Mr. Corliss, you'll have to excuse me. I have a pressing meeting I've completely forgotten. Ms. Lockhart will be more than happy to conclude your tour." He hurried toward the elevator.

"Dr. Barbieri, you haven't answered my question," Corliss called out. "Dr. Barbieri, my story isn't fin—"

But the elevator doors had already closed.

Norlake Xenotransplant Center

Once the best kickball player and prettiest girl in her third grade class, Brenda McCarthy now lay comatose, an intravenous drip inserted into her arm, attachments peppering her small torso, a thick tube leading from her abdomen to an extracorporeal liver assist device softly whooshing next to her. Hair disheveled, eyes drawn, her mother's head lay beside her daughter's as she held the little girl's limp hand.

Without entourage, Emery slipped into the room, stood by the foot of the bed for a moment, and watched his tiny patient.

"Oh, it's you doctor," Ms. McCarthy said, lifting her head.

"Let me again apologize for postponing the operation," he said softly. "There were unavoidable delays at the Sacrifice Center. They've assured me that the liver will arrive no later than seven A.M. tomorrow morning."

"I hate hospitals." The child's mother looked at the tower composed of a compact computer atop intricate arrays of tubes connecting a plethora of different distillation filters, charcoal columns, oxygenators, and pump. "Ugly looking machine, isn't it?"

"I don't care what it looks like," he said, glancing at the device, "as long as it removes the toxins in Brenda's body and prevents brain damage."

Ms. McCarthy looked up at him. "Am I doing the right thing?"

"Brenda has fulminant liver failure. A transplant's her only option."

"But she was so healthy just a few weeks ago." Sobbing, "How could it happen so fast?"

"Hepatitis B can sometimes just overwhelm the liver."

She wiped her eyes. "You're sure you can't use mine? A piece—"

"We've discussed this several times, Ms. McCarthy." He tenderly held her hand between his. "If we use part of your liver, three months from now, Brenda could be right back in this room with less chance than ever, unless there's another family member who'd be a willing donor."

She shook her head. "It's always been just the two of us."

Emery pulled up a chair and placed a great arm across her shoulders.

"Maybe I should wait for a—human donor. She's at the top of the waiting list—"

"She's *near* the top of the waiting list. It could be two, maybe three weeks. Brenda doesn't have that time."

She shivered. "Just the thought of a pig's liver in my baby's belly—"

"Ms. McCarthy, as we speak, Brenda's blood is being filtered through billions of pig liver cells. When you think about it, is there really any difference between a device that uses animal cells and a full organ—except that the animal organ will provide your daughter the same quality of life as a human one." He pulled up a chair and sat beside her. "We've reviewed the risks, the aftercare, the possible complications. Is there anything I haven't told you that you need to know, or explained in more detail?"

She shook her head.

"In a sense, the timing couldn't be better. The FDA only approved the use of these liver transplants in the last few weeks. For months prior, we weren't allowed to perform them, because the clinical trials had been closed and the FDA was still reviewing the data. If Brenda had become ill then, our only option would have been to wait and pray for a donor—pray for some other little girl or boy to die."

She clasped her daughter's hand tightly. "A friend told me to wait for a human one."

"I want to remind you that I have performed more liver xenotransplantations than anyone else in the world."

"Yes, Dr. Emery. I know you're the best." She brushed back her daughter's hair. "Can I think about it?"

"Of course. It's a difficult decision." He stood. "I don't want to seem callous, but I must know by eleven P.M. tonight. Because if Brenda isn't going to have that organ, some other desperate child will."

SEVEN

VERITY HEALTHCARE CONSULTANTS

Scott rummaged through the pile of medical journal articles, memos, and client communications. A photograph of a young boy peeked from beneath a stack of handwritten notes. Scott accidentally sliced his index finger on a sharp corner of the photo's silver-plated frame. A drop of blood splattered across the boy's piercing eyes. His skin suddenly felt icy. With a tissue, he wiped the stain from the smiling boy's face, a young incarnation of his own. *Sorry, Andy.*

"I need an eleven-letter word for dejected," a baritone announced from the doorway.

Scott looked up. John Gavin, Verity Healthcare's Senior Vice President, stood in the doorway. The man had a flattened nose, a jaw that dropped too far when he spoke, and exceedingly dark eyes that narrowed to lizard-like slits when he smiled. He liked to show his gold Rolex watch and, most of all, hear himself talk, though Scott reluctantly acknowledged that his comments were often on-target. Though adept at slithering through an opening in corporate hierarchy without angering those he passed on his ascent, Gavin was a momma's boy at home, enduing his first fifty-three years with an egocentric, domineering mother who had eroded away most of his self-esteem before she had died. Gavin was a man of extremes: a career bureaucrat living a pendulum existence between fear and mania, constantly extinguishing fires.

"So naturally you thought of me," Scott said. "Try 'crest-fallen.'"

Gavin opened the paperback book cradled in his hands and counted the blocks on the puzzle. "That'll work." He ambled around Scott's messy desk. "House cleaning?"

"Just reorganizing, Jack."

Gavin checked the hallway, then slowly closed the door. "Come here, and take some papers from the desk, for appearances." After Scott complied, "Now, it'll look as if we're discussing a specific project. Talk facing the window. It reduces eavesdropping or lip-reading."

"Okay Jack, who's getting axed?"

"I'm in a fight for my life, and like it or not, you're being dragged in." His eyes shifted toward the hall. "Senator Bannerman's here."

"He's just a public servant. You smile, you schmooze. He'll promise, he'll bull—"

"There's two types of politicians: the inane and the malevolent. Make no mistake, Senator Bannerman has a subcommittee chairmanship, inexhaustible backing, and a fireball forward philosophy. And right now, my friend, you're standing directly in his path."

"Me? What did I do?"

Gavin drummed on the pane. "Too good a job."

"You're not making sense."

"Privatizing the National Xenotransplant Registry has been Bannerman's special project. He's put a lot of time and money, as well as a chunk of his reputation behind it. The work you did before you came here puts all that in jeopardy."

"You mean when I was with The Society for Ethical Medical Advancements?"

"Yeah, whatever." He added, "And let's not forget that PTS's billion dollar Sacrifice Center is in his home state."

"Jack, my audit demonstrated that IRACT files are accurate. He'll have my corroborating testimony next week. What more could he want?"

"It's not the audit you just finished. It's your past."

"My activities before I came here are none of Bannerman's business."

"The ranking minority member on the committee, Senator Morton, came into possession of some of your reports. His wife had died of complications from kidney failure following xenotransplantation, so he was already skeptical of the whole process. Starting to get the picture?"

"It's still fuzzy."

"Then let me clarify it for you." Gavin wiped the perspiration from his lips. "On the one hand, you have IRACT, dedicated to promoting xeno technology, compiling data from thousands of transplant patients showing how safe and effective it is—confirmed by the audit we here at Verity performed. On the other hand, there's the auditor—you—who once railed against xenotransplantation and issued several prominent white papers for an activist group opposing xeno technology. And the same person—*you*—responsible for both audit and report. The committee chairman supports the Institute and xenografting. The ranking minority member, not only is skeptical, not only has his own political agenda, but is personally involved. And, on top of that, at stake is control of all data in this country that supports a $20 billion industry, an industry that is, at present, a monopoly."

"So Morton saw one of my reports—"

"And went ballistic. It could embarrass Bannerman, not to mention devastate the reputation of this company. Your personal flip-flop on the issue raises the specter of impropriety."

"I haven't flip-flopped. And you know me, Jack. I've never cheated—"

"Of course not. But are you willing to say that you were wrong? Naïve, maybe?"

Scott crossed his arms. "The company's going to let Bannerman fry me."

"Singe, maybe." Looking away, "And it's them, not me."

"Don't hand me crap! You're top management, for God's sake. Shouldn't—"

"Look, there's billions involved. Bannerman's precariously positioned. He can't risk having you testify that your papers before coming to Verity are correct. You've just said that you're not willing to denounce your earlier work. That kind of testimony could put the Institute in a bad light, maybe even jeopardize privatizing the FDA registry. Your credibility, and Bannerman's aspirations, would be destroyed. So the Senator is going to carefully, selectively discredit the work you performed prior to your tenure here at Verity—show that it was flawed while still preserving your credibility as auditor of the Institute's files. He'll probe you, look for weakness, so that when you testify, he'll be able to preempt Morton. If Morton waves one of your reports in front of the committee, Bannerman wants the perfect rebuttal in hand." He placed an imposing hand on Scott's shoulder. "Sorry, but you don't have much choice."

"I could resign. Tell you all to shove it up—"

"This is a U.S. Senate Subcommittee Chairman, not a company tribunal. If Bannerman wants to make an example of you, he can pursue you long after you've left Verity Healthcare. Then you'd be alone."

Scott focused on the man's wide pupils. "How deep will he probe?"

Gavin glanced away. "There's nothing I can do. There's nothing any of us can do. Scott m'boy, look, take some unpleasant advice. Senator Bannerman's going to try and walk all over you. Let him."

IRACT
Executive Lounge

Barbieri was about to barge into the executive lounge, when on the other side of the closed door, a voice screamed, "I don't have to justify anything to you! Goddamn it, leave me alone!" followed by a second, sedate, muffled voice, the words indistinguishable. *Wasn't Stone supposed to be alone?* He waited a moment before quietly knocking.

"Who is it?" the angry voice asked.

"It's Barbieri. Are you alone?"

"Yes."

"Then, if you're done with your phone call—"

"I wasn't on the phone, but I did expect you an hour ago. Come in and stop wasting my time!"

The door creaked as it opened. Damara Stone, PhD, sat alone, posture perfect, staring at the laptop on a coffee table. Long strawberry blond hair fell over her taupe leather dress and draped her muscular shoulders—shoulders seemingly incongruous with her petite, slightly emaciated five-foot four-inch frame. Generously freckled with crescent lips and high, sloping cheeks, her face would have been angelic, but down-turned creases around her mouth, shaped by a perpetually dour expression, had aged it beyond her thirty-eight years. But it was Damara Stone's misty blue eyes that both captivated and troubled Barbieri. He likened them to a video he'd once seen of a lake atop the Greenland tundra, so clear and colorless that it reflected the sky. He'd often find himself staring into those ultra pale blue eyes, seeking their bottom, but finding only a reflection of his own. Approaching Damara Stone was like a male black widow spider seeking its female: compelled by nature, likely to wind up a meal. Even after three years, her frequently unannounced visits to the Institute unnerved him as profoundly as the first. "Damara—"

"Quiet!"

At a party, he'd once described her to Emery as 'beautiful, brilliant, and brutal.' Beautiful was obvious. Brilliant in that, in just her early thirties, she'd become Vice President of Research and Development at ApothePharma Pharmaceuticals—supposedly PTS's CEO had personally recruited Damara Stone for the Senior Vice President of PTS's Whole Organ Enterprises after a surprise resignation from ApothePharma. Brutal in that she pushed projects through the FDA's regulatory process with unmerciful efficiency while keeping a tight reign on the Institute's research and data collection activities.

After an exaggerated tap on the laptop's screen track, Dr. Damara Stone glanced at him. "You want to know why I ordered Foster in IT to shut down the Network? Then come here."

Barbieri complied. Stone's laptop screen displayed a tree of subdirectories on the left side, individual files on the right. She used the tracker to point to the subdirectory **STAT-COM/TRACT**, then clicked. The file names on the right side of the screen changed. Each listed file had a byte size and date of construction. Barbieri surveyed the top of the list:

KEAL1199_017
KEAL1199_16
KEAL1199_015
KEAL1199_1006
KEAL1199_1005

" 'E' series patient listing files?"

"Stat summary files, too." She clicked on a file. "A patient report batch from the Tryonville Center."

Barbieri stared. *Transformed* patient listing files? On a laptop? That's a hell of a security breach."

She continued scrolling down the list. "My laptop, but not my files."

"Damn, how much is on here?"

She ran a finger over the track screen. "Quite probably every raw and transformed file."

"It all fits on a laptop?"

Stone shook her head. "Amazing that someone supposedly in charge of so much information could know so little about it. Patient listing files are small, only about 25 to 50 Kb. Batch statistical summary files even smaller. All total, two to three Gigs, max."

"Who?"

"Copying transformed files requires someone with both access and expertise to circumvent security measures."

"Meaning you, me, Foster, and Cruz."

"We'll exclude me," she said with an icy smile, "since I'm in charge."

Barbieri let her crack pass. "It sure as hell wasn't me."

"You have the access, but not the fortitude."

"If it was Foster, you'd have had him bound and gagged. So it's Cruz?"

Stone's smile dissipated. "We downloaded these files directly from her home PC."

"Maybe Evelyn had a reason. She could have been working on them at home."

"Are you defending her?"

"No, certainly not." Barbieri hesitated. "But those files are useless without the Institute's program. I know it's a bad breach, but—"

"In case you've forgotten, Verity Healthcare completed an audit a few weeks ago. If they should get hold of these files—"

"Why would Evelyn do this?"

"Probably an attack of conscience—like Todd." Stone directed the screen's arrow to a new subdirectory and clicked twice. A new folder marked *AIMS* appeared. She clicked again. It was empty. "She probably also copied the transforming subprogram."

"AIMS? Damn, we've got to find out who Evelyn was working with!"

"That won't be easy—now."

"Oh no, tell me you didn't!" He gazed directly into Stone's bottomless eyes.

"I told you six months ago to dump her when things started deteriorating with Todd. Since he set up the System, he probably created a back door and gave Cruz the key."

Barbieri put his head in his hands. "You didn't have to kill her!"

Stone opened the top left drawer and removed a cellular phone. "Funny how you were so anxious to clip Todd. He was your best friend for years, yet all he ever did to earn your wrath was call you a fraud and give you a black eye. But now with Cruz—." She pressed the power button and proffered him the phone. "If you wish to lodge a complaint, just give him a call. The number's pre-programmed."

Barbieri turned away, gazing at the oppressive clouds outside his window.

Stone punched a preset number on the cellular. "It's me," she said into the phone. "Last night, did you leave the target's system on?" A static-ridden voice answered. "Good. Is the password deleted?" She nodded. "Wait till you hear from me." She disconnected, activated her laptop modem, then began scanning the file management system on Cruz's home computer. A minute later, she located another folder.

"What're you doing?" Barbieri rasped.

"Trying to determine whether Cruz had any pathology summary files on her home PC."

"How the hell would she get access to those?"

"She was in charge of the databases, remember?"

"At least those files are encrypted."

"Which guarantees nothing," she said. "So far, we've been lucky. I haven't found any of those in the files downloaded onto this laptop."

"If it's not on your laptop, then either she never had any or they've been deleted. Either way, there's no problem."

Stone rapped on the keyboard. "When a file is deleted, it's not destroyed. The record is just marked for deletion and no longer displayed. If it hasn't been overwritten, then the file is often still in there, retrievable and—" She stopped, leaned back, and covered her mouth.

EIGHT

The overcast permeating the windows matched the gray of Verity Healthcare's Executive Conference Room: the blended berber carpeting, the nubby fabric soundproofing the walls, even the tinge on the polished forty-foot rectangular table. Scott sipped coffee near the demonstration board at one end of the table, a black disposable pen in front of him. At the far end of the table was United States Senator Stanford Bannerman. He leaned to his right and started quietly conversing with his top aide, David Price, Esq., who nodded obsequiously each time the Senator subtly gestured with his index finger. Verity Healthcare's President, M. Jessica Tremayne, sat three seats to their right, her hands folded, as if in prayer, a fixed diplomatic smile plastered across her face. Verity's Senior Vice President, Jack Gavin, stood behind her, adding artificial sweetener to his tea at the coffee service set-up on a side table against one wall.

Cool air rushed across the back of Scott's neck from the

door opening behind him. He glanced back just as Vincent Ingenito, Verity's Junior Vice President and Scott's direct supervisor, hurriedly entered. Lean, olive-skinned, five-foot-five with tightly-cropped curly black hair, a dense, square moustache, and deep-set brown eyes, Ignito nodded respectfully at the VIPs. "Sorry for the delay."

"We still need a moment," Price, the Senator's aide said.

Ingenito stepped behind Scott's chair, leaned down, and whispered, "What did Gavin say to you?"

"He warned me about this meeting," Scott returned, "and Bannerman's agenda."

"What else?"

"He was nervous." Scott looked directly at his boss. "More nervous than you."

Ingenito hissed through his teeth, "That's bad. Worse than I thought."

"Is there a problem?" Gavin asked from behind them.

Ingenito jumped. "No—no I'm just giving our man here a little pep talk." He patted Scott's shoulder, "We'll talk later." He joined the others at the far side of the table.

Gavin glanced at the door. "Where's Rogers?"

"I gave him a couple of days off."

"He should be here."

"I didn't know about today's meeting until after I'd already given him the time."

Gavin leaned in close and whispered, "Scott, the Senator wants to be absolutely certain that there are no surprises when you testify at the hearing next week. The audit his sub-committee ordered generated more than $2.2 million *net* for the firm, but the prestige and PR are worth twenty times that." Pursing his lips, "It's all just politics. We help him look good and there's no telling how grateful he'll be. I mean, take a good look at the man!"

Strapping, with deep blue eyes, ruddy complexion, thick shock of silver hair with every strand in place, and the physique of a power back, Senator Stanford Bannerman of the Commonwealth of Virginia presented a camera-perfect image that would complement a business suit, rolled up white shirt sleeves, blue collar and hard hat, or knitted polo.

"Presidential handsome," Gavin continued, patting Scott's shoulder. "Prove to me again that you are the man I hired." He returned to the others.

"Let's get started," Tremayne announced.

Scott gazed at M. Jessica Tremayne, CEO and President of Verity Healthcare, in her olive green dress with big black buttons that accentuated her matronly figure, plain face, and pallid complexion. The woman was as tenacious as she was unattractive—chucking the corporate glass ceiling, ridding herself of an abusive husband, founding and growing a successful company while raising three children, alone. But more important to Scott, she was fair-minded.

"As everyone in this room is aware, Senator Bannerman is Chairman of the Senate Subcommittee on Labor, Health and Human Services and Education," she said, her mouth listing left as she spoke, the remnants of an old stroke. "About a year ago, his subcommittee awarded this firm a contract to audit patient records maintained by the Institute for the Research of Animal Compatible Transplantations, which collects data on xenotransplantation patients. The audit was to include processing, collection and collation of data submitted from source documents at participating medical centers, results of tissue and serum specimens from patients, family members, and medical center staffers, as well as an independent statistical analysis of the Institute's databases. Verity Healthcare was commissioned to assess how well the Institute keeps patient records and whether its findings are accurate. The chosen test topic was renal xenotransplantation."

"Chosen because it's the largest whole organ application of xeno technology," Bannerman said, his rich voice rooted with a genteel, melodic accent.

"Verity Healthcare completed that audit under the auspices of Dr. Scott Merritt," Tremayne continued. "Well within the allotted timeframe, I might add."

"Before we go into the specifics of the audit, Ms.

Tremayne, I have a few questions for the doctor," the Senator said. "It could help divert unfriendly fire some of my fellow committeepersons might steer his way."

Gavin raised his chin and glared; Ingenito peered at his lap.

Scott glanced at them. *They expect me to go politely to the slaughter?*

Bannerman nodded to his top assistant, David Price. Scott quickly appraised the attorney: aquiline nose, slate-colored eyes, nut-brown hair with a sharp part on the right where his scalp showed through like a dry riverbed, and a toned body probably shaped by regular gym visits and 10K runs. He had the quintessential demeanor of a conservative senatorial aide: confident, predatory, and operating within but always testing his master's limits. He wore a dark tweed suit and button-down white collar shirt with a golden tie-pin, but Scott sensed that the man would have easily fit into judgment garbs worn during the Salem witchcraft trials. Price opened a rich leather hard-frame briefcase, pulled out an ivory folder, and buried his face in it. "Good morning, Dr. Merritt," he began. "Let's see how you—*merit*."

Scott stared down Senator Bannerman's counsel. "That's *priceless*." With his right hand, he removed the cap of his black pen. Quickly, one-handed, he slid the pen down his palm, shoved the cap on the other end of its shaft, removed the cap, slid the pen up his palm, and snapped the cap back onto the point. The pen trick: part nervous habit, but mostly to prove to himself that he still had the dexterity of a surgeon.

"Let's see. A Bachelor's in biochemistry from the University of Virginia, a Masters in Biostatistics from Rutgers. A medical degree from the University of Pennsylvania, brief internship, followed by a Captaincy at," Price looked up from the folder, "my records are a little unclear. Was it Elmendorf or Eilson Air Force Base?"

"I was based out of Elmendorf in Anchorage, but they'd often shuttle me to Eielson near Fairbanks to service the Sixth and Ninety-seventh Bomb Wings and the 354th Fighter Wing."

"As repayment on your school loans," Price stated.

Senator Bannerman lightly touched Price's sleeve. "For services we in this room and this nation respect and gratefully acknowledge," he said, his voice velvety, as if delivered from a podium.

"Of course," Price added quickly. "Did you ever get used to that cold?"

The rapidly moving pen slowed in Scott's hand. An enveloping frigidity crept into his fingers, numbing the tips, stiffening his joints, cracking his skin. His hands remembered the pain. And though he had loved Alaska, he swore he'd never have to endure that kind of bitter cold again. "In time and after a fashion."

Price glanced at the folder. "Then on to a rather lengthy residency in orthopedics from the University of Pennsylvania. That made you several years older than most of your fellow residents." Looking up, "It seems that by the time you physicians are ready to start, you're middle-aged and by the time you're prepared, you're ready to retire." Holding up his hand, "Sorry, that was rhetorical. Nonetheless Dr. Merritt, you became a general partner in a very successful orthopedic practice. And after all those years of schooling, of military service, of residency, of building a practice, after all that time, suddenly, four years ago, you stop practicing." With a curt smile, "Now you work for less than half of your previous salary."

"Closer to twenty percent, after taxes."

Price leafed through the folder for a full minute. "Dr. Merritt, based on your clinical experience, what would you say the probability is for a 23-year-old woman, of normal weight with an unremarkable medical history, to develop a fatal pulmonary embolism following arthroscopic repair of the anterior cruciate ligament of the knee." Glancing back at Bannerman, "A pulmonary embolism, a 'PE', is a blood clot that travels through the body and lodges in the lung."

Scott twirled the pen faster. "It depends."

"Certainly less than one in a thousand, wouldn't you say, doctor?"

"It can happen," the pen racing along Scott's palm—a blur in his hands, "to the best of us."

"No one's saying that it's your fault. We're just here trying to calculate the odds." Price returned to his folder. "And then the odds of a 25-year-old construction worker, also in perfect health, in for repair of a torn rotator cuff, dying of an anesthesia mishap? Less than one in ten thousand, to be sure. And before you object, isn't a surgeon like the captain of a ship, responsible for everything that transpires on his watch?"

"That's how it's perceived."

"And the odds of a 33-year-old housewife, in for an open reduction with internal fixation, dying—"

Scott slapped his hand on the table. "You have no idea what it's like to be a surgeon, to *physically* hold a life in your hands. No, your hands just carry the McCarthy briefcase—"

"Mr. Price, I find your line of questioning inappropriate," Tremayne interrupted. Glancing at Bannerman, "Please sir, throttle back."

Bannerman touched Price's shoulder. The Senator's assistant continued, "I merely wanted to point out that the odds of these three incidents are one in ten billion. And if one considers that these three incidents happened all in one week, well, Dr. Merritt must have been the unluckiest surgeon in the history of medicine." Before looking through his folder, Price faintly smiled at the sight of Scott baring his teeth. "Tell me Dr. Merritt, do you remember Mrs. Rose Thornton? Your patient, four years ago, underwent a standard hip arthroplasty? Your partner, Dr. Benjamin Waltham, had to rush in to relieve you. That incident led to the breakup of your partnership."

"I remember."

Price looked up over his folder. "In fact, that led to your retiring from medical practice, didn't it?"

"Damn it, I said 'I remember!' "

"You froze during surgery," Price declared. "But that description wouldn't be completely accurate, now would it?

More like," glancing down at the folder, "diplopia, paresthesia of the lower extremities, and ataxia? Symptoms of an attack?"

Scott sat straight up, put on his glasses, and stood. "Yes, I have multiple sclerosis—relapsing-remitting multiple sclerosis. I developed it four years ago. Everyone in this room knows I have it. I'm not ashamed. It's not who I am, it's what I deal with."

"No one's implying shame, doctor." Thumbing through the folder, "Just a bit of clarification on your condition. I believe you self-medicate with injections of Interferon IA—a rather old treatment—weekly, every Sunday night. With the whole host of unfortunate side effects that often follow, why inject yourself right before the work week?"

"Less disruptive to my family. This way, I get a whole healthy weekend with them," glancing at Tremayne, "while still putting in a full, productive workweek."

Price noticed Tremayne's slow nodding agreement. "And those symptoms?"

The bastard wants to humiliate me! Do I tell him all about the arthritic pains, the fevers, the sweats, the vision problems, the weak limbs, the burning-buzzing-numbing pain in my legs like a cranked-up funny bone, and all the other little indignities that go with it? For an instant, an image flashed of how bad it could get, of how severely the disease had affected some people he'd known. "I've been lucky."

Price countered with a cross-examiner's ruthless smile. "I'll bet you didn't feel that way when your malpractice insurance carrier quadrupled your insurance rates because of your affliction—and no one else would cover you for surgery."

For a moment, Scott was gowned, gloved, masked, back in the O.R., a bountifully-stocked and arrayed instrument table to his right, surgical nurses and residents gathered around the draped patient comfortably sedated on the operating table beneath hot lights, the anesthesiologist's nod, but most of all, his hands craving to rescue a damaged limb. "Surgery was all I ever wanted to do."

Price flipped through several pages of Scott's file. "That explains why you stopped performing surgery, not why you gave up on all of medicine."

Scott walked ominously toward Senator Bannerman's counsel. "Does this make you feel like a big man, Price? Or maybe you'd like to prove just how big you are?"

"Scott, please sit down," Tremayne said sharply. Turning to Bannerman, "And respectfully, sir, if your assistant continues to debase Dr. Merritt, I'll have to end this."

Bannerman leaned over and whispered into Price's ear. The counsel's posture relaxed as he nodded obsequiously. Price frowned at Scott. "I'm sorry about your affliction, doctor. Let's hope that you continue doing as remarkably well as you appear." To Verity's president, "Of course Dr. Merritt deserves our respect and admiration for what he has accomplished in spite of his illness. I just have a few more questions."

Scott returned to his seat, his fists clenched.

Tremayne looked to the Senator, who nodded. "Proceed," she said to Price, "for now."

Price turned to Scott. "Dr. Merritt, how many attacks have you had?"

"All total, four since I was diagnosed."

"Including that unfortunate incident with Mrs. Thornton four years ago?"

Scott resumed his pen trick, rapidly removing and returning the pen's cap. "I hadn't been officially diagnosed at that time." He smirked. "Who's to say?"

"I take it that it's possible for you to have an attack without people around you being aware of it?"

Scott hesitated. "Yes."

"And to your knowledge, have you ever had an attack and been unaware of it?"

"No. MS isn't like epilepsy."

"Then tell us about one of your attacks."

Scott shrugged. "They're infrequent, usually preceded by an illness, bronchitis, pneumonia, something of that order.

Often brought on or exacerbated by stress. Typically there's loss of vision in my left eye, like a dark curtain moving from the edge of my field of vision inward—or fuzzy, like looking through saran wrap. My wrists, my legs grow weak. I've fallen a few times."

Price scanned the file. "Let's return to those three patients who unexpectedly died on your operating—"

"In no way did I—nor would I—ever allow my illness to compromise the safety of my patients!"

"You mean the ones who died?"

Scott took a couple steps, stretched across the table, and catching Price by surprise, grabbed the attorney's folder and flung it against the wall. Gasps arose around the room.

The attorney condescendingly smiled. "Once news of your illness became public, your malpractice insurance carrier quickly settled out of court. Eagerly, I might add."

"I wanted to fight. Their lawyers didn't."

"You still haven't answered my question. Dr. Merritt, were you—"

"That's enough, Price!" Tremayne snapped. "We're well aware of the circumstances under which Dr. Merritt left private practice."

"Are you certain that you know *all* the circumstances, Ms. Tremayne?" Price asked.

She glanced at Scott. "I'd like to think so."

Price looked to the Senator, then to Scott. "Dr. Merritt, let me ask you a strictly medical question. Are hallucinations a common consequence or symptom of relapsing-remitting MS? Or any type of MS for that matter?"

"No."

"So then you would say that there's no medical basis for hallucinations or *visions* being associated with MS?"

"Didn't I just say that?"

Price nodded. "And have you personally, Dr. Merritt, experienced any hallucination or vision that you might consider possibly associated with your affliction?"

"*Mild* hallucinations are a possible side effect of steroid treatment following an attack," Scott paused. "But I've never experienced that."

"I was thinking more along of the lines of while you were in surgery."

"Certainly not." Scott looked around the room. "Though it is possible I might have daydreamed for an instant about some Tahitian beach." A few chuckles arose from Verity's senior staff.

Unblinking, Price said, "Perhaps while you were standing with a scalpel over one of those unfortunate patients who—"

"Never there!" Scott blurted.

Price reached into his briefcase and pulled out another folder. "According to one witness, you've gone into several 'trances' during which you've talked about a plague decimating the world. Millions of people laying dead, rotting in abandoned streets. Another witness reported similar episodes, except that you were floating in some generic intensive care unit, 'ground zero' I believe you called it, where the pandemic would begin—a pandemic caused by xenotransplantation gone awry—and that you were the only one on Earth who could prevent it."

Scott reached for the file. "Where did you—"

"There are at least seven other witnesses who've seen or overheard similar incidents." Price said, smoothly passing the folder to his other hand, beyond Scott's grasp. "Including the anesthesiologist who was present at the very last surgery you performed."

"An eternity ago," Scott whispered.

"An admission, doctor?"

"You little bastard, I—"

"So, we're left with four possible explanations," Price said. "One, you have somehow found a way to violate the laws of physics and nature and can actually see into the future. Two, these visions are some heretofore completely unique, never before or since recognized consequence of MS. Three, you are in strong need of psychiatric counseling. Or four, your visions are just manifestations of your own personal bias against xenotransplantation. Which do you think applies, Dr. Merritt?" Everyone in the room turned to Scott, except Tremayne glowering at Price. "This does lead directly into my next series of questions, Ms. Tremayne."

She grimaced. "I'd like to move onto the more important issues ASAP."

"Certainly," Price said. To Scott, "Dr. Merritt, after you left practice, you worked as a volunteer for a time for the Society for Ethical Medical Advancements?"

"I needed to establish writing and consulting credentials in a new profession. SEMA appeared perfect," Scott said. "It's an honorable non-profit alliance of concerned medical professionals who—"

"Recognize this?" Price asked, reaching under his seat and propped a thick, yellow bound report on the table.

"A treatise I co-authored while working for SEMA," he hissed.

"An elegant condemnation of whole organ xenotransplantation." Price let the report slip through his hands. It thumped onto the table. "Though a little verbose."

"Expecting me to denounce it, Price?" Scott grinned. "Over your dead body."

"Scott!" Tremayne started. "That was uncalled—"

"Your executive summary here lists twenty-five reasons why xenotransplantation and xeno research should be stopped outright," Price said, thumbing through the report. "Most are outdated. The FDA is satisfied with the current efficacy and safety data on various xeno technology applications."

"Well, duh! That's why we're here today, Price, because of the Agency's less than stellar job as National Xenotransplant Registry."

The Senator chuckled. Price waited until his boss' laughter subsided. "As your treatise is rather lengthy and I don't have copies for everyone, I'd like to read aloud the last few paragraphs from the executive summary, if I might." Before Scott could object, Price read:

Xenotransplantation circumvents the skin, the gastrointestinal system, and other natural barriers designed to prevent transmission of disease-causing viruses, bacteria, prions, and other infectious organisms among different species, and most especially between animals and human beings. This greatly increases the risk of xenosis: transmission of an animal virus to a human host via xenotransplantation.

All donor (source) animals potentially harbor viruses that exist within the animal's organ matrix, or lay dormant for years or generations, within the animal's own DNA. This latter group—known as endogenous viruses and includes retroviruses—if introduced to a new species host environment with a depressed immune system, might activate, mutate, and/or combine with human viral components and create an organism with dire infectious characteristics. If the odds against such a viral recombination were as low as a million-to-one, then based on the projected increase of xenotransplantations over the next ten years, the United States will face a potentially catastrophic plague once every three years.

Proponents of whole organ xenotransplantation contend that pathogen-free animals can be genetically-engineered and maintained in "germ-free" environments. Proponents of xeno technology also contend that polymerase chain reaction (PCR) testing of animal (source) organ DNA, along with increasingly sensitive and varied assays for viruses and viral products in these animals, eliminate the risk of xenosis. These assertions are unproven—it is not possible to screen for unknown viruses.

The above concerns are based not only in fact, but also in history. Have the world's governments forgotten that at the end of World War I, twenty million people died during an influenza epidemic from a virus that originated in pigs, the same animals used today for xenotransplantation? Have these governments forgotten the hundred million plus people who died from HIV, which originated in African primates? We cannot prevent calamities by developing 'better, cleaner, disease-free' animals for xenotransplantation. Therefore, the Society urges permanent cessation of all whole or partial organ xenotransplantation and, in its place, supports ethically sound measures that would increase the availability of human donor organs, and increased funds to expand research to develop practical artificial and/or synthetic organs.

Around the turn of this century, Klaus Hammer wrote that in order for xenotransplantation to succeed, humanity must learn to outwit evolution. We wish to add that if humanity chooses this course of action, we could find ourselves extinct.

Price closed the thick yellow document and positioned it so that Tremayne and the other Verity officers could read its title: *The Global Threat From Xenotransplantation.* "Ms. Tremayne, why would you place the author of such a document in charge of auditing the Institute?"

Tremayne gazed stiff-jawed at the senator. "Dr. Merritt is not only our top analyst, but his unswerving attention to detail has made him a very thorough, efficient auditor."

Price turned to Scott. "Do you still believe in that document's conclusions?"

"That's what the report says, Price," Scott shot back.

"But that isn't what you really wanted the audit to conclude, now is it?"

"What I want is irrelevant. What I believe is irrelevant. What matters is the way in which I conducted the audit—professionally and without bias!"

"We'll come back to that." Price slowly smiled. "Your mother was quite ill. What did she suffer from?"

"Kidney failure. End-stage renal disease," Scott growled.

"She was on dialysis for years, wasn't it, *before* she underwent kidney xenotransplantation."

"Before I finished the audit, Price. Before!"

"It must have been terribly difficult, watching your mother die from complications following xenotransplantation, a medical procedure you find scientifically and morally reprehensible. A procedure that you spent years fighting. Surely you two must have argued before she agreed to the surgery."

"That's none of your damn business!"

"She died shortly after transplantation. How did that make you feel?"

"How do you think that made me feel, you Goddamn—"

"Gentlemen!" Tremayne barked.

Price cracked his knuckles. "What I'm getting at, doctor, is didn't you want to prove that xeno was ineffective? A public health hazard even?"

Scott pounded a fist into his other hand. He edged toward the attorney. "You're damn right I did!"

Price cocked his head at Scott and deliberately blinked. "Coupling your personal convictions and your mother's death with your—for want of better terminology—*dangerous visions,* why didn't you?"

Scott wiped sweat beading on his forehead. He wanted to pick up Price by the throat and throw him out the window. He wanted to tear Senator Bannerman apart for orchestrating this. But most of all, he wanted to demolish his own immovable pillars of ethics and morality obstructing him from what was likely the greater good. "That would have been wrong. Being a lawyer, it's beyond your understanding."

"Not touché, doctor. Cliché." Price chuckled as he reached into his briefcase and placed a red-bound document on the table. "I needed to know whether this audit of yours is correct as is."

"IRACT's record keeping is accurate to 99.99%."

"Then there are no confirmed cases of xenosis—transspecies infections."

"Your question has been answered."

"One last thing, doctor." Price leaned forward and whispered, "Are you still having those visions of yours?"

Scott started toward the attorney, but Ingenito stepped in front of him. "Forget that little ass-wipe, he's nothing," the junior VP whispered in Scott's ear. "I'm just a couple pieces shy of assembling the whole dirty puzzle. If you—"

"Excuse my overzealous assistant, Dr. Merritt," Senator Bannerman said. "I regret having to put you through that. But I had to be certain for myself that your work *and you* are, indeed, unbiased. My subcommittee is charged with providing leadership for the health and safety of this nation. There's no arguing that, theoretically, xenotransplantation has inherent risks. We must maintain our diligence to eliminate, or at the very least, minimize those risks. Years ago, as part of the agreement allowing xeno technology to move forward, it was decided that a National Xenotransplant Registry had to be established to monitor patients and providers alike, to safeguard against potential epidemics. At the time, it was thought that FDA, which regulates drug and medical devices in this country, would be the natural repository for such an activity. That thinking was woefully wrong. But bureaucracy, cutbacks, apathy, they've all crippled FDA's vigilance. Hence, our reasons for wresting the National Registry from that government bureaucracy and awarding it to the Institute."

Ingenito gave Scott a long, lingering, pensive look before stepping back. They both returned to their seats.

"Not to mention the projected millions in savings by privatizing the operation," Scott said, pulling in his chair behind him.

Bannerman smiled. "I am not a supporter of big government."

"Are you soliciting my vote, sir?" Scott asked with a measured touch of sarcasm.

The Senator bowed his head. "I admire men of strong conviction. I know you still oppose xeno technology, which doubtless made this project particularly burdensome for you, but by verifying that the Institute's records support xeno, you personally are helping ensure the public's safety. And isn't that SEMA's ultimate goal?"

Politicians. They twist the truth so well, Scott thought, picking up his pen.

"Senator Morton, my esteemed colleague from Ohio, is skeptical of privatizing the Registry." Bannerman picked up the yellow report. "He obtained a copy of this treatise, which contradicts the audit, and is particularly disturbed that you authored both reports—the *pro bono* one scathing xenotransplantation and the remunerated version praising it. He will be unmerciful when you take the stand. Which is why you had to go through this unfortunate grilling this morning."

"I'm sorry, Dr. Merritt," Price added. "I truly am."

Tremayne said, "Senator Bannerman is here today, off the record, to give Verity Healthcare the opportunity to avoid the appearance of impropriety."

Ingenito asked, "Senator, I'm not an attorney, but isn't it inappropriate for a committee member to, uh, coach the witness?"

"I just came here to clarify some outstanding issues." Bannerman laid both documents flat on the table. "Now, I'm satisfied."

"Wonderful." Tremayne glanced up and down the table. "If there's nothing further to discuss, then I believe we can adjourn."

Bannerman stood. "I look forward to your testimony next week at—"

"I have a question for the senator," Scott announced.

Tremayne's head whipped in his direction. The others instantly followed. "Scott, the Senator has a train to—"

"I have time for Dr. Merritt's question," Bannerman said. "Lord only knows, after what the poor man has been through this last hour, he's entitled."

Scott disregarded warning stares from his colleagues,

"With all the effort your subcommittee has expended on xenotransplantation, why hasn't it ever introduced '*presumed consent?*' "

"What's 'presumed consent?' " Ingentio blurted.

"It's law stating that a dying or dead person is presumed to give his or her consent to donate his or her organs, unless otherwise specified," Scott answered. "Presumed consent can't be overruled by a family member."

"Right you are, doctor," Bannerman said. "The committee felt that presumed consent is more an issue for the states than the federal government. A number of states already ask people if they want to donate, and include donor status on drivers' licenses."

"Many don't," Scott said. "Congress has the power to implement it, nationally."

"That's a rather involved discussion involving a number of sensitive issues."

"It's been implemented successfully in Spain and other European countries."

"Which have far smaller populations," Bannerman returned.

"Presumed consent could potentially reduce the demand for animal organs."

"The committee is in receipt of a number of assessments clearly showing that the supply of donated human organ will never come close to meeting demand, especially for patients on dialysis."

Scott once again twirled the pen in his hand at blurring speed. "Were those assessments provided by Paradigm Transplant Solutions—which coincidentally, has its Sacrifice Center in your home state?"

"Dr. Merritt!" Tremayne gasped.

The senator grinned. "If you'd like, I'll have those assessments delivered to you personally by week's end."

Scott nodded. *But not in time to make a difference.*

"When one gets down to brass tacks, Dr. Merritt, xenotransplantation is just another medical procedure. One of thousands performed daily."

"With all due respect, Senator, I'm the only man in this room who's ever performed surgery. Take it from someone who's had his hands inside another human being—this is not just another medical procedure."

The senator turned to leave. "And why not, doctor?"

The pen stopped dead in Scott's hand. He held it like a scalpel. "When I performed surgery, I risked the life of my patient. When a xenotransplant specialist performs surgery, he's also risking the lives of his patient's neighbors down the street."

NINE

Scott shoved papers into unlabeled folders piled on his desk. Two banker boxes lay at his feet. A third, unassembled, leaned against a filing cabinet.

Hands in pockets, Gavin quietly ambled across Scott's office and stopped in front of a chair piled with papers. He picked up the package from Dylan, glanced at it, then absently placed it back on the desk. "Planning on working at home?"

Scott gazed at the package, then tossed it across the room. It struck his open briefcase and fell inside the well. The top half of the briefcase tottered, and closed on it. "You hung me out to dry. All of you."

"The Senator needed to see for himself how you'd react. Your job's not in jeopardy."

"The hell with Bannerman, with IRACT, with Verity, and with you, Jack."

"When you first applied here, I didn't know what to make

of you. But I saw something special, and I fought to hire you. I don't want to lose you now."

"At such a critical juncture, you mean."

"Scott m'boy, you're exhausted. Take some time off. Take that pretty wife of yours to lunch or something."

Scott snorted. "Way ahead of you, Jack. She's coming into Philly this Friday for lunch. Someplace special."

"Oh? Where?"

"*Tout a Vous.*"

"At the Bourse? Excellent choice." He took a deep breath. "Look, I'm clearing your schedule for the rest of the week. Take some personal time. Just be at the Washington Grand Hyatt by Monday afternoon."

Scott grabbed the travel folder protruding from a stack of yellow papers and slid it into his coat pocket. "I'll think I'll take you up on that."

"Great. What's more, I'm going to arrange for you and your clan to have the company condo on Sanibel Island for two weeks, either at the end of this month or beginning of next. Candice and the kids will love it."

Scott picked up his briefcase. *Think you can buy me that easily?*

Gavin draped his arm around his employee. "I know you're understandably angry. But here's some sound advice for anyone working in the corporate world. Ask yourself this: 'Do I want to be right, or do I want to be happy?' "

IRACT

". . . but Cruz might not have made additional copies, in which case we're chasing shadows," Barbieri said.

Stone continued to evaluate files downloaded into her laptop. "Cruz had a guest in her townhouse last night. Unfortunately, I don't have a name or a license plate. But," pulling out a small black notebook from her jacket, "I have this."

"Am I in there, too?"

Stone rendered a chilling smile. "Barbieri, Edward. Began medical career at Cornell. After treating his first patient, found he couldn't stand the sight of blood. After treating his second, found he couldn't stand the sight of patients, so he switched to radiology. But his radiographic interpretations were—creative. After two divorces with fat alimony checks leading to bankruptcy, he discovered that he performed his best diagnoses in board rooms and his finest surgeries on banquet room floors, leading him, circuitously, to these cushy confines."

"I live for the day you finish here."

"Till then, you and I and our respective organizations are stuck with each other."

"Like brothers, each with a knife to the other's throat." Barbieri sat back and crossed his arms. "Did Evelyn have to die?"

"If your question isn't rhetorical, you're an even bigger fool than I thought."

Barbieri sighed. "I take it that PTS hasn't made any new inroads."

She nodded. "Which probably still surpasses your techno-boobs downstairs."

"Damara, what if the problem's insoluble?" Barbieri wrung his head in his hands. "Did you ever *consider* the possibility of going public? Maybe the FDA—"

FDA. FDA. The sceen on her laptop blurred. Dr. Damara Stone found herself back at ApothePharma Pharmaceticals in the office of the company president, a bald, furrow-browed little man seated behind a $25,000 desk. She was Vice President of Research and Development. To her left stood Executive VP, Lawrence Gainly, a husky man with polished teeth and salesman's smile. In the distance, beyond the president's expansive window, was a misty, ominously-shrouded Boston skyline. On the desk, the old man's hands fumbled with a certified letter, a rejection letter from the FDA. The company's anti-asthma drug was "not approvable," and reading between the lines of text, never would be—$350 million of research and development, wasted. The company would survive, but not all of it.

Gainly's words came out in slow motion. "Sir, I told you this would happen if we listened to Dr. Stone. We should have cut our losses back in Phase I. Now we're . . ."

You goddamn liar! she thought. *You forced me to push this drug through! I told you it was going to fail. We had plenty of good chemicals in the pipeline, but you only wanted the blockbuster!* As Gainly continued politely berating her, Stone gazed from his eyes to ApothePharma's president. This was pure show; the decision had already been made. It didn't matter that she had dozens of memos backing her position: her office was probably sealed, she had no hard copies, and doubtless those memos were being deleted from the server as Gainly spoke. The only question was whether they were going to fire her or let her resign. With her meteoric rise in the company, she had unintentionally cultivated a reputation of brutal efficiency. Finding another job might be simple—or impossible.

Damara glared at Gainly, his thick shock of reddish hair, the deep creases in his great forehead, his big thick lips blabbing, blabbing. And to think of all the times she had had him inside of her—and enjoyed it! Uncharacteristically, she continued to say nothing. A thought exploded on her consciousness, repeating over and over, louder and louder. *That's the last man who's ever going to betray me!*

". . . hear me, Damara?" Barbieri asked. "Maybe we should go to the FDA and—"

Stone shook her head, chasing away the memory. "Don't tell *me* about the Agency! The first thing they'd do after declaring a moratorium would be to force the company to recall Diabend and Tremulate."

"But the problem doesn't affect—"

"The two drugs are SPF-4912-based. That's all the Agency will see."

"But public outcry—"

"Would quickly turn against us." She pivoted toward him. "Are *you* turning against us, Eddie?"

"No-no, of course not. I'm just so tired of all of this."

A smile slowly emerged beneath blue, frigid, unyielding eyes. "No one wants this resolved more than I do," she declared. "No one."

"But in the meantime, as Senior Vice President of PTS' Whole Organ Enterprises, you're raking in the major bucks."

"You idiot, no officer or primary stockholder can sell a single share of equity until the Problem's fixed. It's the only way to maintain security and prevent a panic sell-off. Not to mention keeping the lot of us out of a federal penitentiary."

"And just what is your share, Damara—$5 million, $10 million?"

Stone calculated her potential profits once the transplant center franchising kicked in, combined with projected global expansion. She laughed. *$60 million!*

"Fine. Don't tell me. What are you going to do with it? Build some glass tower with your name inscribed in gold letters? Or maybe blow it all on sycophants and servants?"

The one-word answer instantly popped into her: *Fire!* She quickly returned to her black book, picked up the phone on the table, punched in Evelyn Cruz's extension and PIN, and put the female electronic voice on speaker phone. It said:

Two messages. Message #1. Wednesday, February 2nd, 9:35 A.M.

A matronly voice then said, "Ms. Cruz, this is Amare from Dr. Craig's office. The doctor's running late today, so we need to push your appoint—"

Stone pressed two numbers. The electronic voice said:

Message #1 deleted. Message #2. Wednesday, February 2nd, 11:47 A.M.

A male voice then said, "Evelyn, it's Dylan. I left a message for you at home, but I'm leaving one here, too. I've finagled a few days off. I'd like to see you in Boston after the funeral, maybe have a nice long weekend? Oh, I took care of your package. You could've asked me instead of pulling that cloak-and-dagger stuff. Please call, I miss you. Bye."

She saved the message and slammed down the receiver. "Who is this Dylan?"

"Some junior consultant at Verity. Been dating Evelyn for several months."

Stone stood and slinked toward him. "You knew Cruz was dating someone at Verity and didn't see fit to tell me?"

He looked away and smiled. "Isn't it in that little black book of yours?"

"Give me his home phone!"

"I don't even know his last name."

She opened the door. "Go search Cruz's office for Dylan's home phone."

Barbieri shook his head, shoved his hands in his pockets, and ambled out of the room.

Alone, undisturbed, Stone sat quietly and began formulating a plan, creating an equation with people as elements undergoing constant modification, rearrangement, reformulation. She plotted initial condition, cause, effect, desired response—and the intervening steps between them, seeking the optimal route between cause and effect. She knew the likelihood of perfection was small and laden with missteps, errors leading to 'what if' and the consequences of 'what if that goes wrong.' Each contingency required a unique solution.

The phone rang. She picked up the receiver. "What is it?" She paused. "Got it."

She hung up and took a wireless phone from her jacket so that the call couldn't be tracked to the Institute. She punched in the numbers, then said, "Hi, is this Dylan Rogers?" After the reply, "Nice to finally talk to you. I'm Catherine Benis, one of Evelyn's closest friends. She must have mentioned me to you," she said, drenching her voice with naïvete. "Tragedy about Dr. Todd. I know she's really broken up."

She rolled her eyes as she listened. "That's why I'm calling. Evelyn tried to reach you earlier but couldn't." She looked at her watch. "Yes, Dylan. She asked me to tell you that she won't be staying overnight in Boston. She's flying into Newark late this afternoon and she wants you to be at her house about seven." She tapped her foot as she listened. "That's why I'm calling. You'll find the key in the second flower pot." Flipping to page Cruz in her notebook, "Her security code is 1749322. Got that?" Shaking her head, "Nothing I can remember—except that she said to bring 'something special.'" Nodding, "Great. Seven o'clock. Bye, Dylan."

Cruz Townhouse
Cranbury, New Jersey   6:55 P.M.
As Dylan Rogers parked his black coupe in front of Cruz's townhouse, his headlights illuminated the vermilion Mustang's license plate: IRACT10. He got out of his car, walked to the front of the mustang, and felt the hood. It was ice cold. Obviously, Evelyn wasn't home—unless she'd taken a limousine from Newark.

Carefully, he headed across the frosted cement to the front door. Her house was dark, except for lamplight filtering through living room curtains. He rang the bell and knocked to be sure she wasn't home, then dug his fingers into the flowerpot beside him and unearthed a pair of keys. Reading off the scrap of paper with her security code, he disarmed the security system, then opened the door.

The living room appeared exactly as he'd left it last night. He removed his overcoat and checked the flashing red light on the answering machine. The caller ID box registered two calls, both much earlier in the day: the first from him and the second from an IRACT extension. On the pad by the phone, Evelyn had scribbled a note about a dental appointment, but there was nothing about her flight or transportation from the airport. He went upstairs to check if she'd left any airline information in her bedroom. Her room was immaculate: no clothing rejected during packing, no residual creases from suitcases packed on the bedspread, no last minute items left behind on the nightstand. He opened the closet. A tall, dark shape peered back. He yanked the chain on the closet light. Staring at him was a black, upright vacuum cleaner.

"Get a grip, Dylan."

He whiffed a foul odor emanating from the spare bedroom. He followed it around the room's computer workstation and bookcase to an attic door. It smelled like the dead cat someone had left rotting in the dumpster beneath his own apartment's bedroom window. He turned the knob—it was locked. He shrugged and headed into the ivory-tiled kitchen with color coordinated side-by-side refrigerator, gas stove, and microwave, and helped himself to a bowl of honey-coated peanuts, which he took into the den and deposited on a coffee table near the gas fireplace. He plopped on the couch, clicked on the TV, and channel surfed.

". . . states are called 'commonwealths,' " the game show announcer said.

"What are Virginia, Pennsylvania, and Massachusetts?" he responded concurrently with one contestant. He propped a pillow behind his back, folded his arms, and loosened his tie. Eight commercials later, his eyes fluttered closed.

Evelyn floated across the room, her cream laced chemise trailing in a gentle breeze. Gliding to his side, her gown shimmered, then parted, exposing bare flesh. Long, slender fingers reached out and pulled his face to hers. Her tongue penetrated his mouth and danced along his, a warm wet thickness. She caressed his hand and guided it over her breasts, down her smooth skin rising and falling with ecstatic breaths, and between her legs. Her touch counseled his hand, moving it back and forth. She grew wet, her aroma—strong, searing, assaulting his will. His tongue slid down her neck, her breasts. Her free hand formed an *o*-ring and plunged it between his legs as he reveled in the satiating roundness of her breasts slowly converging around him, over him. He opened his mouth to breathe—her flesh blocked it. He struggled to free himself, his lungs fighting for air. Choking, he rolled off the couch, banging his knee against the coffee table.

Dylan opened his eyes. There was no Evelyn.

The blurry room spun. Head pounding, stomach rumbling, the air tasted foul, smothering. He hacked through burning lungs. A high-pitched hiss emanated from the gas fireplace. Something clattered in the kitchen. He crawled toward it.

Gasping, he rolled into the kitchen. The oven door lay open, its unlit burners hissed. A man wearing a gas mask stood by the microwave. Dylan struggled to his knees. The man whirled and kicked him in the ribs. He fell back, unable to draw a breath, to scream from the pain consuming his spine.

The man stuffed wads of tin foil into the microwave, slammed its door shut, and set the auto timer. Swooping down, he hoisted Dylan onto his shoulder and carried him down the stairs, through the recreation room, and out the back door into the garden.

Brisk air bit Dylan's skin, but refreshed his lungs. The man rapidly traversed the knoll beside the townhouse and circled around front. He dumped Dylan into the passenger seat of the Mustang, scanned the street, then slid behind the wheel. With Evelyn's keys and headlights off, he drove her car two blocks down the street, parked in front of a dentist's office, and waited.

Blinding white light bathed the car.

In the distance, a fireball spread upward, outward. Billowing smoke catapulted into the dark. The ground shook. Heat rippled through cold night air.

The man checked his rearview mirror. The Cruz townhouse and the one adjoining it had disintegrated. A third spewed flames.

Dylan tottered forward and vomited.

The man looked from the puddle on the carpeting to Dylan and back. "Look what you did! Now I have to drive with your stink!" He punched Dylan in the face.

Dylan smacked his head against the car door, and fell unconscious.

TEN

14 Lancelot Way
Royalton Village Estates
Villanova, Pennsylvania   *6:45 P.M.*

Scott finished checking the main floor of the house and
headed into the foyer. His footsteps on the bare tile echoed
off the domed ceiling and chandelier that even now color-
fully refracted ambient light filtering through old laced
curtains from the outside lighted walkway. The eat-in double-
kitchen, the formal dining room with adjoining elevated
platform for the baby grand piano, the spacious sunken living room with bay windows, the bright sunroom, and the
great circular staircase leading up to the five-bedroom upper
floor—all empty, dark, silent.

It was his dream-house, the place he'd always hoped
would remain his home, and now far beyond his means. On
staff at the Hospital of the University of Pennsylvania, his
future as an orthopedic surgeon was promising, he and
Candice were house-poor for the following two years, unable to afford even basic repairs, let alone make the house

inviting. As his practice grew, the house bloomed. Eight years ago, he'd brought his first child, Brooke, home to bare walls. Five years ago, he'd brought his second, Andrew, to half-finished floors. There were two more available bedroom upstairs, and a lifetime with Candice to fill them.

Scott checked the answering machine on a pedestal table, the only piece of furniture left in the house, by the base of the staircase. Nothing: no calls, no messages, no possibilities. He headed up the steps.

The disease had changed everything. The disease had ended his desire for another child: how could he bring one into this world knowing that child might soon have a deteriorating wheelchair-bound father? The disease had ended his surgical career. Without the adrenaline-powered thrill of surgery, Scott found medicine little more than a plodding series of differential diagnoses. Highly trained but unprepared for a world outside of medicine, he'd spent most of the first two years on an odyssey of self-discovery, trying to create a new career for himself. Much of his time had been spent doing volunteer work for the Society for Ethical Medical Advancements, charging the windmills of the medical establishment to keep his mind off suicide.

Scott reached the top of the staircase.

For years, much of his income had been poured back into his professional corporation. His final buyout figure from partner Benjamin Waltham wound up being substantially less than he'd hoped. With a huge mortgage on his house, combined with the mortgage and fees on the condominium he'd bought for his mother, half of his savings disappeared within months. Even after landing his position at Verity Healthcare, he knew he was never going to be able to keep his dream house. Three months ago, he capitulated.

Scott sauntered down the deserted upstairs hall, then stopped at what had been Brooke's room. Though dark, in his mind, he could still see its bright pink walls and Barbie motif. That last day in the house, his little girl had been so mature, talking about her adventure in a new house even as she wiped her teary eyes. Andrew, just a few years younger, had to be dragged screaming out of the house.

The realtor had found the Merritt family a house a quarter of the size with a postage stamp yard in a stable neighborhood. Worse, the same realtor hadn't been able to sell this dream house, leaving them with two mortgages—three counting his mother's condominium. Scott had fired the realtor and assumed the burden of selling this house himself.

The phone rang. Scott headed quickly toward the stairs. Just after the outgoing message on the machine finished, he heard Candice's voice. "Scott, it's me. Are you there?"

He leaned over the railing, picked up the receiver, and turned off the answering machine. "Yeah, I'm here."

"I thought I might find you there," Candice said.

"It's Wednesday. You know I always check the house Wednesday evenings. I thought I'd take care of this first," Scott answered. "Why didn't you call my cell phone?"

"You forgot to turn it on again. House okay? Any interest?"

"House is fine. No takers."

"The realtor had said that we were handicapping ourselves by setting the price too high in a depressed market."

"Candice, we need to get out from under."

"Could it just be that you really don't want to sell, so you're sabotaging the effort?" She sighed. "It's just a house, dear. It's a place, not a home. Your home's here, where I am, where your children are. Where you're loved."

"I *will* sell this house!"

"Scott, I know you've gotten a raw deal. You entered a noble profession, worked hard, always held yourself up to the highest standards. Always put me and the children first. And you've come through all the adversity with your head up. We're all proud of you for it." She paused. "But I'm so worried about you. You've taken on too much. If you don't stop driving yourself this hard, you're going to put yourself in a wheelchair ahead of your time."

Norlake Hospital
Lecture Hall

Filling three-quarters of Norlake amphitheater's five hundred seats, the audience was unexpectedly large for an in-house grand rounds presentation. Emery surveyed the usual smattering of students from a nearby medical school, residents serving in other disciplines, colleagues, selected Norlake senior staffers—and several people in the audience who had notepads and pocket recorders poised.

"Nice turnout, eh?" asked the man seated beside Emery at the table.

Emery turned to the President of Norlake Hospital, Charles Nickelson, a short, stocky man with monogrammed cuffs, oversized ears and a turtle-like neck—the result of lousy plastic surgery. "Charlie, who exactly did you invite?"

"Ralph Demartre, *Cleveland Plain Dealer*," Nickelson whispered, surreptitiously pointing to a man in a blue-pinstripe suit in the front row, center section. "Lisa Brannon, *Pittsburgh Post-Gazette*," pointing at a matronly brunette a few rows back, "and Jay Morello, *Washington Post*," pointing at a portly man in the near side section. "I called in a few favors. Thought you'd appreciate the publicity."

"Charlie, this doesn't change anything."

"We'll tackle those issues tomorrow. Meanwhile, I suggest you keep this sweet, short, simple, and quotable." Nickelson turned on his microphone and began a long-winded, glowing introduction of Norlake Clinic's Director and world famous xenotransplant surgeon.

All these reporters. I hope they're just writers for the science sections, Emery thought, *and not investigative reporters.*

This was a time of vulnerable successes. The Senate Subcommittee hearing scheduled next week, at which he was to testify, was virtually guaranteed to strip stewardship of the

National Xenotransplant Registry from the FDA and transfer it to the Institute over in Princeton. Later this week was the complicated maneuver with MidEast Partners, a deal that could go very public, very ugly if their CEO decided to fight and cast unwanted attention on PTS' Whole Organ Enterprises. The FDA's recent approval of porcine-to-human liver xenografting using PTS' SPF-4912 pigs as organ donors had ignited a fresh wave of strident protests by animal activist groups and anti-transplant organizations. Here at Norlake, an impending wildcat strike by nurses in the xenotransplant center could generate a severe backlash if clinic nurses chose to ally themselves with anti-transplant activists. One of his own residents, Sarah Novia, was coming close to deducing the problem. And his last conversation with PTS' elite team had been chilling: not only had they revised their previous optimistic estimate of twelve to eighteen months, but now they were euphemistically using terminology like 'indeterminate future.'

". . . discussion on 'Overcoming Xenograft Rejection,'" Nickelson said. "Please welcome Dr. Carlton Emery."

After a warm reception, Emery rose and strutted to the whiteboard like a gladiator. He clipped a body mike to his lapel and began drawing, his body concealing the board from the audience. After a moment, he finished and stepped aside, exposing a stick-figure person on the left side and a rudimentary drawing of a pig on the right. Facing the audience while pointing at the figures, "Can anyone out there tell me the main difference between these two creatures?" He paused. "Don't be shy."

"One has four legs and the other two," one person shouted.

"A more developed brain," a baritone declared.

"For which?" Emery quipped. The audience chuckled. "Come on people, you can do better."

Someone yelled, "One winds up on the breakfast table beside sunny side eggs."

The crowd laughed.

"Close." Emery pointed at the young man who'd made the

comment. "Since the end of dinosaurs and the explosion of mammals on this planet, the immune systems of each species has slowly, successfully learned to recognize what constitutes its 'self' and what constitutes 'non-self'—that is, foreign. Our bodies recognize bacteria and viruses as foreign and attack them. So does a pig's. That specificity works on much larger scales. Place a human heart in a pig's body, and that pig's immune system will destroy the human organ in hours. Place an unmodified, *barnyard* pig organ in a human being, and the same thing happens. The difference is seventy-five million years of evolution." He put down the drawing marker in his hand. "At an International Workshop on Xenotransplantation, back in 1998, Claus Hammel said that we must overcome nature's protection of the individual—and outwit evolution." Emery sighed. "No small task. The human immune system is very effective. So effective that, in fact, it has not only learned to recognize what is unique to the species, it's learned to recognize what is unique to the individual. It's challenge enough to transplant an organ from one human being to another, which we call *allotransplantation*. The obstacles are far greater when we try to transplant a life-giving organ from another species to a human being, which we call *xenotransplantation*." He placed his hands behind his back and walked toward the edge of the stage. "How many of you are blood type O? Could I please see a show of hands?"

Nearly half the audience raised their hands.

"How about type A?" he asked. Twenty people raised their hands. "Type B?" A dozen. "Is there anybody out there with type AB blood?"

In the back row, Nurse Christina Forman rubbed her temples, trying to squelch the pounding that wracked her head. Though her shift had ended hours ago—and surprisingly they hadn't 'requested' that she put in another as usual—she'd needed an excuse to hang around the hospital to talk to some of the other nurses. Every day-nurse was furious with

Administration's unrelenting demand for extra hours, coupled with wage freezes, shrinking benefits, decaying job security, and increasingly difficult working conditions. Tonight, she'd confirm that the nurses on the evening shift were fed up, too. Unfortunately, all of Administration's demands were within the legal limits of their last union contract, so technically, nothing was actionable until the contract expired a full year from now. However, Christina was certain that most nurses were angry enough to stage a sick-out. Hospital administrators, already suspicious, were closely watching known 'malcontent organizers' and were ready to move quickly against anyone trying to organize a wildcat action.

Which was precisely why Christina had to organize it. She had a good relationship with Emery—some said too good— and Emery was the root of the problem. It had all been to provide some security for her husband, Dave, a tile-layer, who hadn't been steadily employed for almost three years, and her pair of young boys. Smiling with a little extra ass-wiggle at a man she loathed was small payment. But now that Dave had made the union and with it, steady work, it was time to parlay that distasteful false friendliness into a weapon to improve conditions for herself and her fellow nurses.

The pounding in her head worsened.

"O, A, B, and AB are names for the different types of sugar molecules on our blood vessels and red blood cells," Emery said. "Those of you with type A have billions of A-type molecules throughout your bodies. Those of you with type B have B-type molecules. The same for type O. These molecules, called *antigens,* can be recognized by an immune system. Take blood or an organ from a person with type A blood, then transfuse or transplant it into a person with type B, and that person's immune system will produce *antibodies* from their immune system, specifically their T-cells, that will recognize type A as foreign, and bind to those antigens so they can be attacked." He strolled across the stage. "And that's just within the same species. Imagine the difficulty in xenotransplantation, grafting an organ from one species into another. Our bodies have awesome mechanisms for recognizing itself and for rejecting what it considers invaders." Emery meandered back to the whiteboard and wrote, his great frame obscuring the contents. "There are the four types of barriers we must overcome to enable a body to accept a transplanted organ." He stepped back, revealing a list on the board:

Hyperacute Rejection
Acute Rejection
Delayed Xenograft (Antibody-mediated) Rejection
Chronic Rejection

"In a hyperacute rejection, the human immune system instantly recognizes a transplanted organ—and destroys it within hours." On the board, he drew a tube with a dandelion-like attachment on its interior. "That represents the blood vessel of any organ we graft. And this," writing 'GAL', "the sugar galactose. Like our O, A, and B antigens, this sugar is found on the interior surface of blood vessels in viruses, bacteria, and nearly all mammals, except primates. The Gal sugar is the same as that found in many types of bacteria and viruses. Shortly after birth, our immune systems learn to recognize Gal as a foreign antigen and so construct antibodies to fight it. Unfortunately, our immune systems can't tell the difference between a bacteria with Gal and a transplanted pig organ that has it, so any transplanted pig organ containing Gal sugars on its blood vessels is immediately attacked by primed human antibodies that bind to these molecules on the new organ. This activates a complex cascade of proteins called *complement*. Once this hyperacute rejection process begins, nothing—nothing stops it. The complement proteins destroy the transplanted organ in hours." He took a deep breath. "I've watched it happen right before my eyes."

Except for a muffled cough, the audience was silent, attentive.

"Beyond hyperacute rejection, evolution has placed additional obstacles to prevent interspecies organ grafting. If the recipient's immune system is not already primed to produce antibodies, then it has B-cells that can begin to recognize the foreign antigen and develop antibodies. That process, *acute rejection*, similarly can destroy the new organ in weeks. Drugs that suppress the immune system, such as cyclosporine, tacrolimus, and newer agents such as GSMab715 fusion antisense DNA and monoclonal antibody proteins can fend off the slow attack, but they also impair the recipient's immune system, rendering that person extremely susceptible to infection." Placing his hands behind his back, "Even if the recipient fends off this rejection, there are long-term problems. Delayed graft rejection, for one. Chronic rejection, for another, in which an organ is slowly rejected after years. We don't know why some patients develop chronic rejection, nor is there much we can do in these cases. But at least with a xenograft, you can always get another organ." Shaking his head, "Not always so with a human donor."

It had started with a simple, annoying drip in the back of Christina's nose. Now, her whole throat was raw, scratchy. Her head pounded in synch with her heartbeat. The hairs on her arms had stiffened, chilling her. She touched her forehead. It was warm, sweaty.

". . . leaving us with a choice of two approaches for treatment," Emery continued. "Either make the recipient's immune system adapt to the foreign organ, or make the donor's organ compatible with the recipient's immune system. Tell me with a show of hands, who among you would like to take drugs to depress your immune system and leave you open to constant infection and re-infection, for the rest of your life?"

As he expected, no one raised a hand.

"Who among you would prefer to have the donor organ genetically engineered so that your body would eventually accept the new organ?"

Smiling as everyone raised their hands, "Naturally. It's vastly superior, both near- and long-term, to adapt animal organs to fit human needs instead of continually pumping dangerous chemicals into our bodies. Generally, patients who receive xenografts from miniature swine strain SPF-4912 do not require immunosuppression drug therapy as intensely or as long as patients receiving allografts, organs from other human beings."

Christina felt light-headed as she stood. The floor wobbled beneath her and she felt Emery's eyes searing her neck as she struggled down the seats in her row and into the aisle.

Emery stared at her as she trudged out the back, the door slowly drifting closed behind her. Why had she left in the middle of his lecture?

"Carl, are you all right?" he heard Nickelson whisper from the table.

Emery shook off his lapse of strength. He headed back to the whiteboard, erased the previous list, and replaced it with a new one:

1. Gene Knockout
2. Intrabodies
3. Effective, Safe Vectors Carrying Human Genes Into Porcine Hosts
4. Cloning

"These technologies have made it possible for miniature swine or porcine strain SPF-4912 to supplement the ever-growing shortage of human donor organs. First, gene knock-out technology. It's exactly what it sounds like—the ability to knock out, that is, remove undesirable genes from an animal's genome, its DNA structure. These changes were introduced into stem cells, which are primitive cells that have the potential to become any specialized cell, such as a liver, kidney, or brain cells. Second, intrabodies. These genetically-engineered antibodies are produced by the pig's own cells. Intrabodies actually interfere with the pig's chemical processes within its own cells, either in the nucleus or surrounding tissue. As a result, certain proteins in pig cells that would otherwise cause rejection in a human host never have the opportunity to develop." Emery deliberately slowed his pace. "Third, non-viral vectors. Vectors make it possible for genetic researchers to insert new genes into a cell's DNA. Without vectors, we wouldn't have been able to insert pivotal human genes into the transgenic animals that we use today for organ grafting. And last, but not least, cloning. In March 2000, PPL Technologies cloned the first pigs, mak-ing it possible to produce vast quantities of identical, genetically-engineered animals suitable as donors for human medicinal applications. And in December of the following year, that same company cloned five piglets—I believe their names were Noel, Angel, Star, Joy, and, uh, Mary— that were missing the alpha 1,3-galactosyl transferase gene, a critical milestone in creating animal organs suitable for human recipients and which we will discuss at length shortly." Hands in pockets, he slowly approached the edge of the stage. "Today, there are hundreds of thousands of strain SPF-4912 miniature swine—all genetically identical, all derived from one single pig. Cells taken from pig strain SPF-4912 have been used to virtually cure insulin-dependent diabetes, Parkinson's disease, and show enormous potential for the treatment of Alzheimer's disease and even spinal cord injuries. Thousands of former dialysis patients have successfully received strain SPF-4912 kidney transplants. The FDA recently approved SPF-4912 liver transplants. Results from current clinical trials with SPF-4912 heart transplants appear promising."

Emery waited for Morello from *The Washington Post* to look up. "The complete process for converting the common barnyard pig from a smorgasbord of breakfast meats to a repository of life-saving medical miracles is actually far more complicated, involving a slew of genetic manipulations that we will be discussing at length. Some key genes that have been eliminated from these pigs include enzyme alpha-1,3-galactosyl transferase, or GT for short, and Porcine MHC Class II, short for Major Histocompatibility Complex Class II, known to be responsible for causing hyperacute organ rejection. Some key genes that have been inserted into these pigs include the human gene coding for sugar type "O', protein decay accelerating factor, or DAF, along with key human MHC Class II genes. These enabled us to successfully transplant SPF-4912 organs into human beings. Only fifteen years ago, no patient who received a xenograft organ survived more than eight weeks. Today, we have patients surviving *years*, and still going strong. And we can always improve animal source donors through genetic engineering. Not so for people."

In the fourth row, left side, he spotted resident Sarah Novia slightly shaking her head. *The Washington Post* reporter was sitting only half a row to her right. If the reporter noticed Novia's apprehension, he might begin asking the wrong questions.

Emery turned directly to the reporter. "An old fear of xenotransplantation was that the animal source organs were filled with viruses that would run wild in a human being recipient, perhaps even spread into the general population—a process called xenozoonosis, or xenosis for short. Years ago, researchers discovered two retroviruses—viral particles that had become incorporated in some distant past into pig DNA—porcine endogenous retroviruses, PERV strains A and B. People feared that these non-functioning viruses would suddenly wake in a human host and wreak havoc." He snickered. "After tens of thousands of patients who have received pig organ transplants, not one patient has ever died from a pig viral retroviral infection. Why?" He spun toward Novia. "Because these animals are kept in sterile environments. Because they're constantly screened for potential viruses. Because we've removed every possible retrovirus that might have inserted itself into pig DNA. And because we know the pig's entire genome structure, every aspect of its DNA, we'd know if any new retrovirus inserted itself into these animals. The FDA has certified it."

Beneath Interstate-95
Delaware-Pennsylvania State Line   *11:07 P.M.*
Stone wrapped her fur coat snugly around her chest, recessed into the car's leather upholstery, and stared out the rear window. Her car sat in a dark, deserted gully between sixty-foot high cement columns. The distant clump-clump of trucks speeding along the interstate bridge overhead relentlessly pounded.

She closed her eyes. More than the cold chilled her. She'd sworn she'd never again be in a place like this: at the bottom of a deserted ravine, at night, in the back seat of a car, with a man. She closed her eyes and tried to create a wall of blackness to fend off the memory. Instead, she summoned it.

Fourteen, friendless, fighting loneliness, Damara had accepted senior Bobby Webster's invitation to a movie. But he'd picked her up late, and she didn't want to sit in a cold, dark theatre anyway; she needed someone to hold her, some way to feel warm, wanted. So after a couple of hot dogs and fries, she went willingly with him to Limekiln Ravine, beneath the bridge. She remembered the touch of his hands on her shoulders, her breasts, his lips pressing hers, his tongue dancing in her mouth. She knew that must have made her feel good, but she could no longer remember sensations of pleasure—only pain. His hands delving between her legs, ripping away her pantyhose and panties, spreading her legs. His fingernails scratching her thighs. *I'm bleeding!* Her free hand shooting out, striking him under his double-chin. She watched him fall back. Saw herself open the door, tumble into the dark, run across frozen mud, hide behind a bush, and listen to her date scream obscenities, his headlights bouncing wildly in circles until they retreated up the access road. And she remaining still, freezing in the dark, until morning.

Stone rubbed her eyes, ripping apart the memory. From the back seat, she glimpsed Clayton, her driver, in the rearview mirror: his thick graying hair, broad dark eyes, straight nose anchored on a bushy moustache, and double-chin—almost an aged version of Bobby Webster. Stone knew nothing about Clayton, not family, not even his background. He operated quietly and efficiently—that was enough. "I'm freezing. Turn the engine on," she told him.

"It's not safe to leave the engine running too long while the car is parked," Clayton said. "Carbon monoxide."

And he is experienced with that. She shivered. "They're late."

"It's two hours from Princeton."

"We'd know by now if that moron, Phillips, hadn't forgotten his wireless. And if that other moron, Buchanan, had left his on."

Waiting. I'm always waiting! She drifted in the darkness—back to the ApothePharma parking lot, three Fridays after she'd resigned. It was late, dark, raining, and deserted, except for that bastard Gainly who'd just remotely unlocked his Mercedes. She'd waited for hours, planning to pull her car up right next to his and scare the living crap out of him. She fantasized that she'd goad him, he'd take a swing, and she'd be 'forced' to use some of her second degree black belt skills in self-defense. Gainly stood next to his driver's side door. Her headlights out, she put her car in drive, and floored it. She sped toward the spot right next to his Mercedes. A hundred feet. Fifty feet. Gainly, distracted, dropped his keys on the asphalt, and knelt to find them— directly in the path of Damara's car. She swerved to miss him. Her car thumped, as if it had run over a curb. And thumped again.

"They're here," Clayton announced.

A pair of bobbing headlights belonging to a tan station wagon warily proceeded down the rock-strewn road and parked in front of the sedan. Lit by her sedan's headlights, two men emerged from the station wagon: one, a bulky giant at six-foot-six; the other, short and sinewy, brandishing a gleaming automatic. The shorter man tripped as he approached the sedan. His gun nearly misfired.

Stone put down her window. The big man stuck his head inside the car. He smelled vile. "Went off without a hitch."

"Cruz's car?" she asked.

Buchanan, the shorter man answered, "Right where you told us to leave it."

Stone caught a glimpse of his oversized .44-caliber Desert Eagle automatic. "Lose that. The ballistics are too distinctive. And next time, turn on your phone." To the big man, Phillips, "*And you*—you forgot yours, *again*—and left me sitting for two hours, not knowing. You've screwed up twice in as many nights. Do it a third time and you're finished."

"Fuckin' bitch," Phillips muttered.

Stone calmly stepped out of the car, and stared at him a moment. "I didn't hear you."

He glared at her. "I said f—"

She delivered a spinning hook kick directly into his groin. He crumpled in high-pitched agony. "Be grateful I'm wearing riding boots and not stilettos." Looking over her shoulder at his partner, "Now, get our guest." She got back in the car.

Dylan Rogers was slung into the seat beside her. Sleeves torn at the shoulders, right eye swollen, jaw dangled unevenly, he reeked of vomit and sweat. Buchanan piled into the front passenger seat. Clayton handed Stone a pocket flask. She steadied Dylan and poured a swig down his throat. "Hundred proof. Feeling better?"

"I knnoww you," he slurred. "You're the one who—called. Where's Evelyn?"

Stone stared at Dylan, trying to anticipate how the man would react, how he'd confront death, possibly for the first time. She remembered her first: Gainly in the parking lot, dead, his chest crushed by the wheels of her car, his blood pouring onto wet asphalt. She had vomited, which fortunately driving rain washed away, along with Gainly's blood. After subduing the initial shock, she had picked up Gainly, put him in her car, drove to a remote wooded area in Connecticut, and buried his body. The following morning, she'd had her car meticulously detailed. The police questioned her twice before focusing on a thief found in possession of Gainly's Mercedes the following week.

Now Damara, you know Gainly wasn't your first, a voice inside her chided.

Shut up! she thought back.

"Oh God!" Dylan exclaimed. "You killed Evelyn! You killed her, didn't you?" He flung back his head and sobbed.

Stone took a moment to wash away Gainly's death. She re-entered the present with a soft melodic voice. "Dylan, this is an opportunity—"

"You're going to kill me, too."

She removed her gloves. "I could've let you die in the explosion." She plopped three stacks of $100 bills in his lap. Dylan picked up one and held it to the car dome light. "That's $5000," she continued. "There's $10,000 more in your lap and another $15,000 in my purse."

"You kill my girlfriend, then want to bribe me?"

"Forget Evelyn Cruz. She was always James Todd's property. Every touch, every kiss, everything that ever passed between you was meant for Todd. Tell me Dylan, while she was wrapped in your arms, did she ever call out *his* name?"

"I don't believe you."

"Denial is the first stage of healing," she whispered in his ear. "Cruz was Todd's queen in his game against us. The two of them were blackmailing some very powerful people."

"You're lying."

"You saw how she lived: expensive home, *Architectural Digest* interior, classic car, six-digit bank accounts. Pricey for a Database Administrator, wouldn't you say?" As he took another swig. "If she cared for you, would she have embroiled you in blackmail—by giving you that package?"

"I don't know what you're talking about."

"What was in the package?"

Buchanan reached out from the front seat and brushed the muzzle of his automatic against Dylan's forehead.

"I don't know. I swear."

She looked to Clayton. "I think we're going to have to kill—"

"Wait! It felt like—there was a CD." Trembling hands brought the flask to his mouth. "But I didn't open it."

At Stone's glance, Clayton holstered his gun. "Dylan, let's pretend that it's story time and I'll tell you a tale about Cruz. Once upon a time, not long ago, we began finding extra patient listing files on the Institute's system. We investigated and found that they contained fallacious data, manufactured files cooked up by her and Todd. Enough fraudulent data to shut down fifteen years of research and land the lot of us in federal prison. Todd and Cruz both threatened to publicly release their fake data—unless we paid, and kept Cruz on staff, presumably to continue corrupting our data. So we paid, and paid, but that dear, sweet girl wouldn't keep her end of the bargain."

Burying his face in his hands, "So you blew up her house—"

"In case she'd hidden files there."

"You expect me to believe this?"

She squeezed his inner thigh. "You can refuse to cooperate or lie or try to escape, in which case you won't survive this hour. Or, you can do exactly as I say, and keep the

$30,000 down payment on this." She handed him a brown folder.

"What is it?"

"An off-shore account, opened in your name, for a quarter million dollars. I need a pair of eyes and ears at Verity Healthcare. Consider this your signing bonus."

Dylan gazed into the dark.

"I'm going to ask you some questions," she said slowly. "I'll ask each only once. Now, do you still have the CD?"

He shook his head.

"Good, that wasn't hard. Are there any copies?"

"None that I know of."

"Anything else in the package?"

"Like I said, 'I don't know.'"

"Where is it now?"

"I delivered it," he coughed, "to Mer—ritt."

"Merritt? Scott Merritt? The auditor?"

"Yes, yes."

Stone clamped her hand hard on his scrotum. "Where is he now?"

"His house, I guess. Please let go!"

"Did he upload the CD to Verity's mainframe?"

"I don't know! I left it with him this morning!"

Clayton interjected, "We don't have time for both operations tonight."

"You're right." To Dylan, "Where's Merritt live?"

"On the Main Line at—he's at Royalton Village Development on Route 352. Please—"

She released him. To Buchanan, "You deal with Merritt." To Clayton, "While you and I finish with Dylan."

There is no shame in not knowing—the shame lies in not finding out.
—A PROVERB

THURSDAY, FEBRUARY 3

ELEVEN

Scott leaned precariously on the rail rimming the fifteenth floor balcony. In the distance, light reflecting from the Monument of the Revolutionary War's Unknown Soldier seeped through Washington Square's barren treetops. A block beyond lay Independence Hall. Hannah, Scott's mother, had always loved this condominium, its Old City locale, its spacious rooms, its hardwood floors. *I wish I hadn't had to sell this place, too.* He closed the sliding glass door, and headed across the great room and down the hallway filled with boxed photographs: aged wedding photos of his parents, baby pictures of him and older sister Celia, impromptu pictures of the family frolicking on a Florida beach, camping out by a frigid Maine lake, posing against the yawning Grand Canyon. He focused on a photograph of his father standing proudly beside Celia in her gleaming white gymnastics uniform, her arms akimbo.

Celia had been the first, and the worst, of his haunting hunches. He had repeatedly dreamed that his father, while driving Celia to the state invitational gymnastics tournament, slid on a patch of black ice along a treacherous curve near Scranton, sailed off the road, and slammed head first into a drainage ditch, the wheel crushing his father's chest, Celia crashing through the windshield. That wasn't precisely how the fatal accident happened—but they did die in their car on a hilltop curve in Scranton. As with all his hunches, it had been tantalizing close to the truth, yet different enough to be coincidental. But his dreams of millions dying and ground zero for the plague had persisted so long, so maddeningly long.

Scott stumbled into the unlit den. His knee struck a sharp edge and tripped. Annoyed, he kicked the nearest object in the dark: his briefcase. He groped toward the freestanding lamp in the corner and turned on the light.

Half the size of the living room, the den contained a white couch, coffee table, recliner, stereo, secretary chair, and computer sitting atop a desk he'd built for her from a kit. Next to his briefcase, open against the back wall, was a brown package wedged under the couch. He picked up the package and examined it. *This is what Dylan gave me.*

He ripped open its stapled edge. Out tumbled a CD followed by a piece of paper with scribbling on one side. *All right, let's see what's so important.* He booted the computer, shoved the CD into the driver, selected an executable file, and clicked. "What the hell is this?"

IRACT

From the comfort of the Institute's executive lounge, Stone observed the deserted street at 14 Lancelot Way in Royalton Village Estates via the tiny camera attached to her man Buchanan's tie. She peered into the monitor as he approached Merritt's front door, removed a slender cordless cylinder with a rake-like projection from his pocket, and delicately inserted it into the lock. The rake vibrated as it opened the pin and disc tumbler cylinders, neutralizing the lock.

Merritt's house was dark. She switched the camera to infrared while her man checked the downstairs. "There's no heat sources," she said into Buchanan's earpiece. "Check the second floor." She watched him climb the stairs and checked the bedrooms, bathrooms, and closets: nothing.

"Everything's cold," Buchanan said. "Looks like Merritt hasn't been here for weeks. Why don't you try asking Rogers again. Less politely."

Stone turned to her second man, Clayton, seated behind her. He went into the adjoining room. Muffled screams penetrated the walls. Moments later, Clayton returned. "Rogers says that he heard that Merritt was getting ready to move, but that maybe he already did."

She noticed an answering machine in the foyer. "Try that," she ordered Buchanan.

He hit the 'play' button. An electronically-generated female voice said:

You have one message. Wednesday, February second, 7:02 P.M. Candice's voice said: "I thought I might find you there . . ."

Buchanan played the rest of the conversation. "Sounds like a wife."

"Ya think?" Stone rolled her eyes. "Find out where she called from."

He checked the numbers on the machine's caller ID and dialed. A woman answered on the seventh ring. "What? Who is it?"

Buchanan did not answer.

"I know it's you, Scott. What are you doing at the house at this hour?"

Buchanan hung up.

Stone coldly smiled. "What was that number?"

TWELVE

Scott shifted away from the monitor. Hardwood peeked through printouts with column upon column of patient treatment dates, biopsy results, medical examinations, radiographic findings, probabilities, and graphed distributions strewn across the floor. After five consecutive hours, Scott's lower back ached, his rear was numb—and calculations from the files on Cruz's CD kept repeating the same undeniable answer. He looked down at a neatly organized stack of four hundred pages that had taken him the better part of the night to calculate—and kicked it. "Barbieri and the rest of you lying bastards, I'm not going to let this go!" he yelled at the papers exploding across the room. But what really bothered Scott was the unavoidable phone call that he instinctively feared, but knew he must make. Lightheaded, the dark room gently spinning, he picked up the receiver. *Forgive me for putting more than my life at risk.*

Norlake Xenotransplant Center
O.R. #7

Standing over little Brenda McCarthy's exposed abdomen, Emery mentally reviewed how the surgery had proceeded: the porcine liver, having arrived from the Sacrifice Center hours ahead of schedule, had been successfully anastomosed at the appropriate vascular sites, and the bile duct attached with accompanying tissue resection. To circumvent obstruction of the bile duct postoperatively, he'd successfully inserted a T-tube stent to maintain patency, monitor bile production, and assess the xenografted liver's function. Soon, it would be time to close. Emery initially planned to order that the patient be administered antisense-GSMab715 postoperatively to minimize the already small chance of early rejection. As with many patients, despite all indications that the organ would function well for years, the little girl might need another transplant. If so, there were always more pigs.

Emery felt a little lightheaded. His thoughts drifted away from the surgical well, back to yesterday's rounds. *Folcroft, another mistake. I can cover my own mistakes, but I can't cover everyone else's all the time. Those idiot residents were supposed to pick up her problem in the history and physical! I'm exhausted even before my days begin. How long am I supposed to keep this up? They have got to find that answer—and soon!*

A nurse beside him patted his profusely sweating forehead. Emery stood immobile, staring into space.

"Something the matter, doctor?" asked the nurse.

Emery looked down into the surgical well. The transplanted liver was intact, well-positioned, and without signs of leakage at joined vessels. He glanced around the table— and slowly focused on Novia. *And on top of all of that, I'm sick of being saddled with chicken little!* He pointed a bloody finger at her. "You, in my office, first available opening!"

Forman Household
4314 Canyard Street
Cleveland, OH 6:50 A.M.

Christina Forman stood over the plastic cutting board, a can of tuna fish in one hand and a jar of chunky peanut butter in the other. Was it Evan who only ate tuna for lunch, or his twin, Ethan? With her throat so dry and sore, her shoulder and back muscles so stiff and achy, and the relentless pounding, pounding of each heart beat through blood vessels in her head, she could not think. She slammed both containers on the kitchen counter and whimpered.

Light, shuffling footsteps approached the doorway behind her. A six-year-old boy with dark curly hair and wearing flannels with American League pennants wandered into the kitchen. "Mommy, you're making so much noise."

Christina knelt beside him and gave him a hug and kiss. "Mommy's sorry. What would you like for lunch today, Evan, tuna fish or peanut butter and jelly?"

"I'm *Ethan!*" You love Evan more than me!" He ran screaming out the doorway.

Heavy, methodic footsteps descended the staircase. Christina, already crouched, leaned against the counter, slid down till she was sitting on the floor, and stared at the kitchen table legs coated with dog hair. In the doorway appeared a burly man with a faded tattoo of an eagle with a snake in its mouth, six-pack abdominals, and perfect white teeth. He knelt beside her and draped his arms around her shoulders. "You're very warm. Don't go in today."

She turned toward him. "Dave, I have to. I'm the one coordinating the strike. Without me, it all falls apart."

"You're sick." He helped her to her feet. "You're not going to do anyone any good."

Christina struggled to the sink and splashed cold water on her face.

"Don't do this. You're a great nurse. You'll find another job."

"That clinic supported this family the three years you were out of work.

"The hell with that place!"

"Now that things are working out, I owe it to my friends there to see that their families have the same—"

"You don't owe those nurses nothing!"

She tried to stand, wobbled, nearly fell over.

"Christina, you won't make it through the day."

Straightening her back, "My temp's only one hundred. I'll drink plenty of liquids and take an anti-viral and Motrin." She rubbed his shoulder. "It's going to be all right."

THIRTEEN

Calculations paraded before Scott. Digits whirled by with intoxicating rapidity as the statistical program compressed hundreds of man-hours into minutes. Scott still had lingering doubts that he was examining it all too analytically, without clinical insight, without compassion.

The doorbell rang. Scott minimized the screen of ongoing calculations, stumbled across the littered floor, and opened the front door. Ryan Knight stood grinning: six-foot-one, sparse frizzy-haired, and beneath his woolen coat, a corpulent frame. It didn't matter that Ryan's hands had grown so chubby that his gold-plated watch dug deep into his wrist and his wedding and pinkie rings near strangulated his fingers. Scott saw him, would always see him, as his stick-figured friend from grade school who never failed to lap him around the track. "Come on in."

Ryan looked at the boxes haphazardly stacked across the

living room floor and foyer, and peered around the corner toward the hallway. "Candice here?"

"She's home with the kids."

"Her choice? Or yours?"

"You sound like my mother."

"I've known you almost as long." Ryan shifted the bags in his hands. "Scott, I know you're the doc, but you shouldn't be doing this all by yourself. Overexertion, lack of sleep, you could catch a bug, maybe develop a fever. And with your condit—"

"This is more important. I need your expertise."

Ryan broke into a wide grin and slapped him on the shoulder. "You're lucky you got hold of me today. I'm taking Janine and the kids out west for a couple of weeks. We fly to Phoenix tomorrow night."

"If I know Janine, she'll kill you if you don't help her pack."

"All I need to know is when the flight leaves and what to stuff in the luggage. Now, what's going on?"

With one finger, Scott beckoned him into the den. Ryan stopped short in the doorway. Piles of paper lay strewn across the couch, the coffee table, the carpet. "This—on top of packing?"

Scott swatted away a pile of papers on the couch, "You might remember, I audited patient data files kept at the Institute for the Research of Animal Compatible Transplantations. It's a xenotransplantation database registry that collects and reports on outcomes of all pig organ transplants. Over the past four months, I've analyzed all of their files on kidneys."

"Obsessed, more like it."

He looked around the room, as if searching, and shook his head. "This is a mistake. I shouldn't have called you."

"Hey, it's me, Ryan. The one who passed you notes in fifth grade, taught you how to throw a boomerang through the principal's window. How to drink Slivovitz in college. What's wrong?"

Norlake Hospital
Emery's Office

From the confines of his wing-back chair, Emery patted his fingertips and watched Norlake Hospital's President, Charles Nickelson, squirm on the other side of his desk. "A separate full-service lab dedicated exclusively for the Xenotransplant Clinic? Separate admissions facilities? Separate nursing staff? Separate clerical and support staff? Separate billing? Two percent of the gross generated from Norlake's *non-transplant* services?" Nickelson shouted. "What right do you have to demand a piece of this hospital's revenue that has absolutely nothing to do with your clinic?"

"Charlie, Charlie, how quickly you forget. Norlake was teetering between bankruptcy and hostile takeover. *I* brought this place back from the brink. My transplant center delivered a large patient load, extensive facility service utilization, national prestige, a dozen major research grants, and overly-generous endowments from the area's elite that guarantee the hospital's solvency for the next ten years—that is, as long as I and my Xenotransplant Center remain here."

"You're being unreasonable. The Board's pressuring—"

"*You* don't know pressure."

"Carl, what's going on?" Nickelson softened his tone. "We've had a great relationship since Day One. Have I done something to break your trust?"

It's the other way around, old friend. He said, "You're the same you've always been."

Nickelson stood, walked to the great window, and stared out at Lake Erie in the distance. "No matter what people do to the water, it's still beautiful. Had a chance to get out on your boat, recently?"

Emery gazed out the window. He tried to focus on the piece of Lake Erie that peeked around Nickelson's silhouette. Tried to feel the brine spray gently kissing his face, titillating his tongue as he plowed through the churning waves.

Tried to transform the great lake into the Chesapeake, into home. "Not really," he whispered. Turning away from the window, his voice hardened. "But if I'm lucky, I may get a few days before I testify in Washington next week."

Nickelson sighed. "Your demands on hospital staff are instigating a nurses' revolt. My sources tell me they're going to stage a wildcat walkout within days. Are you deliberately trying to drive a wedge between yourself and Norlake?"

I built Norlake. Think this is easy for me? He rasped, "It's business. Just business."

Nickelson looked back over his shoulder at Emery. "Whose? Yours or PTS'?"

Emery slammed a pen down on the desk. "Okay, you want to hear the real truth? Here it is. As you're well aware, I'm a major stockholder and board member in PTS' Whole Organ Enterprises. Breathe a word of what I'm about to tell you, and you'll be living with attorneys the rest of your life."

"You can trust me, Carl."

He swiveled nervously in his chair. "Xenotransplantation technology is proliferating. Whole Organ Enterprises represents the largest new growth market for PTS, what with porcine kidney organ transplants, and now recent FDA approval for liver transplants. And as sole approved manufacturer and distributor of porcine organs for transplant, we've captured the market while our patents remain in force—"

"And with xeno-based drugs that have virtually wiped out insulin-dependent diabetes and Parkinson's, PTS may soon become one of the world's most profitable companies," Nickelson said. "What could possibly worry management?"

"The same force that battered and ultimately beat down health care providers." Emery cracked his knuckles. "MCOs—managed care organizations. Health insurers control the money."

"They have for decades. So what?"

"With the projected huge increase in the number of patients to undergo kidney xenografting—patients who would otherwise have remained on renal dialysis—the health insurance industry is predicting substantially diminished revenues, possibly negative growth. Their actuarials are going ape shit."

"So PTS is worried that insurers will band together and force you to drop the price." Nickelson smiled at Emery. "It's collusion. Fight it in the media. You'll win."

Emery picked up a folder from his desk. "This is a copy of a letter drafted by the Health Insurance Association of America. It's been sent to eight *friendly* United States Senators."

Nickelson took the folder. He whistled as he read. "They want Congress to pass legislation regulating the 'horrific' costs of xeno organs that could potentially damage the U.S. health care system and lead to unfair rationing based on economic status, with the poor especially penalized." He looked up at Emery. "They also want to regulate the cost and supply of xenograft organs. They make a strong case. PTS would face quite a battle, both on the Hill and in the media."

"We have a better solution." Emery delivered a smug smile. "We're going to drop the price ourselves within the next few weeks."

"That should cool any congressional initiative. What's that got to do with your demands here at Norlake?"

"The 'R and D' behind genetically engineering pathogen-free animals and meeting FDA's almost unimaginably difficult standards has been spectacularly expensive. The lost revenue will have to be made up, somewhere."

"I see," Nickelson nodded. "The transplantation centers."

"Precisely. PTS's Whole Organ Enterprises is ready to start buying group practices of xenotransplant physicians around the country—we're calling them Network Centers—at which PTS will make organs available at substantial discounts."

"While charging full price to physicians in non-network centers."

"Sure. PTS recoups the lost revenue from the other services provided at physician practice Network Centers, circumvents government action, and ensures a modicum of control over xeno technology, even when current patents expire."

Nickelson sighed. "How far is the process along?"

"That's proprietary, but I could close Norlake's Xeno-transplantation Center today and still walk away with $320 million."

"I know you, Carl. You can't walk away."

Emery put his feet on his desk. "I've already submitted a bid to buy Gloria Dei Mercy Hospital."

Nickelson swallowed. "That was—you?"

"However, I can withdraw that bid up to the last day of this month," whispering, "should I find cause."

Nickelson gazed down, rubbed the sweat from his upper lip, then stood. "When can you have a contract on my desk?"

"Tomorrow."

"I—hospital counsel will need time to review the document."

"Take all the time you want, until I get back from Washington." Emery smiled. *He bought it. They were right—the financial story is an excellent cover.*

FOURTEEN

Hannah Merritt's Condominium
Scott beckoned Ryan to the computer desk. He slid the mouse across the pad, and clicked.

A graph appeared on-screen.

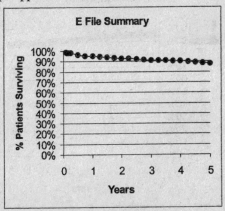

Ryan, stepping behind Scott, placed one hand on the chair, the other on the desk. "I'm a computer network systems administrator, not a statistician."

"This is a standard survival graph, called a Kaplan-Meier curve. It's a plot of the probability of patient survival over time. I generated it using all survival data from patients listed in IRACT's database who had kidney xenotransplants. So, looking at this graph—"

"Oh, I get it! At one year, about 95% of the patients survive. At three years, about 90% survive, and at five years, about 88% survive. Pretty good results, aren't they?"

"These are files that IRACT recorded and *entered,* hence the designation *E.*"

"I'm guessing files you audited," Ryan said.

"Right. Everything's in order. But look at this." Scott clicked a window option in the menu bar, selected a file, and double-clicked. Nothing happened. "It's responding a little slow. I'm simultaneously running some other calculations." Before Ryan could ask, "I'll show you those in a minute."

The screen burped, displaying another survival curve, labeled *R* summary files.

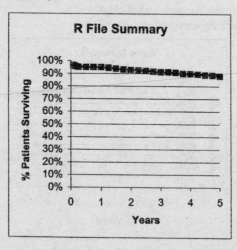

"This survival plot is based on *raw* data received by IRACT directly from xenotransplant clinics around the country, *before* the data were entered and processed. They're designated as *R* files." Scott said. "Except for the occasional human error slipping through quality control, raw and entered data should be identical, because it's the same information from the same patients."

Ryan pointed to the screen. "Well they are. See, you've got 95% survival at one year, 90% at three, and 88% at five years, just like the other."

"That's what I thought—until I began to realize that the shape of the raw summary file seemed odd." Scott half-smiled. "I'll superimpose them on the same graph."

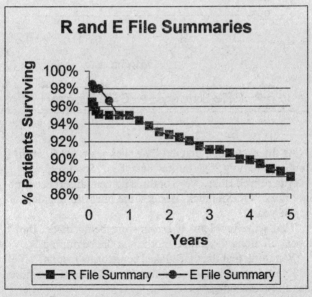

Ryan shrugged. "Doesn't seem to be much, just a little deviation between the survival lines in the first few months. The lines converge after one year."

"Take a closer look." Scott selected another graph.

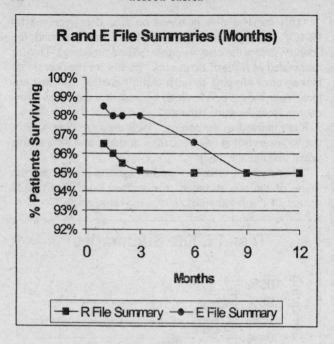

R and E File Summaries (Months)

"At three months, entered data files show 98% survival compared to only 95% for raw data files," Scott said.

Ryan peered close. "Two or three percent difference probably doesn't mean much. Besides, the lines are identical after one year."

"That's the problem. If errors were being made, they'd appear all along these lines, not just at the beginning."

"You think that the place faked some of its results?"

"Ryan, I spent months auditing IRACT's data. I've never seen these outcomes."

"That doesn't mean they're bogus."

Scott clicked on a square and a circle. "This is an abbreviated summary of an IRACT data listing for an individual patient from files LRDK1800-098 and LEDK1800-098 as of this past Friday." The screen displayed:

FILE: LRDK1800-098   FILE: LEDK1800-098
Patient: Merritt, Hannah L.   Patient: Merritt, Hannah L.
ID: LD317NSC   ID: LD317NSC
Start Therapy: 2/3/14   Start Therapy: 2/3/14
Current Status: Deceased   Current Status: Deceased
Date of Death: 3/15/14   Date of Death: 3/15/14

"Your mother?" Ryan asked.

Scott slowly nodded.

"Well, the raw and entered data on her are the same. So their info on her was properly entered."

Scott clicked on another square and circle. The screen displayed:

FILE: LRDK1800-142   FILE: LEDK1800-142
Patient: Crossland, Sarah   Patient: Crossland, Sarah
ID: LD814NSC   ID: LD814NSC
Start Therapy: 5/3/12   Start Therapy: 5/3/12
Current Status: Deceased   Current Status: Deceased
Date of Death: 5/18/12   Date of Death: 11/12/12

Ryan touched the screen. "Again, they're the same—oh, except for the date of death. Probably just a data entry error."

Scott brought up patient listing files SEAL0235-101, SRAL0235-101, JEZN9342-053, JRZN9342-053, DEPK1181-232, and DRPK1181-232, then compared the 25 to 33 patients in each file. Data for each patient were identical in *E* and *R* files, except for those who'd died within three months of transplantation. Several of those patients had their reported dates of death listed four to eight months later than the actual date.

"Maybe it's not deliberate. Some incompetent data entry clerk—"

"C'mon Ryan, no natural error sequence could account for these differences. Look at the way the entered data flattens off at 95% around half a year. It's deliberate."

"How'd you get this stuff?"

"A colleague is having an affair with IRACT's Database Administrator, who must've had a falling out with her employers. The stuff was quite literally shoved into my hands."

"So you think IRACT pays people to fabricate data?"

"Not likely. There's thousands of patients that need constant tracking and updating. Cheating on a grand scale is hard work. A growing database requires more staffers, thereby increasing the security risk."

"Must be software."

Scott's mouse glided in his hand, dancing, clicking across its mouse-pad dance floor. A series of alphanumeric characters spread across the screen. "AIMS, short for the Allocation and Integrative Modeling System—a resident program designed to sit inside the SAS statistical program, the prime software for pharma houses and the FDA. Using the patient's social security number as identification and a programmable algorithm, AIMS transforms genuine patient survival data into whatever outcome the user specifies—all while sorting patient data listings and tracking updates."

"Probably not that difficult to design. Some of my people, especially the ones who dream in code, could do it in their sleep. But," placing a finger to his lips, "it doesn't make sense. If IRACT was really trying to cook their books, wouldn't they have manipulated the data to show better long-term results? Like a 99% five-year survival rate, instead of 88%? What difference does it make padding the 3-month survival rate?"

Scott clicked on the program's toolbar. A blue bar marking JOB 58% COMPLETE occupied the center of the screen. "I'm running the calculations as we speak. Ryan, if it's what I think, then the crisis I've been telling you about all these years—the one you've scoffed at—is already here."

Norlake Xenotransplant Center
3rd Floor Supply Closet   3:02 P.M.

"There must be another way," head floor nurse Yancy said, a plump woman with tight-curled auburn hair, silver cross earring studs, and shaded glasses.

"There is," Christina answered, gazing through hot, painful eyes at the nurse ten years her senior. "Keep working daily double-shifts, six days a week, without biohazard comp, for a cost-of-living increase and shrinking benefits until our contract expires."

Yancy straightened her white uniform. "I'm day-shift nurse rep, and I can tell you the union—"

"Has already told us that, like it or not, we're stuck with the contract." Fever scorched Christina's face, her neck. She felt her legs buckling. She reached up and seized a strut on the metal shelving unit to bolster her. "We're on our own. Always have been."

The older nurse squeezed a box of packaged needles on the shelf beside her. "I could try going again to Nickelson to—"

"Nickelson isn't running this hospital. Emery is." Christina delivered a deep, phlegm-filled cough, partially covering her mouth.

Yancy touched Christina's quaking shoulders. "God girl, you sound awful!"

Christina strained to stop her body from shaking. She felt fever creep from her chest into her extremities covered with goose bumps. "We shouldn't stage our sick-out against the hospital." Nearly losing her balance, "We should focus it where the power is." Turning drooping eyes, "Here. In this clinic."

Yancy nodded. "That'd send a message all right."

"We'll start calling in sick for day-shift, Monday. That way, morning xenotransplants will be canceled. The rest of the hospital staff will temporarily make up the shortage and care for clinic inpatients, but there'll be no elective procedures. Norlake will go on, but we'll be hitting Emery where it hurts—his pocket." Closing her eyes from the pain in her aching back, "And when the TV cameras show up, we vent against Emery, not the hospital."

A smile slowly engulfed the nurse rep's face. "I like it."

"Have everyone meet at my house, Sunday afternoon." Christina violently coughed, spraying the air.

Yancy reached out and touched Christina's forehead. "You're burning up. Go home."

She tried to swallow. Her parched throat burned. "Not until I talk to Roberta Brown, the evening-shift rep."

"Roberta won't be in till four."

"I'll make it. But would you handle the midnight shift?"

"Sure, hon."

Christina fought the alternately cramping and sharp pains in her stomach. "Come next week, everyone will know just what's going on here!"

Hannah Merritt's Condominium

"What's it running?" Ryan asked as the blue bar on-screen inched closer to the right, its bold letters displaying: JOB 72% COMPLETE.

The CPU deep within Scott's computer ploughed invisibly through layers of data.

"Hundreds of thousands of calculations," Scott said.

"Yo! I mean what *exactly* is running?"

Scott picked up a pen and quickly began his pen trick, rapidly removing, then replacing its top. "IRACT's compiled records on more than fifty thousand patients who've had kidney xenotransplants. The place went to great lengths to fool me into believing that 98% of the patients survive three months after surgery, instead of 95%. Something is happening in those first three months postop."

"But it's only 3% of the patients."

"Don't get me wrong, kidney xenotransplantation works. But by lying to their auditor—me—they risked losing everything. Three percent isn't all that much, so it can't be the numbers *per se* who died that worry them. It's got to be the reason *why* they did."

Ryan sat on the couch and comfortably crossed his legs. "Probably just padding their numbers. You're making too much of it."

"I am not paranoid."

Ryan crossed his arms. "It's the 'visions' I'll bet. You still seeing the one about some transplant center?"

Scott slowly nodded.

"And the one with millions of dead people laying around in piles?"

"That too."

"By any chance, have you seen me in any of those piles?"

Scott slapped Ryan's knee. "Not funny."

Ryan shrugged with a smirk. "How do you know that those two dreams are even related?"

"I just do."

"Can't argue against logic like that," Ryan said sarcastically. He watched Scott walk over to the window, gaze out at the scattered lights from the office towers across the park, and lean over with clenched fists. "In all the years we've known each other, you've never directly asked me *the question*. Were you afraid it'd wreck our friendship? Mark you as Captain Weird from Planet Ten?"

Scott pounded on the windowsill. "Consider it asked."

"Then my answer's simple." Ryan paused. "Your daymares, nightmares, visions, whatever—they have the same chance of coming true as anybody else's. No more. No less."

Scott whirled around.

Ryan smiled at the surprise on Scott's face. "Not the answer you expected, huh?"

"After all that's happened over the years?"

"Who are you trying to convince?" Ryan asked. "Me or you?"

"So many times—"

"You were wrong."

"And plenty of times I was right. Remember that time in sixth grade when I dreamed that Joe Camery would be struck and crushed by a truck?" Scott asked.

"That kid spent half his time playing in the street and the rest running between parked cars. Chalk that up to inevitability," Ryan countered.

"What about our English teacher, Mrs. Falbert? She suffered a heart attack and dropped dead on the floor?"

Ryan stretched out on the couch. "The woman weighed more than her class combined and was always eating from the four basic food groups: fat, grease, chocolate, and Twinkies." Looking down at his own pot-belly, "Guess I shouldn't talk, huh?"

Scott sank into the chair beside Ryan and hung his head. "What about—Celia and Dad?"

"Come off it!" Ryan jumped off the couch and stood over his friend. "You hated being schlepped to Celia's gymnastic meets. I remember you throwing tantrums to keep from going. The day of the accident, that was the only time you ever managed to get out of it, right?"

He nodded.

"Think there's any possibility you might have felt guilty? That maybe if you went, the accident would never have happened?"

Gazing up at Ryan, "I warned them not to go!"

"I've talked to your mom about this over the years. She never remembered any 'warning' from you."

"It must have been too painful," Scott rasped.

"Or maybe that's just how *you* remember it."

"You're wrong, Ryan. Wrong!"

Ryan put his hands on his hips and towered over Scott. "I should have told you this a long time ago. I love you like my brother—if I had a brother—but this thing about you has always bugged my ass! I don't know if it's guilt, déjà vu, or some defense mechanism to make you feel special, but you don't have ESP and you're certainly not clairvoyant. Hell, you lose every week in the football pool! So give it up already, you are not Johnny Smith and this is not Stephen King's *The Dead Zone!*"

JOB STATUS 76% COMPLETE, read the blue bar on the monitor.

Scott slowly stood and faced his best friend. "God I hope you're right."

Norlake Hospital
Emery's Office

Emery watched the tiny monitor inlaid in a corner of his desk that everyone, even his secretary, Clara Bender, thought was part of his computer system. In reality, Emery used it to check on events in his outer office from a camera and microphone hidden in the drop ceiling—a necessity given the climate at PTS and the Institute. He wryly smiled as he watched Dr. Sarah Novia tightly cross her legs and glance around the outer office at his thirty-five proclamations of academic achievement from Berkeley to Bucknell, chiseled on plaques of bronze or silver plating, or written on parchments with embossed golden seals.

"Quite a man, isn't he Mrs. Bender?" he heard Sarah ask.

The silver-haired woman seated at the desk looked up from her console. "Hon, you don't know the half of it."

Bender had been with him too long, perhaps knew too much. But she was also an asset, knowing how to anticipate his needs, from airline tickets to insurance billing. It had taken years to break her in—he didn't relish replacing her with some gum-chewing ditz like Barbieri had over at the Institute.

"Did the doctor seem upset?" Sarah asked.

"Dr. Emery generally only sees residents three times a year. Mostly for evaluations. You're not due till next month."

Emery turned off the monitor and buzzed his secretary. He swiveled his chair toward his great window with its panoramic view of Cleveland with Lake Erie in the distance. Sarah entered, gazing around the inner office that seemed to have no walls, only flat surfaces shrouded by diplomas, awards, affiliations, acknowledgements, testimonials, newspaper clippings, letters of distinction, and photographs of him shaking hands with political celebrities, including two U.S. presidents and the governors of Massachusetts, Ohio, and Virginia.

"Sit please. I need another minute," he said. He heard her accidentally knock over the photo album on his desk of his wife and children. He swiveled back and buried his head in a folder on his desk. "You have an undergraduate degree in mathematics, correct?"

"Yes sir, Ohio State."

"And you were in a PhD program in pharmacology for two years? What made you switch from laboratory work to clinical practice?"

"I suppose the clincher was seeing the people I help in person."

Emery scratched his beard. "So in your opinion, clinical practice is more important than theory?"

"Not more important. More desirable, for me."

"Yet you seem to place theory above the welfare of our patients, as exemplified by this," he said quietly, holding up a manuscript entitled:

Porcine Endogenous Retroviruses (PERVs): Calculating the Probability of a Global Pandemic Arising From Xenotransplantation
submitted by Sarah K. Novia, MD

"Dr. Emery, I wanted your comments before submitting it to—"

"You're in training to become a transplant surgeon," dropping the manuscript like dead weight on his desk, "not a virologist."

She tried to hide her clenched fists. "That doesn't change the validity of the work. This needs to be heard."

"So that's what this is all about." Emery leaned back and locked his hands behind his head. "Proving to yourself and your uncle that you *earned* this position—that I didn't hand it to you because you're niece of the world-renowned Dr. Theodore Salsbury, father of modern xeno-transplantation, co-founder of the Institute, and my long-time colleague."

"Dr. Emery, I've never solicited any favoritism during my residency, nor do I believe I've ever received any."

"True enough." He sat up and rearranged sheets of her manuscript. "You have the potential to be an outstanding xenotransplant surgeon one day. The clinic fellowship is yours—if you want it." He observed her fists unclench and a smile slowly spread across her face. "And if you can get over two big hang-ups." He paused, watching her moisten her lips with anticipation. "First, you did get your residency here because of your uncle. Are you strong enough to accept that?"

She sighed. "I will, in time."

He nodded. "A fair answer."

"And the second?"

"This paper!" he bellowed, thumping her manuscript. "Sarah, you're spoiled! Do you know what it was like for transplant surgeons before xenografting?" Emery's eyelids grew heavy. "Watching your patients slowly die, knowing that their only hope was for a transplant—a transplant that had to come from some unfortunate soul," he said softly, re-membering faces of patients—some familiar, some he'd thought forgotten, sitting teary-eyed in his office—patients he'd never had the chance to save. "Waiting desperately for that phone call from the Organ Procurement Organization telling you that an organ is available. Knowing that at least one of every four patients you see will never receive that call. And if that call came from the organ donor coordinator, usually in the middle of the night, too often the human donor organ is damaged or diseased. You're left between choosing a compromised organ that could kill your patient—or waiting for another to become available before your patient dies, knowing damn well that you're praying for someone else to die." He cleared his throat and opened his eyes. "The worst is for children." He rapped his fist on the desk. "I've been to that place way too many times. I won't go back—not without a fight!"

Sarah pursed her lips. "I—appreciate what xeno technology has done for medicine."

"Do you, young lady? Effective synthetic organs that provide patients with a decent quality of life are decades away, pushed back by years of politically-forged restrictions on embryonic stem cell research. Even if growing human whole organs from human cell cultures becomes technically feasible, we may have to wait generations for unwarranted moral and ethical questions swirling around stem cell research to settle. No, the politicians and the social fringes have left us little choice. The xeno solution is the only answer to the horrendous shortage of donor organs for the foreseeable future."

"Our duty as physicians extends beyond the patients we treat. Our actions may place the community at large at risk."

"A *theoretical* risk, Novia. I cannot allow *this*," crumpling her manuscript, "to see the light of day."

Sarah's eyes shifted to her work, now a heap on his desk. "Dr. Emery, I've estimated—no, *under*estimated—that there's an annual 2% to 6% probability of a pandemic arising over the next ten years, based on widespread whole organ xenografting of SPF-4912."

"You've based your entire paper on SPF-4912 having endogenous retroviruses buried in its genetic structure—unknown, unsuspected, undetected retroviruses that have somehow managed to elude twelve years of preclinical and clinical research, intense FDA scrutiny, and hundreds of thousands of healthy, successful patients."

"Absence of evidence isn't evidence of absence," she said.

"You have no reason to suspect that such a retrovirus exists in SPF-4912."

"Dr. Emery, let's not forget what a retrovirus is. A retro-viruses is a RNA virus which, with the right enzyme, converts into DNA and inserts itself into a host cell's DNA. Porcine retroviruses, PERVs, are descendants of retroviruses that may have incorporated into the genetic structure of pigs eons ago. They might have been damaged by mutation over the course of evolution," leaning forward, "but they may still hold onto their ability to produce viral proteins—awakening from dormancy to infect the cells of another species—us."

"Pure speculation."

"Not speculation. Endogenous retroviruses, stuck in animal DNA and passed on from generation to generation, have been identified in pigs, cats, mice, and baboons. More than two hundred different copies are in human beings. In fact, they may comprise 1% of the entire human genome."

"Just an evolutionary consequence," Emery said.

"But with two clear dangers. One, retroviruses can destroy immune systems. Look at AIDS/HIV. And two, they can integrate themselves into the genetic structure of host cells."

"Novia, these aren't living retroviruses, anymore. They're *endogenous* retroviruses—ancient, broken down pieces of DNA that have been absorbed into an animal's genetic structure—defective and permanently damaged by mutations over hundreds, maybe thousands, of generations. They're no more alive unto themselves than the DNA sequences coding for my toenails. They aren't invaders—they're our heritage."

"Evolution doesn't account for transplanting pig organs into human beings—totally new environments—and genetic manipulation to avoid the human immune system, the last natural line of defense."

"There's nothing to indicate that such a virus would, even if it could."

Sarah released an exasperated breath. "Dr. Emery, viruses are extremely adaptable. Introduce pig endogenous retro-viruses to human endogenous retroviruses in a human host, and you set up the possibility that these two ancient, broken down viruses will combine, synergize, and reactivate. Perform enough xenotransplantations and eventually the genetic combination between the two viral sequences will click, creating new, recombinant viruses, one possibly deadlier than either of its predecessors. Even if the odds are a billion to one against for any given transplant, the chances are reasonably good that we could unleash such a virus sometime within the next twenty years."

"Were that possible, which I don't believe for a second, we'd detect—"

"We've given our 'humanized' pigs the ability to fool our own immune systems. Cells transplanted from animal organs can migrate throughout the human body, hide in brain cells, liver cells, anywhere. We might unintentionally give this new hybrid virus time to become an extremely efficient killing machine," she said. "Our screening assays might not be able to detect a recombinant human-pig hybrid virus. By the time we find out that it exists, it could have been carried all over the world."

"No such combinations between human and animal endogenous retroviruses have ever occurred, in culture or in subjects," Emery declared.

"A new hybrid virus, being a retrovirus, could be incorporated into human germ cell lines." Raising her voice, "Meaning that survivors might pass the hybrid virus on directly through their chromosomes to the next generation! We might never get rid of such a plague!"

"Let's not get irrational." He scanned through several pages of the disheveled manuscript.

She gazed at him. "This doesn't frighten you?"

"It would—if I believed it was even remotely possible."

"You don't believe diseases jump from animals to people?" she asked.

"You mean *zoonosis*? No, it's not a common phenomenon."

"The hell it isn't," swallowing uncomfortably, "sir. AIDS

came from the simian retrovirus, SIV, jumping from monkey to human, and mutating to become HIV. If HIV had been airborne, it might have decimated the world, not just Africa."

"The genetic makeup of monkeys is too similar to ours—which is why we don't use them." Emery paused. "Evolution has made pig DNA so different from ours that it virtually eliminates the chances of a pig virus infecting people."

"The 1918 influenza epidemic came from a mutated swine virus. It killed twenty million people!"

"Novia, people have butchered pigs for millennia. Every day, workers at meat packing plants around the world slaughter thousands upon thousands of pigs. Can you cite me even one case of a human being coming down with a PERV infection?"

"Meat packaging is not medicine."

"Then let's talk medicine." He put his feet on the desk and crossed his arms. "Pig valves have been used as substitutes for heart valves in patients for more than forty years, without incident."

"With all due respect, Dr. Emery, pig valves have been treated with glutaraldehyde. That tissue is as dead as plucked hair."

"It still has pig DNA which, according to your speculation, could serve as a repository for potentially lethal PERVs, doesn't it? And pig skin has been grafted onto burn patients for more than seventy years—without pig viral transmission."

"Skin isn't a whole organ planted internally, doctor."

"Not a convincing argument," he said. "Thousands of diabetic patients in clinical trials in the U.S., New Zealand, Sweden, and dozens of other countries underwent pancreas islet cell transplantation from pigs. Not one patient developed an infection from a pig virus."

"Yes, but—"

"Novia, what about the millions of insulin-dependent diabetics who've been injected with Diabend and have had their diabetes virtually cured by using islet cells from the SPF-

4912 pancreas? Same thing for Tremulate, which has pig brain cells encapsulated in a polymer used to treat Parkinson's disease. With the FDA's nose in everything, don't you think such a super-virus would have turned up *somewhere,* either in the clinical trials or the years of follow-up since the drug's release?"

"Respectfully Dr. Emery, those are examples of transplanted cells, not whole organs," Sarah insisted. "PERVs could be hiding in the matrix composing porcine organs."

He pointed a finger at her. "Now you're reaching."

"But that doesn't mean that there aren't other PERVs that we don't know about lurking dormant somewhere in SPF-4912's genetic code."

"Novia, all endogenous retroviruses have a similar portion of genetic sequence that codes for a protein envelope. This envelope protects the virus when it comes out of the host DNA. If that portion of the retrovirus DNA is damaged, the virus can't produce its envelope and therefore can't survive on its own. This same genetic sequence has been found in the retroviruses of cats, mice, pigs, baboons, and yes, people." He shifted his weight. "We have powerful genetic probes, be it your polymerase chain reaction tests, tests for possible PERV antibodies, Southern blot hybridization tests—all constantly searching for any DNA sequence in SPF-4912 that could potentially represent a previously unidentified PERV."

"Probe screens only detect what they're designed to test for. It's impossible to guarantee that SPF-4912, or any animal for that matter, is free of retroviruses."

"Sarah, you've personally assisted me on more than two hundred and thirty-one xenotransplant procedures. Have you seen even one postop case of PERV xenosis?"

"It only takes one incident to start an epidemic."

"Which is why the Institute for the Research of Animal Compatible Transplantations keeps such detailed records on every xenograft patient and close family members." He sat up. "Like your uncle, as a co-founder of the Institute, I'm dedicated to maintaining this vigil against possible xeno-

zoonotic infection. There'll be no plagues under my watch."
He sighed, gazing almost fatherly at her. "Your paper will
promote panic."

"I was hoping it would stimulate thoughtful discussion."

"This field of medicine lives under a Sword of Damocles.
The very first case of a pig retrovirus even suspected in the
death of a transplanted patient will slam the door on this
technology." He leaned forward, and pointed. "And you're
helping to make it happen."

"Dr. Emery, how could—"

"By putting that idea in some fucking shyster's head who'll
manufacture a case. Or hadn't you thought of that?" He held
back a smile as she looked down. "I thought not." Snorting,
"What's Uncle Theodore have to say about all of this?"

"I haven't shown him yet."

Softly, "Sarah, you're one of the brightest residents I've
ever had. You have great hands to go with that mind, a real
passion for the welfare of your patients and your work, as
well as some of what I've lost—idealism." He reached out
and touched her hand. "I can't stop you from publishing, so
let me help you." He waited until she turned to him, her eyebrows scrunched. "Your paper is filled with unsupported assumptions. Wouldn't it be better it you had a little more data
to go with those assumptions?" Emery sat back, locked his
fingers together, and smiled. "Say about twenty-thousand
patients? Institute registry data. I'll give you clearance to examine all the data you'll ever need. And all you need do is
agree to hold off submitting it until you've at least seen it."

She straightened up in her chair. "When might that be?"

"There's the Senate Subcommittee hearing next week,
and some time for the political dust to settle. I'd say about a
month—maybe six weeks."

"That seems reasonable. Thank you so much for offering."
He stood. "And now if you'll excuse me, I—"

"There's just one other thing," she blurted. "Uh, yesterday, you stopped me from changing Mrs. Folcroft's dressing
and DC'd her immunosuppressants." Disregarding Emery's

tightening jaw muscles, "Over the past few months, I've seen you show a heightened concern for certain patients."

Glaring at her, "What do you mean by *certain?*"

"I'm not sure. I have some notes—"

"It's time you and Uncle Theo had a little chat!"

Hannah Merritt's Condominium

JOB 98% COMPLETE.

Scott pointed at the monitor. "The disk my research assistant gave me had more than 50,000 patients, each with 400-plus pieces of information. From that mountain of data, I had to find a way to explain the difference between patients who died right after transplanting—the ones IRACT is covering up—from those who really survived."

Ryan looked at the blue bar onscreen creeping towards completion. "A giant equation?"

"A single equation of 400 variables for 50,000 patients would blow out my system. So I created ten different scenarios—each containing some of the key variables, like weight, age, and different aspects of medical history. I'm running them all in tandem, like assembling building blocks."

The screen displayed:

JOB COMPLETE
- Display All Parameters
- Select Parameter Characteristics
- Cancel

He clicked the second button and entered: **P<0.001.** "I told the program to select variables in the best scenario that have less than a one-in-a-thousand chance of being wrong."

The screen displayed: β_{Hanoi}

Scott turned completely around and gazed up at his friend's perplexed expression. "Remember the so-called Hanoi flu that was going around several years ago?"

"It didn't infect a lot of people, but those who were got really sick."

Pointing at the screen, "This indicates that patients who've had Hanoi flu are far more likely to die within weeks after a kidney xenotransplant than those who didn't have that flu."

"Maybe IRACT doesn't know."

"They know. They must."

Ryan paced up and back. "Then why didn't they exclude patients with Hanoi flu?"

Scott minimized the statistical software display, opened his PC's main directory, went to the CD drive, and double-clicked on a file. "That's why I need your help."

Ryan grimaced. "I'm a systems/network manager, not a statistician."

Scott pointed at a jumble of numbers in an interference pattern that abruptly appeared on-screen. "These files were on the CD my assistant gave me. They're encrypted."

Ryan studied the interference pattern on the screen.

Scott slid to the far end of the room, sank in the couch, and dropped his head between his knees. "I don't want to drag you into this, but I have no one else."

"Your mom was a nice lady." Pursing his lips, "She had the Hanoi Flu, didn't she?" Ryan pursed his lips. "You know, her record wasn't altered like the others. Whoever fabricated this must have known that your mother's record would be the first place you'd check."

"Exactly." Scott lifted his head. "They set me up."

IRACT   6:10 p.m.

Barbieri leaned against a cubicle in the IT department as Stone approached, her shoulders uncharacteristically drooped, hair tousled, face drawn, eyes downcast. "Evening Damara, you look like hell."

"How kind of you to notice," Stone replied, glaring. "I thought you were going to New York."

"Tomorrow morning."

"This meeting between Foster and me is private. Now I've had a long day, a longer night ahead, and I have to be on the road shortly, so—"

"Found Merritt yet?"

"I never mentioned Merritt to you. Which one of my—"

"Amazing how fast one can fall into disfavor with one's bosses." Grinning as she raised an eyebrow, "*He* wants to hear from you before you set out on your little expedition tonight."

"You know about that, too?"

"We should *both* talk to Foster."

Glowering, she followed him into IT's main conference room, a windowless chamber with beige walls, matching carpet, and an oval conference table with twelve separate inlaid keyboards. Four giant screens covered the walls. Barbieri sat on the opposite side of the table and propped up a bruised leg. To his right, Randolph Foster, the IT Department Director, a gangly young man in corduroys and a gray turtle-neck shirt, was hunched over. Stone seated herself opposite Barbieri.

Foster ran his fingers over a keyboard. Files containing individual patient names and personal data, byte size, and hospital/clinic/medical institution streamed across the screen beside the quotation. "We know that Evelyn Cruz assaulted the System. Now, I've analyzed the contents of information retried from Dr. Stone's laptop and reconstructed what I could from files deleted on Evelyn's PC. She apparently copied raw patient listing data, transformed patient listings, the AIMS program itself, and encrypted files containing summaries of specimen and assay outcomes. What bothers me is how Evelyn managed to do it."

"How so?" Stone asked.

"We all assumed that she bypassed security lockouts and copied the files from her desk or another in-house terminal. But I checked the activity on her terminal, by her username, and by keystroke and file activity at every workstation in the building. None of the files on Evelyn's PC or laptop were copied on-site."

"But on Monday, Cruz was seen, *in her office,* copying files onto disks," Stone said.

"I traced that. It seems she'd been using a statistical program in our system to forecast T-bill rates over the coming year. That's all."

Barbieri glared at Stone. "Then finding these files on Cruz's home computer—"

"Was serendipity," Foster finished. "Exactly what I discussed a few hours ago with Dr. Barbieri."

Stone's misty eyes narrowed. "Foster, if Cruz didn't hack in on-site, she must have hacked in online through your security system."

"As you know, when any of our reporting medical centers wants to send us data electronically, they can't direct access the file server. Whether by direct modem through Electronic Data Interface or through our website, they first have to pass through our firewall. Evelyn was a good database administrator, but didn't have much expertise hacking. I don't think she could have done it unless she already had a key."

Stone snarled. "How do you know Cruz didn't use a legitimate password?"

"None of the passwords accepted through the firewall by EDI originated from Evelyn's phone exchange, much less her house."

"She could have faked another phone number."

Foster shook his head. "Evelyn isn't a *phreak*. She doesn't have the skills to hack into the telephone network and temporarily change her number. However," tapping on the keyboard, "I reconstructed this from a partially destroyed file in her PC." On screen appeared:

k # * 3.

"The remnants of a 21-character password, a back door buried deep in our System. Something I wasn't privy to." He glanced from Barbieri to Stone. "Dr. Stone, I spoke to Dr. Barbieri because you weren't available at the time."

Barbieri folded his hands behind his head, putting his feet on the table. "So I suggested to Randy that he call Dr. Emery and Dr. Salsbury to see if either of them knew anything about master passwords or back doors into the System."

Stone fell back against her chair and closed her eyes. "What did they say?"

Foster pursed his lips. "Dr. Emery, well, he's not a pleasant man. He screamed that he had no idea what I was talking about, but that my job was on the line if I didn't fix the problem immediately. Dr. Salsbury, on the other hand, was very nice, but said he was retired and knew nothing of any master password."

In a bit of hot water, are we Damara? the voice that had chided Stone earlier taunted. She countered it by playing full volume Wagnerian opera in her mind.

"Who set up the back door, Randy?" Barbieri asked.

"Probably Dr. Todd." Foster blushed. "He and Evelyn had quite a thing going, or so I heard."

"Umm, umm, what about a core shutdown, then restarting with an archived copy?" Stone asked, appearing distracted.

"There's no way to know how long Todd's back door has been in the System. His password's probably been sitting there for years."

"What about shutting down selected areas of the mainframe server and—"

"Blindly poking our heads in for a look is risky. Anyone smart enough to leave a back door would leave behind other surprises. A trojan horse. A worm. We could wake up tomorrow morning and find all of our patient data so subtly changed that we'd never know it, or completely rewritten, completely destroyed, even transmitted off-site."

"Our immediate problem is keeping anyone with this password, out. At least through next week," Barbieri declared. "What do you suggest?"

"Lock down all remote access," Foster suggested.

"No!" Stone snapped.

"We can't," Barbieri echoed. "The Senate Subcommittee hearing begins next week. Randy, I need a working alternative."

Foster tapped on the keyboard. Data files raced across one of the screens. Patient names, phone numbers, and pertinent data whizzing by in hypnotic procession. "I could record all incoming calls and match communications against area codes and exchanges of participating institutions. We could then generate a list of phone numbers that don't appear to match. If we're lucky, we might be able to trace it back to the hacker. But that means restricting access to EDI and temporarily locking out web access."

Stone sighed. "Do it! But we'll have to re-open website access before the hearing."

Barbieri nodded, then looked at his watch. "It's late, Randy. You've done a great job."

The IT Director stood, nodded, then left.

"Let me capsulate your position, young lady." Barbieri shaped his hands like a steeple. "I may be in charge of the day-to-day running of this facility, but *you* are responsible for computer and general security. Your negligence enabled a glorified clerk to not only copy critical files that could cage us for forty years—which considering some of our investors might be the least of our worries—you allow those files to fall into the hands of the only man alive who could demolish us at the hearing *and* allow him to get hold of a golden key to our mainframe—all while you run around like a decapitated chicken."

"Merritt is not a problem," she said through clenched teeth.

"I know what you're planning, dear Damara. But what if he doesn't contact them between now and the hearing?"

"How did you—"

"Knowing a man's strengths and weaknesses in the abstract isn't the same as knowing him. You've never met him, never talked to him. You don't really know how he thinks."

"And you do?"

"I met him at a cocktail party," he snickered. "I can get him for you."

"I don't need your help."

Barbieri shook his head, regarding her as if she was a puppy spending its final night in an animal shelter. "You can't spend your millions if you're in pieces rotting in a land-fill." He stood and walked to the door. He turned the knob.

"What's your price?" she called as he turned the knob.

Without turning to face her, "I'm getting on in years, now. I haven't put away as much as I should have. My current annual salary doesn't provide enough to help me retire comfortably."

"I could force the information from you."

He turned. "There'd be no way to guarantee its accuracy—until it was too late." Smiling as she rolled her eyes, "To get $500,000 a year annuity, I'd need a principle of, oh, $5 million."

"You're out of your mind!"

"You could persuade senior PTS officers to increase the corporate contribution to the Institute for continued research—"

"While you cut corners and pocket the difference."

He grinned. "Something like that."

She shook her head and lightly pounded the table. "You'd have to wait to spend it, just like the rest of us."

"I have faith in science."

She hissed through her teeth. "Agreed. This conversation never took place."

"Good. Be in my office in fifteen minutes."

"Why?"

"Because partner, that's where the fax will arrive."

The Peninsula Beverly Hills Hotel
Beverly Hills, California

Hope Wheelan gazed out at the reporters and graciously smiled. She knew exactly how to present herself: regal pos-ture, stylish dressed in a ochre St. John suit and matching Jimmy Choo shoes, and accessorized with Patek Phillipe watch, David Yurman jewelry, and Prada handbag—all orig-inals. Her cinnamon-colored hair was exquisitely coiffed, designed to bring out the natural beauty of her tanned creaseless face. Though fifty-eight, she had a well-toned musculature honed by $1,500 an hour personal trainers and kickboxing instructors. This was not like the dark times: the media assembly was ostensibly favorable, or at least, non-hostile. Publicly, Hope accepted her apparent role as a footnote to these proceedings. Privately, she took pride in knowing that she was the power driving this beneficence.

While listening patiently to presenters, Hope turned and looked down the long head table at her husband of twenty-five years, Alexander, standing by a covered easel. Though he'd lost most of his curly black hair, he still had the firm physique she remembered from his youth. The few lines that had crept onto his face had added an extra touch of virility. With one eye shielded from the cameras, he shot her his characteristic quick double-wink, and mouthed 'Happy Birthday.'

". . . and dedication to seeing that every child who . . ." droned the woman at his side.

This donation, though public, was a deeply personal gift for Hope. Her mother had been beaten countless times by her alcoholic father; Hope herself had lost her virginity to the man at age nine. She had managed to escape; her mother never did.

". . . for battered women all over this country."

A distinguished looking gentlemen beside Alexander stepped to the easel, picked up a corner of the cloth covering the display, and announced, "This donation comes from Mr. and Mrs. Wheelan's *personal* assets, not from their wonderful foundation noted for its support of the needy here and around the world. We are overwhelmed by the Wheelans' generosity." The man pulled back the cover from the easel, revealing an enlarged check for $50 million. "This is for establishing Hope Wheelan Outreach Centers for Abused Women and Families all across North America."

Hope smiled for the barrage of glittering camera flashes as she joined her husband by the podium.

A deep, penetrating voice arose from the onlookers. "Mr. Wheelan, do you think this gift atones for the thousands of people whose jobs you've eliminated over the years?"

Hope covered her mouth. "Bastards! Won't they ever let go?"

Candice Kleisher Merritt stood over her two children playing with their dinner on the kitchen table. Nearly capitulating in her thirty-minute fight to get them to eat, she gritted her teeth as she watched Brooke, her eldest, picking her food while her son, Andrew, sat beside his sister, his arms defiantly folded.

"I hate ravioli!" Andrew declared. Five years old, he had the same face as Scott's, except cherubic and without the distinctive red flecks in his lagoon blue eyes. He put his hands over the top of his curly russet hair and scowled.

"Andrew, if you eat your ravioli, you can have two pickles," Candice said, extracting onion bits from sauce in his plate.

"Three!"

"None."

The boy reluctantly punctured a piece of cheese-filled pasta.

Candice turned to her eight-year-old girl with cascading hair and sparkling azure eyes looking down at her plate: her ravioli lay crushed beneath a mountain of grated parmesan. "Brooke, you're not the only one at this table!"

Brooke gazed up, her face etched with the same intractable expression as her mother. "All you do is yell!"

"Almost eight o'clock," Candice muttered as she glanced at the clock. "Much too late to feed the kids. I just can't help it." In a louder voice, "Eat or no dessert!" Out of the corner of her eyes, she glimpsed the image in the mirror on the far wall: a petite figure with long, dark, thick hair. Candice had worked hard to restore her body to the time when she'd first dated Scott. But her face had grown sallow, tired, worn—not so much from the battle between youthful beauty and age, but between endurance and adversity. She headed into the living room, sat down, and absently sipped the day's sixth cup of coffee while she stared at the phone.

Her mother, Edith Kleisher, placed her teacup on its saucer and pulled her glasses down from the bridge of her nose. Silver and black hair framed dark brown eyes inspecting her daughter's preoccupied face. "Relax sweetheart. They're children, just like you were."

Candice's bloodshot eyes refocused on her cup. "You're sure that you'll have no problems taking care of the kids for the weekend?"

"We'll all have a wonderful time." Edith squeezed her daughter's hand. "And I expect you and Scott to do the same in Annapolis."

"Remember, on Saturday Brooke has karate in the morning at nine and Andrew has indoor soccer at noon."

"They really teach kids soccer at that age?"

"Mob ball—they kick each other more than the ball. I've left you directions, an itinerary, and phone numbers where we'll be." Checking the phone on the table, "He always calls the kids before bedtime when he's away."

"Scott has a lot on his mind."

"Who's your child—me or him?"

"Don't you know by now?" Her mother smiled knowingly. "You both are."

The swirling spoon in Candice's coffee created a tiny vortex, its funnel warping the liquid's surface. "I should've forced Scott to share the responsibilities. What kind of wife lets her sick husband take on everything?"

"A compassionate one. One who understands the importance of her man's dignity."

Candice glanced up from the still swirling tea, "Scott tells me that sometimes wherever he looks, his mind sticks this— this stopwatch in the corner of his vision, like some *High Noon* Western movie. And it's ticking down the 'usefulness' of his life, of our time together as husband and wife." She dropped the spoon. The vortex in her cup died. "I'll never forgive myself if it makes him worse before his time."

"My little girl," Edith mock scolded. "*Now* who's taking on everything?"

"Mother, people with MS are seven times more likely to commit suicide."

Edith slid her chair closer to Candice and began stroking her daughter's hair. "Not Scott. Not ever. He's like your father, a military man."

"Daddy was a Marine with two tours of combat. Scott was an Air Force Base surgeon who spent most of his time treating frostbite. You can't compare—"

"Both draw strength from discipline and order. Sweetheart, your father, God bless his soul, drew it from experience. Scott, from his exposure to people who did and that love of his for military strategy. God makes good men by giving them their own sources of strength." She rubbed her cheek against her daughter's hair. "And good women, too. When we lived on Millington Road and you were little, I watched you play at the park across the street. You were always the field marshal directing others how to play. You'll come through this. You can't help yourself. It's in your genes. It's in Scott's, too. You're both stubborn, you're both strong, you're both winners."

The chimes rang the half-hour. Candice wiped her eyes with a napkin, and called out, "Dinner's done, kids! Bathroom, both of you! Anyone not here and ready in five minutes spends a boring weekend with a cranky mom!"

The house reverberated with small, harried footsteps, followed by water rushing through pipes. Brooke appeared in the kitchen carrying a small overnight bag, an oversized woolen coat, and a plastic sled. A straw hat, front brim folded back and accented by a paper sunflower, sat incongruously atop her golden hair.

"Is that your idea of a winter hat?" Candice asked.

"It's stylish," Edith said, smiling at her granddaughter.

Andrew followed, dropping a satchel filled with games and puzzles on the floor. "When's Dad gonna call?"

Edith bundled him up, buying his and his sister's cooperation with the promise of ice cream. Candice accompanied them out the kitchen and down the driveway illuminated by tiny black lanterns inset along its grassy perimeter. Shivering, she helped them pile into her mother's ancient Oldsmobile.

Across the street, four houses down the block, a man put his coffee mug on the dashboard. A grin spread across his wide face as he watching Brooke bend over and climb into the back seat of the grandmother's car.

FIFTEEN

Scott came up behind Ryan and placed a cold bottle of dark beer beside the computer tower. "You've been at this for hours. It's getting late. Have a cold one—for the road."

Ryan's eyes remained fixed on the numerical streams flowing across the monitor as his fingers pounded the keyboard. "Do you have any idea what it's like being with Janine the night before a trip? It's like she's in labor. She only wants me nearby so she can torture me."

"Packing! Damn, I forgot about Annapolis!"

"Looks like both of us might be happier—and safer— Wait, wait!" The numeric streams flowing on-screen abruptly terminated. "I think I've got it!" Orderly rows of jumbled letters appeared:

```
  1 GATCTTAAATTCACTATTAAGGGGATATGAAAGTATAAAGCCTTAAAATACGAAGCAAGT
 61 CTTGTTTTATCAACCAGATTCTAGTATTTTAATTAAAATACATATTTCTAACAATGAATT
121 CTCCTGTACCTCTCAGAGACCAGAGCCACTACCTCTAAATGTTTGCTGTTGTTGTTAGGA
```

```
181 ACTGGCCAATAAATGGTCATTTTTGTGGTCGCCATACCTGAGATGAATTGAGGTTGATCA
241 TAGACTTAAATGGAAAATTTAAAACTATAAATCTAAAAGCTAATGACATTTATCTTTGTT
301 CAATGTGTATTTTATCCCTATCCCCCCATGAACATGGAAAGAATGTTTTCCCACTATAGC
361 ATACAGACTCTGAAGTTTTTTCTTTGTGTATTGTTCATTGTTCAGACTTAACAAGTGTTA
421 TTAAAATATTAAAATGTATACTAAGTACTATTCAGCAATGTTAAGGACTAAAATGTTACA
481 ACATGTTCCATGATACAACACAGATAAACTTCAGTGCCAGTGAAAAAGTTAGATGCAAAA
```

"Naah, sorry. Nothing but junk. Let me—"

Scott lunged toward the desk, knocked Ryan's hands from the keyboard, and bumped him from his seat. Quickly, he began scrolling down through the alphanumeric rows.

"What is it?"

Scott continued scrolling. "Genetic code. A nucleotide sequence."

```
3181 GACAGCCCTTCATGCTGACCAGGATGTGGAACAACAAGAATGTTAATTCACTGCTAGTGA
3241 GTATGCAATGTGGTCTAGCCACGTTGGAAGACAGTCGTCCAGTTTCTTAAAAACTGAAC
3301 GTACTCTTACTATACCAATTAGCAATTGTGCTCTTTGGTTTTTATTCAAGTGAGTTGAAA
3361 GTATCTGTCCACTCAAAATTTCTGAAAAGATGATAATAGAAGCTTTATGTGTAATTGTCA
3421 AAACTTGGATTTGCAACCATTGTCCTTCAGTAGGTAAATGGATAAATAATCCACCGTACA
```

"Oh yeah, I remember Bio 101," Ryan said. "*G* for guanine, *C* for cytosine, *A* for adenine, *T* for thymine. Nucleic acids, they make up DNA. So what kind of DNA?"

Scott scrolled through the balance of the four-letter sequence, then began scouring through dense text that followed. He slammed his fist on the desk. "Viral."

Forman Household
Cleveland, Ohio

Christina let herself in through the sliding glass door and hobbled across the back of the house to the kitchen doorway. Her husband, Dave, sat at the table with Ethan and Evan, both playing with their bowls of macaroni and cheese. The boys jumped down from their chairs, and charged her.

"Mommy, want to hear what I did today?" Evan asked, clinging to her left leg.

"Gimme a ride, Mommy," Ethan begged, clinging to the other leg.

"Owwwwww!" she moaned.

Dave zipped around the table. "Get off her, boys," he said, grabbing the collars of their shirts and gently peeled them from her. "Your mother's not feeling well. Watch some TV in the other room. Cartoon channel only. I'll be with you guys in a few minutes."

Christina collapsed into a chair.

"Feel better, Mommy," Ethan said, giving her a little hug. Jealous Evan followed before Christina and Dave went into the den.

"Okay nurse, where's it hurt?" Dave asked.

"Head. Neck. Throat. Stomach. Every joint in my body."

He touched her forehead. "You're burning up." He strode to the first floor powder-room, returned with a prepped digital thermometer, and shoved it beneath her swollen tongue. A moment later, the thermometer beeped. "A hundred and two degrees. You just had to knock yourself out, didn't you? Was it necessary?"

One red eye peeked up at him. "It's flu—nothing more. Sleep, rest, liquids. Already taking—"

"If your temperature goes up one more degree, I'm taking you to the hospital!"

SIXTEEN

Scott floated above the central nurses' station. The staffers below him were busy, oblivious to the frazzled woman in a worn blue coat who wailed outside of Room Three-Something-Something, the last two digits smeared. A cadre of faceless white-coated doctors walked through the double doors at the far end of the wing. He gazed at the bright red embroidery stitched on one doctor's coat. An orderly pushing a gurney passed in front of him and blocked his view. The doctors walked beyond his vision. That had not happened before. Over the orderly's shoulder, was a placard. The lettering—

"Hey Scott!" Ryan called. "Something the matter?"

The hospital wing evaporated., replaced by his computer monitor filled with dense technical text. Scott rubbed his eyes, wishing those day/nightmare-hunch/visions-whatever-the-hell-they-were would just stop hounding him. "No, nothing's the matter."

Ryan peered into Scott's eyes. "You had that weird, far-away look. You in déjà vu land again, having one of those—"

"It's late," he said, pointing at a travel clock sitting atop a stack of boxes in the corner. "You'd better call your wife."

"Janine's gonna be pissed." He pulled out his wireless phone. "Here goes nothing," he said, punching in his house's preprogrammed number, and holding it loosely beside his ear. "Hi Janine, it's me." Shrill tones bled from the receiver. "Yes, I know we're going away tomorrow." The voice again rose, a piercing crescendo. "I know it was inconsiderate, but Scott needed me." He ambled toward the couch. "What do you mean you've been trying to reach me for hours? I've been here the whole time." His face scrunched. "Janine, wait a second. Have you been calling with the automatic speed dial, the one programmed in my den's phone?" He nodded. "That explains it. You've been calling his old house number. We're at *his mother's* place. Guess I didn't make that clear." He paced the length of the room. "About an hour. I promise I'll reprogram it when I get home." He nodded incessantly, then closed with a perfunctory 'I love you.'

"Trouble in paradise?" Scott asked, returning his attention to the monitor.

"I forgot to reprogram the phone. Janine kept calling the wrong number by accident." Ryan said. "You'll find a bunch of angry messages next time you check your old house's answering machine."

Scott hunched forward, staring at the monitor illuminating the dark room. "I've been so wrapped up in these files that I forgot to call Candice. The kids are spending the weekend at their grandmother's and I didn't even call to say good-bye to them."

"I have to go soon. I'm not going to have time to decrypt the rest of these files. I'll take them out West with me and finish them there." Placing a pudgy hand on Scott's shoulder, "And don't give me an argument."

Scott's stomach felt queasy at the thought. He said nothing.

Ryan swiveled his friend around to face him. "You've had enough time to read through most of the files. Now, what about that virus?"

"It's—highly technical."

Ryan rolled his eyes. "Take a shot at it!"

Scott slowly rubbed his hands, as if prepping for surgery. "Paradigm Transplant Solutions spent years and enough money to build an aircraft carrier to develop a miniature swine for xeno—"

"I didn't mean start at the *very* beginning."

Scott said, "One huge potential drawback to xenografting is the risk of transferring animal viruses, hidden deep in the donor organ, into human beings."

"Retroviruses?"

"Uh-huh. Type C, specifically porcine endogenous retrovirus—PERV. Little pieces of viral genetic code incorporated into the pig's genetic structure that lay dormant and are passed on to succeeding generations, theoretically for thousands to millions of years. To get SPF-4912 pigs approved for organ transplantation PTS had to prove to the FDA that the animal tissue was safe—that it was free of PERV viruses. The Agency was quite impressed."

"Probably wasn't hard to do," Ryan said. "I've heard drug companies cheat all the time."

Scott made a "T" with his hands. "Time out, old buddy. That's a common misconception. They rarely do, because it's cheaper for them to go back to the drawing board and do additional research or cut their losses rather than risk a deluge of lawsuits by knowingly releasing a faulty product. But mostly it's tough enough for them not to screw up clinical trials. And if you want to fudge data, you've got to be able to run the clinical trial right in the first place—which they often don't."

"Is that what happened to PTS?"

Scott nodded. "This documentation shows that three and a

half years ago, PTS researchers discovered a previously undiscovered retrovirus in the pig strain, designated PERV-DS, the 'DS' standing for 'Damn Shit.' "

"Named by somebody totally frustrated or with a sense of humor." Ryan sat down, propping his elbows on his knees. "Leaving them between a rock and a hard place."

"Believe it or not, it wasn't entirely their fault. PERV retroviruses are genetically similar to retroviruses found in many species. Researchers tend to hone in on three key genes: *gag, pol,* and *env*—which can be identified by standard testing, such polymerase chain reactions, PCRs. But PERV-DS isn't like any other PERV. It doesn't have those key genes."

"And so went undetected."

Scott shook his head. "PERV-DS is so damn small, only around 6,100 nucleic acid base pairs long. You saw its genetic structure earlier. By itself, an archaic piece of formerly living DNA that Nature seemingly forgot, harmless to pig or man. But when—"

"It synergized with Hanoi Flu!"

Scott grinned. "Not bad for a computer geek. Hanoi Flu was a virulent, airborne, but non-lethal influenza-like virus that swept through the Midwest and East Coast several years ago. Most people had a natural resistance, but those who got quite ill apparently also retained some vestiges of the virus. So," holding up one hand, "Here you have PERV-DS, a long-dormant virus with unpredictable properties." Holding up the other hand, "Here you have Hanoi Flu, with possibly very virulent pieces and the ability to be transmitted through the air." He slammed his hands together and rubbed, as if molding a ball. "Mix them together in a human host with an impaired immune system. Add in the capacity to mutate. What you wind up with is a breeding ground for new viruses spawned from PERV-DS-Hanoi combined. Repeat that, 100,000 times a year, and sooner or later, xenotransplantation with SPF-4912 organs will create a deadly virus almost unrecognizable to the human immune system. A super-virus."

Ryan nodded thoughtfully. "I'm assuming PTS can't just knock out the PERV like the others?"

"PERV-DS is latched onto key genes throughout SPF-4912's genetic structure. Every time they try to knock it out, they wind up taking essential genes with it that prevent organ rejection. From a practical standpoint, removing PERV-DS makes SPF-4912 pigs no better for xenotransplantation than those raised in a barn."

"Why don't they just go public? There've been no out—"

"Patients have died," Scott snapped. "There'd be a slew of state and federal indictments, followed by an avalanche of wrongful death suits. Xenotransplantation would be finished."

"They could instruct doctors to exclude patients with a history of Hanoi Flu."

"Like I told you a few hours ago, that raises questions that PTS can't risk answering."

"Then they could issue a recall. Claim that they only just recently discov—"

"Not without jeopardizing their flagship products."

Ryan involuntarily shook his head. "I don't understand."

"Diabend is the only treatment marketed in the world that actually cures type 1 diabetes. Tremulate is the only treatment that cures Parkinson's disease. Both agents generate profits for PTS in excess of $20 billion annually. Both are based on SPF-4912 pig extracts. Once FDA learns that SPF-4912 cells carry potentially lethal viruses, it would suspend sales, even though neither product carries the virus. That'd cost PTS billions in lost revenues and re-testing before the company could petition for reinstatement," Scott said. "Plus maybe ten years to clone a new pig strain in sufficient quantity for thousands of organ recipients."

"Where's IRACT fit into all of this?"

"Five years ago, PTS had planned to launch IRACT, ostensibly to continue monitoring for possible PERV infiltration. In reality, it was intended to be a lobbying center. With the advent of PERV-DS, PTS dumped $250 million-plus into IRACT, which it then used to independently gather and analyze tissue samples from xenotransplant patients around the country. That way, by using IRACT as its primary surrogate research center, PTS wouldn't have to gather the specimens themselves or perform any other activities that might draw unwanted FDA attention—or public stockholders for that matter."

Ryan pressed his temples. "Don't they realize the terrible chance they're taking?"

"After three years, despite all the setbacks laid out in these documents, there are scores of memos here from PTS senior officers who still believe they'll beat it." Staring beyond Ryan, "They're also trying to maintain tighter control of patient selection by limiting organ availability to 'franchised' xenograft medical centers—run by transplant surgeons who have a financial stake in the problem. All while they're expanding globally."

"You've got to take this to the police."

"Sure. I'll hand over the files and spend the next six months giving them a crash course in biostatistics and virology. In the meantime, they'll want to know where I got this," he said, grabbing a stack of papers.

He grabbed Scott's hand. "You could go to the media."

"Who do you think the public's going to believe: a washed-up surgeon with MS and possible mental impairment or a multibillion dollar corporation that found the cure for diabetes and Parkinson's disease?"

Ryan stood up. "What are you going to do?"

Scott looked out the window. "My best bet is to get these files to the hearing on Tuesday. At least everything will be out in the open."

"And in the meantime?"

"Go with Candice to Annapolis. It's probably the best way to lay low."

"Anyone know where you'll be staying?"

"*I* don't remember where I'm staying."

"Have I ever got a headache." Ryan massaged his temples. "Where will you leave the information?"

"At my e-mail address."

"If they're on to you, that'll be the first place they'd look." He went to the desk, tore a corner from a sheet of paper, scribbled on it, then handed it to Scott. It read: **obfusc8@it.upenn.edu;jlkdpsyv.** "My departmental address and password. Nobody else uses it. E-mail me and/or upload files of everything you need there, and I'll e-mail back any info there that I might come across while I'm out west."

Scott folded the paper and inserted it into his wallet between portraits of Andrew and Brooke.

They meandered into the living room. Ryan grabbed his coat, headed for the door, then slowly turned back. "IRACT's Database Administrator had to know that these files are just copies and, therefore, in and of themselves, useless in a court of law. IRACT can archive the originals, destroy what's on their computer system, and no one could prove otherwise. I'm thinking that maybe she had a back door into their mainframe. Did she leave a password?"

Scott shrugged. "No."

Ryan stuck his face three inches from Scott's. "Oh yes she did."

"What makes you say that?"

"It's obvious. Their Database Administrator gave you the disk so *you* would be the whistleblower, not her. And since she clearly wanted you to succeed, but take all the risks, she had to give you all the tools to do it. So she had to include some sort of back door, or else all this," pointing at the papers and the screen, "proves nothing."

Scott grimaced. "I told you, she didn't—"

"Why do you think I'm always inviting you over for poker? Because of your scintillating personality? No, it's cause I can count on your stake for my spending money. Now," holding out his hand, "give!"

Blushing, Scott reached into his pocket and handed him a scrap of paper. "This is a copy of what came with the CD."

Ryan read: **k4aA+.>#OCMqb*j,130vx.** He shook his head. "You were going to let me leave without this?"

Scott sighed. "I've got a real bad feeling about whoever uses that password. I don't want it to be you."

"I don't believe what can't be quantitated, and everything can be reduced to ones and zeros." Ryan stuffed the paper in his pocket. "The evidence is somewhere in their system and I'm the best one equipped to find it. Leave this to an expert. I've hacked into phone systems and temporarily changed numbers before. They'll think the call is coming from some neighborhood church instead of my house." He patted Scott on the shoulder. "Don't worry, I know what I'm doing."

North Wilmington, Delaware   *11:19 P.M.*

Stone slowly opened her eyes after a short, restless nap and wiped condensation from the car's passenger window as they sped down the interstate. "Clayton, are we almost there?"

The car's driver, her most reliable man, clenched his jaw. "Yeah."

She looked in the right sideview mirror. There were no trailing headlights. "Where are the others?"

"Disposing of Cruz's car," Clayton said flatly. His jaw clenched again. "They'll meet us there."

She looked at the man's profile. Eyes narrow, nostrils flared, jaw clenched—he was angry. "What's bothering—" Her cellphone rang. "Yes?" She listened a moment. "Keep them there until you hear from me." End call. "The others have Merritt's kids and mother-in-law secured in a safe house," she told her driver.

Clayton's eyes remained fixed on the road. "Won-der-ful."

"You disapprove?" The man said nothing. "Did Boston get to you?"

"Todd was necessary. His family was not."

"He might have told his wife."

Clayton turned from the road to her. "And his children?"

The car passed an eight-foot internally lit sign proclaiming 'Verity Healthcare Consultants.' Clayton turned into the parking lot, drove down the central road between rows of halogen lamps, then circled the trapezoidal building, dark except for a single office light from the southeast corner of the seventh floor.

"You didn't have doubts last night," she said.

"Last night, we didn't have," opening the glove box and removing a piece of paper, "that."

"The fax? It's just floor plans and security measures."

"Anyone providing that much detail about Verity that quickly would've already searched for the files on their own. Which makes what we're doing tonight, extraneous."

"I disagree, and I'm in charge."

That's telling him, Damara, sounded the sarcastic voice in her head.

Clayton drove to the rear of the building, parked obliquely to the loading platform, and shut off the headlights. A pair of headlights appeared behind them. Stone removed folded papers from the glove box and shoved them into her black jeans. She and Clayton then put on two sets of latex surgical gloves, fitted ski masks over their heads, and aligned wireless headsets with precut ear holes in the masks. "Everybody hear me?" she asked.

"Reeve, yeah," answered a man from the other car.

"Uh-huh," answered Thane, Reeve's partner.

"There's a light on in the top corner of the building. Is somebody up there?" Reeve asked.

"Shouldn't be," she replied. "There's no janitorial service on Thursday nights. See any activity?"

"Nope. But there's a car parked in front of the main entrance."

They circled to the main entrance and spotted a four-door Hyundai angled between two lines in the second row: its left front tire was flat; its windows were iced over.

"Be on guard," she said as they swung around to the back of the building. "Once inside, there's no biometrics or other security. Get in and get out, clean." Placing a hand over her mouthpiece, "Clayton—"

"If the CD's there, I'll find it."

"It's probably not hidden, so if you don't find it in ten minutes, hit three other offices on the same floor as decoys." Taking her hand off the microphone, "Thane, take my car around front. Get us out at the first sign of trouble. And sound off at five minute intervals."

As Stone and Clayton got out of their car, Thane, the black-clad rotund driver of the second car, took Clayton's place behind the wheel and drove off. Reeve, the second man in black, carried a knapsack. When Clayton held out his hand, Reeve slapped it with a small canister from his sack.

Stone scanned the two closed-circuit cameras: one swiveling on its base, the other partially hidden in an alcove. "Get moving."

Clayton jumped onto the platform and hugged the near wall, his shoulder scraping its frigid surface. On reaching the corner, he pivoted and side-stepped across the loading dock. Ignoring the moving camera, he slid along the wall until his back was flush against the steel door. At arm's length from the camera, he reached up and sprayed its lens, then swiped the card he'd taken from Dylan through the slot on the wall. The door clicked. He checked inside, then signaled all-clear.

The three passed through the internal loading bay. Thirty paces later, they stopped at a corridor junction. Stone directed Reeve towards the computer server room at the third door on the left. With Clayton, she continued to a stairwell across from an elevator bank midway down the building's long side. She proceeded up the stairs to the second floor landing while Clayton climbed to the fourth floor. Gingerly, she opened the fire door and peeked around the door-jamb.

* * *

Exhausted, Verity's vice president Vincent Ingenito sprawled across three swivel chairs in the seventh floor conference room. Papers lay strewn across the rectangular table, overhead projector and floor. "What was the damn emergency?" he muttered. "This stuff wasn't due for two weeks. All of a sudden, it's got to be in tomorrow? What a jerk!" He plunged into a stack of papers on the seat to his right. "Where's that directory?" He snapped his fingers. "That's right. I lent it to Merritt. It must be in his office."

By flashlight, Stone groped through the pitch black second floor.

"Server room secure," she heard Reeve announce on her headset. "Now searching for backups."

"I'm in Merritt's office," Clayton announced through her earpiece. "Fourth floor hallway lights are on. Same for the second?"

"No. Keep on guard."

"Five minutes," Thane chimed.

Stone explored two rows of cubicles before identifying the one marked 'Dylan Rogers.' She sat at his desk and turned on his computer. The monitor illuminated a patch of the black room that occupied the entire second floor. After logging in with Dylan's username, the computer network awaited his password. "I killed him too soon," she muttered. "Ah, no matter. He's left it here somewhere." She checked for stick 'em scraps around the monitor, under the mouse pad, under the desk, in the top drawer and found his password taped to the bottom of the keyboard.

"Got it," Reeve announced. "Eighty gigabytes. Four days' worth of company backup data."

"Good. I'll have it checked later at the Institute." She finished rifling through Dylan's desk: nothing.

"Ten minutes," chimed Thane.

She ordered a list of all new files Dylan had created in the last week: six client letters and thirty-five internal e-mails—none of them attached or referring to Institute files. "Reeve, there should be an old wooden desk in the corner of the room. Pull out the lower left drawer and reach into the back section. You should find an unmarked manila folder with stapled papers. Look up Merritt's employee number and password."

As Reeve relayed the info, she entered the password and began searching. After only seconds, "There's no Institute files on Verity's mainframe—at least nothing from Rogers or Merritt," she told the group. To Clayton in Merritt's office, "The CD?"

"I don't think it's here," he answered.

"Fifteen minutes," Thane chimed.

"Clayton, toss three offices next to Merritt's. Meet me at the docking bay. Ten-minute ceiling. Reeve, get down to the bay. We're leav—"

"Aaaahhh!" a voice screamed through Stone's earphones.

Thane nervously eyed the black glass building as he sat outside in his car, engine revving.

A fourth floor window exploded. A man shot into the air, arms flailing, somersaulting, shrieking as it fell. He struck a parking lot lamp. Sparks showered the pavement. The metal pole collapsed. The body folded backward, ricocheted, and struck cement. The pole clanged like a broken bell, then rolled slowly across the ground and into the gutter.

Thane sped his car to the site and skidded to a squealing stop. The man on the pavement lay in a pool of blood, the left arm twisted around the right elbow, three quarters of the face smashed. A chunk of the man's back had been sliced by the pole and singed by hot halogen vapor light.

* * *

Stone burst into Merritt's office. Wind whipped her face. Papers flew across the room, funneled into mini-twisters. The Wilmington skyline twinkled through jagged glass as air whistled through the shattered window wall. In the dark, behind the desk, knelt a man, wheezing in synchrony with the room's rushing air. "Clayton?"

A man's head turned in the shadow, as if just becoming aware of her.

Thane yelled through her earphone, "Clayton's dead!"

She drew her automatic. A figure moved out of the shadow, picked up the desk phone, and hurled it at her. It struck her hand. The gun flew into the dark.

The man lunged, his body blotting out the skyline. His right hand smashed into her face. She reeled against the wall. Her body bounced back like a tennis ball. Through dulling pain, she focused on his hand, grabbed his thumb, and jammed it back. Steering his hand in a power arc, she slung it behind his back, tipped his torso forward, and front-kicked him between his legs. The blow struck his inside thigh. He winced, but shot his leg back, full force. His heel struck her abdomen.

She doubled over, releasing him. The man staggered two steps towards the window and collapsed to his knees, unable to catch his breath. She straightened up, ignoring the fiery pain in her stomach, and lunged at him. The man gazed up at her like a submissive dog. She knocked him to the floor. "You're not Scott Merritt."

"No, I'm," panting, "I'm—Vincent Ingenito."

Damara swung his right arm high behind his back, like a post. "Too bad—for you." Firmly gripping the wrist, she squinted, then kicked the arm above the elbow. It snapped. Ingenito wailed. Dropping the limp arm to the floor, she pulled the other arm back, lifted him to his feet while tipping him forward like a wheelbarrow. And ran him toward the window.

"Noooooo!"

She launched him, through jagged glass, into the dark.

Ingenito's right foot slipped in front of her ankle. He disappeared over the edge. Stone fell forward, following him into space. She careened out the window, into the cold night air. And felt the exhilarating terror of uncontrolled falling.

Frantically, her hand plucked at air. Grabbed the headset ripped from her ears. The ground rushed toward her.

Below her, a muffled thud—Ingenito's body splattering on the ground.

Something pulled her back, yanked at her shoulder with fiery pain. She looked up. The trailing wire from her headset was wrapped around a corner of the bookcase. Her body swung precariously against the outside of the building, dangling by her headset mouthpiece. She groped for the windowsill four inches beyond her reach. The cord slackened, then stiffened. The microphone weakened. Stretched.

She looked down. Felt herself slipping.

And now we come to the end, the voice in her mind said.

"You want me to die?" she screamed, her body rotating in the wind.

That would save us both a lot of misery, it said.

"Oh, oh, G—"

Praying to God? You must be an optimist, thinking He'll listen to your prayers.

"Like He listened to yours?" The cord slipped. "I'd rather die."

A hand dangled in front of her. "Stone, gimme your hand!"

"No. You're not real."

"You crazy, Stone? Gimme your fuckin' hand!"

She looked up: Reeve stretched precariously out of the window, emphatically gesturing at her with his outstretched arm. She clasped it, planted her feet against the building, and pulled as he strained to hoist her up. She clambered back over the edge, and fell heaving onto the floor.

He stood over her, hands on hips. "You hurt?"

She shook her head. "Let's get out of here. We'll get Merritt tomorrow."

Death does not take the old, but the ripe.

—A PROVERB

FRIDAY, FEBRUARY 4

SEVENTEEN

Bleary-eyed, trying to focus on the monitor, Scott clicked the last file attachment, then hit the SEND button. The e-mail disappeared into cyberspace. Both e-mails with IRACT's bogus files attached were now gone: one sent to his own address; the other to the address Ryan had given him. Now, no matter what happened to the computer in his mother's apartment, the files were safe.

No one knew where he and Candice were going for the weekend. By the time he appeared late Monday afternoon-early evening in Washington, it would be too late. Only a few hours later, he'd be testifying in front of the Senate Subcommittee. Scott particularly looked forward to seeing Barbieri's face—the obnoxious, slimy bureaucrat he'd had to deal with during the long months of the grueling audit—when he would use powerful buzz phrases before the Senatorial panel: how IRACT was risking the lives of every American citizen; how IRACT was threatening national security. He edited and re-edited the words he'd use just before clicking the mouse and retrieving IRACT's own fraudulent files. He applauded himself as he replayed the shock, the outrage that would erupt from the genteel senators on the dais. And Senator Bannerman, that condescending bastard, what would he do? Probably start with inquisitorial tactics worse than his dwarf hatchet man Price. But Scott had the power of statistics behind him, and with each attack Bannerman would launch, Scott could counter with the record of some patient who supposedly had lived for months but had actually died within days after xenotransplantation from a virus hidden deep in the transplanted pig organ. Yes, Bannerman, would face a major scandal, and probably have to find himself new backers for his presidential bid—assuming he survived.

That's the way it should happen. But sitting by himself, in the dark, Scott couldn't *feel* that. Despite all the precautions he'd taken, somewhere, somehow he'd made a mistake. People around him were going to suffer.

Barbieri's Office, IRACT   8:15 A.M.

Barbieri typed furiously on his laptop. His two-part lecture on Institute-projected demands for xenotransplantation, scheduled to be addressed to the nephrology convention, was far from complete.

His secretary, Amanda, buzzed him. "Mr. Foster's here. He says it has to do with a standing private matter between you two."

Barbieri minimized the PowerPoint file on-screen. "Send him in."

Foster entered, nervously rubbing his hands.

"I'm catching a train to New York in an hour. What is it, Randy?"

"Some time ago, you said that if Dr. Stone received any—sensitive communications, that you might be willing to find some *special funding* for—"

"*If* it proved useful."

"There's, uh, there's a file named *Kompromat*. I've decrypted it. You can find it under this directory," he said, handing him a slip of paper. "Doctor, when you're done, *please* remember to toggle back on the encryption key. If you leave the file naked, Dr. Stone will know." He nodded and left.

Barbieri located the file on the server and accessed. *Looks like PTS will be paying me sooner than I'd hoped.*

Emergency Room, Norlake Hospital

Christina gazed up at Dave's blurry face. Even through the haze, she could see her husband's worried expression. She tried calling his name, but only gurgling sounds arose. Her chest burned. Overhead, fluorescent lights rushed by. She felt herself moving, cradled within his tender arms. It was so hard to breathe. And cold, so very cold.

Dave shouted. People yelled around her. She felt her body ripped from Dave's arms. Slammed onto a cold, flat, padded slab. Faces she did not recognized pierced the twilight enveloping her. No, not all the faces were unfamiliar: there was Nurse Mocarelli's concerned expression, and Dr. Silverstein's stern face. But they worked in Norlake's Emergency Room. Why were they here in her kitchen?

Someone pulled back her eyelids. Something jabbed her arm. It did not hurt. She reached out for a breath of air. None came. Her mind fought for that breath, but she sensed her body laying, impotent. She opened her eyes. The twilight darkened. Far off, a tiny voice wailed. Was that Dave, crying?

EIGHTEEN

Scott opened his eyes a crack. A starfield raced before him.

He pulled back. Slowly focused. The starfield was the screensaver on the monitor. Daylight peeked through the drawn blinds. He glanced at the clock. "Shit! I'll be late!"

He stumbled into the master bathroom, brushed his teeth, trimmed his beard, and took a hot shower, the water soothing like an afternoon massage in a Japanese bath house. Before putting on his blue suit, he gazed out the window at the overcast sky. It looked like snow. He turned on the TV to hear the forecast:

". . . story is a bizarre connection between a mysterious death at a New Castle county, Delaware medical consulting firm and Wednesday night's tragic Middlesex County, New Jersey, gas explosion," the anchorwoman said. *"Lena Dunn-Martin has this live report. Lena?"* A moment later, another woman resumed, *"I'm in the parking lot of Verity Healthcare Consultants in the peaceful, community*

of North Wilmington, Delaware—a peace shattered around midnight last night when Vincent Ingenito, a senior company official, either jumped or was shoved to his death out of a fourth floor window . . ."

Scott froze. On-screen, the camera focused on a broken parking lamp and remnants of a bloodstain.

". . . ware authorities are seeking Dylan Rogers, a company employee, for questioning. Rogers disappeared two days ago, and authorities suspect that he may have been the last one to enter the building last night . . ."

"They got to him!"
On-screen, file footage of a fire scene at night titled 'Cranbury, NJ, Wednesday night':

". . . tentatively linked him to the spectacular gas explosion that rocked a residential section of Cranbury, New Jersey, two nights ago—a fire now labeled arson. The deadly explosion, at the home of Evelyn Cruz of the 200 block of Remington Road, killed seven people, sent another twenty-one to the hospital, and destroyed or severely damaged six homes. Middlesex County detectives have identified a car damaged in that explosion as belonging to Rogers. And Delaware state police have found Cruz's car abandoned less than a mile from where I'm standing. The FBI . . ."

"Dylan's dead," Scott rasped.

". . . that Rogers may have had an affair with Cruz. More than $250,000 had been deposited in Rogers' bank account this past week . . ."

Scott felt lightheaded. Cold waves rippled through his chest. Icy tendrils crawled down his legs. *Discipline*, he mentally shouted. *Discipline*.

He felt himself back in the operating room, standing over his blue draped patient, his gloved hands awash in blood, his forehead damp, his nostrils irritated by tissue burned by high-powered bone cutters. The patient's bone unexpectedly shattering, the surgical implant now useless—his first emergency, the dread of not knowing what to do. Then, remembering the solution he'd taught himself in that first tumultuous O.R. outing: stand back, clear the mind, *make time pass slowly for you.* An answer will come. Maybe not the correct one, but at least one not made in panic. He remembered turning to the surgical nurse, his hand outstretched, confidently demanding a self-retractor, and discovering for himself the practicing surgeon's creed: often wrong, but never in doubt. Candice had dubbed it 'doctor-mode.' Whatever its name, it was the core of confidence, of strength.

Scott took a deep breath, strode into the den, shoved a rewritable CD in the slot, and began copying all the files. Systematically, he gathered the papers littering the floor, took them into the hall, and tossed them down the refuse chute. When he returned to the den, he took a brown envelope from his briefcase, scribbled an address on it, shoved the newly written CD inside, and sealed it.

He checked the clock. It would be tight.

Knight Residence
Montgomeryville, Pennsylvania
12:35 P.M.

Ryan Knight, working his laptop like a pianist, sensed familiar footsteps approaching from behind. Quickly, he hit the screen saver and turned around with an exaggerated smile. Janine Knight stood two paces behind him, her arms folded, piqued. Dark eyes, set against a ginger-skinned face, she glared. "What are you doing?"

"Just finishing up before we go," he shot back quickly.

"Like what you were working on late last night with Scott?"

"He was having problems—"

"We're flying out in a few hours. Have you packed your toiletries, your shirts, your underwear, your hiking shoes? Checked to see that I did for you? And what about the kids? Have you seen that they're packed? Taken any travel games for the plane? Called the airline to check on our flight?"

"No. No. No. No. No. And uh, no."

"Why bother? You have me to take care of every—" She noticed the photograph of a five-year-old girl with glowing smile, dainty features, and ponytail protruding from a blue baseball cap with a large script 'A', who sat gleefully atop Ryan. It was the last happy photograph of Alyssa—and the first time Janine had seen it since her child had died six years ago. "I didn't know we still had that picture of her. Did you just find it?" She stepped forward and put her arms around Ryan's neck. "There are times when I think you've locked memories of her away in some dark corner of your mind and thrown away the key." As he looked away, "What happened?"

He shrugged.

"If you're going to brood the entire trip, you can stay home."

"I can't explain it now, but what I'm doing is for *her*." He kissed her hand. "Remember when they said they had an available—"

Someone lightly rapped on the door. "Mommy?"

"Wait a minute, Jonathan," she said to the child in the hallway. Eyes glistening, "Do what you must." She walked to the door. "But do it in fifteen minutes. Then, you're mine."

Ryan turned his attention to the laptop screen as the voices of Janine and his youngest son faded down the hall. At his touch, the bottom of the laptop screen read: **78 Files Copied**. "That's the last batch. Now, to make sure they're protected."

He tapped on the keyboard. A file name and password request appeared center screen. He entered a series of keystrokes that the file server rejected, then typed the genuine password. After a long, lingering gaze at Alyssa's smile, he terminated the connection to IRACT, restored his genuine phone number through the phone system, closed the laptop, and removed the line to the wall jack. As he started to leave, he glanced at the phone. "Oh, what the hell."

He picked up the receiver, but before he could phone Scott, he heard Janine scream from the other room, "Time's up, Ryan! Logoff!"

"All right, all right." He pressed the speed-dial button on the phone, then touched the number '4.' Bell tones sounded in a rapid, familiar sequence. The answering machine at the other end picked up after four rings:

> This is the Merritt household. Leave your name and num-
> ber after the tone, and we promise to get back to you just
> as soon as we can. Please don't hang up. Beep.

"Hey Scott, Ryan here," he said quickly, quietly. "I used the password to get inside IRACT's system. Listen, what you and I saw was only the surface. There's more to this, *a lot* more. Check your e-mail. I'm taking copies of all the downloaded originals with me. Anyway, my flight leaves around 5:15 and gets into Phoenix around 10:00 P.M., Philly time. Hope everything works out for you guys this weekend. May the boomerang be with you."

As he hung up the phone, Ryan had a nagging feeling. Something he was supposed to do with the phone? Something he'd promised Janine?

Former Merritt Residence:
14 Lancelot Way
Royalton Village Estates, Villanova, PA   12:47 P.M.
The answering machine clicked off.

IRACT   12:59 P.M.
Stone was sitting quietly in the IT conference room when in burst Foster. "Put it through here," he called to one of his

sysops before the door closed. He slid into a chair at the near end of the table, locked his eyes on the screen covering the opposite wall, and began pounding on an inlaid keyboard. A series of phone numbers and accompanying names scrolled up on the screen. "With web access down in the last hour, we've received sixty-two calls, excluding one listed as anonymous which we blocked from accessing one gateway."

"What about the anonymous call?" Stone asked.

"Probably a telemarketer. Now, after eliminating phone calls coming through directly to staffers, four accessed the Electronic Data Interface for transmitting patient data. Three were from pre-approved sources—that is participating medical institutions and phsyical offices or homes. But the last one." The screen displayed one number and identification: Santolini Pizza, Montgomeryville, PA.

Stone shrugged. "Any laptop with a wireless—"

"The call came from the restaurant's *incoming* line. You can't make outgoing calls on it; it's for taking orders, only. Unfortunately, the connection was terminated from their end before we could act. And no ma'am, I don't know the damage."

"Run that exchange number against employee records, med centers, vendors, anything on record." Stone put her hands to her throbbing temples. "So what now, a core wipe?"

"You don't burn the house down when just your back door's broken," he said. "Plus I don't want to take the chance that our phreak will call back, find we're using archived files, and *really* get nasty. We can't risk a catastrophic System collapse before Tuesday."

"So what *are* you doing?"

"Running file comparisons between all current and archived data and statistical files. We have data entry staffers checking, by hand, every file updated since Monday. We've locked down EDI for the next couple of hours while data entry catches up. But finding a Trojan horse—"

"No excuses, Foster. Something is sitting on the Institute's mainframe. Something that will blow up in our face." She straightened her back and brought her scorching eyes to bear upon him. "You will find it!"

NINETEEN

Bourse Building
Old City, Philadelphia, PA   1:20 P.M.

Scott bounded up the stairs. A great banner draped across the foyer of the Bourse building welcomed visitors to an architectural linchpin of Old City Philadelphia. The lobby opened into a grand concourse surrounded by columns with terra cotta ornamentation supporting the upper levels. Two sets of fire-tower staircases with marble-inlaid landings and delicately-crafted iron railings led to the atrium's upper floors. Overhead, bowed steel girders upheld a skylight and the modern office building above it. The nineteenth-century Carlisle redstone building, which had once served as America's first commodity exchange with ship captains announcing on its floor the arrival of their vessels filled with sugar, grain, and fine textiles, now had a food court serving egg rolls, corn dogs, and cheese steaks.

The restored Victorian clock on the third floor railing warned Scott that he was already twenty minutes late. He glanced behind him to see if he was being followed, then dashed up the nearest tower staircase to the second floor. A man with thinning blond hair and wearing a gray tuxedo stood at attention behind a podium marked *'Tout a Vous.'*

"I'm Dr. Merritt. My wife—"

"This way please," the host said as he led Scott along a walkway between the main glass-enclosed dining area and a row of tables abutting the rail leading to Candice's table. "Enjoy your meal, sir." He spun on his heel and left.

Scott surveyed his surroundings: four tables were on Candice's near side, six on her far side. Most patrons were sipping coffee or tea, their checks face down on their respective tables. No one seemed to notice him. Satisfied, he placed his hand on his wife's shoulder and bent to give her a gentle kiss. A figure in black from long thick hair to seductively simple dress to low-heeled leather boots, she looked up with eyes he'd never been able to resist. A bloody Mary with protruding celery stalk straddled a rumpled napkin lay in front of her on the table. "Sorry I'm late."

She pointed to a glass of watery scotch rocks. "Your drink's getting warm."

He sat down and shoved the glass aside, caught a passing waiter's attention, and ordered Caesar salad for two. "Candice, I—" He heard a faint, disquieting ringing behind him. It compelled him to turn around. He scanned the restaurant, but none of the patrons that he could see was using a wireless. Perhaps someone behind the glass at the far end of the restaurant?

With lunchtime ending, people filed out, the smells of seafood and perfume following them. One woman, who wore a wide-brimmed chestnut hat partially obscuring her light blue eyes, had a particularly strong scent—powerful, but not sickly sweet or choking—as she passed their table. By the time their salad arrived, only two tables remained occupied.

"I found street parking, but there's less than an hour left on the meter. If we're late, they'll tow my car," Candice said after three forkfuls of romaine.

"Sorry. I had to drop something off."

"What?"

"I can't tell you," looking around, "here."

"I understand." She leaned toward him. "There are spies everywhere!"

Scott could not smile at her sarcasm. Tenderly, he took her hand. "Through it all, I realize that the one single shining brilliance, the best possible partner I could have hoped to chose to share my life with—is you."

Her eyes grew moist. "I love you, too, which is why I'm so worried about you. If you continue pushing yourself at this pace, you could burn away whatever time, long or short, that's left. You could bring on the very thing you're trying to avoid."

"And if I don't, I could waste what fully functional time I have left before my health deteriorates."

"You don't know that will happen."

"I don't know that it won't," he whispered. "You have to let me self-regulate."

"Okay. Start by making it a priority to enjoy our moments, our *nows*." She caressed his hand. "That's all people ever really get. I could walk outside after lunch and get hit by a bus. Stop trying to cram everything in, or you'll miss what you've got. A wife who loves you. Healthy, happy, intelligent, and God bless them, creative children who adore you."

"It's like—" he sighed, "it's like I feel myself looking through my own eyes, sitting at a screening of my life. And whatever I do, wherever I am, I see that stopwatch ticking."

Her hand brushed against her glass and tipped over the remains of her drink. Disregarding fingers of bloody Mary staining the tablecloth, "Then turn it off! You're taking ridiculous risks. I mean, what did you possibly think you'd gain by checking the old house at two in the morning?"

He squinted one eye. "What are you talking about?"

"Wednesday night. You called me at two in the morning."

"You're mistaken."

"It was you."

"Candice, I did not call you at two in the morning. And certainly not from the old house!"

"Scott, I checked the caller ID box next to the bedroom phone. You called me from the house."

"What did I say?"

"Nothing. There was just dead air." She bit the end of the celery stalk. "I don't think a burglar would be calling—"

"Oh no." His eyes darted around the concourse. "Who did you tell about our lunch?"

"Just mother. Neither of us have had much of a social life the last few months, what with the move and trying to sell the old house and the condo—which is why we're going to have this lovely weekend. Now, would you mind—"

"Vince Ingenito is dead." Scanning the atrium, "Someone threw him out a window."

Candice held one hand over her mouth. "Oh my God!"

"Behind you. Don't turn around! To your left. Look at the reflection in the glass. See those men three tables over?"

She glanced at the reflection of one gray-suited man sipping coffee, his companion with tight-curled brown hair speaking in animated gestures. "The one on the left is cute, the one on the right's wearing a toupee. What does—"

"When did they come in?"

"Umm, sometime before me."

The man sipping coffee rubbed his ear.

Scott tossed cash on the table. "We're leaving," grabbing her wrist, "now!"

"But Scott, we haven't even—"

"Don't argue! Now!"

He half-dragged her out of the restaurant and down the fire tower stairs. Their footsteps echoed across the deserted great floor. As they headed toward the Fifth Street exit, out of the corner of one eye, he spied the two men hastily pay their bill and hurry toward the stairs.

Candice said, "My car's parked on Fourth."

"Forget your car!"

"But our luggage is in the trunk."

They exited into the cold overcast. Scott, weaving a tortu- ous path between tourists milling around and posing for pictures, dragged his wife behind him like a dinghy. As they reached street level, he yanked her alongside him. They danced between onrushing cars. A blue Toyota grazed his free wrist; a bus skimmed behind Candice, the turbulent air from its wake rushing up her dress. Across the street was Independence Hall, a red brick and beige wood eighteenth-century anachronism against concrete and steel towers, the presiding statue of George Washington guarding its main entrance, along with concrete security barriers. "This way!"

Candice freed her wrist and stopped, refusing to move. "This is crazy. Who are we running from?"

"My car's on the other side of Independence Park. If they didn't know where I was, they probably don't know where I'm parked."

"They?"

The man with the brown curly hair appeared at the Bourse entrance. Candice watched the man's eyes systematically scan the crowd, like high-wattage searchlights. His gaze met hers. Scott saw her freeze—her face consumed by a moment of pure, perfect terror, when prey instinctively recognizes hunter. Standing a full head above the crowd, the man's eyes locked onto Candice. He began hacking his way through a cadre of German tourists, then bullied through a crowd on the curb. A woman with short blond hair and silver raincoat, inadvertently shoved by the crowd, flew off balance into the street. A red checkered cab struck the woman's back, snapped her spine, and carried her fifteen yards down the street. Rubber tires squealed against blood-soaked asphalt.

Traffic halted. The man, swept by the surging current of the crowd, lost eye contact with Candice. Immediately, he produced a cellphone.

"Candice, we've got to go!"

They ran down the thoroughfare away from the Constitution Center and headed toward Independence Hall. Before them lay Chestnut Street, busy with school buses and charters. They dashed haphazardly across the street, amid screeching sudden stops, and cut around to the back end of the Hall, as close to the middle of three red brick arches connecting the west wing with the Hall's main body as security barriers permitted.

"Why don't we get the security guards?" Candice asked, frantic.

"They don't have guns."

They stood in Independence Square, a small plot of winter grass under the auspices of the black, patina-free statue of Commodore Barry, his rear to the Hall. Directly ahead, south, was Walnut Street, running one way from east to west. Independence Mall Road West, running one way north to south, bounded the square on the right.

"My car's two blocks down on Pine Street," Scott snapped.

A green sedan, paralleling them to their right along the Mall Road West, stopped in the middle of the street. The driver stuck his head out the window and scanned the square. He found them.

"They'll cut us off." Scott checked the park: Walnut Street, dead on, ran one-way westerly, and the street grid pattern would prevent the sedan from turning left for two full-sized blocks. They could lose their pursuers if they headed left, easterly, into the heart of Independence Park. But it was all open ground. "This way!"

They sprinted behind the statue. The driver of the sedan gunned the vehicle down the street. Screeching, the car turned left at the corner.

"Scott, he's going the wrong way!"

The green sedan streaked down Walnut Street, against traffic. Began closing in. Cars in oncoming traffic swerved out of its path. The sedan careened off four parked cars on the right. Three cars, horns frantically blaring, swung around it. A dark blue SUV veered right, lost control, struck a lamppost, and sent it crashing onto pedestrians on the crowded pavement. The sedan clipped a black Porsche, and drove it head first into a stone retaining wall.

Six strides ahead of Scott and Candice lay the cobblestone extension of Fifth Street between Independence Square and the rest of the National Park—a perfect place to be cut off.

On the other side of Fifth Street, the traffic light on Walnut Street changed. The driver of a Camarson Brothers fish and produce truck checked traffic to his right, then drove into the intersection.

The green sedan slammed into the left side of the truck cab.

A body exploded through the windshield, smashed head first into the side door of the truck, landed on the crushed hood, and rolled off, inert. Through the blood-soaked driver's side window, a man twitched.

Scott stopped. Stared at the man laying dead in the street. "Celia?"

"Scott! Scott!"

He checked Candice. "I'm all right."

They ran with her through what had been the heart of colonial America. Repeatedly, he glanced behind them. No one was following. They stumbled past the Parthenon-facade Second National Bank, around the red brick house of Carpenter's Hall, and emerged at the park's edge.

Candice panted. "Now where?"

Scott scanned the horizon. Checked again behind him. "We might make it. Come on."

He led her out of the park. The surrounding neighborhood was primarily old townhouses, their doors barred with heavily fortified wrought-iron fences. They stopped at Front Street, both panting, hands on knees. He looked behind him and thought he saw a lone figure several blocks away. Ahead lay a pedestrian bridge over Interstate 95.

"Scott, where are we going?"

He led her across a wide bridge flanked by terraced gardens and high iron rod fences. "There!" he said. At mid-span apex, they could see the Delaware River. In the distance stretched the skyline of South Jersey's entertainment complex. The tram across the river was inoperative. The only readily available access: the RiverLink ferry docked by the pier below. Quickly, they trampled across the bridge. On the far side, Scott jumped down the stairs two at a time with Candice close behind. They reached the ticket booth as the RiverLink prepared to shove off.

"One way or round trip?" the ticket agent in the booth asked.

Scott shoved $25 into the plastic slot. "Doesn't matter. Just two."

The attendant shrugged and handed him two blue stubs and change. The three-foot iron gate to the dock was closing. Scott turned back to his wife and helped her swing her legs over the barrier. The ferry began pulling away. She stood motionless.

"Jump, Candice! Jump!"

Seizing her arm, he leaped with her across the widening gulf between ferry and dock.

They landed feet first on the ferry deck and rolled into the railing. The only other passengers on deck, two elderly women, scurried away from the commotion. Scott looked back and scanned the dock: there was no sign of pursuit. He helped Candice up.

"It's all right, Scott whispered. He kissed the top of her head, feeling her body quiver. "It's all right." He led her below deck to passenger seating and gently deposited her in a red vinyl bench. "I'll be back in a minute."

Candice fiercely clutched him. "Don't leave!"

"I'm going to get the captain to radio to shore. The police will be standing by when we reach the Jersey side. We'll be safe."

Scott returned to find Candice hugging herself, rocking back and forth.

"They were going to kill us!" she sobbed.

He pulled her close, "They were chasing me. You just got in the way."

"Who were they?"

"My guess is that they're somehow tied into IRACT."

"Why would *they* be chasing anyone?"

He told her of the fraudulent patient listings. When he finished, she shook her head.

"You don't believe me?"

"Of course I believe you! It's just—" She sniffled. "I have to call Mother. Tell her to take the children some place safe. Scott, what are we going to do?"

Peering through the porthole, "We're going to get through this, Candice. When we get to the other side, we'll—" He stopped and put his face in the porthole. "Stay here!" He leaped up the stairs.

On deck, the ferry had docked on the Philadelphia—not the Camden, New Jersey side of the river. Two muscular men with earphones and blue suits stood ominously between him and the bobbing dock. One pulled an automatic from his shoulder holster and aimed it at Scott's chest; the other produced a pair of gleaming handcuffs and plastic identification.

"Are you Scott Skylar Merritt?"

There was nowhere to go. Scott straightened his back and faced them. "Yes."

"Federal agents. You are under arrest."

One man forced Scott's arms back and secured his wrists with handcuffs. The other tilted his head down and shoved him forward.

"What's the charge?"

"Computer crime. Violation of United States Code 1243 and information theft in accordance with the Federal Computer Fraud and Abuse Act. You have the right to—"

"Candice? Candice!"

Someone shoved Scott into a car. A blunt, metal rod struck the back of his head. Bright white flickers swam in his vision. Something sharp stung his neck. He collapsed.

In Transit   3:18 P.M.

For Emery, having logged more than a million air miles to seminars and trade shows, a first class seat was necessity, not luxury, for his massive frame. Still, airliner luxury did little to ameliorate the whine of jet engines and high-altitude air pressure that pierced his ears like pins. A stewardess appeared with an inviting smile and a leather-jacket menu. The choices: filet mignon with hollandaise, trout in light dijon, and Cornish hen a l'orange. Experience had taught him to stick with beef.

The Captain's gruff voice, piped into the cabin, welcomed passengers aboard the flight from Cleveland to Washington. *". . . We have an estimated time of arrival at Reagan National Airport of 4:40 P.M. Currently, the weather is overcast and thirty-three degrees, and latest forecasts are that the city's going to be spared the brunt of the Noreaster bearing down on the Jersey coast."*

Maybe it'll miss the Chesapeake, Emery thought before picking up the passenger phone. His secretary, Clara Bender, answered his call on the third ring. "Afternoon, Clara. What do you have for me?"

"A representative from PTS called, very apologetic about last trip's mix-up and, absolutely, positively guaranteed that the limo would meet you at National on time," she said.

"I've heard that before. Next?"

"Randolph Foster, the System Administrator from the Institute called about an hour ago to tell you that, due to technical problems, EDI will be down for several hours today and web access out for the next few days."

Emery shook his head. "You wouldn't believe what he was bothering me about earlier. The clinic?"

"Running smoothly. However, one patient, Mrs. Folcroft, expired shortly after you boarded."

Emery squinted as unfiltered sunlight glared in his eyes. He lowered the window shade. Sometimes he wished he was more like his wife, Grace, secure in her unflinching piety, her mindless faith. But Grace hadn't spent a career facing down imminent death. She only had to care for the children; he had to care for every patient entering his clinic—while containing the destructive potential of the only cure. "She was a nice woman. Send an appropriate floral arrangement to her home, along with confirmation cards of gifts in her name to the American Kidney Society and the Institute. Oh and make certain that the Institute receives a comprehensive report on the patient, including pathology-autopsy findings."

She paused. "The high-priority report, *doctor?*"

Was that sarcasm? he wondered. "Yes, the usual for these cases," he told her. He heard Clara mutter on the other end. *Oh yes, that was sarcasm. Why does she do this? It takes so long to break in a new assistant. I can't deal with one more problem right now.* "You know, I haven't seen you and Gunnar in almost a year. You two ought to come over to the house for dinner soon. How's he been feeling anyway?" Emery asked, knowing very well that Clara's husband was unemployed with chronic back pain and totally reliant on Clara's insurance for his long-term physical rehabilitation.

Clara responded after a long silence. "Of course doctor, the high-priority report."

Damn you, Clara, why the hell did you force me to do that? he thought. "Anything else?"

"I'm sad to say that one of the clinic nurses passed away this morning—Christina Forman."

"I saw her yesterday. She was fine!" Emery exclaimed. "What was it? Car accident?"

"Her husband brought her in the ER this morning with a very high fever. Her lungs were filled with fluid. Pneumonia maybe. She died before they could get her upstairs."

Emery squeezed the phone. "What was the diagnosis?"

"There's talk about some nasty new flu strain. An autopsy's scheduled later today."

Emery put his head in his hands. "Make certain that our pathology group is in charge of that autopsy."

"The clinic's?"

"I want *our* clinic personnel there, Clara, not those from the hospital."

"That will step on more than a few toes."

Through gritted teeth, "If there's any resistance, call Nick-elson and tell him that because Nurse Forman worked exclusively in my clinic, I'm under contractual obligation to provide a comprehensive pathology report to the Institute. And emphasize that the jury's still out on the matter he and I were discussing earlier. You won't have a problem after that."

"I'll send the family the usual flower and donation package—"

"No. Make them out a clinic check for—twenty-thousand dollars," Emery blurted, half-wishing he could take it back, half-wishing he'd promised more.

"That's *very* generous of you."

But why? he could hear in her tone. "We take care of our own, Clara. You know where to reach me. I'll check in tomorrow." He hung up.

Tell me this isn't happening. His laptop already stowed in the overhead compartment, Emery took his palm computer from his jacket pocket, and accessed the Norlake Hospital employee database. Two minutes later, he finished scanning Forman's comprehensive medical history. He leaned back, sighed in relief, and ordered a full glass of merlot from the stewardess: Christina had never contracted Hanoi Flu.

KECT Studios
Los Angeles, California
The "green room" at KECT-TV had salmon walls, a pair of beige couches, and assorted black-backed folding chairs, but not a touch of green anywhere, including the scores of photos and promotional posters of Paul Empire, host of the weekly interview show, *The Empire Report*. Hope Wheelan dug her fingernails into into the seat cushion. If only she'd been more forceful and insisted on sitting beside her husband during the on-camera interview, instead of watching from a monitor in the studio's green room. That bastard, Paul Empire, wouldn't have dared ambush him.

". . . deny that for fifteen years, you'd buy corporations, break them up, squeeze out their liquid assets and holdings, then sell the pieces for a tidy profit, do you Mr. Wheelan?" Empire asked, leaning over the desk microphone, his red tie flashing in guest Alexander Wheelan's face.

Hope's eyes narrowed as she watched the squat man with a bulbous nose, down-turned lips, and grating voice that had three settings: loud, obnoxious, and intolerable.

Alexander Wheelan warmly smiled at host Empire and placed delicately folded hands on the desk. "Too many corporations had grown fat and complacent, particularly in upper management. In some respects I'm owed a debt of gratitude."

"Gratitude? For—"

"American firms have never been stronger." Alexander looked directly into the camera. "Despite globalization of many industry jobs, employment and wages are at an all-time high. Many of those who lost their jobs have learned new skills offering better long-term opportunities. Most who permanently lost their livelihoods were in upper management, enjoying perks while producing little or nothing. I've brought along charts to demonstrate."

Hope beamed as she watched. Alex was more prepared than he'd let on.

"Sorry, there isn't time," Empire smirked. "Forty weeks a year on the charity circuit. Could there be just a twinge of guilt for all the lives you've ruined?"

"Over the past few years, I've donated more than three-quarters of the corporations on the *Fortune* 500 list. And I don't solicit clients to use my services so I can be philanthropic with *their* money. Now, you tell me who should have a guilty conscience."

"Philanthropic funds which, apparently, you can afford."

"The Cassandran Strategic Fund has been very successful, thank God."

"Especially since underwriting upstart turned pharmaceutical giant Paradigm Transplant Solutions, which many analysts predict will be one of the world's top corporations by the fourth quarter of this year," Empire said.

Alexander smiled. "We've had our successes."

Hope glanced at the clock beside the monitor. *Your timing is perfect, dear.*

"Phenomenally successful," Empire, said. "Seeding PTS has made the Cassandran Strategic Fund one of Wall Street's most successful. In particular, your investment house caters only to the super-rich." Glancing at the camera, "Many of your critics think it's done *too* well for them."

"We've been investigated by the Securities and Exchange Commission since Day One. They always give us a clean bill of health. Cassandran Strategic offers a wide variety of funds for investors with $50 million or more. I won't apologize for knowing where key stocks are headed before my competition." He paused before looking into the camera. "I've been able to benefit my investors. But what personally gratifies me is the hope that I'm able to provide for those less fortunate."

Empire grimaced as the studio director, talking through his ear jack, informed him that he'd run out of time. Gracefully, he wrapped up the show with a hint of tomorrow night's guests.

Hope hurried from the green room to her husband who was having his make-up removed. She glared at Empire two chairs away. "You've got a hell of a nerve—"

"Your husband knew the score before he ever set foot in here," Empire shot back.

"You ought to be ashamed of yourself!"

"So should your husband for the way he slapped the American worker across the face."

Hope smacked his face. Empire spilled onto the floor.

"You mean like that?" she asked.

Alexander scooped up his wife in his arms and led her out of the studio.

"I'll sue your ass, lady!" Empire yelled from the floor.

"Have your attorney contact my legal department. We'll see who eats whom!"

Once outside the building, they climbed into their waiting limousine and headed for the airport.

"I'm sorry, Alex. I just can't stand watching you treated like that," she said.

"That cardiokarate works wonders." Alexander repressed a chuckle.

Hope leaned into him. Her lips parted. Her cell phone rang. She gave him a quick kiss, then answered it. She listened a moment. The glow evaporated from her face. "There isn't time. Replace him with one of theirs." She paused. "You heard me! Do it!" She hung up.

"What was that?"

She stared out the limousine window. "Problems with the help."

Philadelphia International Airport   6:27 P.M.
"*. . . apologize for the delay. It should only be a moment now,*" the cockpit voice droned. Sounds of subdued wing engines and hissing air filled the cabin.

Sitting upright, clutching both armrests, Ryan peered out the cabin window at the dark exterior lit by faint blue runway lights. Tiny frozen droplets pounded the exterior glass. The airport terminal, shrouded in icy mist, glimmered in the distance. A tight stream of warm air from the overhead nozzle struck his cheek.

Janine caressed his hand. "An hour delay in this kind of weather isn't so bad."

"I didn't see them de-ice. They're supposed to de-ice at least every forty-five minutes!"

A pair of young hands seized his seat and yanked. "Yo Dad, I saw 'em de-ice a couple minutes ago. You're acting like a big baby!"

Ryan craned around at the boy with an asymmetrical crew cut and taunting grin. "Steven, sit back and put on your seat belt or so help me, I'll force this plane back to the terminal and you'll spend the week with your grandmother."

Janine twisted around and checked on her two other children in the row behind her. A little boy sat in the middle seat with an oversized bear he danced on his knee while his sister chewed gum and stared intently out the window.

"Maybe this wasn't such a good idea," Ryan muttered.

"He's just scared of flying," Steven interjected.

"Steven, shut up!" Ryan and Janine said in unison.

After their son turned around, Janine flicked back a strand of hair crossing her cheek, "You haven't been the same since you were at Scott's last night."

"I don't follow."

"Alyssa's photograph. The one you said you threw away the day after—she died. The picture you found too painful to keep."

His eyes darted around the cabin, at first, deliberately avoiding the seat in front of him, then glancing too long at his laptop sealed in its black travel case.

"What have you been up to?"

The engines whined. The voice from the cockpit said: *"Ready for take-off. All flight personnel please be seated at this time."*

The plane swiveled leisurely around a light at the runway's edge, the wings eagerly thundering like a dragster gunning a newly overhauled engine at a red light. The plane lurched forward, rapidly building speed. Its wheels spun away concrete. Gently, it tipped back. Friction between runway and rubber reverberated through the cabin. Sensing ascent, Ryan stiffened his neck against the force driving him deep into his seat. Outside, the dark ribbon of the Delaware River grew slender. To the right, below, the marshy wildlife preserve near the oil refinery spread for miles—a tract of utter darkness nestled in city lights stretching to all horizons. Sounds of roaring engines and rushing air overlaying the shrill whine inundated him. He closed his eyes and started counting slowly to one hundred.

The cabin shuttered. He felt his body tilt. His stomach churned. He opened his eyes. The plane was abruptly turning.

The cockpit voice announced: *"Ladies and gentlemen,*

we're experiencing some technical difficulties and will be returning to the termin—

The floor lurched. The cabin pitched forward.

A great force reached out and tried to tear him from his seat. People screamed in front of him, behind him—a cacophony mixed with the engine crescendo.

Janine's hand squeezed his, her hammered white gold ring slicing into his palm.

The cabin violently spun upside down—right side up—upside down.

A heavy vinyl bag from an overhead compartment slammed against his head. A mask dropped onto his lap. Fell back toward the ceiling. Upside down, a flame atop a refinery tower zipped by the cabin window.

A blinding fireball swept down the aisle.

TWENTY

Scott opened his eyes. Darkness.

Frantically, he shut his eyes. Reopened them. Everything was absolutely black.

Scott felt enclosed—a burlap cloth, saturated with perspiration and saliva, covered his face. *A hood!* He couldn't catch his breath. Started gasping for air. *I'm blowing off too much CO_2. Slow my breathing. Slow—it—down!*

The adrenaline chilling his chest, his back, subsided. Scott realized that he was sitting in a chair, his hands tightly bound behind his back by what felt like a sturdy electrical cord, his ankles locked together behind him. He pulled on the cord twice; it tightened around his wrists. His fingertips tingled.

"Struggling makes it worse," a distorted voice warned.

A drop of sweat rolled down Scott's forehead onto his glasses. He tried to wipe it. The cord dug deep into his wrist. "Where's Candice?"

"Safe," the unnatural voice answered.

"I want to see her."

"Of course you do."

That voice—electronically warped? "Where the hell am I?"

"Secure."

"Who the hell are you?"

"The one asking the questions," the distorted voice answered with a lilt.

Choosing his next words carefully, "Since when does the FBI get off incarcerating people like this? I'm not saying another damned word without an attorney!"

The interrogator's determined footsteps traversed tiled floor, the forefoot striking simultaneously with the heel. *Feminine. Someone accustomed to wearing high heels,* Scott thought. He smelled a scent, primal, compelling—but familiar, growing more powerful as he felt a face lean close to his.

"We must play poker some time. Even with your face covered, you can't bluff. You know that our little charade at the river was for the spectators, not you," the voice stated. "Do you have my files?"

"What files?"

A hand struck Scott's chin. His head recoiled. Razor pain shot from the base of his skull, down his neck. Then, a spinning wooziness.

"Lie again and I'll hit you lower. Do you have any files that belong to the Institute?"

"Yes."

"I assume then you've seen them," the voice said. "Question is, have you analyzed them?"

The darkness, the impending torture, the answer he dared not give, the fate of Candice hanging in the balance—panic began welling up. He fought it by again trying to make time pass slowly for him—and the calmness that it brought. And he remembered something about detecting lies through voice volume, tone, and cadence.

"Have you analyzed them?" the voice shouted.

Scott answered very slowly. "Yes."

"And your impression?"

Weakness invites attack. Answer the same way as before. He slowed his breathing, then monotoned, "I was right all along."

Footsteps crossed the room. "You were going to make them public."

"Uh-huh."

Footsteps circled around him. "Patients and their families love us. They write about us in newsletters, talk about us in chat rooms, endlessly blog us, lobby their Congressmen, parade before their state capitals. We answer their prayers. Who are you to snuff that out?"

"Snuff out. Is that what you did to Dylan Rogers?"

"Rogers is beyond your concern. Or anyone else's." A distorted snorting sound, "Just what the world needs—another self-annointed savior." A sharp knuckle struck Scott's chest. He groaned, fire-pain radiating between his seventh and eighth ribs. "A rather flawed one at that. But one with 'visions'—that's a nice touch."

Scott turned directly toward the voice emanating just beyond the darkness of the enveloping burlap. He hoped she could feel his glare.

"Don't be angry, Dr. Merritt. We're more alike than not." The interrogator's voice whispered, "Each of us is suffering. Each of us being consumed within our private purgatories, haunted by visions—though mine are somewhat less noble that yours."

I have a lunatic at my throat!

He heard the inquisitor walk in front of him. A door opened and a second pair of footsteps crossed the room. Those footsteps were distinctive, peculiar: one side scuffing the floor followed by a powerful heel strike. *Definitely masculine.*

"Ever hear of the Strength Deployment Index?" the interrogator asked.

"No."

"Fascinating little test describing individual personality strengths. Imagine a color-coded triangle. In one corner are the 'blues,' the people who are loyal, fair, the ones who want to help. In another corner, the 'greens,' the droll, the analytical, the anal-retentive, the ones who relish process above product. And in the third corner, the 'reds,' the successful salespeople, the CEOs, the ones who matter. If you held a meeting, the reds would set the agenda, the greens would bore the meeting with charts and figures, and the blues would bring the cookies. You, Merritt, are pure green, envisioning yourself Don Quixote, when the truth is, you're bound to sacrifice your worthless little life to prove something pointless while the rest of us march merrily away . . ."

Scott felt the prelude closing. In a moment, he sensed that the interrogator would again put hard questions to him. The key to his survival was withholding just enough truth now so that he could barter the rest later. *Answer slowly. Establish the pattern.*

"Now where are my files?" the voice shouted.

Scott counted to ten before answering. "On the computer in my mother's apartment, 439 South Seventh Street, Apartment 1518."

"Password protected?"

He paused. " 'Janus,' the two-faced god."

"The CD from Rogers?"

He paused. "It's there, too."

"And additional copies?"

He paused. "In my e-mail address, 'Scotmer1@aol.com.' Password 'blackhole.' "

"Who has copies?"

"No one."

A spiked heel drove into the top of his left foot. He yelped.

"Who—has—copies?"

Sweat stung his eyes. "No one."

The interrogator paused. "Let me rephrase that. Who else has *seen* the files?"

Frantic, he searched for a viable alternative to the truth.

"It's not easy giving up someone close, is it? Most people spend their lives looking for friends. They're lucky if they finish with just two or three good ones standing over their coffin."

Something clicked. Ryan's voice said: *"Hey Scott, Ryan here. I used the password to get inside IRACT's system. Listen, what you and I saw was only the surface. There's more to this, a lot more. Check your e-mail. I'm taking all the downloaded originals with me. Anyway, my flight leaves around 5:15 and gets into Phoenix around 10:00 P.M., Philly time. Hope everything works out for you guys this weekend. May the boomerang be with you. Click."*

"Odd way to end a call. Some sort of male bonding rite?" Scott shrugged.

"He broke into our System this morning. The address he mentioned, was that the one you just gave me?"

Slowly, he nodded.

"The message was relayed to me at *Tout a Vous*. You and Candice really should have stayed for dessert. They make a raspberry chocolate tort to die for."

In the restaurant, the woman with the hat! That's why the scent is so familiar!

"We searched your empty house and found nothing. Why did your friend leave that message there?"

Damn it Ryan, couldn't you have remembered to program your phone? "I don't know."

"I'll have that password, now," the voice commanded.

"Which password?"

"The one your friend used to bypass our security," both volume and intensity of the electronically distorted voice increasing. "The one he got from you, from Rogers, from Evelyn Cruz, from Todd! The master password!"

How am I going to answer this one?

"Now will you look at the time? A quarter past the hour. We should be able to get an update." A radio clicked on: *". . . issued general alarms. Once again, American Airlines*

Flight 841 from Philadelphia to Phoenix crashed just before 7 P.M. this evening shortly after take-off. The plane struck one of the huge holding tanks at the Ensolco Oil Refinery, setting off a spectacular blaze still roaring out of control. Tragically, there appear to be no survivors. All 171 men, women, and children— lost in this terrible crash. No word yet on the cause, but several sources have raised the possibility of ice build-up on the wings. Compounding this tragedy is what one source quoted as 'potentially the worst fire in the city's history' and the severe ice storm paralyzing the Tristate . . ."

Darkness dissolved away into a bright, cloudless, warm sky. A freshly mowed lawn, the scent of summer, early June. The old ribbon-pointed, stone school stood before him, the upper floor corner office's great windows flung wide open. 'Come on, do it, do it,' echoed from the other side of the building. Scott looked down. His left hand held a polished yellow and black wooden boomerang. He felt himself draw the boomerang back, behind his ear, take three strides toward the building, and launch. The boomerang sliced through air, gracefully whirling, ascending, sailing toward the near side window. It disappeared into the principal's corner office. He trembled as he waited, waited. A wild scream from the other side of the building? Adrenaline surged through Scott's arteries, seeming to force the bloodflow backward. Success or failure? Who could tell from that scream? With lanky frame and straight brown hair, eleven-year-old Ryan appeared from behind the school, and waved the boomerang over his head in triumph. Gleefully, he ran toward Scott.

A clenched hand struck Scott's right cheek. "Merritt, have we come to an understanding?"

Scott licked a trickle of blood from the corner of his mouth. "Yeah. You're going to kill me and Candice. Why the hell should—"

"On the contrary. Hoods, voice modulator, proof that I've gone to considerable effort to spare you, your wife, *and* your children."

He shut burning eyes. "You—have—my kids?"

"Are you going to pass out on us?"

"I want to see them! Now! Or you'll never get that password!"

"The children aren't here."

"Then Candice."

"I can have her phone—"

"No, I mean here! In person!"

The interrogator hesitated. "What makes you think we'd keep her here?"

"Because your next logical step is to parade her in this room, put a gun to her head, and tell me to answer or else."

The interrogator strolled across the floor. A door opened, then slammed. He listened as the rhythm of the female inquisitor's gait and the silent male accomplice faded. Ignoring beads of sweat searing his eyes, he began mentally constructing possible escape plans. Footsteps approached. One set belonged to the interrogator. The door opened. He heard a click, presumably a light switch.

"Scott?"

Candice's voice! "Are you hurt?"

"No."

He heard her shoes screech across the room, followed by subdued whimpering.

"Just tying her up," the interrogator said.

"Candice. Quickly—are you blindfolded?"

"Uh-huh."

"Since you got here?"

"Yes."

"I've kept my word, Dr. Merritt. I'm waiting on your end of the bargain."

He counted silently to ten. "I don't know Todd's password."

"Scott, what do these people want?" Candice interjected.

"Quiet Mrs. Merritt, for your sake, your husband's sake, and your—"

"It was too much to remember—twenty, no twenty-one digits," Scott said. Lowering his voice, "But, I know where it is."

"Where?"

"Also on the computer in my mother's apartment."

"You'd better—"

"It's there."

"Good. We'll check this very minute." He heard the captors open the door and the lights click—off?

"When you see I'm telling you the truth, maybe we can make a deal," Scott called.

The footsteps halted. "What could you possibly offer?"

Staring in the direction of the door, "I'm supposed to testify before the Senate subcommittee on Tuesday. What if— what if I agree to give testimony supporting IRACT?"

"In exchange for?"

"Candice, for starters."

"Scott, I—"

"Quiet, Candice!" To the interrogator, "Each of us gets what we want. Once my testimony's in the Senate records, I won't be able to recant a word without risking perjury. What do you say?" *You bitch!* A very long silence followed. Scott tightened the muscles in his neck, his arms, his chest— anticipating punishing blows that might strike him anywhere, from any angle.

No response. The door closed. Footsteps faded down the hall. He waited for the sounds of their return. And waited.

"I think they're gone," he said, releasing a pent-up sigh. Candice's muffled whimpers drifted from across the room. "Don't cry, hon. I'll get us out of here," he whispered. He strained to lift his right thigh. The bindings cut deep into his wrists. Two numb fingers caught his pen as it fell out of his pants pocket.

ENSOLCO Oil Refinery
Southwest Philadelphia

George Terrill watched the reporters clamber around his sedan, each of them trying to peek in through fogged windows and probe for some new facet of the ongoing story. His car crawled to the police barrier and stopped. A slicker-clad officer, his eyebrows and moustache covered with ice crystals, shined a flashlight into the driver's side. He checked Terrill and the entourage's credentials, and matched it to the blue-lettered license plate before waving it on. The car proceeded slowly through an armada of fire engines, hoses, ladders, and tankers. Men in full fire-fighting regalia battled the fire raging a thousand yards away. The car swung right and parked near an RV-sized vehicle with a plastic sign marked 'Operations.' Wiry, with chiseled nose and recessed jaw, Terrill stepped out of the passenger-side rear and stared, oblivious to sleet splattering his face. Less than three hours till midnight, and the sky was as bright as midday.

Half a mile away, pillars of fire over the remnants of refinery storage tanks erupted. Orange flames burst into the sky, illuminating the wind. The air tasted acrid. Thick smoke clouds formed as gusts whipped them toward the cacophony of sirens, cries, and unnatural thunder. Intense heat distorted the horizon like asphalt baking on a hot summer day. Ice covering the sedan began to melt.

A young woman with bronze hair stepped out of the front passenger seat. "My God!"

A heavyset man with a wide face opened the driver's door. "The Gates of Hell!"

Terrill silently led the pair into the command center. The Philadelphia Deputy Police Commissioner, four battalion chiefs, city and suburban county officials, and Ensolco Oil Refinery representatives stood around a table strewn with blueprints. Phones rang. Peripheral personnel answered on headsets. People shouted. Terrill strode up to a man with black, thinning hair standing at the near side of the table. "Deputy Commissioner Hopple?" Terrill held up his identification. "FBI. George Terrill, Special Agent in Charge, Philadelphia Division."

"So they dragged out the SAC himself," Hopple said. "Yous guys here till NTSB shows?"

Terrill glanced around the room. "I need your attention for a few moments."

"We're fighting a fire here, mister."

"Sir, this really cannot wait."

"And this fire can?"

Terrill leaned over, whispered in the Police Commissioner's ear, and walked out the door. His colleagues followed like puppies. A moment later, Hopple joined them outside in the tempest.

The woman whispered in the rotund man's ear, "Hey Cicero, what did he say?"

"I'll tell you, Kamen, when I think you can pull it off," the agent responded.

The four of them climbed into the car, Terrill and Hopple in the rear.

Terrill began, "My associates, Special Agent Cicero," motioning toward the heavyset man in front, "and Special Agent Kamen," nodding at the woman. "Commissioner, I've been trying to reach you for more than an hour."

"We're got a major crash. An oil refinery fire that may take a big chunk of southwest Philly with it. Toxic gas blown by fifty mile-an-hour winds, a quarter-million people we might have to evacuate across iced-over roads. And in an hour, thirty-five thousand people are going to pour out of the Flyers-Bruins game and the rock concert less than two miles from here!" Hopple spat. "We're fucking busy!"

Terrill stared at him.

"The mayor's daughter was on that plane." Hopple shook his head. "Man's a basket case. Calling me every fifteen minutes, asking if I've found—. She was my goddaughter."

"Sorry for your loss."

"When's NTSB arrive?"

"A team's coming up from DC, but the airport's closed and the roads are impassable. It took me an hour to crawl the half-mile from Terminal A."

"So you're the stand-in?"

"In part. I don't suppose you've recovered the cockpit voice or digital flight data recorder?"

"No. And what do you mean 'in part?'"

"What I tell you stays in this car." Terrill ran a hand through his short-cropped hair. "A cargo handler servicing this flight was found dead. His neck had been broken, professionally. With the foul weather on the tarmac, a hood up over the man's head, the handlers saw just another one of their own."

"I have a cousin who works over at the tower. He overheard a controller who said that he heard the pilot report two distinct 'pops' before it dropped off-screen. Goddamn fuckin' terrorists!"

Terrill nodded. "It's preliminary, but we suspect two separate explosions on board. Initially a small one, probably not sufficient to down it, but enough to force the pilot to swing back to the airport, followed by a second, devastating one, possibly centered around hydraulics."

"Why plant two?"

"There's open fields and marshlands with less than ten feet of water on the other side of the airport. You could have a soft landing, minimum casualties. But turn the plane around, aim it at a refinery, and then bring it down, and you guarantee a wipe out. So until NTSB and our own teams arrive, please have your people sift through everything coming out of that fire. Key in on pieces of detonators, triggers, circuit elements, charge blocks, fuselage or metal pieces with radiating or grooved striations from a central source. Stow it all under guard while a temporary hanger site is secured."

"Don't count on identifying blast chemicals from the fuselage. The inferno out there probably fused any number of petroleum-based products into the metal wreckage. Unless we're dealing with some unique spectroscopic signature, the refinery fire's going to mask the results."

"Much appreciated. And please secure a perimeter around the refinery complex." Terrill released a long, heated sigh. "This might just be the opening shot for something much bigger."

TWENTY-ONE

"How're you coming?" Candice asked.

Concentrating on the pen that he'd awkwardly slipped between his thumb and third finger, Scott's mind watched the pen slowly whittle away the cord securing his hands behind his back. Though slippery with sweat, he gently guided the pen back and forth in long, purposeful strokes, like a familiar scalpel handle with a number-ten blade gracefully separating tissue layers in a bloodless field. His hands remembered. "Almost there."

The binding was probably insulated electrical cable, but could be slowly, tediously cut. Painstakingly, he'd stripped away the thick, plastic insulation, exposing tiny wire strands that bit his fingertips like fire ants. Surgeon hands delicately maneuvered the pen's blunt tip between a single strand and the rest of the bundle, and with a confident turn of the wrist, snapped the strand before moving onto the next. Then the next.

The cord slackened. His hands identified a classic square knot—the type he'd tied himself tens of thousands of times with nylon on absorbable sutures—strong, secure, but with a weakness. He slid a fingertip into the small cavity in the center of the crossing knot cords, and flicked his wrists. The bindings slid off. He ripped off his hood and untied his feet from the chair. Slowly, his eyes grew accustomed to the dark room. Candice was hooded, slumped, and bound to a chair by his side.

Scott stared at her. For a moment, he forgot the danger outside the door. He'd loved her long before the day he'd knelt in the park to propose. Candice—the one who'd fixed the frequently overflowing downstairs toilet, the one who'd read stories to the children and nursed their pains, the one who'd turned the cow path of his life into a freeway. He released her hands.

Candice clasped her arms around his neck as he untied the cord around her ankles and removed her hood. She gazed at him, her face drenched in sweat, eyes wide, tongue visible between parted lips. His lips moved close to hers. She gave him a quick hard kiss. "Now what?"

Scott inventoried the room: industrial tile flooring, drop ceiling with acoustic tiles, inset fluorescent light boxes, heavy steel door, open closet with wire hangers, 1950s-style government-issue gray-green metal desk, and a large window with unrolled black shade. He tiptoed to the door and put his ear to the metal—not a sound. He placed his hand on the knob and turned: locked, as expected. He crossed to the desk and picked up his keys. The wallet beside them had been rifled, though its its contents appeared intact. He pulled out the portraits of Brooke and Andrew, and checked between them: the paper with Ryan's e-mail address and password was still there. He shoved the wallet in his pocket and told Candice to check the window.

She pulled up the shade. Orange light bathed the room. "Look!"

The skyline blazed beneath billowing black clouds. Dark terrain lay between them and the fire.

They probably crashed Ryan's plane by remote from here. He pointed at the distant blaze. "That's the refinery, two or three miles straight away. See the ground between here and the fire? It's marshland, the Heinz Wildlife Preserve, and our way out."

"Through a marsh? At night?"

"You can skirt the edge, toward the fire. There's got to be an army of firemen and cops out there. It's a few miles, but you'll be in the dark, and relatively safe."

Candice looked beyond the tiny ice pellets beating the window to the frozen grass below. After a twenty-foot drop, the ground fell away, a steep embankment disappearing into dark marsh. "What about the door?"

"Solid steel—and no lock to pick on this side."

She stared at the embankment and bit her lower lip. "I can't go that way. I'm—my acropho—"

"We have no choice. They're armed, they outnumber us, and face it, we're just an out-of-shape, middle-aged couple. We just can't charge blindly out that door."

"We got loose, didn't we?"

"They don't consider us a threat to escape. If they did, they'd've bugged the room. And if that was true, they'd've been in here by now." He strode to the closet, grabbed a dozen wire hangers, and handed them to her. "Take them apart and stretch out the wires." He began rummaging through the metal desk drawers.

"Now what are you looking for?"

He produced some paper clips, half a dozen pens, an old pad of paper, and a small Phillips screwdriver. "Hook the ends together, securely." Screwdriver in hand, he picked up a chair, positioned it beneath a fluorescent light box, stood on the seat, and quickly pried off the fixture's two-by-four foot clear plastic cover which laid on the floor.

"Run the wire from the fixture to the knob. Turn on the light and electrocute them when they come in. Smart idea, dear," Candice said.

Scott cocked his head and looked from the light to the door. "I hadn't thought of that. There must be a wall switch on the other side of the door." He added, "But at best, it'd only slow one of them down." He removed a second cover near the door, sat on the floor and, with the screwdriver, bored a hole into a corner of one sheet.

"What on Earth are you doing?" she asked as he moved to the second cover.

While fixing one end of the wire through the hole in the plastic cover, "I'll lower this out the window. When you jump, it'll break your fall, and you'll glide down the hill on it, like a sled."

"That won't support the both of us!"

"We go separately. You first."

"There's not enough wire to lower the other piece!"

"When you land, the plastic around the hole will give way. I'll retract it and reuse the wire."

"I can't do this!"

"You have to!" He placed an arm around her quivering shoulders. "They're going to kill the kids."

She pushed his arm away. Shrank back into the far corner of the room. "Oh my God! Oh my God! They have our children? And you didn't tell me? When were you going to—"

"Candice, you've got to be strong! We have to get out of here!"

"Maybe we should stay put. Yes, yes, if we cooperate, they'll let them go. You said you told them everything. Then— then there's no reason for them to hurt the children if—"

"Candice, they downed a commercial jet! Killed hundreds of people—just to get Ryan!" Moving closer to her, "We've got to be certain that at least you escape."

She turned to him and gaped. "You're not coming, are you?"

"You and I have to split up. *You* have to get to the authorities. I can't."

"We go together or not at all!"

"This isn't a conventional kidnapping. There's no money, no exchange. When they come back, they'll think they have everything they want—the information, the kids, us. They won't deal—unless they believe I'm holding something back. And that'll only work if they believe I'm running around on my own, keeping them off balance—giving them a reason to keep the kids alive, if only for a few days—while I find out exactly who has them and where they're being held."

"I know you. You're going to trade yourself for the children."

He took a deep breath and gazed longingly at her. "Candice, it was you who had faith in me. Faith that I would build a life after practice. Faith that I would get through my—disorder. Won't you show some of that now?"

She grabbed him. "I can't lose you!"

"You won't." He caressed her cheek. "I'm in 'doctor-mode.' "

She seized him by his neck, pulled him toward her, and gave him a long, penetrating kiss. Tenderly, slowly, she released him.

He hooked one end of the hanger-wire assembly through the hole in one plastic sheet and pointed out the window. "Once you get to the preserve, go left, parallel to the fire. Stay out of the marsh. In weather like this, you'll get hypothermia a lot faster in water than in air. It's dark now, so they can only follow on foot. About two miles down is a driving range. You'll see lights from the automall across from an access road. Go diagonally across the range, and then another couple hundred yards down the road. There you're sure to find help."

"What about you?"

"I'll follow you," Scott said. *Unless they're after me.* He lifted open the old window. Ice pellets struck his face as he hooked the other end of the wire to the windowsill and lowered the plastic sheet. The makeshift sled dangled by its edge against the embankment.

Terrified, Candice climbed onto the windowsill. Shivering, clutching the wall, she looked back. "How will I know if—if—"

"The house, apartment, everything's sure to be bugged."

"My voicemail at work. You know the access code. At least this way I'll know if—"

"You too. I love you, you know."

"I always have."

He expected one last look from her. She closed her eyes, and jumped.

Scott stuck his head out the window. He heard a muffled thud below. The wire, hooked around the windowsill, vibrated, then flew out into the ice storm. He glimpsed Candice gliding into darkness and waited for some distant noise—scraping, splashing, a cry. He heard only wailing wind. Scanning the darkness, he counted the seconds, promising himself he'd wait just a bit longer before risking to call out her name.

In his far left field of vision, a shadowy figure moved. He whispered a 'thank you' before checking the remaining hanger wire. Only eight feet left—not enough to lower another makeshift sled. He looked from the door to the open fixture overhead. *It's worth the try.* He broke off pieces of wire, wrapped them around the main trunk to form a pair of two-prong connections, stood on a chair, and removed one fluorescent tube. Bracing for an electric shock, he shoved the prong connections into open sockets, but the wall switch outside the room was off. As he wrapped the other end around the doorknob twice, the lower half of the window, laden with ice, suddenly slammed shut. Its glass panes shattered.

Footsteps clambered up steps, then quickly converged from both directions outside the door.

It's too soon!

The wall switched clicked. The room lit up with a faint hum. The doorknob turned—and vibrated.

"Yee—yee—yee—oooowwwww!" a voice screamed from the other side of the door. The vibration stopped. "Goddamn fuckers! That hurt! Get 'em! Get 'em!"

Metal exploded through the door, around the knob. Bullets whizzed by his head. Without thinking, Scott picked up the plastic sheet, ran to the window, and took a flying leap, head first, into the dark.

Falling. Falling. Falling.

His chest struck the ground.

Plastic sliced his fingers. He shot forward, down. Ice chips rushed up his nostrils, seared his nose. A wave of frigid water tore away his plastic shield. His outstretched limbs bent back, his torso slammed against semi-frozen muck. He landed on his back—freezing water creeping into his ears, his mouth, his nose. He felt himself slipping away.

White-hot pain permeated his sinuses—like a blade on fire plunged into his skull, and being twisted over and over. The pain forced him up—out of the water. Dizzy, he doubled over, and vomited. He splashed cold water against his mouth, and vomited again.

Slowly, he opened his eyes.

Scott sat in partially frozen goo, his feet stuck in muck below the dark surface. In the distance, the refinery fire raged. But there were no voices, no signs of pursuit. Wobbly, he stood and headed toward a distant string of incandescent lights. Muck sucked at his legs.

The ground grew firmer; the lights, brighter. Scott stumbled onto an access road. Ahead were lit signs, glass-enclosed showrooms, and rows of cars gleaming in stadium lights. He staggered between columns of minivans, dropped down, placed his hands on his knees and panted.

". . . checking it out," he heard an unfamiliar voice come from one or two rows of vehicles away. "No sign of 'em yet."

Scott pressed against a minivan and closed his mouth. He wished the wind would stop so he could listen for footsteps. Dead ahead, on the horizon, the fire burned. In the foreground, across the road, lay an open field with low rectangular markers stuck in the ground: the driving range. And—something moving behind the nearest one. *No!*

"It's Phillips. I spotted the woman," the voice said. "No sign of Merritt." After a pause, "Course I won't take out the wrong one!" He emerged from between a pair of sport coupes, pulled an automatic from his coat pocket, and aimed it at the figure across the road.

Scott planted his right hand on a car hood. Using it like a cantilever, he hoisted himself feet first over the vehicle. "Candice!"

She stopped, stood upright, and gazed back at the car lot.

The gun fired.

Candice crumpled behind a yard marker.

Scott's feet struck the big man's wrist. The weapon flew out of the his hand, clanged against a hubcap, skidded along asphalt, and disappeared beneath a bright green car. In his follow-through, Scott smashed his ribs against a sideview mirror, landed on the side of his foot, twisting his ankle. His lower leg on fire, he curled up on the ground.

The man approached, his features hidden in the glare of the bright lights behind him. "That was convenient." He pulled out a wireless phone and pressed a button. "It's Phillips. The woman's down. And I've got Merritt laying out in front of me, nice as you please—alive."

Wind masked the high-pitched response from the man's walkie-talkie cellular. Head pounding, Scott gazed at the man's legs. A calmness washed over Scott: the man's movements, the voice emanating from the walkie-talkie, even the once-howling wind, slowed. Doctor-mode. Anatomical drawings of the lower extremities that he used to keep on his offices' patient treatment rooms flashed through his mind. "Twenty—five."

Phillips stepped closer. "What'd ya say?"

Scott's feet shot out. Struck the outside of the man's right leg.

The knee exploded. Scott felt ligaments ripping open. Phillips dropped the phone, screamed, and fell to the ground, his face grotesquely distorted in agony. Clutching his leg, he rolled on the asphalt. Scott grabbed the wireless, lifted it high over his head, and slammed it into the man's skull. Again. Again.

The man's hand reach up toward Scott's throat.

Scott smashed the phone with all his strength against the man's forehead.

Phillips lay still.

"Twenty-five pounds of pressure breaks the medial collateral ligament of your fucking knee!" Scott struggled to his feet. He could not see her. "Candice! Candice! Answer me!"

His right ankle throbbing, he hobbled across the road toward the driving range. "Can—dice!"

The wind howled.

Do not venture into a foreign monastery with your own rules.

—A PROVERB

SATURDAY, FEBRUARY 5

TWENTY-TWO

Dazed, ankle inflamed, eyes fixed on the yard marker where Candice had fallen, Scott staggered across the driving range. He stumbled on a range ball. Slammed his forehead against the frozen ground. Crawling on his knees, he neared the sign. Fearful, he peered behind it. Candice was gone.

Relieved, terrified, he searched the field lit by the refinery inferno. Wandering from yard marker to yard marker, he called her name, the wind carried away his hoarse cries. Was she dead a few yards away? Or bringing help?

The storm intensified. He wanted to believe that she was only wounded, that she'd escaped. But the sinking feeling within began to overwhelm him. *Candice is laying dead somewhere, and I can't find her!* Shivering, he wanted to close his eyes, lay down in the ice, and join her.

The cold was a familiar, detested enemy—relentlessly biting and burning his skin, taxing his condition, penetrating his limbs, his chest, trying to freeze his soul. To survive the long winters at Eielson AFB, he'd signed an uneasy armistice with that enemy by letting its pain pass over him and finding its hidden beauty. For a few nights, he found that beauty in the form of brilliant aqua blue streaks and shimmering lights across the sky, the aurora borealis. Scott looked up at the starless, lightless night—and remembered the many times he'd described that fire sky display. *Candice may be gone, but I'm the children's only hope. But where do I begin?*

He looked down. His hand still gripped the goon's cellphone. The once *Star Trek* communicator-like phone was gnarled: one side half-crushed, the other dented, its back panel gone, leaving an exposed circuit board. Its metallic-blue flip hood with external LCD that would have displayed the caller ID, was cracked, irreparably broken. Scott gently lifted the phone's hood; it fell to the frozen ground. Inside, six of the phone's plastic keys were permanently sunken into its silver casing, its color screen, splintered, useless. Besides a slew of digital features, the phone once had always-on wireless web and e-mail access, text messaging, and probably an internal scrambler. But one button on the phone appeared intact—perhaps the only one that mattered. Tenuously, he lifted his finger, and pressed.

A quick snapping. Nothing answered.

"Shit, I'm—"

"Phillips, what the hell have you been doing? Do you have him or not?" a female voice shouted from the phone.

The walkie-talkie! It works!

"Phillips, where are you?" the voice blasted from the bent speakerphone.

The tone, the inflection—so familiar. *The Inquisitor's voice!* "Dead, I hope!"

"Is—is that you Merritt?"

"Damn right it is! You killed my wife, you—"

"Should I kill your children, too?" the voice responded softly.

"Touch them and, I swear, IRACT'll be on network news!"

"I'll call that bluff. We've searched your mother's condo and *both* your houses. If you had anything more, you'd've already tried bargaining your way out."

"I backed up everything on *another* CD that I mailed, with full instructions, to a friend in a TV news department. He'll have it Monday. So, in the next ten minutes, unless you prove that *both* my children are alive and well, you lose." He hung up. *What have I done? I've severed the only link—*

A shrill note reverberated in his hand. He gazed at the wireless. Hesitated before answering. A tiny whimpering voice called his name. "Daddy?"

"Oh Brooke, are you all right?"

"I'm so scared!"

"They hurt you, cutie?"

"I want to go home!"

Scott sank to his knees. "Brooke, cutie, listen to—"

Rustling sounds. Another voice, much softer, subdued. "Daddy?"

"Andrew? Are you—"

"Watching cartoons."

"Andy, it's important that you listen to your grand—"

The connection terminated. He stared into the dark. A moment later, his phone rang again. "Satisfied?" the woman asked.

Scott got off his knees, stood erect, and pulled back his shoulders. "Release them now and I'll tell you where to get the CD."

"Do I sound like a fool?"

"A straight swap, then. Me for the kids. Once you—"

"The CD, *immediately*. Then I'll release them."

"I—I can't. I told you, the CD is physically in the mail. I can't possibly get it to you before Monday." Scott tried to fight the wind blowing ice in his eyes. He wanted his children now! To leave them in that monster's hands for two full days: would they survive? *Do I have a choice?* "We'll trade on Monday," Scott declared, speaking from his diaphragm, using a deep, resonant, compelling voice he'd used so successfully in his practice on indecisive patients. "*I* pick the location. And *I* get to speak to the kids at a time of my choosing *before* the exchange. That way, you'll be certain to keep them alive. Raise or call!"

She did not reply.

"Last chance—raise or call!"

She cursed under her breath. "Agreed. But there's two points. One, if you use the phone—"

"The phone's broken. Only the walkie-talkie works."

"Nonetheless, let me assure you, if you call any other programmed number on that phone, your children will—"

"And your other point being that I don't contact the police or the FBI, right?"

"I wouldn't." She lowered her voice. "We're everywhere."

ENSOLCO Oil Refinery

Exhausted, Special Agent in Charge George Terrill stepped out from his trailer. Freezing ice crystals pelted him back into alertness. He turned toward the fire—and noticed a partially-clothed woman, wrapped in blankets, being accompanied by a firefighter.

Two TV camera crews saw her, too. They started converging.

Terrill broke through one news crew and joined four uniformed patrolmen. Shielding the woman in blankets, they helped her onto a gurney. Terrill listened carefully to the woman mumble as they lifted her into an ambulance. The vehicle's doors slammed shut. It drove off amid tape rolling and hoarse local reporters.

After the ambulance disappeared, Terrill turned toward the hell freezing night, the skyline illuminated by huge refinery tanks ablaze. *How could anyone survive* that?

The Wheelan Jet
In Transit Over the Texas Panhandle

On one side of the cabin, Hope Wheelan's face remained buried in index charts, projections, and forecasts. Alexander, on the far side, stretched across a plush couch, and double-winked at his wife. "Hey kid, care for a diversion?"

Peering at him over her reading glasses, "If I finish before we reach Washington," she said, faintly smiling, knowing he sometimes regretted making her president of Paradigm Transplant Solutions—but only because it took her from his side, from his bed. By shrewdly acquiring key genetic engineering technology, Hope had transformed PTS into a global giant, making Cassandran Strategic Funds one of Wall Street's top-rated—and all leveraged using 'unconventional' investors.

"I'd sacrifice a few million to have you tonight."

"How you'd hate yourself in the morning."

Alexander got up and ambled toward her. He touched her cheek.

Her wireless rang. She picked it up as he sat beside her, rubbing her shoulder. After a moment, she looked down and released a shuddering sigh. "Where is he now?" Looking out the window, "I don't care! Arrange a meeting!" She disconnected. To Alexander, "My largest investor is threatening to bail. That could start a sell off of PTS. Possibly destabilize the entire fund."

"I'll go with you."

"You promised you'd let me run the company the way *I* wanted. *I* will handle him."

"What about your meeting in Washington?"

"I'd forgotten." She sighed. "It's too important to postpone. I'll have to swing the client meeting afterward."

"And where would that be?"

"Aruba."

"Aruba's beautiful this time of year. Who exactly is this gentleman that you've kept me in the dark about for so long? I trust this is a *business* meeting."

"Jealously is unbecoming."

"Aruba's only a skip from South America. Tell me that this man is not a drug lord."

She looked away. *I should be so lucky.*

### Interstate-95, Philadelphia Area					1:58 A.M.

As her car crawled through traffic paralyzed by ice, Stone appraised the sinewy silhouette of the man who filled the back seat, Clayton's replacement. She knew even less about him than she had about Clayton, except that this man worked directly for one of the Investors, that he exuded a patient, controlled brutality, and that he made her skin frostier than the already freezing car. "Krysha, have you sterilized the site?"

The man in the shadows slowly folded his hands. "Sufficient to stifle forensic teams."

"And the cellphones?" she asked.

"All replaced. All clean. Except of course for the one linking you with Merritt—which your man's incompetence forces you to keep," he finished with a stern flourish.

Stone replayed his voice in her mind, analyzing his speech. It was thick-tongued, especially heavy on the *f*'s: British, superimposed on German? Real or affected? And 'Krysha'—an interesting name. She took out her palm pad and initiated a word search on it. "Speaking of Phillips, what did you do with him?"

"Which part?" The car speeded up. "It was hoped that your aberration could have been concluded this evening," Krysha said, slowly enunciating each syllable. "This not being the case, you will be needing my services for more than just the aircraft."

"I didn't order you to bomb that plane."

"Your blundering left me no choice."

"Listen you insolent bastard. I'm—" He palm pad beeped. She looked down at her search results—and placed her hand over her chest and slowed her breathing. "I, uh, I need you to

assist Hailey and Buchanan to guard Merritt's kids. I'm—
holding you in reserve."

Krysha pursed his lips. "A dreadful under-utilization of
my talents."

Ensolco Oil Refinery

Special Agent in Charge Terrill brushed icicles from his hair
and trudged back through the storm to his Operations trailer.
Inside, Special Agents Cicero and Kamen stood over a map
of the airport. Two other agents, cramped along the far end,
chattered on headsets.

"Philly PD found a woman in a field at the periphery,"
Terrill said. "No ID."

"A survivor?" Agent Cicero asked.

Glancing back at Agents Cicero and Kamen, "Jane Doe
had been shot, right shoulder. Entry wound looked like a
nine-millimeter. She was half frozen, dressed as if she'd been
in a business meeting and dumped in the sleet. She was inco-
herent, mumbling about someone kidnapping her children."

"Where is she now, sir?" Kamen asked.

Rubbing his frozen hands, "On her way to the hospital."
To Cicero, "Post her room, both sides. Run her through
NCIC. Get her statement. I want a name to go with that face
before breakfast."

Kamen asked, "Do you think there's a connection
between—"

"Two points always form a straight line, Agent Kamen.
Not necessarily three." Terrill slipped on a pair of reading
glasses. "They originally found her here," he said, pointing
on the map to the northwestern tip of the refinery. "There's a
driving range, a road, car dealerships, a wildlife refuge, and
some developments near the marsh that've seen better days.
And, what's here?" he asked, pointing at the western edge of
the map.

"An industrial park," Kamen answered. "Small busi-
nesses, mostly. Partially occupied."

"The JD had been dumped in the marsh."

"She say that?" Cicero asked.

Terrill wryly smiled. "Her feet were muddy. Ankles, too."

"That doesn't necessarily prove—"

"It's winter. The ground surface is frozen, but not in a marsh. Also, her fingers were sliced between knuckle and tip, as if she'd cut them holding a piece of ice."

Cicero motioned them to the map. "If we draw a straight line through the marsh, we wind up with this site right here, part of the old shipyard."

Terrill shook his head. "Cut through four miles plus of swamp in the dark? Unlikely." He traced a new line with a ruler. "The woman was heading toward the fire. Assuming she skirted the marsh, that eliminates the residential developments," tracing out the woman's projected path on the map with his ruler, "and leaves us with the driving range." He drew a second line intersecting the marsh periphery with the first line, connected the tips, and shaded in the resultant triangle.

"That's Kimbrough industrial park," Cicero said.

"Let's see where the flight path went." Terrill picked up a red marker and superimposed a sweeping, inverted parabolic curve. The airliner's aborted return path passed through the heart of the triangle.

"Jees!"

"Okay Kamen, she could be a witness to whoever brought 841 down." Turning to Cicero, "You and the others over there coordinate with Philly PD. Canvass anyone with a potential line of sight on the place. Search every room in that complex and every inch of ground between that's not on fire."

TWENTY-THREE

Medical Library of the University of Pennsylvania
Philadelphia   **10:00 A.M.**

Freezing, Scott glimpsed his reflection in one of the fifteen-foot-high tinted windows by the medical library's main entrance: his hair was disheveled, his shirt collar torn, his suit jacket covered with caked muck, and he probably smelled like swamp when the wind wasn't carrying away his odor. As an alumnus of Penn's medical school and former attending at its hospital, Scott had often seen derelicts, looking very much like his reflection in the window, hanging around campus—and wondered what could have made them sink to such depths, and why they would even want to survive like that. At another time, he might have appreciated a lesson in humility. But now, shivering in an alcove, he gazed at the remnants of the badly damaged cellular. Had its web and e-mail features endured the pummeling, Scott wouldn't have needed to crawl back to Penn—which had seemingly been so glad to see him depart years ago.

A matronly redheaded librarian unlocked the door and

glanced disapprovingly at him like a German shepherd patrolling its turf. A few minutes after she and a few other staffers followed her inside the double door, he limped on his swollen ankle to a young woman sitting at the front desk. The student clerk's eyes narrowed, her nose wrinkled, but before she could say a word, Scott produced two maroon and white plastic cards from his soggy wallet: one alumnus and one out-of-date faculty ID.

She studied them. "Wow Dr. Merritt, are you—"

"It was one hell of a party."

Ignoring whispers from the reference librarians, Scott headed directly to the first row of workstations, sat in front of a console, and accessed Ryan's e-mail address. The last message read:

Date: Fri, 4 Feb 11:31:01 EST
From: <obfusc8@it.upenn.edu>
To: <obfusc8@it.upenn.edu>
Subject: IRACT
Scott:
The password worked old buddy. Got in.

Copied all data and stat files, real and faked. Copies are downloaded and will be attached in a follow-up e-mail time-delayed until Sunday when we will be able to talk. (Knowing you, if I sent them now, you'd call me the minute you got them. And Janine would kill me if we talked the first couple days of our vacation!)

Left a nice little program they won't soon forget. Had it copy all data/stat files into a new folder in the mainframe. Folder and files are hidden. To retrieve, go to IRACT folder: /Commun/MF/Data/Fox. It's password protected—you know, HER name.

I found the money trail. Took some doing, but decrypted. It's in a file named 'Kompromat.' That has all the an-

swers. Talk to you Sunday or Monday from AZ. Till then,
may the boomerang be with you.
Ryan

PS—Don't worry. Won't trace it to me. Told you, leave it
to a pro. ☺

Scott gazed down for a moment, silent, knowing those
words were the last he'd ever hear from his lifelong friend.
He printed the message and stuffed the hard copy in his coat
pocket. Unfortunately, Ryan's e-mail with the critical attachments wasn't going to be available till tomorrow, at the
earliest. In the meantime, he'd go online to search for the
whereabouts of the IRACT officials. He clicked on the internet explorer icon. The screen displayed the Penn homepage.
A message box suddenly appeared center screen:

> *Server maintenance scheduled from 10:15 A.M. through
> 2:30 P.M.*
> *Internet access will be unavailable during these period.*
> *We apologize for any inconvenience.*

"It's always something!" he muttered. Ignoring an avalanche of shushes, he headed to the rear of the library, and
slipped between the 'I' and 'J' seven-foot high shelves of
current journals. Four paces in, three rows up to his right, he
found it: *The Journal of Xenotransplant Investigations*. He
turned to page two of IRACT's newsletter. It was filled with
stock photographs of Barbieri and the three co-founders.
Scott studied their faces, trying to decide which of them had
ordered his children kidnapped. After reaching a decision,
he scoured the journal's February listing of seminars and
speaking engagements:

Feb. 5 (Sat) & Feb. 6 (Sun)—Dr. Edward Barbieri, Institute Chief Operating Officer. Lectures on "Effective Procedures for Relieving Residual Pain Following Renal

Xenotransplantation." American Society of Physical
Therapists for Long-term Transplant Management.
Plaza Hotel, NYC.

Feb. 8 (Tue)—Dr. Carlton Emery, Institute President
and Co-Founder, and Dr. Edward Barbieri, Institute
COO. Testimony before the Senate Subcommittee on
Labor, Health, and Human Services and Education for
the purpose of establishing the Institute as the National
Xenotransplant Registry.

Feb. 19 (Sat)—Dr. James Todd, Institute Co-Founder.
Round table discussion . . .

"Damn it! Nothing else for February!"

Loud 'shushes' blew in between the stacks. He closed the
journal and threw it back in the stacks. "Wait a second!" He
snapped his fingers, spun around at the 'I' shelves, and
picked up the latest issue of *The Institute Update*. "I was
looking through this Wednesday morning." He leafed
through its four-color glossy front section filled with adver-
tisements trumpeting the latest innovations in xenotransplantation and entreating managed health care administrators to
meet them in person at the Annual Xenotransplantation
Symposium, the weekend of February 4 through February 6.
He continued to page 14A. "There!" He ripped the page
from the journal, the sound slicing through the silent library,
and stashed it in his torn suit pocket. Ignoring his throbbing
ankle, he strode through the library and stepped into the cold
gray morning—his plan already formulated.

Norlake Xenotransplant Center

Exhausted and in her second consecutive shift, Nurse Yancy
dreaded this last-minute, clandestine meeting in the supply
closet with her counterpart, Nurse Brown. Insufferable, stiff,
Brown would have made a great trustee/guard in a woman's
penitentiary. "I owe it to Christine's memory," she muttered.

Nurse Brown sneaked into the supply closet and soundlessly shut the door. Narrow dark eyes set against her dark complexion, Brown looked down the glasses perched on the end of her nose. "You have two minutes."

Yancy repeated the litany of working condition abuses that Christine had expounded just a few days ago while standing exactly where Brown now stood. Then said, "We all meet after the wake tomorrow. Six P.M. at O'Neill's Pub."

Brown tugged at her lower lip. "No one from Administration would be suspicious if a bunch of us went out afterward. It'll work."

"Especially with Emery out of town."

"Speaking of Emery, did you hear that he sent Christine's family twenty thousand dollars? He's never sent more than a card to any staffer!"

"Wow! Why?"

Brown leaned toward Yancy. "Maybe our beloved Dr. Emery is feeling guilty."

Yancy abruptly sneezed, covering her mouth a half-instant late. "Sorry." She felt an annoying drip at the back of her throat. "Guilty? About what?"

"Dunno, but the clinic's pathology team performed the autopsy, not the hospital's. Emery's order, I'll bet. It should be interesting when they release the cause of death."

Crystal City Hotel
Arlington, Virginia   12:28 P.M.

Carlton Emery turned up his nose at the plate the waiter set before him: dried out chicken cordon bleu, over-steamed broccoli, and tawny-colored carrots. He took a small bite of the entrée, grimaced, then reached for a pad of butter, imprinted with the Crystal City Hotel emblem, and smeared it across a hard roll. "Why must everything taste like chicken, except chicken?"

To his right at the round luncheon table sat Steven Griffith, CEO of Great MidEast Health Partners, a top ten nationally-ranked managed healthcare company. Trim, with puffed black hair and a barber shaven face that paradoxically displayed boyish naiveté and viper cunning, Griffith held his fork with perfectly manicured hands and speared the last forkful of mixed greens on his plate. "You tired of rubber chicken too, Mrs. Wheelan?" he asked Hope to his right.

The President of Paradigm Transplant Solutions demurely smiled. "I adapt my palate to fit the occasion."

Griffith locked his button brown eyes on the man at Hope's right. "I must say I'm surprised to see *you* here, Mr. Wheelan."

Alexander Wheelan straightened his silver-striped tie and politely smiled. "Just a guest of my lovely wife."

"But of course." Griffith scanned the partitioned ballroom, from burgundy tracery carpeting to crystal chandeliers, before settling on the two vacant chairs beside Emery. "Carl, is Theodore coming or not?"

Emery reached for another roll. "Oh, our good Dr. Salsbury will be 'mosying' along, sooner or later. He's supposed to be meeting his niece."

"I was looking forward to chatting with him," Griffith said. Turning toward Hope while ignoring Alexander, "So, what does PTS want with Great MidEast Health Partners?"

"Great MidEast is the most rapidly expanding integrated health provider in the country," Hope started. "You're already the largest health provider in Ohio, Kentucky, Indiana, Illinois, and are planning to enter Iowa, West Virginia, Pennsylvania, and New Jersey by year's end. With 20.5 million HMO/PPO members in your network and complete or partial ownership of fifty-seven major hospitals and clinics, you, sir, have personally made Great MidEast a force to be reckoned with." She handed MidEast's CEO a thick, bound proposal.

Griffith quickly perused through the first few pages. His eyes widened. "You want to purchase twenty-five of our facilities?"

"Yes, Mr. Griffith. Located in six major metropolitan regions and ten semi-rural."

He scanned the proposal. "For $2.2 billion? A little under priced, considering they're all profitable, don't you think?"

Hope shifted in her seat. "If you'll examine the proposal carefully, you'll note that we're seeking only to purchase *select clinics* within your medical centers, not the hospitals themselves. PTS would only have autonomy of the clinics. And although PTS would retain all revenue generated by these clinics, Great MidEast would retain revenue generated by ancillary and support services, such as pharmacy and physical therapy—arrangements similar to those anticipated to begin shortly at Norlake Hospital."

Griffith turned to Emery. "And what did your hospital administrator have to say, Carl?"

Emery put down the butter knife. "What he had to."

Turning from Emery, "Mrs. Wheelan, your offer is still significantly less than MidEast might obtain on the open market, were we so inclined. Which we are not."

"Mr. Griffith, the number of patients expected to undergo kidney xenotransplantation is expected to double, perhaps triple over the next few years," Hope said. "Not to mention the FDA's recent approval of liver xenotransplantation." She pulled out a calculator and began entering figures. "In addition to the cash offer, PTS will provide Great MidEast with a sliding scale percentage of gross revenue generated, less direct costs and physician fees, from these clinics. That would yield approximately," showing Griffith the calculator's display, "$350 million the first fiscal year and $450 million the second. Enough to dwarf perceived inadequacies in the initial cash outlay."

Griffith put aside his salad. "PTS is a pharmaceutical house. Why burden itself with clinics?"

Hope sipped her coffee. "More efficient distribution of xeno organs. And making certain there's an adequate network of qualified physician providers to perform these transplants."

"Your own network of preferred transplant specialists?" Griffith shook his head. "Does PTS plan to limit the distribution of animal organs to its proposed network of preferred physicians?"

She put down her cup. "That, sir, would be illegal."

He grinned. "What I meant to say is that transplant surgeons in PTS' network of clinics might be able to offer *discounted* organs to health management organizations, Blue Cross, and health insurers in general."

Hope knowingly smiled. "Why Mr. Griffith, that action would almost certainly land us in court facing antitrust laws, since the company has a monopoly on animal donor organs."

"But by operating within the umbrella of a health insurer such as Great MidEast, you make that case far more difficult for legal challenges," he declared. "Implying that PTS must be engaged in such discussions with other health insurers in other regions of the country."

"Your reputation precedes you." Hope smiled. "We plan to implement a unified network of clinics nationwide by the end of the calendar year."

Griffith leaned back and tossed the report on the table. "Why is PTS embroiling itself in a health provider network?"

"To make certain that the company continues to have a strong market for distrib—"

"We both know PTS won't face any significant competition for upwards of ten years. A few minutes ago, you stressed the importance of autonomy. Why, Mrs. Wheelan, why?"

Emery noticed Alexander Wheelan's perplexed expression. *Is it possible she managed to keep the truth from her husband? Could he really be in the dark?*

Hope patted the corners of her mouth with a napkin. "I believe I've made our reasons clear enough, Mr. Griffith."

"And if I reject your offer?"

She smiled, looked down, and brushed away a few scattered crumbs in front of her.

Emery stopped eating. "Steven, I've known you a long time. Trust me, you'll be a whole lot happier if you take the deal."

"My hands are tied until next fiscal year, beginning October," Griffith said.

"PTS must be operational in your key sites within the next sixty days."

"Come now—the forms, the paperwork, the impact studies, the hearings, the state Insurance Commissioners—you couldn't possibly ram it through the bureaucracies that fast, even if I said 'yes' this minute. Nonetheless, well played, Mrs. Wheelan. Call my people in the fall."

She looked to Alexander, then back to MidEast's CEO. "We can't wait that long."

"My hands are tied. I have a Board of Directors to answer to, Mrs. Wheelan."

Hope ordered a waitress to freshen her coffee. "If I didn't know better, I'd think you were stalling to check us out, then buy us out."

Griffith turned up his palms. "PTS would be an excellent acquisition."

Hope glanced at Alexander. "Cassandran Strategic, which owns controlling interest in PTS, has procured twenty-five percent of Great MidEast stock, and controls proxy rights to an additional twenty-six percent." She pushed away from the table. "In short, Mr. Griffith, as of this moment, *we* own *you*."

"Impossible!"

"Check it out if you'd like," she said flatly.

Griffith pointed at Alexander. "You! You're behind this!"

"No, Mr. Griffith," Alexander said softly smiling. "Hope is."

Griffith glared, grit his teeth, sank bank into his chair. "Then why the charade? If you people really had controlling interest, you wouldn't have pretended to kiss my ass."

"You're an excellent administrator. We want you to stay on—"

"And keep silent. Which is probably why you don't own fifty-one percent outright."

Hope leaned closer. "That too."

Griffith snorted. "My silence will come at a high price."

"Yes," she whispered, "yes it most certainly will."

"You seem to have things well in hand," Emery said to Hope. "Any further need for me?"

"No, and thank you for your assistance. You'll find the cabin cruiser gassed and the house fully stocked," she answered. "Enjoy the rest of your weekend, Dr. Emery."

Hope turned to her husband. "Now I have to get to that investor meeting. Is the jet prepped?"

Alexander nodded. "I'll finish up here." He kissed her as she started to leave. Then whispered in her ear, "Hope, why exactly *do* you want to control a provider network?"

Sarah Novia eyed the men's bathroom door. Dr. Theodore Salsbury, illustrious transplant surgeon and co-founder of the Institute—her Uncle Theo—was taking an extraordinary amount of time, no doubt a product of his advancing years and a slow, drawn out, recovery from hip surgery. She glanced at her watch, half-hoping her uncle was stuck in the facility for another half-hour, anything long enough to miss the luncheon underway in the ballroom—and Emery.

One set of double-doors to the ballroom behind her burst open. *Damn it!*

Emery charged through. "Novia, where is he? I want to finish up and get out of here."

Sarah pointed to the men's room. As if on cue, the door slowly opened an Salsbury appeared: bald, liver-spotted, but with a grandfatherly smile and an old style handlebar moustache that made him look like the man sitting atop the Monopoly® Community Chest. Knobby, arthritic hands helped guide his walker.

Emery beelined toward Salsbury, nearly knocking over the elderly man. Sarah watched him gesticulate furiously, his face reddening. Salsbury stood quietly nodding, his twinkling eyes never leaving Sarah's, his face still bearing his great smile. Emery abruptly left. Sarah approached her uncle like an apprehensive schoolchild to an miffed teacher.

"Let's go back to the house," Salsbury said, the broad smile still fixed on his face, his sonorous voice without anger, without disapproval. "I have a wonderful and enlightening weekend planned for us."

The porter had just finished carting Emery's bags through the hotel's front door to the awaiting gray Lincoln when Emery's cellular trilled. The surgeon checked the number, then placed the phone against his ear.

Dr. Michael Valsamis, the clinic's chief pathologist, said, "I've completed the Constance Folcroft autopsy. There were protein fractions fully consistent with the PERV-DS envelope present in four separate tissue biopsies. There's no doubt now, Carl. This is a virulent mutation."

Emery muttered, "And that, Griffith you pompous ass, is why we need our own provider network."

"I didn't catch that," the pathologist on the other end of the cellphone said.

"Never mind. Forward all specimens and findings to the Institute. Let Barbieri know it's coming. Standard procedure. Uh, hang on just a second." He scooted into the Lincoln and passed a tip to the valet. As he closed the car door and headed into traffic, "Now what about the nurse, Christine Forman?"

The pathologist's sigh burst like a gale in his ears. "Carl, you're not going to like this . . ."

TWENTY-FOUR

Philadelphia Impound Lot #2
Delaware River Site   2:34 P.M.

You've reached the office of Candice Merritt. I'm not at my
desk at this time, but if you'll leave your name, telephone
number, and message—

Scott pressed the '#' on the pay phone, then punched in
'0630,' her personal ID. Heart racing, he waited for the electronic voice: *You have no new messages.*

That was the third time in the last five hours he'd accessed
Candice's voicemail. Still, no message from her. She could
have been injured or forgotten in the heat of that frenzied
moment, but the pessimistic voice inside him was growing
louder.

He gazed across the six-lane highway of Columbus Avenue. Positioned between the Interstate overpass and dilapi-
dated buildings stretched a football field-length parking lot
surrounded by barbed wire fence: Philadelphia's notorious
Center City Impound Lot #2. He scanned the street. There

were no parked cars nor, apparently, was anyone watching. Ankle throbbing, he hobbled across the street to a two-room cinderblock building beside the lot gate and stopped in front of a window with implanted microphone flanked by 'Cash Only!' signs. A squat man with a Phillies' *P* on a red baseball cap appeared at the window. An unlit cigar protruded from his weathered face, like a finger stuck in a folded accordion.

"You've got my wife's car," Scott said.

The man shoved a pen and form through a slit under the glass. Scott filled out the paperwork and handed it back with his driver's license and photocopy of his car registration. The man inspected it. "Nine-year-old four door white Volvo. PA license plate FLK7935," he said, lumbering past a security guard reading a newspaper. In the back of the office, he handed Scott's paperwork to a young woman seated beside a computer monitor. They talked briefly, continually glancing at Scott. A few minutes later, the man returned the license and registration. "Yo, that's $150 for the tow, $180 for storage. Comes to $330, cash."

Scott shook his head and dug into his wallet. With the $300 he kept hidden in a slot behind his photos, he had only $6 to spare. Reluctantly, he handed it over.

The attendant counted the money. "Section 'C,' row two, middle. Up and to yer left."

Receipt in hand, Scott glanced past him to the young woman at the desk talking on the phone before limping past nine rows of cars. He honed in on one with a caduceus in the rear window: Candice's white Volvo. With his spare keys, he opened the trunk and found a full-sized brown leather suitcase with matching tote and hanging bag, water jug, filled red plastic gasoline container, emergency road kit, and a first aid package. *Hope you kept it in the usual place.* He unzipped the small pouch in the front of the suitcase, felt inside, and withdrew a bank envelope. Scrounging through the main body of the suitcase, he found two additional envelopes. A quick check in the emergency road kit exposed a fourth envelope stuck between magnesium flares. He checked the contents of each envelope. *That's $800 in cash and traveler's checks. Smart woman!*

In the hanging bag he found a dark blue sports jacket, pants, shirt, fresh set of underwear, and a pair of comfortable walking shoes. He unlocked the driver's door and tossed the entire outfit into the front seat. Next, he rummaged through the first-aid kit and found an old elastic wrap. Leaning against the trunk, he gingerly removed his right shoe and sock. His ankle was angry, swollen, painful to the touch. Clinical experience told him it was badly sprained, and required rest, elevation, and probably a soft, flexible cast. The best he could hope for now was to temporarily stabilize the joint. He rolled the elastic bandage around his ankle in a classic heel lock that his hands joyously remembered, then tested the wrap. For the first time since the injury, his ankle did not ache. He stepped inside the car, and closed the door. When he emerged, he was wearing fresh clothes, though a pungent odor persisted. "Almost forgot."

He slipped back to the trunk, removed a screwdriver from the road kit, walked to the next row of cars, checked around to see if he was being watched, and removed the license plate from a maroon Buick. He hustled back to his car, the plate hidden beneath his jacket.

Moments later, the Volvo halted at the front gate. The attendant looked superciliously at him before raising the yellow barrier. Scott's car rolled onto Columbus Avenue. A mile down the road, it turned onto a ramp beneath a large green sign marked 'Interstate 95 North, New York.'

Three cars behind him, an indigo-colored sedan followed.

Hospital of the University of Pennsylvania (HUP)
Philadelphia

"Mrs. Merritt?" a gravelly voice asked in the darkness. "Mrs. Merritt?"

Candice's eyes fluttered open. Flesh-colored blurry

shapes hovered over her. She felt herself laying on her back, with slowly awakening sensations of sheets pressing across her body, of electrode pads pasted to her chest, and of tubes, one stuck in her right arm, another naggingly snaked between her legs into her bladder. Her left shoulder throbbed. The room spun counterclockwise in synch with the beeping ECG monitor and the pounding in her head.

"Where—where am I?" she heard herself ask. Her dry lips hurt as she formed the words, and the voice sounded so raspy, distant, not hers.

"At HUP, Mrs. Merritt. Several doctors on staff recognized you from when your husband worked here," the voice responded. "You've been shot in the left shoulder, but you're going to be all right."

The blurry, flesh-colored shapes coalesced into faces: a man with sharp, chiseled nose and chin, and a woman with brownish-blond straight hair closer to the foot of her bed. Their faces drifted to her left with the slowly revolving ceiling. "Who are you?"

"We're with the FBI. I'm Special Agent Terrill," said the sharp featured face. "And this is Special Agent Kamen. We're here to ask you some questions about a kidnapping."

"Oh God, it's not a dream!" Candice turned her head away. "Did you find Scott?"

"No, just you, alone, unconscious, in a field near the refinery fire last night. Mrs. Merritt, earlier today, when you were partially sedated, you were saying that someone had taken Brooke and Andrew. Specifically, Iraq. Has your husband—"

"Not Iraq. IRAC—T!"

"That's what I'm saying. Iraq. Have terrorists—"

"No, no! IRACT!" Candice strained to widen her eyes. "I-R-A-C-T. Institute for Research of—it's, uh, it's some transplant institute. They have my—babies!"

Kamen looked to Terrill. Both shrugged. "Who from this transplant—"

"Maybe some woman, Scott said. "He wasn't sure."

"Did you see her?"

Candice found herself back wearing that oppressive hood, breathing in her own sweat, tasting that terrible, numbing fear. "No."

"What about her voice?"

"Dis—torted."

"Mrs. Merritt, do you know where you were?" Agent Kamen asked.

"Somewhere near the airport."

"Do you remember a building or—"

"Dark. A room. That's all."

"Mrs. Merritt, I know it's painful, but think back. Put yourself back in that room. Was there anything—anything at all distinctive about it. The walls, the paint, the furniture, the view?"

Candice closed her eyes. Took a long, pained breath. "No. Nothing."

"How about when you escaped? The grounds outside? Where you were walking?"

"A marsh. A hill."

"Any landmarks? A building?"

She shook her head. "All I remember is jumping out a window—into mud. Running. Running—then Scott's voice. God, they shot me!"

"Who shot you? The people from this transplant research institute?"

"Uh-huh."

"Why?"

She tried to remember Scott's rushed explanation on the ferry, but his words seemed so technical, so convoluted. "Killing people by numbers," she rasped, not understanding her own words, unable to clarify. Her throbbing shoulder burned.

The federal agents looked quizzically at each other. Kamen continued, "Mrs. Merritt, where is Scott now?"

"Out—looking for them." With a halting sob, "If they didn't—kill him."

Terrill softened his tone. "Do you or your husband know a Vincent Ingenito?"

"Scott's boss."

"And Dylan Rogers?"

"Research assistant."

Terrill paused. "Mrs. Merritt, while you were under, you were also saying something about a Ryan and Janine Knight. What can you tell us?"

Candice's eyes crept shut. She could feel herself spinning faster. She fought it, but the only answer seemed to embrace the darkness. "Blew up their—plane."

"Who blew up their plane?"

Her breathing slowed. "IRACT has Brooke and Andy. Probably Mother, too."

Terrill whispered to Kamen, "Was the husband ever booked on that flight?"

"No record of it, sir," Kamen answered. "But the Knights were."

Eyes shut, losing consciousness, Candice reached out and touched Terrill's arm. "Save them, please!"

Terrill took her hand and patted it. "We'll do everything in our power. There's policemen right outside your door. You rest now. When you're feeling better, we'll talk again."

As Terrill and Kamen reached the door, Candice called, "Scott said I should leave a message on—work voicemail. Let him know I'm alive. Or he won't know I am."

Terrill said, "Give me your PIN number, and I'll leave a message."

Terrill led Kamen into an unoccupied patient room. "Before anyone—and I mean *anyone* on staff enters that room, I want confirmation, in person, by another staffer. Stick with this witness, Kamen. Either she has the key, or her husband does." He pulled out a wireless.

"You can't use that here, sir," she said. "Interferes with pacemakers and the like."

He shrugged, picked up the phone on the table by the hospital bed and heard a dial tone. "This one's still connected," he said, dialing his divisional office. "It's Terrill. Seems there's a link between Merritt, his company, the bombing, and a probable kidnapping. Here's what I want. One, get surveillance teams out to the wife and mother-in-law's addresses. Forensic teams in and out ASAP. Two, get me anything and everything about an organ transplant organization, acronym IRACT, that's India-Romeo-Alfa-Charlie-Tango. Finances, functions, backers, products, research, personnel, you name it. Find out who's in charge of the place, and put 'em under full surveillance." His head bobbed. "Three, go over the ground again between the refinery and Kimbrough Industrial park. Key in on buildings directly overlooking the marsh. Four, find Merritt. Update me every two hours. And assemble available team leaders for a task force meeting." He hung up.

Kamen looked quizzically at him.

"Something bothering you, Bonnie."

"Why would this research center blow up the plane? I mean, if you wanted to kill someone, why do it publicly? Wouldn't you prefer someplace quiet, like an alley? Why draw attention?"

Terrill leaned against the stripped bed. "Go on."

"It'd only make sense if you wanted to kill someone—and get rid of 'something' that they had, something dangerous. But suppose you weren't sure *where* that 'something' was, or even *what* it was. Just that it was on the plane—with them."

"You're suggesting that the bomb was meant to kill the Knights?"

"More than that. I'm thinking luggage, probably carry-on," she answered. "Since a handler was killed, whoever did it probably had ample access to stowed cargo. If he'd found what he wanted, he'd've probably disposed of the Knights later, quietly."

"So what are we looking for?"

Eight-year-old Brooke Merritt's earliest memory was of crawling backward down creaking stairs from her grandmother's kitchen onto a cold, concrete basement floor, the thunderous oil furnace suddenly clanging, the old wooden door snapping shut behind her, and the screaming—screaming that had made her dizzy until her mother had rushed down and scooped her away. Now, here, this place brought out the same pure terror. The cellar's only light came from flicking images on the TV. Her wrist was tied to a long cord, anchored to a pipe in a corner, as was Andrew's beside her. They could not wander far from that pipe and the tiny fraying carpet—their only protection from the damp, freezing floor. Andrew rocked back and forth, clutching the remote control, staring at the uninterrupted parade of cartoons. Brooke had screamed and screamed. No one heard. Andrew hadn't uttered a word since the men had bound them in the cellar. There was one window—but too tiny to squeeze through, even if they weren't bound. The only way out was up the stairs into the kitchen, where someone always stood guard.

The lock on the door clicked.

"Please let it be grandmom and the police!" Brooke whispered, huddled in her coat.

The door opened. A large man, wearing a skeleton mask and carrying a tray of food, entered. He gave Candice and Andrew each a can of soda and a microwaved pastry that smelled like pepperoni pizza. Andrew leaned to his right as the man crossed between the TV and him, so as not to miss an instant of cartoon time.

"Oh please mister! Let us go! We won't tell anybody! Please, please!" Brooke cried.

The man with the skeleton mask said nothing. As he crossed in front of her, she extended her right leg. He tripped and flew forward. Brooke curled up, paralyzed, not sure whether it had been an accident.

The man righted himself like a Ninja. Brooke shrank into

the corner. Without a word, his left leg exploded out and struck Brooke's thigh. She shrieked as the door slammed. The lock clicked.

Andrew slid timidly next to her, put his arm around her heaving shoulders. On TV, a roadrunner stood in midair while the pursuing coyote plunged into a deep canyon. Poof.

TWENTY-FIVE

Scott's old white Volvo flashed its left turn signal, eased into the center lane, gently passed the minivan ahead of it, and then leisurely returned to the right hand lane.

Trailing five cars behind, Stone's henchmen mimicked the maneuver in an indigo Chrysler. Reeve, angular, long-legged, wearing pinch sunglasses and a long black duster, squirmed in the passenger seat, having spent much of the last two hours bumping his head against the ceiling as Thane, the driver, seemingly hit every bump on the New Jersey Turnpike. Reeve pointed at the white Volvo. "Think Merritt spotted us?"

"Naah." Thane's belly chafed the steering wheel. "See how nonchalant he's driving?"

"Tail a man seventy miles, you'd think he'd catch on." Reeve glanced at the back seat passenger. "Wouldn't you, MacLellan?"

The third man assigned to tail Scott shrugged. Buzz cut

hair, eyes forward, back straight, MacLellan had remained silent since the trio had picked-up their quarry at the impound lot.

"It's getting dark!" Reeve snapped as they passed beneath a twenty-foot green sign. "The road divides up two miles ahead. Cars only in the left three lanes, mostly trucks in the right lanes. Merritt could go either way."

"He'll go left, the cars only lanes," Thane said, his extra chin wiggling as he spoke. "But the truck lanes're faster cause nobody's admiring the view."

Scott's car signaled left and passed in front of a tractor-trailer. Thane followed behind the truck.

Reeve's wireless rang. "Yes, Dr. Stone," he answered. "We're still heading north on the Jersey Turnpike, approaching the Brunswick exit. We think he's heading for New York."

Scott's car shifted to the far left-hand lane—cars only.

Thane compensated, using the intervening truck as a shield. "Told ya."

Reeve continued, "No ma'am, we won't move in until we see the—"

Scott's car picked up speed and swerved right across six lanes of traffic just as the highway divided. The tractor-trailer behind it slammed on its brakes. Rubber screeched with a blaring horn. The trailer's rear shimmied right, left, perpendicular to its cab—and the entire truck slid across the road. The three cars ahead of the Chrysler disappeared.

Thane swerved left, missing the truck's sliding rear by inches, then back to the right as its jackknifing body followed. The truck tipped, paused pregnantly—and spilled on its side. Momentum carried it across the road, metal grinding concrete. Sparks erupted around them.

The Chrysler escaped. Behind it, cars slammed into the jackknifed trailer section.

They sped across the middle lane of the left side of the highway. A sturdy guardrail separated them from the truck lanes. "Where is that bastard?" Thane yelled.

MacLellan pointed. "Ten car lengths up. Left lane. On the *other* side of the barrier."

Though the white Volvo raced only a few hundred feet ahead of them, miles of continuous guardrail separated them.

"I'm gonna get that fucker!" Thane yelled.

Reeve hung up on Stone. "Forget it, where can he go? There're just a few marked exits from the road. He can't get away."

Thane slammed on the gas pedal. The gap closed to five car lengths.

For the first time since Philadelphia, Thane saw Scott's profile as they zipped by a small placard marked 'Z1000' atop the guardrail. "A thousand feet. It'll work."

"Slow down. You're doin' over a hundred!"

A thirty-foot opening appeared ahead—an opening intended for enforcement and emergency vehicles to cross between sections of the divided highway.

"No, don't do it! Don't do it!"

Thane spun the wheel right. The car launched up a crown in the road and flew between the guardrails. There was an instant of exhilarating, terrifying flight. The front wheels nose-dived into asphalt. Reeve's forehead struck the dashboard. The car rocked violently as they raced up the right hand side. Scott's car weaved through traffic less than ten yards ahead.

Reeve wiped blood from his forehead. "Do that again and I'll blow your brains out!"

MacLellan pointed at a passing blue sign. "Coming up on a service area. It exits from this lane. If he's bugging out here, he'll slow down."

The Volvo accelerated. Thane closed to within four car lengths.

The ramp appeared. Scott's car veered right through the last opening in the guardrail. Swung directly across three truck lanes. Big rig brakes squealed. Another tractor-trailer jackknifed.

Scott's Volvo darted up the truck entrance to the service area and disappeared. The Chrysler raced beyond the gap in the guardrail, beyond the car lane exit, beyond the service area.

"Shit! Shit! Shit!" Thane veered the car toward the guardrail, slammed on the brakes, and sat behind the wheel, seething.

"It's okay," Reeve said. "All Merritt can do is hide in that rest stop or continue heading north on this road. We can wait him out."

"Dumb ass, in an hour it'll be dark and we won't be able to see shit!" He looked out the rear window and put the car in reverse. Infuriatingly slow, the car eked backward. The slightest movement of his hands on the wheel translated into an exaggerated swerving of the car as it backed up. Twice, he scraped the right rear door against the guardrail and overcompensated by veering into oncoming traffic. The entrance loomed a half-mile behind them. "Fuck this!" Thane shifted into drive and floored it.

Wheels spun on road shoulder. The car shot blindly into traffic. A thirty-five-foot parapet appeared on their right—a ramp, the exit from the service area—shrinking as it paralleled them. The exit ramp was almost eye-level. Thane lifted his foot from the accelerator and spun the wheel sharply right. The car swung completely about, facing opposite to traffic. Rear tires screeching, he accelerated exactly as the spin came under his control, and sped up the exit ramp, opposing traffic. Cars swung wildly from side to side as they plowed the wrong way. A hatchback grazed the guardrail. A minivan struck the parapet.

Reeve shut his eyes.

The trio found themselves in a well-lit parking lot near two banks of gas pump islands. Seventeen full-sized rigs sat diagonally parked to their left. Straight ahead was a red-roofed plaza with a food court offering hot dogs, hamburgers, chicken, frozen yogurt, and gourmet cinnamon buns. Thirty cars sat in the near side restaurant parking lot—none white Volvos. They coasted to the far side of the plaza. The main lot was nearly filled with cars and minivans. People walked briskly between their vehicles and the plaza. Systematically, Thane drove up and down the parking lot. Still, no white Volvo. He pulled into a vacant spot.

"Out of ideas now that demolition derby's over?" Reeve asked.

"Shut up! If he slipped by us and got back on the pike, we're fucked," Thane said. To Reeve, "You check the restaurant." To MacLellan, "You search the grounds. I'll stay by the car and watch the parking lot. And remember, we have to take him alive."

Reeve, standing in the center of the food court, watched several hundred people jockeying in line or conversing over early dinner at plastic tables. He knew that his greatest advantage was anonymity and that, in open space, deception was the best means of camouflage. He walked through the courtyard and pointed at different stands, panning all the way around, as if choosing a place to eat with an unseen partner. Hands in pockets, he ambled down the corridor leading to a gift shop, sit-down restaurant, and rest rooms. The gift shop and game rooms, little larger than closets, provided no cover. The only exits were rigged to the alarm system. If Merritt was still in the plaza, he was trapped. Reeve approached the main restaurant.

"May I help you, sir?" asked the hostess.

"Just looking to see if my friend's here." He brushed past her and found only one room lined by naugahyde-covered booths around a central buffet stand—deserted. "Sorry."

He proceeded to the rest rooms. Bypassing the long line outside the women's facilities, he walked directly into the men's room. Inside, six men were washing their hands at sinks while a dozen others were lined up at urinals. Behind them stretched a long row of enclosed stalls. Reeve ambled down the row, checking beneath stall doors, then turned back up the row, like a hunting dog, pacing. Two stall doors opened: neither one had Merritt.

Thane's voice came through on his walkie-talkie cellphone. "MacLellan found Merritt's car parked behind a truck."

Reeve looked back at the closed stalls. The near one opened.

His automatic poised, MacLellan crouched next to the white Volvo sandwiched between two tractor-trailers in the far parking lot. He inspected the empty car a second time before checking the Volvo's trunk. It was locked. He squatted and checked under the sedan and trucks, and tried to peer into deep shadows cast by halogen lights illuminating the truck park. A shiver ran down the back of his neck. He whirled around.

Nothing, except the tractor-trailers looming over him. Delicately, he placed a foot and free hand on the cab and hoisted himself up onto the cab roof. Cautiously, he stuck his head above the top of the trailer.

Nothing.

MacLellan leaped down and checked the car again, this time noticing an ignition key and broken key ring partially obscured beneath the brake pedal. He removed his coat, wrapped it around his hand, and smashed the window with a backhand fist. After clearing away the glass, he picked up the key, cautiously inserted it into the steering column, and turned. The dashboard displayed a red line over the back of the car schematic. The trunk was not firmly latched.

Smiling, he got out and strutted behind the car. "Merritt, get out of the trunk!"

No answer. The background traffic noise from the turnpike seemed louder, more turbulent. MacLellan crept forward, hand on trigger, body in firing position. He placed his fingers under the edge of the trunk, and pulled. The trunk resisted. He yanked harder. Something snapped. The trunk flew open.

A piece of string that had been wound around the inside of the trunk latch dangled. A dazzling red flare ignited—beside a red, two-gallon container that smelled of—gasoline.

A river of flame shot out.

As Reeve exited the food court, he saw flames dancing at the other end of the service area. Gun drawn, he dashed toward fire. Thane, in the parking lot, opened the car door, stepped out, and stared, dumbfounded.

A powerful explosion rocked the ground. Orange flames burst up from a car with a deafening boom, followed a split-second later by its echo off the building. A crowd quickly gathered outside the restaurant.

Four couples passed Thane as they rushed to move their cars. Eyes locked on the fire, Thane did not notice a woman bundled in a long fur coat and with a head scarf approaching the Chrysler. From under her coat, the woman pulled a tire iron and swung it at Thane's back. He collapsed, writhing. The scarf fluttered down across his face.

Scott bared his teeth, threw the tire iron at Thane, stepped into the henchmen's car, and slammed the door. Casually, he drove out of the parking lot, past the service pumps, down the exit ramp, and into traffic.

Plaza Hotel
Midtown, New York City   *6:25 P.M.*
Barbieri bellowed at his date's unimaginative joke. What mattered wasn't what she had said, but that her nipples pierced her red chiffon dress. Petite and perky with well-toned shoulders and waist-length golden hair, she bore a striking semblance to an idealized Damara Stone, except

that her eyes were dull brown, not bottomless blue, and her smile was iridescent, not terrifying. She extended her tongue and massaged his ear.

The elevator halted. The doors opened onto the fourteenth floor. Heading arm in arm down the hallway with her, he walked as if straddling a horse. She followed him into his dark room and gazed out the window at Midtown Manhattan.

"Saturday night. It'll be tough getting reservations." He grinned. "Room service?"

She looked back over her shoulder. "I like my meat *rare*."

Barbieri noticed the flashing red light on the phone: a message was waiting. Ignoring it, he picked up the receiver and ordered a pair of steak dinners and a $200 bottle of wine. He advanced toward her. "It'll be up in about an hour."

"We'll have built quite an appetite—by then." Gracefully side-stepping him, she slipped into the bathroom. "Let me freshen up." The door locked.

Barbieri looked at the light flashing on the phone: a message. He did not want to take that message, but with an unbearably long wait, he needed something to distract himself from being *too* anxious.

She turned off the bathroom light, slowly opened the door, and presented herself to him: lips moist and luxurious, breasts full and supple, legs smooth from delicate ankles to firm thighs. The midtown lights cast an arousing shadow of her sculptured body on the bedroom wall.

Barbieri, fully clothed, sat staring beyond her, the receiver dangling over the edge of his night stand.

She smiled seductively. "Come here."

He remained motionless.

"What's wrong, Eddie?" She turned on the light.

Barbieri's complexion had turned chalky white, his eyes

darting manically around the room. "He's out there—and he's going to kill me!"

Duffey Farmhouse
Bucks County, Suburban Philadelphia

Stone detested driving in the country, especially at night when cow-path roads twisted around stunted hills. Finally, her headlights illuminated a mailbox with the name 'Duffey' imprinted on its side. She slowed the car as she walkie-talkied, "It's me. I'm by the gate."

Turning left at the mailbox, she proceeded past a stone wall to a nineteenth-century farmhouse beneath four large oaks set far back from the main road. She'd chosen this as a safe house because it was secluded, only a short distance from the Institute, but especially because six months ago, the owner, Charles Duffey, had cut her off in traffic, given her the finger, and called her a bitch. She regretted that she wasn't there when her men took Duffey's house and then his life.

She pulled up the gravel driveway, stopped, got out of the car, and by flashlight, carefully crossed the slate stones in the grass and up a set of old worn steps leading to the house. One of her men opened the door and motioned her inside. Sounds from a blaring TV filled the house. As she placed her coat on a foyer chair, he held up a half-eaten Italian sandwich. "Wanna bite?"

"God no, Buchanan. Where are the others?" Stone asked him.

Buchanan led her through a living room with laced doilies on sofa backs and lounging chairs, a grandfather clock, and walls covered by pastoral scene paintings, into a comparably decorated den. One man sat eating from a butler table in front of a TV, the other reclining beneath Friday's *Wall Street Journal*.

"Hailey, turn the volume down!" Stone shouted at the man watching TV.

The stodgy man with deep furrows in his neck wiped the sweat from his forehead and spotted the remote beside a bowl of tortilla chips. Reluctantly, he stood, crossed between Stone and the television, picked up the remote, and muted it. His body blocked the entire TV: last night's footage of Candice Merritt wrapped in blankets being escorted to an ambulance. Hailey picked up the bowl of chips. The image on the TV quickly switched to a reporter standing by an airport runway.

"Any problems with the three of them?" Stone asked.

"Naah, not really," he answered.

"Krysha, anything to add?" she asked the man behind the newspaper.

The man lowered yesterday's closing quotes. The face behind the print had piercing bright blue eyes, a flattened nose, pitted cheeks, thin lips, graying moustache, and long brown hair—a face undoubtedly created by colored contacts, cosmetics, and a partial mask. Only the tight muscles beneath his gray Brooks Brothers suit appeared genuine. "Yes," he said, briefly appraising Buchanan. "Employing that man is a mistake with dividends." His previous strong accent, gone.

"Asshole," Buchanan mumbled before biting off a chunk of his ham, salami, bologna, provolone, and lettuce hoagie riddled with hot peppers.

Stone recoiled from the pungent odor and rolled her eyes. "Krysha, we need to talk. Privately."

Regally, the man stood and accompanied her into the kitchen. The floor tiles amplified the faint sounds of his distinctive gait: his right forefoot brushing the ground before heel strike. As they sat at the table, the TV volume increased.

Stone sat down and supported her head on tired elbows that fit neatly into the grooves in the classic country wooden kitchen table. "They lost Merritt on the Jersey Turnpike. He killed one man and injured another. We were lucky no one was caught." Krysha, posture perfect, gazed at her impassively with unblinking eyes. "We think he's in New York."

"Why?"

"He was heading in that direction. He also left a message for Barbieri that he was going to kill him."

"Flimsy evidence for such a conjecture."

"You didn't hear the message. Merritt threatened to vivisect him. Barbieri, being the pansy he is, panicked. He called my supervisor and begged for protection—"

"Translating to me," Krysha finished.

She rubbed her sore eyes. "Barbieri is the only one at the Institute who Merritt knows personally. Merritt wants to destroy us. We use Barbieri as bait. Merritt bites—you snare him."

"Why should Merritt risk pursuing Barbieri after tipping him off?"

"Desperation."

"At best, an unpredictable emotion." Krysha shook his head. "Your idea is so—*simple*."

"Something wrong with simple?"

"Simplicity is like over-reduced sauce—too salty, too sweet, or too scorched." Krysha strolled to the counter, dumped a package of powdered hot chocolate into a mug, poured in hot water from a teapot, stirred, and presented it to Stone. "Was it your idea for me to guard Barbieri? Or the Doctor's?"

Stone picked up the mug and loudly slurped. "That's not your concern."

He frowned. "But it is for my clients."

"You're on loan. While you're here, you'll do what I order, when I order it."

"Perhaps I have not made myself clear. With the present emergency, your corporate structure is in very real danger of being—usurped."

She dropped the mug. Brown liquid spilled across the table.

Krysha moved his chair before a liquid tentacle reached him. "You've made a mess."

The muscles over her temples tightened. "Tell them," she took a deep breath, "tell them—him that I'll resolve the situation within forty-eight hours."

Interstate-95, Philadelphia Area   8:04 P.M.

Between snowflakes melting on his fogged windshield, Terrill looked out over the arched red columns of taillights stretching along the expressway to Philadelphia's misty skyline. His car had crawled two miles in the last hour; he was going to be late for his own meeting. His wireless phone rang. For the first time in his career, he hesitated to pick it up. In the last few hours, he'd received two calls from United States Attorney General Kress, a dozen from Bureau Director Frakes and assorted Assistant Directors, and an onslaught from Homeland and the National Intelligence Director.

"Urgent call for you, sir," said Tess from his office.

"It isn't the President, is it?" he asked, half-serious.

"No, sir. The man won't identify himself, and we don't have a number yet. But he said you left a message on his wife's voicemail."

Terrill peered at traffic stretching into the fog. Cars on either side blocked jammed exit ramps. There was no possibility of reaching the office in the next few minutes. "Record and trace. Now, patch it through." After a series of double clicks, he said, "Dr. Merritt, I'm Special Agent in Charge Terrill." He heard breathing at the other end. "I'm here to help you."

The voice hesitated. "Is Candice—alive?"

"Yes. Shot in the shoulder, but recovering."

A long hard sigh. "Where is she?"

"I'll take you to her. Where are you?"

"Just tell me where she is."

"Who kidnapped your children?"

"Some woman at the Institute for the Research of Animal Compatible Transplantations. Who, I don't know—yet. The whole damn place is a front."

"Finding conspiracies is the national pastime. A name, Dr. Merritt, I need a name."

"Paradigm Transplant Solutions. We—I have information that could destroy them."

Terrill's car inched forward. "You and who else?"

"Ryan Knight. Check that airliner's passenger manifest. They blew up everyone on that plane just to kill him! They tried to get me again a couple of hours ago. Hell, I had to kill in self-defense, just to get this far!" He paused. "They are going to murder my children!"

"Come in, doctor. We are your children's only chance."

"*I* am their only chance."

"Dr. Merritt, Scott, the FBI—"

"They are not going to release my kids! They certainly are not going to let me live! And even if you get incredibly lucky and arrest your suspects an hour from now, it won't matter, because they won't cooperate in time to make a difference!" Scott cleared his throat. "Being on the run now, you can't enforce your rules on me. So you work your end and let me work mine. I do have a strategy."

"This isn't a board game, doctor. You're obstructing justice."

"Ever studied military history, Special Agent in Charge Terrill? Eurasia? The Khan's conquests?"

Keep him on the line. Let him talk. "I was a Marine Sergeant, Dr. Merritt, an enlisted man, not an officer, like you. I was more concerned with the present and the future than the past. Why don't you tell me all about it?"

The voice that replied was calm, dispassionate. "When the Mongols began a battle, they'd send out a small unit of archers to face the enemy. But instead of protecting them with clunky breast plates and knight's armor, which couldn't stop high-powered arrows anyway, the Mongols would only wear silk shirts. You see, when arrow points penetrated European armor and pierced the skin, they'd often break off and couldn't be removed, eventually killing the soldier. But the Mongols' silk shirts would wrap around piercing arrows, which could be pulled out whole, without killing the warrior. Outnumbered, with little protection and knowing that many of them would be wounded, but not die, they'd ride on the swiftest horses into the heart of the enemy, and engage. Then, at a prearranged time, they'd turn as a unit and retreat. The enemy would pursue them—right into the heart of Mongol forces outflanking them. The Mongols would close the circle, surround the enemy, and cut them to pieces."

"They acted in concert, Dr. Merritt. Alone, you're—"

"I assume you have a private, secure e-mail address?"

"Of course." Terrill slowly gave him the address. "Look, let's meet. We—"

"They think Candice is dead. It wouldn't hurt for you to make sure they believe that. God, I really want to see her."

"You can, Scott. Come in." Traffic began moving. Terrill's car picked up speed. "You're a material witness to an airline bombing. I can't have you running loose trying to get the bad guys all by yourself. That and the fact that you have—"

"The next person who tells me what I can't do because I have MS is going to wind up with my foot in their mouth!"

Terrill said softly, "Keep this up and you're going to get your kids killed."

"Tell Candice that I love her. And that I'm still in doctor-mode." Click.

"Damn!" Terrill connected with his office. Special Agent Cicero answered. "Julian—"

"Already on it," Cicero said. "Payphone in Princeton Junction. Locals'll be there in three minutes. We land there in seven."

But he'll be long gone when you do, Terrill thought as he exited the expressway. "Have someone temporarily monitor my e-mail. And I want Agent Weisner to go to school on Paradigm Transplant Solutions."

"Already on it."

As he cut the connection, Terrill curled his lips, unable to decide whether the father of the kidnap victims was out of his mind with frustration and rage—or an apt strategist with some hidden tactical role for the Bureau.

Princeton Junction

For an instant, Scott's face flushed with relief. He allowed himself a guarded smile. *Candice is alive!* But as he stood on the hill overlooking IRACT, that warmth quickly drained. He envisioned glass and steel exploding, the resulting fire-ball reaching the sky, the kidnappers staggering out the front doors—screaming in agony as flames consumed them.

He glanced down at the barely-functioning skeleton of the damaged cellphone, little more than a piece of twisted plastic and metal in his hand. If only its back piece had survived or even if its rickety motherboard was clean, he could have found the phone's serial number, a clue for that FBI agent. Carefully, he put the tenuous lifeline to his children in his pocket.

Tell me who are your friends, and I'll tell you who you are.
—A PROVERB

SUNDAY, FEBRUARY 6

TWENTY-SIX

Scott slowly washed his hands again as he waited for the fat trucker to finish. Finally, the man zipped up his pants, fixed his belt, grunted, and waddled out of the bathroom. Scott turned toward the long mirror over the row of sinks and stared. The face that looked back was drawn, haggard, and covered a thick layer of fear. He'd eaten, showered, even found a re-charger for the wireless phone's walkie-talkie, his only connection to the kidnappers. The re-charger hadn't helped; the rest of the phone was still useless.

He applied an electric razor to his face and began removing the beard that had covered his face for a decade. As chunks of multi-colored facial hair disappeared from his right jowl, he wondered what lay beneath: unblemished skin or a pitted, cratered surface? He focused on his thinning sandy and gray hair, his next target.

The plan he'd already begun implementing would work.

That FBI agent might prove useful, but not yet. To bolster his determination, Scott created snapshots of Brooke and Andrew in his mind. But he could not clearly see both of their faces: one was fading. He had to call one last time to make certain he was wrong.

Duffey Farmhouse   6:18 A.M.

The cellar door creaked as it swung open. Warm air wafted into the dank darkness. Andrew, oblivious, watched cartoons. Brooke shrank back.

The man with a skeleton mask walked in, put his hands on his hips, and hovered over Brooke. "Get up!"

She braced herself against the back wall, took one step, and collapsed, crying.

The man noticed a red-blue welt covering the length of her right thigh. "Pain in the ass!" He knelt beside her, loosened the cord around her wrist, slung her over his shoulders and carried her to the door.

"You leave my sister alone!" Andrew yelled before plunging his thumb back into his mouth.

The skeleton face slammed the door and carried her up a steep, narrow, wood-slat staircase. Brooke clung to him, whimpering with each jarring step. He stopped on the small landing at the top and dragged open an old oak door. They entered a white-tiled kitchen adorned by fruit-mosaic walls and shelves filled with antique porcelains. A woman with long blond hair and skeleton mask sat at the kitchen table. The man dumped Brooke onto the seat beside her.

The woman promptly waved the man away and took out a cell phone. "Brooke, listen very carefully. Your father wants to make sure that you and your brother are okay," she said in a soothing voice. "When you speak to him, tell him 'everything is fine.' Nothing else. Disobey me, and your grandmother will suffer. Now, what will you say to your father?"

Through big tears, "Everything is—fine."

The woman punched a button on the phone and handed it

to her. "Daddy?" Brooke paused. "Everything is—fine." Sobbing, "Take us home, please, Daddy! I wanna—"

The man snatched her away and carried her back to the cellar.

Stone removed her mask and said into the phone, "Merritt, in any fair exchange, the parties trade what they perceive as equitable commodities. When both parties agree on terms, one shouldn't try to beat the other into submission." Her subordinate, Hailey, led Edith Kleisher into the room. His firm hand forced the elderly woman into the seat beside Stone as the other placed a muzzle of a nine-millimeter automatic on top of her head. "From now on, we're both going to live up to our contract." Muting the phone, she whispered to her captive, "Mrs. Kleisher, it's your son-in-law. Tell him that you and the children are fine, but nothing that would reveal our location or identities."

"I—understand." Edith took the phone. "Scott?"

Stone walked to the sink. Poured herself a glass of water.

"No, they haven't hurt me," Edith said.

Stone ripped a square of paper towel from the wall dispenser.

". . . I haven't seen the children, but I've heard them. They're both fine as far as . . ."

Stone sipped from the glass. Nodded to Hailey.

". . . you are. Scott, is Candice—"

A bullet exploded through Edith's skull. The roof of her mouth shattered. The bullet exited the bottom of her jaw, penetrated her abdomen, burst through the bottom of the chair, and lodged in the tiled floor. For an instant, the woman sat rigid, eyes wide with surprise, as if realizing that she had just died. Her body toppled onto the floor.

Ignoring Scott's screams from the phone, Stone moistened the paper towel in her glass, and wiped away splattered blood on the phone that Hailey dutifully handed her. "You owe me, Dr. Merritt. It's not every man who gets to have his mother-in-law killed, free of charge." Holding the receiver from her ear, "Our agreement was for the children *only*. Before your little escapade, I was willing to throw your mother-in-law in as gratuity, but—stop screaming!" The yelling subsided. "Good, then our original terms remain strictly in force. I expect to hear from you no later than noon tomorrow."

She hung up. "Clean up this mess," she told Hailey as she headed for the back door. "I need some fresh air."

The early morning air was crisp, windless, wintry silent as Stone watched her breath condense in front of her. Some-one/something moved around the corner of the converted barn, thirty yards to her left. Stone drew her gun, turned off the rear porch light, and tread cautiously across the uneven frozen grass. Reaching the barn, she slid silently along its surface, and approached the corner. She took a deep breath, then jumped out, brandishing her weapon.

A man in his late thirties sat calmly on a bench, reading a newspaper: *The Stonyville Gazette*. Chiseled face, patrician nose, sloping cheeks, he sat in a circle of light that had no source.

She shoved her automatic back in its holster. "I was wondering when you'd deign to show."

"Cold this morning," he said, putting down his newspaper, "*and* bitter."

"How the hell would you know? You're not real."

The sky brightened behind the man. A sea of papers materialized on the bench. The print on the papers surrounding him sharpened, many emblazoned with great, bold, red letters: **Past Due!**

"This is tiresome."

"You always summon me when you're at your worst." The ambient light around him glowed. "Have you ever seen me so clearly?"

"It's sunrise. You'll disappear soon."

"That's not dawn." He glanced behind him. "Don't you recognize it?"

The orange light behind him splintered. A sloping mountain and a steeple appeared. Smokestacks materialized, followed by rusting storage tanks, rows of cloistered houses up the mountainside, and a patch of storefronts along a narrow strip of level land—all engulfed in flames. Walls of fire charged each other, unifying into a super-conflagration that burned the town, the mountain, her eyes. He sat passively on the bench, barely visible against the brilliance. "It's your dream, isn't it?" He stood, wading through 'past due' notices. "The town of Stonyville, Ohio. Burning."

"First on my list."

"Is there no mercy in you? Must you make my failure their crime?"

"Yes it was a crime. LaTona's general store was part of Stonyville for three generations. Even when the mine closed, you stayed. You cut prices, gave unlimited credit, donated top quality surplus to the destitute. You helped keep that dawn hellhole alive for years. And then, when things finally began to turn the corner, what did those fine townsfolk do?" She snapped her fingers. "Abandon you for the new Wal-Mart that sold underwear and socks six cents cheaper. Those same fine citizens came to the sheriff's sale. And after they took everything in your store, they came to our house for more." She brushed back tears.

The flames disappeared.

"Such a beautiful name I gave you, Damara LaTona. A name that rolls off the tongue like a brook on a warm, spring day. Why did you change it to that of the town you so detest?"

"*Stone* was your wife's maiden name, remember? And I am stone. What a hideous coincidence that it was the town's name, too."

He shook his head. "I was hoping that you might forgive the town."

"You can't expect me to forgive that ugly place or its people any more than you can expect me to forgive Bobby Webster for raping me. Any more than you can expect me to forgive *you*."

"We always come back to *that* moment." Sighing, "I'm so sorry, Damara. You can't imagine the disgrace, the despair—"

She pulled out her automatic and fired. Bullets passed through him, one ricocheting off a tree trunk forty yards behind him. He disappeared.

Big, heavy snowflakes fell all around her. Five inches covered the ground and no sign of letting up soon. No wind, no bitting cold, just thick accumulating wet snow. Damara looked at her feet—she wore tiny blue rubber boots—a child's snow boots. *I'm seven.* Behind her, Stonyville Elementary School had dismissed early. Instead of waiting for the long, long bus ride and its 'hundreds' of stops before hers, Damara found herself happily running home through the snow. She could hear herself thinking how her mother would be out and how she'd surprise her father. He was feeling so sad after losing his store. Maybe they could play in the snow? Build a snowman?

The gate to her house only opened part way, stuck in accumulating snow. She squeezed through, bounded up the front steps onto the porch, and opened the door with a key hidden under an old planter. The house was silent, and so was she as she crept up the steps. A light was on in Daddy's study. She sneaked closer, carefully avoiding the floorboards she knew creaked. Stone tried to close her eyes, but it didn't matter—she was still seeing through little Damara.

Daddy had a gun in his mouth! Damara and Stone wanted to scream, but couldn't. A floorboard beneath them creaked. Their father turned toward the noise. As it did, the gun went off. The back of his head exploded. What was left collapsed onto his desk.

"You saw me, *then* pulled the trigger!" Stone yelled.

A second incarnation of her father, healthy, strong, and proud, appeared standing beside her. "If you'd come just an instant earlier, if I'd been able to look into your eyes," he said, gazing at his bloody body. "It was just tragic timing."

Turning teary eyes toward his daughter, "My last thought was of how I'd harmed the most precious thing in the world."

"You have no thoughts! You're just my own romanticized version of my father! You're not real! You can't be!"

Both fathers began to fade. "Can you ever be sure?"

TWENTY-SEVEN

Thick glass doors with polished brass handles automatically parted for Scott as he strode into the Crystal City Hotel. The lobby boasted marble floors, textured glass, and two-story mirrors enhancing the perception of opulence. He spied his reflection. The man that stared back was unrecognizable: the thinning sandy and gray hair, the multi-colored beard—gone. The sight of his shaved head, his transformation to baldness, was like viewing himself fifteen years in the future. He'd always equated baldness with advanced age and depleted strength. Now, paradoxically, he felt a glimmer of a newly-revived warrior's vigor. Though not a great disguise, it might prevent him from being casually spotted. From the jacket pocket of the suit Candice had packed him, he withdrew a folded paper: page 14A from *The Institute Update*. The advertisement read:

Paradigm innovations leading to life-giving organs for every *Transplant* patient. *Solutions* for patients in need.

*PARADIGM TRANSPLANT SOLUTIONS—Answers to-
day; cures today.*
WHOLE ORGAN ENTERPRISES DIVISION
Carlton Emery, MD, PhD
Director, Norlake Xenotransplant Center; Cleveland,
OH
See us at Booth #69, Annual Xenotransplant Sympo-
sium, Arlington, VA.

All imprinted over a full-page photograph of a robust Dr.
Carlton Emery, beaming.

Since the audit, Scott had suspected that Emery was the
force behind IRACT. Though they'd never met, he'd seen
the Emery-type too often from medical literature and inter-
actions with colleagues: part true believer, part manipulator,
part showman, part profiteer—all egoist. Barbieri was the
figurehead; Emery, the power. Scott congratulated himself
on his ingenuity. Everything since his escape had been a deception: Candice's car, the turnpike chase, the phoned threat
to Barbieri—all designed to misdirect the enemy toward
New York. His appearance altered, enemy forces confused,
their flank overloaded, their king exposed, Emery would be
vulnerable. Scott would take down IRACT and end the
nightmare with a single, swift thrust.

He glanced at the marquee overhanging a set of escalators
leading to the mezzanine. An electronic bulletin board, listing lectures in various meeting rooms. The first was scheduled for 9:00 A.M. *This is where he'd stay,* he thought. *Trick
is, getting him when he's alone.*

Scott strode to the crowded registration desk and corralled
a young female clerk in a freshly pressed green and white
uniform. "Excuse me, but I was supposed to meet Dr. Carlton Emery in his room for breakfast. Could you just tell me
the room number? I'm already late."

"I'm sorry, sir, we're not permitted to give out guest room
numbers," she said with a wide, blank smile. "However, you
can call up on the white phone over—hold on a moment."

She tapped on the keyboard behind the counter. "Dr. Emery checked out this morning."

Scott shook his head, rubbing his suddenly-throbbing temple. "Did he leave a forwarding address?"

The clerk checked. "Uh, yes sir. But I'm afraid I can't reveal that information," looking up from the monitor, "unless you're with *the company*." Despite her hospitality smile, her apple green eyes directly challenged him.

Scott hesitated. Slowly he clasped his hands behind his back and thrust out his chest. "I should say so. I'm Paradigm's Vice President of Medical Affairs. Now, the address?"

She curtly smiled and checked her screen. "Dr. Emery requested that any additional paperwork or items left behind be forward to Norlake Xenotransplant Clinic, and not to the residence. I have an address for the clinic, but not the residence."

"The residence?"

"Yes, sir. I spoke to him myself. He was quite specific about not being disturbed."

Residence? What residence? His house in Cleveland? He's testifying day after tomorrow in D.C. Why would he go home now for one day only to fly right back?

"Anything else I can do for you, sir?"

Scott shook his head, walked stiffly across the lobby, and drove his fist deep into a plush, velvety chair. *Without Emery, I'm lost. Even if I find him—what about going after Barbieri? No, no, never double back on your diversion. Call the FBI now? No, I don't know any more now than I did yesterday.* He glanced up at a pair of men wearing blue suits, mismatching ties, and gleaming gold watches by the mezzanine railing, in a semi-heated discussion, balancing cup and saucer in one hand and cream-cheesed mini-bagels in the other. *Nothing to lose.*

Scott rode the escalator to the mezzanine. As he neared the conference rooms, he stiffened his back and postured for battle. Emery had never met him; perhaps no one else at the conference had, either.

He stepped off the moving stairs. As he glimpsed the

physicians in finely tailored suits, memories of braggado-cio rushed back to him. Medical conferences had often be-come showcases for doctors to display their successes through diamond pinky rings and wives adorned in de-signer originals. It was the part of the game that he'd al-ways loathed. He brushed past a clique engaged in an esoteric discussion on immunosuppressants and a woman with a pearl necklace arranging pamphlets at the registra-tion desk. The main exhibit hall was nearly deserted. Rows of empty tables set before black drapes displaying corpo-rate logos lined the path through the room. Scott walked to his left, following posted booth numbers. He stopped in front of Booth 69 which had a placard marked 'Paradigm Transplant Solutions' hanging over a table. The booth was closed.

Scott shut his eyes. *Now what do I do?*

"Can I help you, doctor?"

Scott looked over at the adjoining booth. A husky man two inches shorter with a gleaming smile proffered a four-color glossy brochure. The placard behind him read 'Arca-dia LabMed Services.' Literature on the table extolled the world's finest hematological laboratory equipment. "Just looking," he said, mentally checking the company's name against those listed in IRACT's newsletter. *Not a contribu-tor!* Scott took the salesman's card. "You know, I was hoping to meet Dr. Emery." Glancing behind him, "I'm surprised Paradigm has closed up already."

The man shrugged. "Doesn't make sense to me, either. It's like they got what they came for. What that is, I have no idea."

"Is Dr. Emery still in town?"

"No sir, he's off celebrating."

Dangling the salesman's card, "Know where?"

"It's not a 'where.' It's a *what*."

Divisional Office, FBI
Philadelphia, Pennsylvania 12:55 P.M.

". . . potentially changing everything," said U.S. Attorney General William Kress.

Terrill sat at attention, hands folded respectfully on his desk, looking at the face of the nation's chief law enforcement officer on his monitor: a squat man with thick, cane-scarred jowls, receding gray hair, cane-colored glasses and wispy moustache. A brilliant attorney, but this time, dead wrong. "Not necessarily, sir."

"The Director informed me that you want to continue with your current investigation. You could wind up with a lot of egg on your face."

"Or a promotion, sir."

Kress gave Terrill a lopsided smile. "You're on. Prove me wrong, and you'll find a suitably worthy opportunity inside the Beltway for you."

Terrill stood over Cicero who shoved the last of a double bacon cheeseburger with Swiss, cheddar, and Russian dressing into his mouth. "Keep it up, Julian, and you'll need your pipes snaked," he told Cicero.

"You only complain about my diet when something's really bothering you," Cicero retorted.

"You mean aside from the Director himself calling for updates while I'm on the crapper and Attorney General Kress chiming in before I flush?"

"You took the promotion, old friend."

Terrill handed him a folded paper.

Cicero scanned it, then handed it back. "You believe this?"

"They think I'm out on the ledge," he said, snapping the paper. "Do you, Julian?"

"You're in charge. Your gut impression is what counts."

"The feel's wrong. The mind that downed that plane

wasn't enraged. It was cold and efficient. They're willing to let me walk that ledge, but if I'm wrong—"

"Never pictured you as Director."

They walked down quiet halls to a windowless conference room. Special Agents Weisner and March waited with Kamen on the right, and Terrill's assistant who handed her boss a stack of papers before she left. Terrill took his place at the head of the conference table and began passing out the papers. "This was posted on several websites thirty minutes ago. An extremist group calling itself the 'Defenders of the Islamic Peoples' is claiming responsibility. What separates this claim from the eleven others is their inclusion of never-released details of the baggage handler's murder."

"What do we have on them?" asked March, a senior agent with a permanent scowl.

"Nothing I know of. Homeland and the integrated intelligence agencies are all over this. However, the National Intelligence Director and the Attorney General still want a small unit to continue operating under the working hypothesis that the bombing ties into the kidnapping. Namely, us." He paused. "Our resources will be placed on minimum priority, since everything else is being channeled toward terrorism." Terrill scanned the eyes of his agents. None flinched, narrowed, or displayed any signs of objection. "But we will make the rest of the Agency turn on its heel." Turning to Cicero, "Any traces of Knight's luggage?"

"There's little hope of finding any papers intact. If he was carrying info on disk or laptop, it was almost certainly incinerated," Cicero said.

"Anything from his background check?" March asked.

"Nothing of consequence," Cicero answered.

"Forensics is going through Knight's residence and office," Terrill said. "There's no sign of forced entry."

"Implying that whoever killed him knew he was carrying their merchandise," chimed in Agent Weisner, a stout, fair-haired man. A chest cold accentuated his normally coarse voice.

"How'd they know?" asked March.

"He told them," Kamen announced. "He left a message on Merritt's answering machine in the Villanova residence, currently unoccupied. Listen." She played Knight's final message. "We've had the phones in Merritt's current domicile in Paoli and former one in Villanova tapped since yesterday, as well as putting both sites under surveillance," she resumed. "Both were inactive, so we sent teams in. Paoli was clean, but we found *this* in Villanova." She held an electronic chip in a plastic tube. "Someone was listening."

"You ran it through—"

"As we speak, sir. Forensics is also going over the house for blood, fiber—"

"What about Mrs. Merritt's story?"

"She only remembers being in a deserted office building, climbing out a window, and sliding on a piece of plastic into the marsh. Oh also, she might have herself released this afternoon, against doctor's orders," Kamen said.

"If so, bring her here." Terrill turned to March. "How does that correlate with your search?"

"Building Four of the Kimbrough complex borders the preserve, but it's vacant," March said. "Nearly all of those buildings have been vandalized to some degree, but the realtor keeps the power on for showings."

"Somebody may've seen something. Re-canvass," Terrill ordered. "What about the doctor?"

March stretched his arms. "Everyone at the table should have Merritt's bio. His colleagues consider him temperamental. His boss describes him as capable, but difficult. The break-in at Verity Healthcare had at least an inside assist. New Castle county detectives consider him a suspect in Ingenito's murder, possibly tied into the disappearance of his subordinate, Dylan Rogers. Rogers might've skipped the country, but his passport hasn't been used. They found a car belonging to Rogers' girlfriend, one Evelyn Cruz, less than a mile from the break-in. Cruz was killed two nights prior from a gas explosion at her residence."

"How do you know this woman was Rogers' girlfriend?" Terrill asked.

"Merritt's boss, John Gavin, had been informed because of a possible conflict of interest."

"Conflict over what?"

March cleared his throat. "According to Gavin, the Cruz woman was the Database Administrator for the Institute for the Research of Animal Compatible Transplantations. Merritt had finished auditing their records. Several days ago, Merritt's firm discovered 'inconsistencies' in that audit. Someone may have paid Merritt to tamper with research files. Merritt may have paid Rogers who used Cruz to gain access. Then, Merritt killed them. And now the people who paid Merritt want him silent, too, but he tried to beat them to the punch by passing the info on to this Ryan Knight. So, they tried getting to Merritt through his wife and kids. Merritt may be the key to the bombing all right— except that he's probably working *for* the bombers, not against them."

"Doesn't fit his profile," Kamen interjected.

"Funny how everyone around him disappears or dies," March countered. "Especially since his car instigated a series of catastrophic pile-ups on the Jersey Turnpike, that is before it blew up taking some JD with it at a nearby rest stop."

"So where would Merritt go?"

"Princeton area," Weisner suggested. "Within striking distance of the research center."

Kamen shook her head. "It's Sunday. No one's there. He's not going to hang around waiting to be taken into custody."

Terrill turned to Cicero. "Julian, what about those taps?"

Cicero glanced down at his notebook. "Judge Walsh was not his normal smiling self. Nor were the three other judges we approached with our request to tap PTS and IRACT corporate phones and cells, along with their senior officers'. Especially when we can't identify half of PTS' holding

companies. But with terrorism a priority, we should be able
to piggyback trap and trace orders for incoming and outgoing line numbers. But it will take—"

"Push it." Terrill turned to Weisner. "What have you got
on IRACT?"

Weisner said, "We've run superficial background checks
on its executive staff. None have criminal records. We
haven't accessed all employee records, yet."

"And PTS?"

Weisner glanced around the tale. "Paradigm Transplant
Solutions, though publicly traded, is largely privately held,
with more than ninety percent of outstanding stock in nested
holding companies. It's managed largely by Cassandran
Strategic Funds, run by Alexander Wheelan. His wife,
Hope, is CEO. I don't know yet who the other primary investors are."

Terrill nodded. "Stay on it." To the group, "At present,
we've been unable to locate any of IRACT's top personnel
except the COO, Edward Barbieri, who's under surveillance
in New York." To Cicero, "Julian, the video."

Cicero dimmed the lights. A monitor in the front of the
room showed Barbieri standing outside his hotel, looking
nervously for a taxi on Park Avenue. A non-descript man of
average height and weight stood poised behind Barbieri in
the shadows. The man continually surveyed the street, his
eyes frequently glancing up. Once, he stared directly into the
camera. After a moment, a cab pulled in front of the building. Barbieri, shaking, opened the door, reluctant to step inside. The man emerged from the shadow, hurried behind
him, shoved him in the cab, got in and slammed the door in
one fluid motion. The cab drove off.

Terrill rewound the video, freezing the image on the man
in the shadows. "What does this tell you?"

"Who is that?" March asked.

"We don't know yet," answered Cicero.

"A bodyguard," Weisner pointed out.

"Not your typical bodyguard," Kamen said.

Terrill placed his fingers thoughtfully on his temples. "Why not, Agent Kamen?"

"Look at him, sir. That's not your classic, thick-necked bully who enjoys pushing people out of the way. He's recessed in the shadows, out of position to protect his charge." She pursed her lips. "He's not there to act. He's there to *react*—to get whoever's after Barbieri, not protect him."

Terrill nodded and restarted the video. The man pivoted on his hips and effortlessly shoved Barbieri into the cab.

"Definitely military," March said. "Probably special forces."

"Which strengthens my belief that we're on the right track." Leaning over the table, "Now, let's get down to our respective assignments . . ."

After the group filed out, Terrill walked briskly to his corner office and closed the door. His window provided an excellent view of Independence Hall, the eighteenth-century colonial red brick building surrounded by twenty-first-century towers of steel, of glass. He picked up the phone, wiped the perspiration from his forehead, and dialed. "It's me. I'm calling in a favor."

The Grand Irausquin Resort at Eagle Beach
Aruba, Dutch Caribbean

As she was being hustled through the kitchen, Hope pulled her beach robe tighter around her two-piece bathing suit and tried to ignore the white-clad workers staring at her. Beside her, the two men in tan suits and sunglasses who had come for her while she was lounging by the pool, quickened the pace as they neared the service elevator. Though demeaning, these were the arrangements that Hope's most important investor had demanded.

The service elevator deposited them at the penthouse. After checking the hallway, her escorts opened the door to a prairie-sized room with huge, tinted glass windows with a grand vista of Aruba's Eagle Beach and the Caribbean beyond. Six armed men stood, their arms folded, hands inside their jackets—she presumed poised near weapons. An obese but impeccably-dressed man with a black imperial beard stood and extended his hand. The guards at her side led her to him. His eyes narrowed as he leaned toward her. He kissed her hand. Hope's tightly wrapped robe slipped open. She felt his eyes drawn to her chest.

He started speaking in Russian.

The smallest guard stepped forward. "Mrs. Wheelan, I am Pavel Formenkavich Slatokhatov. So good to meet you finally in person," the translator said in American English. "I apologize for bringing you here while so scantily dressed. Let us say that your body is less recognizable than your face. If recognized, one would assume that you were having an affair."

"And harder to hide a recording device," she responded in English, her eyes locked on Slatokhatov.

He smiled and continued in Russian. His translator resumed, "I am—unaccustomed to doing business with women."

Dealing with Slatokhatov through intermediaries and back-channels was one thing; dealing with him in person quite another. Hope's sources had briefed her as completely as possible: he would frequently cite Russian proverbs and quotations from Russian masters, in part to present the image of an educated man, in part to make him seem mysterious. " 'Upon meeting, you are judged by your clothes. Upon parting, you are judged by your wits.' "

"Tolstoy. *Anna Karenina.*" Slatokhatov laughed. "Sit please." A fish platter was placed on the butler table between them. She took a cocktail shrimp and ordered a Virgin Mary to match his 112-proof Posolskaya vodka. They clanged glasses. "I know why you have come," he said, filling his plate with oysters. "Outrage is such a foolish reason for dying."

In a low, slow voice, she said, "An old Russian proverb: 'The same hammer that breaks the glass forgets the steel.' Because *your* man bombed that plane and killed those innocent people, we now have to deal with the FBI and—"

"FBI as steel?" Slatokhatov laughed so hard he nearly spit out his oyster.

"I agreed to have your man replace mine only because of time pressures, not for him to make—rash decisions." She crossed her arms. "His carnage has put everything we've worked for in jeopardy."

"Regrettable, such loss of life. Trust I will properly chastise him when next we meet."

Glancing beyond him to the ocean, "Then there will no further incidents?"

He slurped down another oyster. "You Americans find it so much easier to accept the death of one than the death of a million. You don't understand what it is to be Russian," clenching his fist, "what it is to suffer."

"Oh come on, comrade! Enough with the clichés! This isn't about Russian souls—it's about the $5.4 billion you've invested in Paradigm Transplant Solutions." Crossing her legs, "Your portfolio has an aggregate cash value of $10.2 billion. Would you like me to continue making you a fabulously wealthy man, or would you prefer to cash out?"

"Such a courageous woman. You bargain hard in your *resborka*."

Hope restrained a shudder. *Resborka* was the Russian mafia word for negotiations—loosely translated as "dance of death." Slatokhatov was treating the meeting as an opportunity for her to plead her case. She glanced around at the men, at the guns. For the first time, she realized that they might actually dare to kill her.

"Bearing responsibility for ordering one or two men's death to keep a secret is hard, but now, with so much more blood on your hands." Slatokhatov stood, waddled around the couch, and gazed from his glaring guest to the unfettered view of the Caribbean. His translator resumed, "You are thinking what sort of inhuman beast you have fell in with. I am only the product of what you in the West have made, born from reforms and policies that led to privatization. Just as your husband and you learned to manipulate capitalism to create wealth for yourselves off the backs of workers, so I and my colleagues learned that it was far easier to buy a factory with $10,000 and pressure than with $10 million and financing." Turning back to her, "And now, Mrs. Wheelan, each of our respective capitalisms have met in the middle."

"Mr. Slatokhatov, I am prepared to personally buy back *all* of your shares in PTS—at $10.4 billion. It could be some time before we solve our little technical problem. I offer a quick out—a $5 billion profit on your investment, including a $200 million premium."

He chuckled. "When your husband was in such dire need of heart and liver, and you had to work so hard to make them available—excuse please, *find* them—you realized how profitable it would be to have animal donors instead of people. And so foolishly, you jumped in with your investments— only to encounter this problem with viruses—a problem your scientists warned of for years. Old Russian proverb says that, 'there is no shame in not knowing—the shame lies in not finding out.'"

"I'm willing to up that to $10.5 billion."

"Why did you not go to your husband and tell him that Paradigm was in much trouble? Was it fear of your association with me?"

"Make that $10.6 billion."

"Such a refined woman—such unenviable choices. Rather than lose face, you choose to help manage a criminal enterprise. Old Russian proverb, 'with lies, you may go ahead in the world, but you can never go back.'" He devoured a clam casino and washed it down with vodka. "I much admire your little organization with its little 'units' you keep at—what is the term?—arm's length. The way you use the weak point of influential intermediaries, such as a renowned doctor and—"

"$10.7 billion."

He circled behind her. "Normally, I would never think to deal with a woman, but you are so strong, Mrs. Wheelan. Kidnapping is our way, but you and your organization have shown us a new twist. The irony of this rings like beautiful bells in my ears."

"$10.8 billion. Transferred to your accounts. Today."

"In the old days of the Communists, the people were forced to worship the voice of authority. In America today, you have your own new voice of authority that you freely worship. You call it *data*."

"$11 billion. That is my final offer."

"Correction, that is all you can justify—without your husband knowing the truth."

Slatokhatov sat on the back of her couch. "I once saw one of your American gangster movies. I forget the title, but a young man asked his godfather whether it was better to be loved or feared, to which the godfather wisely answered that it was better to be feared. You, Mrs. Wheelan, bear the burden of trying to be loved." He touched her shoulder. "No matter how hard you try for your husband, it will only last as long as your philanthropy. Your John Rockefeller Junior spent his lifetime in philanthropy trying to change the image of his father, John D. With all the very good he did, did he ever truly succeed?"

Hope gritted her teeth.

"There is anger in your eyes, Mrs. Wheelan. Channel that anger for our mutual profit."

"My offer is exceedingly generous."

"Let me show you what it is to be loved," the translator said. Slatokhatov stood, yelled something in Russian, and snapped his fingers. One of his guards retrieved and handed him a photo album. His translator said, "From a time before I was banned from your country." He sat beside Hope and began turning pages. "David Copperfield," Slatokhatov said himself, proudly pointing to an awkwardly-posed picture of him with the master illusionist. "Tony Bennett," he said, pointing to another picture. "Neil Sedaka, Debbie Reynolds, Don Rickels, Paul Anka . . ." His parade of photos, a who's who of Las Vegas headliners. ". . . Willie Nelson, Connie Francis . . ."

Hope found him as animated as a little boy with a new pack of baseball cards.

". . . Wayne Newton . . ."

Any icy wave swept over her as she realized that she and Alex similarly had hundreds of pictures, posed with famous entertainers and political celebrities, on the walls of their homes and stored in such albums.

". . . old Russian proverb, 'tell me who are your friends and I'll tell you who you are,' " he finished. "That is what it is to be loved."

Hope stifled a long, shuddering breath. Slowly, she took out a tiny, blank notebook and handed it to Slatokhatov. "Your bottom line—the absolute, firm, walk-away price for ending this here, now?"

Slatokhatov's head swayed side to side as he mulled over a figure. He raised his eyebrows, nodded to himself, scratched something on the paper, and handed it back to her. "The figure is based on five-year projected profits."

Hope looked down: *$20 billion.* "You must be out of your mind! That would bankrupt Paradigm and decimate Cassandran Strategic!" She threw the notebook on the floor. "Aside from the fact that I can't possibly come up with that kind of money without my husband knowing, we don't have that much in cash! Even if we did, that kind of transfer would set off bells throughout the financial world."

"Is it not best then that we are kept as silent partners?"

She placed her foot on the notebook. "What if I refuse?"

"If so, you will not leave this room—whole."

She coldly smiled. "Mr. Slatokhatov, did you think I'd come to this meeting without my own *krysha*?"

"A roof? Protection?" he snickered, glancing at his guards. "I see no one here protecting you." His entourage laughed as they brandished their weapons. One man picked up the notebook off the floor and deposited it in Hope's lap.

She smiled demurely. "Excuse me but my Russian is weak. I meant to say *kompromat*." The amusement faded from Slatokhatov's smile; hers grew supercilious. "I believe the rough translation is 'personally damaging information.' It's in electronic form and safely secured. Names, dates, places, account numbers, passwords, records, transfers—all could find its way to those with power to inflict great damage, if not destroy, you and your colleagues."

"You risk much." His eyes darkened. "More than just *your* life."

"As do you. My final offer stands."

"I have invested *years* in this enterprise. To withdraw now so close to success, even with the offer of handsome profit, would cause me to lose face. We continue our arrangement, for now."

Duffey Farmhouse

Bang! Bang!

The cartoon hunter fired his shotgun at the cartoon rabbit. The gun blew craters in the ground while the rabbit thumbed his nose and bounded away. Brooke grabbed the remote and clicked to an old, colorized movie, and held the remote beyond her brother's grasp.

"I was watching!" Andrew screamed. "Gimme! Or I'll tell Mom-mom!"

"I told you, stupid, she's dead!"

Andrew stuck out his tongue. "Naah-unh, butt-head."

"Do you know what 'dead' means? Dead is when you go away and never come back." She wanted so badly to cry. "It's my fault," she whispered to herself. "They killed Mom-mom because I couldn't walk. I made them angry."

"You gonna cry again?"

"We got to get out of here."

"You're the one who knows karate!"

Brooke inspected the enormous welt on her thigh. "I can't stand up! You have to go yourself."

Andrew shoved a thumb into his mouth.

She gazed at her brother. He was a kindergartner and he needed her, the way he had the first month of school when that mean second grader, Kenny Scolari, had bullied him every morning during recess. "We'll go together, but you lead cause I can't walk well, okay?"

"Uh-huh."

"Your wrist's smaller than mine. See if you can pull your hand out."

Andrew jerked twice on the cord. The binding bit into his wrist. "It hurts!"

"Try to untie it."

He dug his fingers into the cord. "Stupid! Stupid! Stupid!" He beat the cord with his free hand, then put two fingers to his mouth and started chewing his nails with a gopher's zeal.

Brooke gazed from her brother to the cord, and back. She had an idea.

Norlake Xenotransplant Center

Sitting at the clinic's central station, Nurse Yancy felt achy, abandoned, anxious. The achiness signaled an oncoming flu. Her feelings of abandonment were probably due the short-staffing since most of the nurses on her shift were attending Christine's funeral. Her anxiousness—that was more difficult to explain. Was it because she couldn't attend the funeral like her co-workers? Was it because of the upcoming job action meeting following Christine's wake? Or concern that an infection was spreading through the ward? She'd been extra vigilant, even checking current records against historical ones. Yes, the current percentage of postoperative infections was significantly higher than the normal upper limit, but there were always natural peaks and troughs in clinic operations.

She glanced up and to her left at the placard presented by the women's auxiliary to the clinic. Outside of Room 372, Mrs. McCarthy, wrapped in a worn blue coat, quietly wept. Several days after her daughter, Brenda's, liver xenotransplantation, the little girl was still critical. Yancy had seen it all too often—family members bravely bearing their emotional burden, until it just became so onerous that exhaustion and even small set-backs broke them.

Two white-coated doctors entered through the clinic's double-doors: residents Collins and Putenkin. Emery himself was out of town and his associates were on call or off-duty. Yancy checked her watch. Her abbreviated shift ended in a few minutes so she could attend Christine's funeral. It was either inform these residents now or let it wait until the next shift. An orderly wheeling a gurney passed in front of her. "Dr. Collins, could I see you a moment?" As Collins lumbered up to the desk, "Doctor, I've been going through the charts, and I want to let you know that I think we may have a spreading nosocomial infection."

"You *think* there's a bug running around the ward?" Collins looked to Putenkin by his side. "Have you informed Dr. Emery?"

"I am informing *you.*"

Collins took a seat, grabbed a chart, removed a pen from his pocket, and began flipping through pages of physicians' written notes. "Well then, Nurse," glancing at her nameplate, "Yancy, I suggest you tell Dr. Emery."

"*You* are on duty."

"Have you called ID?"

"No, I haven't informed infectious diseases. That is your place, doctor."

"I'm not calling in ID based on *your feelings.*" Wryly smiling at Putenkin, "And I sure don't want to be the one to tell Dr. Emery based on that. How about you, Dr. Putenkin?"

"Nyet."

Collins started writing in the chart. "If you're certain, let one of the attendings know, but don't put me on the spot. I've had my dose of punishment for the week."

TWENTY-EIGHT

Except for the wind, Talbot Street, the main thoroughfare of the town of St. Michael's, was quiet. The gift shops and the luncheonettes specializing in soft-shell crab sandwiches were closed, but had signs promising to reopen next month. The main crab house, a great two-story wooden structure with exposed steps to the upper floor, was locked tight, silent for the winter. With his jacket tightly wrapped, Scott looked out across the bay. This marina seemed no different than the three others he'd checked in the hours since making his way to Maryland's Eastern shore of the Chesapeake Bay: nineteen boats docked, one hundred fifty vacant slips. Ears burning from the cold, he walked the wharf, scanning the hulls of moored vessels as they bobbed on the water—looking for the name of the boat the salesman had given him.

A man with a ruddy complexion, glistening green eyes, and hooded parka poked his head from below deck of a boat marked 'Avery Marie, Annapolis, MD.' "Looking for something, mister?" he asked.

"A cabin cruiser named *SS Wally.* Seen it?"

The man grinned. "Might've."

Scott reached into his wallet and pulled out a $20 bill, his eyes never wavering from the man.

The man took the money. "Saw it yesterday. Docked."

"Where?"

"Not in a marina, I'll tell you for nothing. The 'where' costs a bit more."

A biting gust of wind blew back Scott's jacket. He lowered his shaved head and took two $50 bills from his wallet. The man quickly snatched them. Scott glared ominously at him and slowly, one by one, cracked his knuckles. "For that, you'll do more than tell me *where.*"

Duffey Farmhouse

"C'mon Andy, you can do it!" Brooke coaxed.

"It hurts!" Andrew cried.

"You're almost done."

Again, he ground his teeth against the cord he'd continually bitten during the last hour. Only in the last few minutes had the cord shown any signs of breaking. "I hate this stupid thing!"

"Pull, Andy!"

The boy grasped his bound wrist, positioned his body like a lever, and yanked. The cord snapped. Andrew flew backward, reverse somersaulted, and landed deftly on his feet. "That was fun!" He removed the loose binding around his wrist.

Brooke pointed to an old workbench with dirt-covered tools in a corner of the cellar. "Find something sharp."

"It's yucky over there. Bet there's spiders, too."

Thumb in mouth, he shuffled to the workbench and stood. "Get something sharp."

He found a pair of pliers, carried them back to Brooke

with three outstretched fingers, and dropped them at her feet. The tool's arms sprang open on impact, exposing two sharp jaw-surfaces.

"Wire cutters. Dad showed me how to use them." Brooke placed the cord between the jaws, and squeezed with both hands. The vice dug deep into the plastic sheath, but did not sever the cord. She tried again. "Help me!" The boy put his hands on Brooke's. Together, they squeezed. The veins around their neck bulged as they strained. Wire cutter jaws began tearing plastic—then cut through.

Brooke struggled to her feet. Hobbling to the door, she tugged on the handle. It clicked. The door creaked open. "They didn't close it good."

Andrew helped her to the bottom of a steep, narrow staircase. She saw another door straight ahead, then looked uneasily up at the wooden slat stairs. "Andy, you go up the steps. Be real quiet. I'll see if we can get out through this other door."

"You come too!"

"I can't climb stairs with my leg."

"Then I won't go!"

"Okay, okay. Now go up the stairs and let me know if anybody's coming."

"What're you gonna do?"

"Look behind this," she said, pointing to an old padlocked door to her right. "Bet it's dark and scary. Wanna trade?"

Andrew's lithe frame slid swiftly up the stairs, the slats bending gently beneath his weight. A moment later, crouching on the landing, he put his ear to the door.

"Hear anything?" Brooke whispered.

"Yeah. The TV. Clanging like the kitchen table being set. Lots of footsteps." He turned. "I don't—"

The door behind him burst open. Daylight streamed into the cellar, blinding Brooke.

A man carrying a tray appeared. And banged into the boy.

Andrew flew out over the staircase. His arms stretched out

like a diver, his body gracefully arched and flipped in
midair, like a cat innately righting itself—until his forehead
clipped the stone wall. His jaw slammed into the flat surface
of one step. His left temple struck the edge of another step
as his arms crumpled on a cross-slat. His head smashed a
second time directly against pointed stone. His body
dropped to the bottom of the stairs, crashed into Brooke's
legs, and knocked her over. Silverware and two fractured
plates rained on them.

"What the fuck?" the man yelled, running down the stairs.

Brooke screamed. Andrew's arms and legs moved slowly,
purposeless—like a turtle, helpless, on its back.

"Buchanan, what happened?" Some called from the top
of the steps.

"Fuckin' kids got loose. One fell down the steps," he
called as he picked up Andrew.

"Take care of it!"

Buchanan picked up Andrew, kicked open the door, and
shoved Brooke inside. She limped to a corner and cowered
while Buchanan deposited her brother on the floor and took
some heavy-duty cord from the workbench. He bound the
children's hands behind their backs with redundant knots
and slammed the basement door behind him.

Brooke waited until the door at the top of the stairs closed.
"Andy? You okay?"

Eyelids drooped, body swaying, Andrew gazed in the direction of the TV. A cartoon mouse pushed an anvil off a
shelf onto the head of a cartoon cat. Dancing stars paraded
in a circle above the cat's dull-eyed expression. Andrew collapsed head first into his sister's lap.

TWENTY-NINE

Hidden behind a knoll across the road, Scott scrutinized the house on 47 Baycrest Drive. The residence, a two-story white stucco-facade colonial with a circular driveway, was quiet, and had been for the last half hour. All the other houses along Baycrest were boarded up for the winter, but the skipper on the boat had sworn he'd seen the *SS Wally* docked at this house on this shoal; Scott tended to believe him because the house had a rental car with Virginia plates parked in front. He had forced the boat's skipper to come ashore and drop him off near here. It was nearly dark. If this wasn't the place, he would not find Emery in time.

Keeping out of sight, Scott stole across the back of the knoll, crossed Baycrest Road, and cut through a deserted neighboring house four lots down shore. When he reached the Chesapeake itself, he trudged along chilly waters lapping against the frozen shore. Cautiously, he approached the backyard of the white stucco house. The rear of the dwelling had a glass-enclosed sun room that opened onto a patio with in-ground barbecue grill. A slate path led thirty yards from the patio to a private, deserted pier. He hid behind a bush, surveying the side of the house, listening to the lone sounds of bay water slapping the dock. Above the soffit, a second floor window, open a crack, suggested recent occupancy and, possibly, an inactive security system. He slinked to the rear of the house and blew on his chilled hands before grasping the aluminum drainpipe running perpendicular to the soffit. Feet braced against metal brackets, he pulled himself up the side of the wall. Each painful tug strained his shoulders. The drain's cold surface stuck to his fingers, ripping his skin. Panting, he scrambled onto the shingled-surface, checked the window, gingerly pried it open, and crawled inside.

Scott found himself in a sparsely decorated bedroom. Two suits hung in the closet. A gray leather suitcase lay spread open across an unmade bed. He inspected the embossed luggage tag: Carlton Emery, MD, 2322 Herbert Lane, Shaker Heights, OH.

Hands clenched, he tiptoed into the upstairs hallway and peeked into the bathroom. Water dripped from the shower faucet. He checked the remaining rooms on the floor: empty. Deadening his footsteps, he slipped down the stairs to the front foyer and checked the dining room on the left and living room on the right. Both were immaculate and apparently unused. A muffled shuffling sound drifted from the far side of the dining room. Warily, he peered through the doorway and found a kitchen with signs of recent activity: an open bottle of vintage French wine, dirty plates piled in the sink, and a residual odor of broiled fish. The shuffling sound emanated from an icemaker in the refrigerator.

Across the linoleum floor was a den dominated by a large screen TV and entertainment system. Glass encased mahogany shelving units housed finely bound tomes, videotapes, compact disks, and an expensive, hand-carved humidor. Several professional journals, including *The Institute Update,* opened to the photos of the founders, lay strewn across the coffee table by the TV. On the other side of the den, a spacious sun room trapped the late afternoon shrouded sunlight. Beyond the sliding glass door lay the pathway to the empty dock.

Now I wait for his boat.

He turned back and spotted a flat case partially obscured by the magazines on the coffee table: a laptop. And access!

Scott plopped down in front of Emery's computer, lifted the lid, booted the system, and waited as the blue screen filled the monitor. If Emery had it password protected, it might take hours, if ever, to gain access. He held his breath.

Icons slowly populated the screen's wallpaper image, a moon rising over a calm sea with tall sailing ships. The computer demanded no password. Relieved, Scott selected the file search and ordered a search for every file that had the word *'Merritt'* in its title or text. At the bottom of the screen, folder and file names whizzed by. Maybe Emery had left a note—anything with Scott's name might be useful.

No Files Found!

Nothing with my name! He cursed as he began checking Emery's e-mails. There was no record of any incoming or outgoing transmissions about 'Merritt' in the last four weeks.

Scott accessed the web. At Ryan's address, using the password hidden in his wallet, he opened the last e-mail. Once inside, he bundled all the files: IRACT data and statistical files, AIMS, and the *Kompromat* file that Ryan had copied from the bowels of the Institute's mainframe—and sent them all to a place he did not know that belonged to a man he had never seen.

Sweat droplets shimmied down Scott's shaven head. He reached for a tissue inside his coat pocket. A folded sheet of paper fell on the floor. He opened and reread Ryan's last message. Then he clicked on the *Kompromat* file.

Forman Household
Cleveland, Ohio

Nurse Yancy spotted Christine's husband, Dave, slip like a specter among the sixty guests holding glasses of wine or beer, and carrying small paper plates filled with meatballs, carved turkey, or lasagna. There was nothing she could hope to say to lessen his grief, but she had to reach out to him. She caught him trying to duck into the laundry room at the foot of the stairs. "How are you managing, Dave?"

"Fine, Yancy. Thanks for your concern," he monotoned.

"Where are the twins?"

"Upstairs with their grandmother. They're a little under the weather.

"Nothing serious I hope."

"Colds, I guess."

She studied him. He was pale and perspiring profusely. "Are *you* all right?"

"A lot of the nurses weren't very nice to Christine because of her 'relationship' with Emery. Now they're prancing around her rec room, eating her food, drinking her liquor. Some even had the nerve to tell me that she's now in a better place."

"I'm sorry." Yancy felt Dave's forehead: it was burning hot. "*You* need to see a doctor."

Through glazed eyes, he appraised his milling guests. Ten people were coughing. "Listen to them. Some probably have the flu. Maybe the same one that—killed Christine. Maybe one of them gave it to her. Why did it take Christine, and not them?"

FBI, Philadelphia Office

Terrill preferred to interrogate friendly witnesses in the corner conference room with its tinted view of Old City, but under the circumstances, a windowless room was a better choice. He respectfully stood as the door opened. Pallid, hair tousled, arm bound in a sling, Candice Merritt wobbled beside Agent Kamen. Painstakingly, she lowered herself into the chair across from Terrill. "My children?" she rasped.

"We have some solid leads," he said. "Mrs. Merritt, perhaps you should readmit yourself."

"I can't just lay on my back, waiting."

He reached behind him, opened a mini-refrigerator, and pulled out a Coke that he poured into a styrofoam cup. She drained half of it. "There's strong reason to believe that your husband is alive and in direct communication with the kidnappers."

"Can I talk to him?"

"We don't know his exact location, but someone e-mailed us a whole slew of statistical-slash-patient files a few minutes ago. We suspect they came from him."

"I don't understand."

He explained the relevant events of the last thirty-six hours. "Your husband apparently told the kidnappers that you were dead. With your permission, we'd like to release that to the media, and keep you incommunicado for a time."

"Why would Scott say that?"

"We were hoping you'd tell us." Terrill folded his hands. "In kidnapping cases, the family either calls in law enforcement officials, sooner or later, or tries to keep the matter quiet and meet the ransom demands on their own. But in twenty years of service, I've never been involved in a case where a family member hunts down the kidnappers, by himself. It may make a good movie, but in real life, it's incredibly foolish."

Kamen added, "Your husband is alone out there. One mistake, one misstep—"

"That's why I asked you here," Terrill resumed. "I need you to help me anticipate your husband, to get inside his head."

Candice glanced between both agents' eyes. "I'm not sure that's possible."

"You've been married to the man fourteen years. Surely

you can explain what's driving him—why he feels he has to take on the kidnappers all by himself. He was a doctor and I'm sure a very rational human being. He must know his actions are futile, if not counterproductive."

"Futile isn't a word I'd ever use to describe Scott."

Terrill smiled curtly. "How is he dealing with his MS?"

She sipped her soda. "Trying to outrun it, thinking that if he keeps moving, maybe it won't catch him."

"And you don't consider that futile?"

"Who's to say? It's no certainty his condition will deteriorate." Her eyes scanned the room's windowless walls. "Scott once said that 'if I can't hold my grandchild, then someone will rub his cheek against mine.' Does that sound like futility? Besides, he's in 'doctor-mode.'"

"He mentioned that. What is it?"

"A kind of highly charged, focused state of mind. Ever seen a surgeon in the O.R.? Confident, directed, unwavering. All of which Scott had in abundance before he was diagnosed," tilting her head, proudly smiling, "and apparently still does."

Terrill nodded as she finished her soda. "I also understand that your husband has some rather unusual attributes."

She danced the cup on its base. "Let's just say he courses a different plane than the rest of us."

"The visions?" he asked. Seeing the surprise in her face, "I've spoken to a number of his colleagues."

"That's one description," she said. "Not a particularly good one."

"Is clairvoyance better?"

"Now if my husband could see the future, do you think we'd be sitting here like this with," stifling a sob, "my children God knows where?"

Terrill tightly folded his hands. "Then what would you call it?"

Candice stared at him. "I don't know. But I can see you're not going to believe me, so why bother?"

"Mrs. Merritt, I have body parts from one hundred and

seventy people in a makeshift morgue. This nation is gripped by terrorist-induced panic. The media's ready to break down these doors. And in the past two days, I've had to field multiple, and I'd like to add *impatient*, phone calls from the Attorney General and an assortment of U.S. Senators—all clambering for answers. So at this point, I'm willing to listen to anything."

Slowly, "Okay Agent Terrill. Have you ever had an intuition—a gut feeling about something. You can't explain it—you just *know*."

"You don't get very far in this line of work without it," Terrill said.

"It's no different with Scott. He just *visualizes* it, that's all. And it's been a little—stronger since he's been diagnosed."

Terrill leaned closer. "Mrs. Merritt, are dreams driving your husband?"

She looked at the two agents. "Scott believes that an undiscovered virus hidden in transplanted pig organs will find its way into people, mutate, and start a plague that'll decimate the world."

"I—see." Terrill nodded. "And he believes he's the only one who can stop it?"

"It's not like that! He doesn't have grandiose delusions of saving the world."

"Then what?"

She looked down at her lap. "Scott constantly dreams of a clinic or a hospital—he calls it *ground zero*—the place he says it all starts. But he doesn't know where it is. Or when it is."

"Do you believe there's a chance, any realistic chance, that he's right?"

There was a long, uncomfortable silence. Wincing, she readjusted her arm in the sling. "He's been right just often enough to make me wonder."

Terrill motioned Kamen to him and whispered, "When we're done here, have one of the group check on unusual deaths in hospitals affiliated with xenotransplant clinics."

Candice said, "You almost sound as if you believe Scott."

"Mrs. Merritt, I believe that *he* believes. Which means that he may act on it." He added, "Your husband also mentioned 'Mongol tactics.' Any significance to that?"

She nodded. "It's a misdirection, coupled with a trap."

"How would we stop him?"

"You don't." She slowly beamed. "You just plant both hands on the bar and brace for the ride."

Terrill's beeper sounded. He picked up the phone and punched in his extension. "Go." After a few seconds, "I'm not at my desk. I'm going to put you on hold, briefly. Don't hang up!" He pressed the hold button. "Mrs. Merritt, you'll have to excuse me. Agent Kamen would like to talk with you about your husband's work with the transplant research institute."

"Come on ma'am, let's get something to eat," Kamen suggested, hastily escorting her charge out of the room.

After the door closed, Terrill resumed his phone conversation. "This counts, but it doesn't clear your slate." He listened. "I need an ID. I'll e-mail you the photo, usual encryption." He leaned back and stretched his arms. "No Everett, this time, I want it all."

O'Neill's Pub
Cleveland, Ohio   6:20 P.M.

". . . Then it's settled," Yancy declared, looking down the three long tables in the private back room of O'Neill's Pub. Fifty-three nurses stared back. "We start our sick-out Tuesday, first shift, with a seventy-five percent reduction per shift."

Expecting a boisterous response to her declaration, only silence greeted her. Yancy, feeling nauseous, struggled to maintain her voice and composure. "Nickelson signed an agreement giving Emery full autonomy over the clinic. Now, hospital nursing staff and xenotransplant clinic nursing staff are going to be treated as separate entities."

"How do you know?" a woman followed-up.

"I'm friends with Norlake's chief counsel. The signed contract will be on Emery's desk tomorrow morning."

"What's to stop Nickelson from firing us *before* Emery signs?" a diminutive nurse at the second table asked.

"If Nickelson does, the agreement becomes invalid because it calls for a *full* nursing staff. Emery would probably leave Norlake, in which case he'd have to start from scratch. I'm sure he doesn't want to do that." Yancy added, "But in case he does, I have another friend with access to some of Emery's dirty little secrets. Enough to make the bastard think twice about forcing us out, whatever the situation."

"And who would that be?" asked the woman at the far end.

"I shouldn't say."

"Oh no you don't! If I'm going through with this, I want full disclosure!" the nurse followed-up.

"Tell us," another seconded.

Yancy sighed. "Clara Bender, his secretary." She glanced around the room. Nearly everyone appeared convinced.

"How long?" asked a nurse at table three to her left. "I'm a single parent. I can't afford to lose this job."

"When Emery gets back in the middle of the week, you'll see things move. If not—we'll call the local TV stations." Yancy sat down. Her stomach angrily rumbled.

Approving murmurs arose around the tables.

The robust nurse at the end of the first table raised her mug. "To Christine Forman."

The nurses stood and raised their glasses. Yancy lifted her mug to her lips, but her stomach painfully churned. She could not drink her beer. As she gazed around the room, she noticed that she wasn't the only one looking ill.

FBI, Philadelphia Office   9:37 P.M.
Terrill kept his inner office dark, illuminated only by the computer monitor and Philadelphia skyline shrouded in mist. Agent Weisner, fighting exhaustion and the resilient

cold that had settled in his chest, stumbled into his desk. He pointed at Terrill's computer. "May I drive?"

"Go."

He slid his chair in front of Terrill's keyboard and began making entries. "We found this file called *Kompromat* in the attachments e-mailed to you a few hours ago. Watch."

A criss-cross of boxes and flow charts flew across the screen. The boxes contain the names of companies; the lines that connected them graphically displayed in a complex array of intertwined relationships. There were dozens of corporations, each with two to sixteen independent connections. Most lines were in black, but a few scattered ones, at the far left side of the flow chart, had red and green connections.

"What exactly is this?"

"A complex web of money transfers. Specifically, pharmaceutical companies, medical device and laboratory equipment manufacturers, venture capital groups, engineering firms, biotech companies, along with managed care, medical service and consulting organizations. This is a detailed map of the slew of holding companies controlling them." He took out a tissue, wiped his nose. "Now, look at this." He scrolled down. An even more intricate display of non-medical enterprises, including mining conglomerates, food processing/packaging, and oil companies appeared. "All are tied into the Cassandran Strategic Fund under the Wheelan umbrella."

"Verified?"

"That'll take some time." Wheezing, "Something else you should see." He scrolled back up the screen to the boxes forming an algorithm. He highlighted a box marked 'CXG,' then following a maze-like series of interconnecting lines, scrolled further left and up to another box: Paradigm Transplant Solutions. "There's a link between CXG, a holding company of the lines we're tapping, and Paradigm."

"Anything else?"

Weisner clicked the Paradigm box at the far left-hand side of the flow chart. A green line linked it to another box. "This, I believe, is a new acquisition: Great MidEast Health Partners, a major integrated health systems company."

"Who else has seen this?"

"No one. As far as I know, it was just dumped on my desk, unopened, because it didn't fit in with the others. I was the one responsible for everything downloaded from your e-mail."

"Have you told anyone about this?"

"No, sir."

"Keep it that way. You archive a copy SOP. I'll keep an unofficial one."

"Sir, shouldn't we—"

"You've done a great job, Kurt. Now go home," Terrill ordered. "Go home." He waited until Weisner disappeared down the corridor before picking up the phone.

THIRTY

Emery loved the water, but boating on the Chesapeake Bay always brought out special feelings unmatched by decades of sailing on Lake Erie—a profound sense of belonging, of home. Before college, he'd lived on Maryland's Eastern Shore, never far from the water, the staccato humming of fishing boat engines, the aroma of fresh, hot, bay-seasoned crabs. Medical school had torn him away from the treasured bay. He'd long dreamed of establishing a state-of-the-art xenotransplant center near Chesapeake City, but could not bring himself to build it until the PERV problem was solved. In the meantime, professional obligations frequently brought him to nearby Washington. For each trip during the last five years, he'd managed to fit an extra day or two at the PTS guest house on the Bay. Solitude, the absence of responsibility, and unavailability to patient, colleague, or subordinate compelled him to use PTS's thirty-eight-foot cabin-cruiser, even in the worst winter weather. He steered his craft the final half-mile home in the dark. Gale winds had made the placid water choppy, and he knew he'd stayed out much too late. For the last half hour, the storm had relentlessly pursued him.

But he felt another, more powerful storm brewing back home at Norlake. Michael Valsamis, his clinic's chief pathololologist, had reported that patient Folcroft had died of some PERV-DS-Hanoi Flu variant—and preliminary probes of Nurse Forman's tissues showed the same mutation. Valsamis wasn't certain *how*. Had it been by contaminated blood or bodily fluids like sweat or saliva? But he had repeatedly drilled her and the rest of his staff on preventative measures. Could she really have been that sloppy? Valsamis' preliminary report that Christine had died of bacterial meningitis would buy time to find out.

Two hundred yards ahead and to his right, Emery spotted the familiar pattern of his lighted dock. He turned his searchlights on the pier and skillfully maneuvered his vessel home. After quickly mooring, he hurried up the lit path to the patio. Only the outside lights were on; the house itself was dark. He unlocked the sliding glass door as the first frozen rain droplets pelted the back of his neck.

Inside the house, he flicked the light switch by the door frame. The room remained dark. He tried the switch again, but nothing. Relying on his memory of the house's layout, he shuffled across the room. The switch for the den's track lighting was through the doorway and one pace to the left.

Something caught his right leg in mid-stride. Twisted his foot.

Emery lurched forward and spun through darkness. His belly slammed into the floor. Air burst out of his lungs. His head smacked a sharp edge. Bony knees landed on his back. A cold, metal point suddenly pressed against the back of his neck.

"Move, and I'll cut your spinal cord," the voice said deliberately.

"Take whatever you want, please. Just don't—"

"Shut up! Hold still!"

A knife pressed harder on his neck. A hand ran across his back, his shoulders, his arms, his legs. He heard sounds—liquid sloshing in a canister? Something smelled acrid. The odor, powerful, penetrating, drove deep into his sinuses like a searing poker. He coughed. His shirt, his pants were suddenly soaked. More liquid poured down. He tried to lift his head. "What are you—"

"Hold out your arms. Then sit up," the voice commanded. The knifepoint withdrew. Prostrate, arms outstretched, head buried in stained carpet, he heard a familiar snap: the removal of latex gloves.

His chest ached. Slowly, he assumed the position.

"Now cross your legs and sit on your hands."

He complied. The overhead lights snapped on. By the coffee table stood a bald man with a six-inch kitchen knife in one hand, a lit cigar in the other.

"Take anything you want. There's a cabin cruiser out back. Take it!"

The man rapidly exhaled the first few puffs from his cigar. "Don't you recognize me?"

"Should I?"

"Add a beard. A little hair on top."

Emery stared at the face. "I don't remember you. I'm sorry."

"We've never met. But I'd assumed you'd've at least seen a photo."

"I swear I don't know you."

"The name's Merritt. Scott Skylar Merritt, MD."

"The Institute employs nearly—"

"I'm the auditor from Verity Healthcare."

"Yes, yes, now I remember. What—what do you want?"

Scott bared his teeth on the cigar. "What do you think I want, you bastard? I want my children back! Alive! Unharmed!"

Emery stared at the man. Tried to swallow. "I don't know what you're talking about."

"You're a poor liar, not what I expected. Oh, that's right. It's easier lying to patients, because they trust you to begin with."

"Dr. Mer—"

"Pick up the phone and release my children!"

"Have they been kidnapped? Is that it? I'm sorry—I have kids of my own, and I know how I'd feel." Emery involuntarily shrugged. "But I swear, I don't know a damned thing about it."

"When Brooke was in kindergarten, she had a friend who had trouble telling the truth." He took a puff on the cigar. "Can you guess where I'm going? Liar, liar, pants—"

"What did you spill on me?"

"Waterproofer left laying around. Highly flammable." He puffed on the cigar, then inspected it. "I love cigars. This one's Jamaican. I haven't had one in years. My wife wouldn't let me. Extraordinary woman, my Candice was— until you had her killed. And my best friend, killed in a plane crash—thanks to your friends." Taking a long puff, "He was burned alive, strapped to his seat, with his wife sitting beside him. Burning you would be so appropriate on so many levels. Now, I'll have my children or I'll have your life!"

"I had nothing to do with any of that!"

"You're President of IRACT."

"It's a medical research center, not an underworld cartel!"

"You're tied in with PTS's Whole Organ Enterprises."

"Lots of people are! It's no crime!"

With the knife in one hand, Scott used the other to take a lighter from his pocket and rip out a page from the open *The Institute Update.* He advanced on Emery. "Where are my children—or I swear I'm going to give you the opportunity to experience, firsthand, what awaits you in the life following this one."

"I swear I don't know!"

Scott flicked his thumb. The lighter burned.

Emery's eyes fixed on the tiny orange-yellow flame. "I'm not involved!"

Scott held a corner of the page in the flame. The tip browned, blackened, withered.

"Please! I—I know who has them!"

The page ignited.

"You're burning the answer!"

Scott pulled the paper away, and stared at an incinerating photo. He dropped it to the floor and stamped on it. "Prove it."

"I keep—been keeping a journal of these things for years. We all have, just in case."

"I suppose you left it in Cleveland?"

"It's on that laptop."

"Liar! I've already scoured your hard drive. My name isn't mentioned anywhere."

"It's got to be!"

"I'm telling you I ran a title and text file search for anything with my name. Nothing!"

Emery's breath quickened, stuttered slightly with his palpitating heart. "Wait a second. How d'you spell that?"

"M-e-r-r—"

"Two 'r's?" Emery said. "I thought there was only one."

Cautiously, Scott put the knife down beside the laptop, opened the lid, booted the unit, initiated word searches for 'Merit' and 'Meritt.' He located a log file.

"Start with the entry for Friday, September 28," Emery said. "They've kept me out of the loop since I argued against killing Todd. It's all there."

Scott read the file slowly, repeatedly glancing up at Emery. The rain intensified, filling their silence with sounds of frozen droplets pounding furiously on glass. After several minutes, he looked away.

Emery said, "I told you I wasn't involved. I never wanted any part of those kinds of decisions. Adjusting data is one thing, but—"

"Moron! I'd have known this hours ago if you fucking knew how to spell. Now, I'm almost out of time." Scott stood, paced across the room, marching through cyclical patterns of sluggish stepping and manic stomping, debating with and against himself. After a moment, he grabbed the speaker-phone off the shelving unit and slammed it on the table in front of Emery. "You're going to set up a meeting—tonight!"

Salsbury Estate
Henrico County, Virginia

Dr. Theodore Salsbury, the other remaining co-founder of the Institute, luxuriated in his jacuzzi as the warm, effervescent water reduced the load on his reconstructed hip. His estate, west of Richmond, snuggled by the river, reflected his love of water in all its forms. He looked out over his Olympic-size pool and sauna beneath the tinted bubble enclosure, all served up like pheasant under glass. Rain pattered on the dome above him.

"An aperitif, sir?"

Salsbury turned to the diminutive man with thinning gray hair and solemn expression. "No thank you, Efrem. What about supper?"

"Poulet in cook's special peanut sauce. Asparagus with almonds and hollandaise. And Dr. Novia's favorite, pan bread," Efram said. "It will be ready in fifteen minutes, sir."

He nodded, laying both palms on the frothing surface. "Where is Dr. Novia? She went to change almost an hour ago."

"She's next door, sir. In the game room, sitting by the television. Looking rather despondent, one might observe."

"Ask her to please join me now." *I should have told her long ago,* Salsbury thought as his servant's steps echoed across the pool enclosure as he left. *It's probably too late, now.*

Sarah sauntered by the pool, removed her blue terry cloth robe, and placed it by the phone on the round glass table. Her petite one-piece black bathing suit matched the long black hair that framed her gentle face. It was the black that re-ignited that old, lasting memory. "You look distant, Uncle Theo."

"Just remembering a rainy afternoon, some twenty-odd years ago." *Watching them lower your father, my brother, into the ground. You, there beneath the canopy, your long black hair wrapped around your stoic face, standing, unwavering throughout the funeral. Until the end, when you turned to me—the desperation, the helplessness in your eyes.*

"I remember." She faintly smiled. "You raised me, educated me, taught me everything I needed to know about medicine, boys, life. In every sense, you've been my father. Where would I be without you?"

"Hopefully with a man." Salsbury splashed. "Have babies before it's too late."

"Career first. There'll be plenty of time later."

"When you're young, time is like a great jar full of pennies. You can't imagine ever running out."

"You've never mentioned children before. Why now?" A corner of her mouth turned down. "Oh, no. The myeloma."

"My beta-2-microglobulin levels are way up."

"That doesn't necessarily prove—"

"Sarah, my remission's over. You knew this had been coming for some time."

"How long?"

"Twelve months at most," he admitted. She sank to the floor and locked her arms around her knees. He shimmied through the water to her side and took her hand. "I thought I'd wait until tomorrow, but now seems as good a time as any. It's time to start making plans. Mary's gone, God rest her soul. I have no heirs. The looming threat of estate taxes forces me to begin to divest much of my fortune while I'm alive. I've designated you as my sole heir." He caressed his niece's hand. "Shortly, you will be a very wealthy woman."

She weakly nodded. "I'd rather have you."

"Child, listen to me. There's a responsibility that goes with this. One that I've tried to hide from you. Now, you need to be prepared—if only for your own protection."

"Is that what Emery's been badgering me about? And now you?"

He shifted position, his eyes, stern. "There's something

not in my will or codicil, something you must remember. In the main library, I keep a collection of old chemistry texts. In the *Handbook of Physics and Chemistry,* 53rd edition, 1972 to 1973, on the page with the periodic table of the elements, you'll find a key that fits a safety deposit box in the main branch of Henrico-James First National Bank. The page number is the box number." He wiped perspiration from his forehead. "In the event of my death, go to that box, first."

"What's in the box?"

"It's best you don't know for the time being."

She retreated several steps. "What is in the box, Uncle?"

Looking at the bottom of the tub, "Records, transactions, orders, meeting summaries. I've been keeping them for years. Think of it as an insurance policy."

"Insurance? Against what?"

"Recently I've made some—missteps."

"I've had a few of my own." She put on her robe and pulled the collar across her chest.

Salsbury put his hands to his temples. "You're not going to take the fellowship with Emery, are you?"

"Technically, he didn't offer it. *You* did."

"But when he does, you're going to turn him down?"

She folded her hands and squeezed. "I—can't work with that man."

"I know he's a bastard, but—"

"He's trying to squash my research."

"Your speculative article on xenozoonotic infections?" He glanced down at the churning water. "I had hoped you'd reconsidered going forward with that."

"So that's what Emery was yelling at you about." Sarah shook her head. "Why is it everyone, you included, seems so intent on blinding themselves to the danger we court—"

"Do you know what it was like being a surgeon in this field before xeno—"

"Spare me the lecture, Uncle. I've heard it from Emery *ad nauseum.*" She whirled around. "Last time he called me

into his office, I got the distinct feeling that my paper more
than intellectually irked him. It was visceral. I could see
something in his eyes, something he's been trying to keep
from me."

"And what was that, Sarah?"

She leaned in and whispered, "Fear."

Salsbury floated back from the edge of the hot tub, and
stunted a chuckle.

"What exactly is in that safety deposit box, Uncle?"

"I already told you, just a few key records, transactions—"

"If you don't tell me the whole truth now, how will I 'protect myself when you're gone?"

Salsbury's lips were so dry, despite the spray. *If this is
how she reacts to what she suspects, what will she do when
she learns the full truth?* He sighed. *I've raised her too
moral, too naïve.* "Sarah, first please understand that everything I've done for the last twenty years was for you . . ."

* * *

Sarah's hands covered most of her face—exposing only
wide, disbelieving eyes.

Salsbury floated to the back of his hot tub. "When you get
to be my age, and if you've learned a few things along the
way, you come to see truth not as a point of light, but as a
sphere, containing an infinite number of different, but
equally valid, interpretations."

"Sophistry! We're not talking about uncertainty measure-
ments in physics, or differential equations with an infinite
number of correct and incorrect solutions. We're talking
about lying—lying without even the courage to directly face
our victims." She shuddered. "What happened to you that you
could do this? That you could use me like this? I'm your
daughter, in practice if not in fact. How could you send me off
to carry out your obscene lie! Disregard every ethical princi-
ple, every shred of moral decency you ever taught me?"

"Sarah, child, if you could just put aside your disappoint-
ment for a moment, I could—"

"Stop it! You're manipulating me, even now!" She spun away and toward the game room.

Salsbury started to follow, but stopped, sank back into the jacuzzi, and turned his back to her. "Don't leave."

She halted at the doorway. "Uncle Theodore, I need to know before I ask this question that you will tell me the truth. I need you to swear it, on your word as my father."

"I swear it."

"Were you involved," she swallowed hard, "in Dr. Todd's death?"

Silence.

She sniffled. "Did you—murder him?"

He hesitated. "There was good reason. Too many events were irrevocably set in motion." The rain beat louder. "I was protecting you. I couldn't allow the blood on my hands to stain yours."

She rasped, "Who else has died to keep your—our secret?"

He was silent a long time. She repeated the question. Again. Again.

The rain pounded on the dome. He whispered, "One hundred and seventy-one people. I know this is a shock for you, child, but it—it was necessary to save tens of thousands— no, hundreds of thousands more."

"That planeload of people? Oh my God! Oh my God! Oh my . . ." She dashed out of the pool enclosure.

Salsbury sank back into the water, rested his head on the jacuzzi's edge, and contemplated the glass ceiling. A wave of exhaustion consumed him. His eyelids drooped, then closed. In the last three days, he'd barely slept as many hours. Sleep brought the screams of his victims, their faces, burning. It had all happened so fast. His preoccupation with Cruz's CD and its potential repercussions—it had blinded him. Knight had to be stopped, so he'd ordered him stopped—never dreaming they'd go so far.

"Forgive me, Uncle," Sarah said from behind him.

"Forgive you?" he asked. "I'm the one who—"

A black box splashed in the tub.

The water churned. Salsbury's limbs contorted. His fingers contracted. His jaw snapped shut, severing his tongue. His body shook ferociously. His heart fluttered, a bag of worms.

The circuit breaker to the game room cut off.

He lay floating face down in the tub, his arms lapping against the extension cord that reached from the game room to the portable television at the bottom of the jacuzzi. Sarah stood over him, her hands cupped, as if ready to sing in a choir.

The phone on the glass table rang.

Her eyes fixed on the body, she stumbled to the phone. "Oh, hello Dr. Emery," she answered flatly. "It's Novia, the little female resident you love to torture." After a moment, "No, he's not available. Not now. Not ever." She waited. "Because he's dead." She glided toward the tub. "Of course I'm certain. I killed him." Teetering on the edge, she disconnected the phone.

And jumped into the tub.

*What men usually ask for when they pray to God
is that two and two may not make four.*

—A PROVERB

MONDAY, FEBRUARY 7

THIRTY-ONE

The speakerphone's droning dial tone masked Scott's stunned silence. An automated feminine voice finally said: *If you'd like to make a call, please hang up and try again.*

Scott swatted the phone off the table. "Who else beside Salsbury would know where my kids are?"

"I don't know," Emery said. "Salsbury directed PTS covert activities."

"Who'll they call once they find out he's dead? Who's his replacement?"

Emery shrugged. "I suppose someone will be assigned. Whoever it is, it won't be me. I argued my way out of that inner loop."

"But you know who might be next."

"Haven't a clue."

Scott sat on the table and re-lit his cigar. "You don't seem upset about Salsbury's death."

"We were colleagues. We had mutual interests. But Salsbury was a kidnapper. A murderer," he said, looking deep into Scott's eyes. "I am not!"

"Maybe yes, maybe no. But up till now, you've been terrified that I'd set you on fire. Now you look like you're going to chant a mantra."

"Merritt, you're just not the type of person to kill an innocent man."

Scott turned the computer away from Emery, and started working the keypad. "How did you become a demagogue— or should I say, *demigod?* Did you know about the virus in the beginning, but the insidious promise of success kept drawing you in deeper? And you, finding yourself, your family, your career, everything that mattered to you staked on xenotransplantation—and slowly realizing that you were never going to get rid of the virus? Or, did you find out about it late in the process—too late to turn back—and desperately hope that your friends at PTS would find a solution—before you kill half the planet? Or are you a 'True Believer,' convinced of your infallibility as you fly in the face of scientific fact?"

"What a stupid, myopic man you are! We've found a way to save tens of thousands of lives every year! The thirty-year-old mother of three who would have been condemned to a horrible, lingering death, waiting hopelessly for her name to move up on the "magical list," where the only way to advance was at the cost of someone else's life. The lives we save every day—"

"Are balanced against the Russian roulette you play with the world!"

"Does that include the young man in India selling his kidney to support his family at the inevitable cost of his own life?" Emery spat. "Does that include the tsunami of people living longer and developing kidney disease, but being placed on a two-year waiting list they have little hope of surviving?"

"No, you self-righteous, holier-than-thou bastard!" Scott shot back. "The rest of humanity."

"We've been doing it for years. No one's been hurt. We're taking every precaution."

"While trampling across every line of ethics instituted since Hippocrates."

"Which I've never violated on any of my patients. The sinuous veins on Emery's necked swelled, tortuously bulged. "You, on the other hand, charged into xeno with the expressed purpose of destroying it. And why? Because you had a couple of bizarre dreams that'd keep a shrink busy for years! Don't bother denying it!"

"Who are you to take such risks? God?"

"I *was* God. When the phone rang in the middle of the night and I had to decide whether to accept a compromised liver that would probably fail for an eight-year-old girl—or hope a donor with a perfect organ to miraculously appear within the seventy-two hours she had left, I was God. Thank the real God that I'm not anymore! But you, you desk-bound paper-pusher, sitting in your little cubby hole writing reports—what the hell do you know about saving lives?"

"I was a surgeon," Scott declared. "I treated patients, same as you."

"You were a Goddamn orthopod! When your patients died, it was because you screwed up. When mine died, it was because some fucking bureaucrat placed them too low on an allocation list!" Emery glowered. "But now look at you. You're a nothing, a nobody!"

Scott threw an ashtray against the bookcase. "You forget, I'm the man holding the cigar."

"But you won't use it."

Scott slammed a fist into his palm. "You're probably right. But I will use *this*." He held up his index finger.

"Huh?"

He turned the laptop toward Emery. "I've uploaded your log to my mailbox. I lurk in dozens of medical forums. With a touch of this finger, your log will be posted on bulletin boards on every continent." Scott repressed a smile as Emery leaned forward and clutched his stomach. "Last chance, who would Salsbury have ordered to kidnap my children?"

"I don't know for sure," Emery rasped. "But my guess is Stone, Damara Stone, a vice president over at PTS. She's hell incarnate."

"And where? Answer me, or I'll transmit—"

"I don't know! I swear!"

"On second thought—" Scott worked the laptop's screen tracker. "Maybe I won't post it all over the planet. Just," glancing up, "at the FBI."

"You can't do that!"

Scott glanced up from the screen and took a big puff on the cigar.

"You don't know who you're dealing with! Threaten them, and they'll send people out for you in the middle of the night! You'll disappear. So will anyone who asks your whereabouts!"

If only he knew that I'd already sent it there. Scott looked down at the laptop screen.

All two hundred and sixty pounds of Emery crashed onto him.

Scott tumbled back. Slammed his head, his spine on the table. A fist smashed against his jaw. The cigar splattered. Another fist pounded his ear. Stunned, he rolled onto the floor. Emery flipped the table on him, jumped in the air in cannonball fashion, and landed with both feet, full force, on Scott's chest.

His breath exploded. A fist struck his right eye. He gasped for air. Emery's hands, thick and powerful, grasped his throat. Scott tried to cough—couldn't. The hands squeezed.

Darkness spun around him. Imaginary fireflies appeared, induced by his brain starved for oxygen. The load crushing his chest bobbed as the table swayed. His right hand, pinned beneath Emery, strained for the knife. Emery's curses, the pummeling, the fingers crushing his throat—all fading. Scott began to lose consciousness.

His left hand touched something small, plastic-smooth, cylindrical, with a metal edge. Instinctively, his fingers flipped it around.

Emery momentarily shifted his weight.

Scott's hand slipped free. Blind, he held up the object: a cigarette lighter. And flicked.

Emery screamed.

Scott felt that heavy body slip off his chest, roll onto the floor, and bang against the couch. Blindly holding up the flame, he hacked on the carpet, still feeling Emery's hands wrapped around his throat, still fighting for air.

Panting, propping himself on one elbow, Scott opened his eyes. The room slowly focused. The main shelving unit lay strewn across the floor, the laptop smashed. Emery was gone.

Scott struggled to stand. A blast of cold air greeted him. He heard sounds of pounding rain on the sunroom roof and patio beyond the open sliding glass door—and in the dark distance, the muffled churning of an engine. *The boat!*

He staggered onto the patio. Cold, driving rain hammered him. He stumbled to the slate path. Water filled his eyes, clouded his glasses.

The cabin cruiser, with Emery at the wheel, was pulling away from the dock. The gap was widening. Five feet, ten. Almost beyond reach. Scott churned harder. Arms pumping furiously, he hit the dock in full stride just as Emery glanced back over his shoulder. Concentrating all his force into the ball of his right foot, he propelled himself at the boat. His foot skid on the wet boards at take-off. He flew off balance, arms flailing.

And struck starboard aft, directly on the guardrail. Half of him hung precariously over the deck, half hung over the water. Emery throttled up. The cabin-cruiser lurched forward. Scott plunged, spine first, overboard.

Frigid water engulfed him. His body screamed from burning iciness. He burst to the surface, kicking bay water furiously to keep afloat, fighting off numbness beginning to seize hold. His foot snagged something slithery—a loop. He struggled. It tightened as he kicked. Shivering, he lay on his back and allowed his legs to float to the surface. As his right foot surfaced, he saw the boat's line knotted around his ankle.

Emery saw it, too.

The cabin cruiser took off, full throttle. Scott grappled with the knot as the coiled rope straightened—yanking his foot, wrenching his leg at the hip, propelling him backward. His head jerked violently against the back of his spine. At high speed, he skimmed beneath the surface of the icy bay. Surging water ripped his glasses from his face. Though his head skidded only six inches beneath the surface, he couldn't breathe. Couldn't lift his head. His arms waved wildly as he tried to pull his face out of the water—but there was nothing to grasp, nothing to fight the force driving his head back into the bay. He opened his eyes in the frigid water, glimpsing dark, turbulent channels his body created. Again, he began feeling that mind-numbing sensation of blackness.

The cruiser slowed, diminishing the force. Scott grabbed his leg with one arm and lifted his head out of the water. He held the line tight, gasping for air against spray and rain. Without his glasses, the world was a blurry, seamless union of sky and terrain.

A patch of darkness expanded in front of him. Rapidly.

Another pier! He only slowed down to steer me into the pilings!

Scott drove his fingers into the knot's core, and pulled. Two fingernails tore. He realigned his bloody fingers and tried again. The knot weakened, slipping off his foot. Momentum carried his body another thirty yards, the turbulence of his wake slowing him. Legs numbing, he could barely kick enough to keep afloat. He couldn't see the cruiser, but he heard its engines growing faint. Fainter.

The motors roared back. They were bearing down on him—fast. *He's circling back!*

A loud pop echoed across the sky. A bright, sizzling projectile whizzed by his head, and struck the water behind him, illuminating the dark before the bay swallowed it. *A flare gun!*

Scott dove beneath the surface. Frantic, he churned through absolute darkness, away from the engines. The cold drained his strength, weakened his breaths.

His arm banged something round, hard, slippery. He surfaced and found himself beneath another unlit pier. The only sound was of rain pelting the boards above him. *He's cut the engines.*

Scott tried holding onto a piling, but slipped and fell back into the water with a gentle splash. A searchlight swung around, and fixed on him.

A shrieking whistle cut through the air. The dock exploded.

A jagged board slammed onto his back, driving him beneath the lit surface bubbling with heat. He dove deeper, propelling himself with exhausted legs. Instead of resisting his strokes, the deep water slowly began dragging him away from the fire. Faster, further from shore. A minute. Two minutes. His body craved air, burned for it. Regardless of Emery, he had to surface. He fought the current to reach the surface, but it dragged him down, stealing his breath. He felt lightheaded. Then content, almost jovial.

The darkness dissipated, transforming into aqua blue. The water warmed. Sunlight filtered through the surface. He was in a pool, alone with the children. In her green and gold suit, Brooke swam on the surface using her self-styled free stroke. Andrew, in navy blue trunks, doggie-paddled behind her. They called his name.

Can we play battleship and submarine, Daddy? Brooke asked.

You be the submarine! We'll be the battleships! Andrew said.

Yeah! Come on, Dad! Get us! they called from overhead.

Scott held his arms to his sides, tilted his body up, and kicked. At ramming speed, he shot out like a torpedo fired from a submerged sub. He was almost upon them.

He broke the water's surface. Rain pelted his face.

Eyes closed, barely able to hold his head above the surface, he seized another breath, knowing it was probably his last. He felt Emery standing over him. Resigned, he opened his eyes.

In the distance was a tiny blotch of light, the only perceptible light in his indistinguishable blurred world. *He's lost me*.

Sluggishly, Scott paddled away from that light. He didn't know whether he was heading to another shore or out to sea, only that he was exhausted—and could no longer feel his legs.

The Four Seasons Hotel at Georgetown
Washington, D.C.

From her suite balcony, Hope stared at the Potomac, the lights from Virginia reflecting on the choppy surface of the river, the sleet like a gentle swarm of fireflies. Warm hands wrapped around her inconsolable shoulders.

"You've barely spoken since you returned from Aruba," Alexander said. "At our age, life is supposed to get simpler, not more complicated. Let it go."

"Can't. The client—he won't let me go."

"'When you spend enough time with a lion, roaring makes sense.' Old Russian proverb."

Hope slowly turned toward him. "How—"

"Did you really think I wouldn't know about Slatokhatov? Multi-billion dollar investors draw attention, no matter how much insulation they use."

"Why didn't you stop me?"

"If you'd needed my help, you'd have asked." He wrapped both arms around her waist. She started to sob. "You still can."

FBI, Philadelphia Office

Terrill stormed down the hallway, his phone pressed against his ear. "Julian, get your oversized tush down to Henrico County Correctional Facility, Woman's Division, outside of Richmond, Virginia."

"What's up?" returned Agent Cicero's groggy voice.

"One doctor, Sarah Novia, confessed to electrocuting

Theodore Salsbury, MD, a board member of the transplant institute. She says that she has information pertaining to 841."

"On my way." Click.

Upon reaching his office, Terrill headed straight for the bathroom, turned on the cold water, and splashed his face, trying to wash away his fatigue. Six hours sleep in three days—just barely enough to keep him functional. As he closed his bathroom door, his office proper was just as he'd left it: lit only by the mist-shrouded ambient skyline and his computer monitor. But his chair now faced the window, instead of the desk. And a hand, protruded from behind the back of the chair. Terrill drew his gun. "Hands up! Palms out!"

"Nice view you have here, but all things considered, I'd rather *not* be in Philadelphia." The voice was deep, blending broad New England and nasal-stumped mid-Atlantic *a*'s.

"Turn around, slowly. Stay seated and keep your hands in the air!" The man leisurely swiveled the chair about. Though the monitor light bathed the man in sickly gray, accentuating a furrowed face with sunken eyes and thin, cracked lips, his body exuding power, more like the gentle swift graciousness from Aikido rather than the intricate savageness from boxing. "Everett?"

The man placed his hands on the armrests. "I always liked that name. You know it means 'strong as a boat.' I suppose I should go back to using it."

Terrill lowered the gun, but kept it in ready position. "How did you get in here?"

"Tisk-tisk. *You* should be answering that question, not me."

"I'll thank you to get out of my chair."

Everett put one hand behind his neck and stretched. "You invited me, remember?"

"I asked for information, not a visit. Now get out of my chair."

Folding his hands in front of his chest, "Tactics, George. Your comfortable chair here is positioned beside the window, behind your desk, with the only way out, right where you're standing. You have the advantage. Only a fool exchanges high ground for ego."

"Amateurs speak in terms of tactics. Professionals, in terms of logistics."

"Schwartzkopf, I believe." Grinning, "It's been five years. I thought you'd forgotten me."

"Everett, it'd take a lifetime to forget you."

"Surely there's more left of our relationship than verbal parrying?"

"There is." Terrill sat in a chair across from his desk. "The debts you owe me."

"There's more than one?"

"I took a bullet for you in Idaho when you were ATF, and deflected the inquiry so you could go on to your nice career as a mid-level spook in some surreptitious agency under Homeland."

"Make that *upper* mid-level spook." He shook his head. "You know George, I remember one summer I was walking along a two-lane road near a creek by a small patch of undeveloped land. As I rounded a bend in the road, I noticed a groundhog sitting in the middle of the road. Cars are racing by him, and he's just sitting there with this dull, glazed stare. So I went over and lifted him out of the road as best as I could without getting bitten, and deposited him into the woods just a few yards away. The poor thing's back legs were broken. I thought he might make it back to his hole if he was strong, or die in peace if he wasn't. When I went back the next day, he was gone. I was very pleased with myself."

"Such a good soul. What does this have—"

"Four days later I found that same groundhog on the road shoulder, just a few yards up from where I'd moved it. Flies covering the open wounds around his broken legs, his body quaking, he lifted his head and stared at me. Just—stared at me." Everett exhaled. "The pain, the torment, and—yes I know it's anthropomorphic—but the blame in those eyes."

"So what did you do?"

"Picked up a rock and put it out of its misery." Gazed at Terrill with featureless eyes, "I would argue that *not* helping you constitutes payment in full."

"You don't get off that easy. Did you get the photos I e-mailed?"

"The shadow in New York? Yes."

"Who is he?"

Everett cracked his knuckles. "The Defenders of the Islamic Peoples is behind the bombing, or so I hear. Maybe the man in the video is one of them."

"More likely he's the tooth fairy."

Everett snickered. "That contradicts the thinking of your superiors—on both accounts."

"The man in the shadows is more militia than militant. He camouflages, he doesn't wear it."

Everett chuckled. "You could have gone a lot farther than this," gazing around the office, "if—never mind. You're right, the higher-ups are trying to figure out how to gracefully back-off the terrorism card considering how easily they fell for it. By the way, how'd you know?"

"The blast that brought down 841 wasn't a fertilizer bomb mixed in a garage. Or a plastique derivative sitting on the fuel tank. Or a suicide bomber with crude explosives and nails packed around his chest. It was very high-yield explosive, both concentrated and focused with pinpoint precision. Now, if the next statement out of your mouth is a lie, I'll—"

"Let you in on a secret, George. Save your lab some work. The explosive was cubane."

"Not familiar with it."

"Nasty stuff developed by Armaments Research, Development, and Engineering Center at Picatinny Arsenal in Jersey, Army Materiel Command and the More Explosive Program people. Cubane's a cube-shaped, man-made molecular explosive. Fully attachable to other substances to enhance explosives, better fuels. You know they actually toyed with using it as a mini-explosive injected into cancer tumors? Medical wonders never cease—which might explain why it's a reasonably well-kept secret."

"Stolen? Manufactured?"

"Ask the man who's picture you sent me."

Terrill recalled the image of the man in the shadows beside Barbieri. "Who is he?"

"*Krysha.*"

"You got a full name?"

Everett smirked. "Krysha isn't a name. It's Russian for 'roof.'"

"What are you talking about?"

"You're in the dark. I can remedy that."

"In the past, you've been less than forthright."

"Each of us has information the other wants. You just don't know what you have."

Terrill crossed his legs. "What are you offering?"

Everett nodded to himself. "*Krysha* is Russian mafia jargon. During Cold War days, *krysha* was a Soviet term for setting up cover for their foreign agents. Today, it's protection—you can't do business in Russia without crime lords taking their cut. *Krysha* is hired muscle enforcing their extortion. It could be anything—a cheap hit man on the streets of St. Petersburg, militsiya and corrupt bureaucrats, high-tech analytical groups, elite assassins. This guy's particularly nasty."

"Are you saying that the Russian mob bombed that plane?"

"Tell me what you suspect."

Terrill related much, but not all, of what he knew about Merritt, IRACT's involvement, and the connection to Paradigm.

Everett nonchalantly waved his hand. "We know all that. That Institute's been scamming the medical community for years."

"And you let them?"

"It's not that simple."

"It never is with you people," Terrill snapped, taking his chair away from Everett. "The Russian connection?"

"Pavel Slatokhatov, a top boss in Russian organized crime. We don't know his exact ante, but it must be in excess of $5 billion. Presumably with some of his comrades."

Terrill raised his eyebrows. "So she cooked the books—"

"It started out legitimate enough. The Russians invest everything abroad cause the ruble's so weak and their financial system so porous. Hope Wheelan was very bullish on xenotransplantation. She used her husband's funds as a platform to bankroll Paradigm Transplants, which developed very profitable products even before its foray into animal transplantation. She needed major investors." He shrugged. "She wasn't very choosy."

"The Wheelans are billionaires themselves. Why risk working with blood money?"

Everett snorted. "Who knows how the rich think? They'd have to eat money if the rest of us didn't provide the food. Anyway, she only began creative bookkeeping—and I don't mean embezzling—when she discovered that everything was in danger of spiraling down the toilet. You've got to hand it to her, she's pulled it off flawlessly for years—until Merritt and his hacker friend whose remains are spread all over an oil refinery."

Terrill slammed his fist on the table. "Goddamn it, answer the question already! Why?"

"Easy, easy," Everett said, holding up his hands in mock defense. "At one time, the Russian crime lords, the oligarchs, had fully insinuated themselves within the Russian government, smuggling oil, coal, gas, tin, you-name-it, through their contacts and selling it in the global market below established price levels. It made them multi-billionaires. They used the entire Russian financial system as their personal money launderer, and in so doing, decimated the Russian economy. Our biggest worry used to be that the whole

Russian Federation would turn into a full-blown crime syndicate, controlling a quarter billion people, one-sixth of the world's surface, and an unstable, aging nuclear arsenal still large enough to destroy us ten times over. Ah, I miss the good old days." Gazing out the window, "You know what you get when crime goes down in Russia?"

"Freedom? A stable economy?"

"Always the boy scout! No George, you get Islamic extremists dedicated to destroying us with that aging nuclear arsenal." Pointing a finger at the FBI agent, "You can help stop them." He smiled as Terrill folded his arms. "Yes, you. I know you've come into possession of the *Kompromat* file. Forget that you've seen it. Give me all your copies, and I'll arrange for you to land a fish so big they'll promote you to assistant director, no questions asked."

Terrill reflected on the file's contents: a dizzying database of account numbers and records. "Now it's beginning to make sense. Accounts, transactions, passwords, names, contacts—key information threatening their global operations. That's why you sat back and let Wheelan, Slatokhatov, and IRACT operate with impunity. You bastard, the CDC would—"

"We've never been able to get anybody close to the top of the Russian hierarchy. Then this rich broad from White Plains drops in out of the sky and unwittingly becomes our in. We've been very patient. And finally, finally, she gives us this real opportunity to manipulate them, and hold off the separatists. Buy ourselves a little time."

"Paid for with innocent American blood."

"We didn't know about 841 until after the fact."

"That's not what I'm talking about."

"This is a matter of national security. Now Goddamn it, give me that file!"

Terrill stared at his old comrade. "You still haven't given *me* what I asked for."

Everett handed him a shiny beige mini-CD. "Krysha is his generic alias. His formal education was at Cambridge, prior to learning at the feet of former KGB masters. He's fluent in five languages and is rated expert in explosives, weapons, hand-to-hand, and aircraft maintenance and operations."

Terrill stepped around the desk, inserted the mini-CD into his computer's drive, and checked the dossier. "Thank you."

"You won't be thanking me if you see him coming. Because if you do, it'll be too late." He tapped the desk. "And now, *my* file."

"I'll—consider it."

"Getting rid of the bad guys? Your promotion? National security? What's to consider?" He started to leave. "George, don't wait *too* long."

Terrill waited until Everett reached the door. "It occurs to me that there might be a secondary objective to all of this."

Everett stopped. "Whatever do you mean?"

Terrill patted his fingertips. "PTS and that institute are both covering up the existence of a virus that could cause a plague. Could it be that you're letting them, so that one day you can weaponize it, off the books of course?"

"What a waste," he whispered, glancing around Terrill's office. "The file, six hours. No longer."

"Or else?"

Everett hesitated before touching the doorknob. "Don't count on who I was." He shook his head, "Because in the end, old friend, you become what you kill."

THIRTY-TWO

"Andy, no!"

Scott awoke. He wiped a hand across his face. The dream had been too vivid.

The rain had stopped, but his damp clothes clung to him. An icy wind blew across the water, stinging his skin, his shaven head. His world was the bluish-brown water, the blur of the greenish-brown ground, and a shiny blue plastic covering him—a tarp? He remembered last night: the long, desperate swim; the struggle to shore; the tarp he'd found and used as shield against the rain. *Where are my glasses?*

His hands skimmed across the frozen ground. He expanded his search, crawling circularly in a ten-foot radius around the tarp. A twenty-five-foot radius. Still no glasses.

He remembered: they'd been ripped from his face when Emery dragged him through the bay. Glasses and contacts had always been a part of him, from the minute he'd awake to the instant he'd fall asleep. But there, on his hands and knees, he was blind, alone, lost.

He gently patted his pockets. The walkie-talkie/wireless phone was still there, thank God. Gingerly, he took it out of his coat pocket and lightly depressed the one-touch walkie-talkie button.

The back of the phone dropped to the ground. And shattered.

Scott pounded the ground in frustration. *The noon deadline! And all I have is a name!*

He looked up and in the distance saw a white blur. *A house?* He started running away from the bay. The uneven, frozen ground fooled his numb feet. He tripped on hidden holes and bumps. Cold air, pumped through his lungs, stole his strength. As he approached, he detected brown blurs covering windows along its sides. He reached the house—it was boarded up, useless.

Trying to catch his breath, he found himself standing on a gravel path. He scanned the horizon. Except for the house, he saw no differently colored blur patches disrupting the smeared union of overcast sky and land. Barely feeling his feet, he ran down the path. He fell, cutting open his cheek, re-aggravating his ankle.

After several hundred yards, the path emptied into a narrow, black macadam road with smudged, staccato yellow lines. He saw no traffic, no signs, no way to judge whether to proceed left or right. His instincts directed him left. He started out with a hobbled sprint. As the road wound inexorably through deserted terrain, his pace deteriorated. His feet struck the ground like dead weights. The narrow road dumped into a wider artery. Exhausted, he crouched, hands on knees, and saw what appeared to be a road sign. He dashed toward it, nearly banging into the pole before he could read the sign: *MD Route 33.*

He gazed down the highway. A tiny blotch appeared on the horizon. *A car!*

He stuck out his right thumb as the sounds of its engine grew louder. Louder, louder, the pitch dropped suddenly.

The car zipped by him. Silently, he turned to his right and stumbled along the shoulder of the road.

He held out his thumb. Another car, a speeding stationwagon—whizzed by him.

I haven't time for this!

A blur, larger than the others, appeared on the horizon. Scott stepped into the middle of the highway and held out his right hand like a maniacal New Jersey state trooper he'd once seen pull stunned motorists off the turnpike. The deep, resonant horn of a tractor-trailer sounded, its short bursts growing progressively longer, merging into one increasingly high-pitched blare. Scott could not see when the truck passed the point of no return.

The truck shrieked. Slammed on its brakes. He felt the road shudder. The squealing crescendo sliced through his ears like fingernails on sheet metal.

The squealing stopped. Hot, oily air wafted wafted through the air, burning his nostrils. The cab's grillwork and headlights stood inches from his head.

"The fuck's the matter with you?" screamed someone far above and behind the hood.

He looked up at a blurred face protruding from the driver's side window. "Please, take me to the nearest gas station? Just any place there's a phone!"

"You fuckin' blind? There's one right *there!*"

Scott turned around and squinted at a colored blur just above the horizon. *A sign?*

"Now get out of my way or I'll fuckin' run you over!"

He ran down the road. The truck was long gone by the time he stumbled into Whitman's Market and Service Station. The public phone was in a corner of the small parking area. Scott was certain what to do for the first phone call. Over that he had, at least, some modicum of control. Not so for the second.

IRACT   9:47 A.M.

Stone barged through the steel doors outside of the IT department, disregarding the teckkies' anxious stares to either side of her, took the last few strides to the conference room door, punched the code, and slipped in just before it shut behind her. Barbieri, already seated in the blue windowless room, greeted her with "Salsbury is dead."

"I heard," she monotoned, dropping into chairs across the table from his.

"It's hard to believe Theo's gone. And by Novia, no less! I heard she tried to commit suicide by jumping into the water after him, but the dumb bunny didn't realized that the circuitbreaker had already gone off." Barbieri slowly grinned. "Damara, I hear you have experience in these matters. What do you think made her snap?"

Stone's hands clutched the arms of her chair and prepared to pounce. *Is that old bastard saying what I think he is? He wouldn't dare!* She glared at him. "I'll send someone down after tomorrow's hearing to find out and close the matter, permanently."

"So who's next in line?"

"That's not your concern," she snapped, looking at her watch.

"The noon deadline's almost here and Merritt still hasn't called."

Stone's eyes bulged. "How do you know?"

"Merritt visited Emery last night at Paradigm's guest house on the Chesapeake." Barbieri winked. "He fooled you, Damara."

She shook her head. "Emery must have told you. Did Merritt tell him where the CD—"

"No, and that's going to be a little difficult to find out, now," Barbieri clucked. "Emery killed him. Ran him over with his boat." Snickering, "Technically, you being a corporate officer, it was *your* boat."

"You have the body?"

Barbieri put his feet up on the table. "No, but it's a big bay. Chances are it'll never be recovered. And even if it is, ever seen a body that's been in the water for weeks?

"Then you can't be certain—"

"In water that cold, the nervous system shuts down in minutes. There's not a chance in hell he survived."

She tapped emphatically on the table. "Again, what about the CD?"

He shrugged. "A bluff. If he really had one, he'd've forced us to make the next move. But just to calm your paranoid heart, I'll have our contact at Verity look into it."

"Where's Emery now?"

"Carl was a wreck. I advised him to return to Cleveland."

"But he's supposed to testify tomorrow."

"He faxed me his text. I'll read it myself." Seeing her objection, "Trust me, Damara, you don't want him sitting in front of that committee tomorrow."

Stone released a long, soothing sigh. "Finally, I can unload those brats." A knock at the door. "Come."

Foster entered just as Stone's beeper sounded its distinctive staccato squeal.

"I'll let voicemail pick that up. This will only take a minute," she said.

Foster stood at attention by the door with his clipboard. "There've been no unauthorized entries in the past forty-eight hours. And we've been through every byte of untransformed files and AIMS. Would you like us to archive and purge now?"

"No. Our problem is solved," she replied. "Keep everything status quo till five P.M. Then, lock down EDI until ten A.M. tomorrow for the subcommittee hearing when either Dr. Barbieri or I call in. At that time, you can also open up web access. That's all."

Foster left. Stone swiveled in her chair, picked up the phone to check her voicemail. Her back to Barbieri she punched in her extension and her PIN. Watching smug, self-assured Barbieri sitting back, his heels digging into the conference table's polished surface, her hand began involuntarily clutching the receiver, her knuckles whitening as she listened. Slowly, she put down the phone, stood, and ominously approached him.

"What's the matter now?" he asked, his eyes shifting from hers.

"Merritt is alive," she whispered, lingering on each syllable. "And now, he knows *I* am involved."

Barbieri answered haltingly, "With the way you've handled things thus far—"

"He also has the *Kompromat* file! How could such a thing have happened, Eddie?"

Barbieri gazed at his lap. "I don't know what you're talking about."

Her voice barely audible, "What did you do, get Foster to decrypt it, then forget to restore the encryption when you were done?" She slapped his legs off the conference table. Her hands formed knife edges.

"Stop!" His voice had an unexpectedly powerful deep resonance that Stone involuntarily obeyed. "It's your fault for leaving the file on the system. And by taking custody of it in the first place, you've allied yourself with Hope Wheelan against the Investors. That was a mistake." He smirked. "And unless you're very careful from here on in, you won't have the opportunity to make another, *comrade!*"

Emery's Office, Norlake Hospital   10.48 A.M.

Buried in his high wingback chair, Emery stared out his office's great window to Lake Michigan. Cold sunlight glimmering on its choppy waters slowly turned to moonlight. He found himself back on the Chesapeake, the vibrations of the cabin-cruiser beneath him, Merritt dangling from the cruiser's line trailing in the bay, the body driven back beneath the water's surface.

Emery shut his eyes, trying to forget. Yes Merritt was ignorant, narrow-minded, and dangerous. And yes, the man had to be stopped so that thousands of innocents might live. But to willingly kill a human being, much less a brethren healer? The rage that had driven him last night had dissipated, leaving him drained. He looked down at his hands, shaking. *What have I become?*

"Carl, I didn't expect you here," a deep voice sounded from across the room. "Weren't you going to testify on Capitol Hill through the early part of next week."

Emery swiveled in his chair: Charles Nickelson, Norlake Hospital's President, stood on the other side of the desk, a thick, legal-size folder in his hands. "I, uh, it was decided—change of plan." Focusing on the envelope, "Is that it?"

Nickelson placed the folder on the desk. "Your agreement on clinic autonomy. I had legal work on it 'round the clock. I think you'll find it to your liking."

Emery nodded, swiveled away, and closed his eyes to the lake.

"Aren't you going to at least look at it?"

He clamped his trembling hands. "Some other time."

Still facing the back of Emery's chair, Nickelson put his palms on the great desk and leaned forward. "I was going to call you, but now that you're here—. We've learned that the nurses, *your clinic* nurses, are going to stage a sick-out. Beginning tomorrow morning. How would you like to handle it?"

Emery shrugged. "It's your hospital."

Nickelson thumped the folder. "You just demanded and received autonomy for your clinic."

"Do as you see fit."

"This is *your* clinic staff."

After a protracted exhale, "I can't—don't want to deal with this—now."

Nickelson stepped around the desk and spun the chair around until Emery faced him. "What the hell is wrong with you? We only—"

"Not now!" Emery barked, leaping out of his chair. His full bulk towered ominously over Norlake's administrator.

Nickelson glanced down at the folder. "Until you sign, this hospital remains mine. All of it!" He slammed the door behind him.

Emery swiveled back toward the lake. *I deliberately killed another human being!*

His pager beeped. He checked the number, shook his head, and then dialed Dr. Valsamis' extension. "Michael, tell me you have good news."

His chief clinic pathologist hesitated before answering. "This call is coming from your office extension. Are you—"

"I took the red-eye back. The results on Forman?"

"I ran the DNA probes again on separate sealed samples." Valsamis hesitated. "There is no doubt. She contracted the same PERV-Hanoi Flu mutation as patient Folcroft."

Emery massaged his temples. "Did Forman have any compromising medical condition that could have rendered her so susceptible?"

"Nothing in her history. Nothing on the examination table."

"So what you're telling me is that this virus killed a young perfectly healthy woman in less than three days?"

"Closer to two."

Emery smashed his right fist against the armrest. "Transmission?"

"The nurse had a cut on her hand. She probably contracted it from direct contact with your patient's wound or dressing. That might also account for the massive serum viral load I found during the autopsy."

"So the virus is passed by direct contact with infected blood or wound exudate. What about the bodies?"

"Don't appear to be contagious once the host is dead."

Emery whipped perspiration from his forehead. "We were damned lucky."

"I wouldn't say that." Valsamis' voice dropped an octave. "I wouldn't say that at all. I've checked both Institute and PTS databases. This new mutation isn't like any ever before seen."

Emery's mouth grew dry. His pulse pounded in his ears. "Go ahead, Michael. And keep in mind I'm a surgeon, not a virologist."

Valsamis let out a deep breath. "Type A influenza viruses, like the Hanoi Flu, have a lipid shell coated with spike-like proteins. This envelope surrounds eight single-strand RNA segments which code for the virus' structural proteins. It's these surface spikes—and there's fifteen different types—on the flu envelope that react with the human immune system. Hanoi flu was type seven."

"What do you mean *was?*" Emery blurted. "That doesn't change!"

"Unless you add in a wildcard—an undiscovered PERV," Valsamis snapped. "Now we have a completely new type of envelope on a flu virus that the human immune system isn't going to easily recognize. This is a full fledged antigenic shift—a sudden appearance of a new type of influenza that has characteristics distinctly different from the original, potentially with deadly retrovirus capabilities that are, in this case, at least as ominous as HIV. Add in any number of point mutations on the RNA code, and you have an extremely adaptable, highly virulent, constantly mutating, wide host-range capable virus with vast endemic potential."

It can't be this bad! He's overstating the case!

"I know what you're thinking, Carl," the pathologist started. "And I'd be thinking that way too if I didn't know better. But trust me, if this gets out in the open environment, it won't kill everybody, but it will solve the global population crisis for the next hundred years."

Emery hissed through his teeth. "If that's true, then why haven't you already reported it to CDC?"

"Because we still have it contained, as long as the corpses are properly disposed of," Valsamis said. "And because if this synergistic PERV-DS-Hanoi Flu virus mutation goes airborne, then CDC might as well quarantine the country for all the good it will do them."

"But that's very unlikely, right? Right?"

The pathologist said slowly, "Carl, *Bubonic* plague, caused by *Yersinia pestis*, was originally spread by blood-borne transmission—fleas preying on rodents and eventually, people. However, some of the infected developed lung fluid filled with the organism which they spread by coughing. That generated *Pneumonic* plague, which was airborne, and nearly one hundred percent fatal. I took three sputum samples from the nurse's lungs. Each was loaded with the variant virus."

Emery, feeling a little whoozy, tightly pinched his neck. The pain cleared his mind. "Michael, thanks for the worst case scenario, but honestly, equating a gram-negative bacteria with a virus like this? That's quite a stretch. PERVs are retroviruses. Retroviruses are transmitted through contact with infected blood or bodily fluids, not through the air."

"But influenza is. So was Hanoi flu. Now that it's combined with PERV-DS, this new virulent mutation could be, too. If it is—"

Duffey Farmhouse   11:31 A.M.

Stone slammed the pocket recorder on the kitchen table and pressed the 'play' button: *Stone, it's Merritt. Surprised? I have the CD—and the Kompromat file. So now, you've got to come to me. You've got to deal directly with me—6:00 P.M. Washington Grand Hyatt, between the Mall and Convention Center. Main lobby. Just you, me, and my kids. Or else—*

She turned off the tape. "Apparently Emery—"

"One wonders, however, how Merritt came to know such things, and with you in charge of security." Krysha paused. "The existence alone of such a file is extremely distressing to my client."

Stone evaluated Krysha's probing expression. The face seemed different than the one she'd seen a few days ago: the hair thinner, less wavy; the face rounder; and the nose, more bulbous. "You're absolutely correct. It is my responsibility."

"The crux, Dr. Stone, is what you intend to do *now*."

"Meet Merritt where he asks and give up one child without a struggle. That will lull him into believing that if he cooperates, he'll get them both."

"He might not be the only one involved."

She rewound the tape, fast-forwarded it, and looped it

twice at: . . . *you've got to come to me. You've got to deal directly with me* . . . "Listen to that voice. 'Me, me, me,' " she said. "The only one he'll ever trust is himself."

"It could be a trap."

"Which is why I'll need you to follow those two yahoos in the other room. You're my backup."

"Have you cleared your plan of action with Salsbury's replacement?"

"No, his replacement hasn't called in yet."

"That one's afraid of soiled hands." Krysha crossed his arms. "What exactly is your plan of action?" He listened attentively as she spoke. After she finished, "It will have to do. However, I can improve your chances." He dangled a black key ring in front of her nose. "This is a sequence encoded, multi-channel programmable transmitter."

"Transmitter for what?"

Norlake Xenotransplant Center   2.15 P.M.

The usual swagger in Emery's gait was noticeably missing as he proceeded through the clinic with residents Collins and Putenkin firmly in tow. Aside from the sounds of monitors and equipment, the place was remarkably quiet. Only three nurses were on duty, less than one-fifth of the usual contingent, and those few handled their tasks with an invoked silence. After reviewing the charts, Emery found that nearly forty percent more of the patients had signs of systemic infection than normal. Little Brenda McCarthy had also slipped into a deep coma.

Emery had spent most of his waking hours within his clinic's confines, in tune with its frenetic pulse. His clinic was a living entity, strong, vibrant, a champion perpetually combating premature death. But now, he felt it exuding weakness, fatigue, loss of hope—like a patient succumbing to a long, grinding disease. Still shaking from his ordeal at the bay, Emery did not know whether that feeling emanated from the clinic itself, under attack from the deadly hybrid virus, or originated in his mind, fearful that it might happen.

With residents Collins and Putenkin shadowing him, he strode up to Nurse Yancy. Her chin was propped on her head, her body lackadaisically slumped in a chair by monitors inset at one end of the central nursing station. "Yancy, I thought your fellow Florence Nightingales were starting their sick-out tomorrow!"

Yancy gazed up with bleary eyes. "They *are* sick."

"I'm supposed to believe that?"

She slurred, "As of right now, I don't give a Goddamn what you believe, *sir.*"

"Sit up straight! Get your chin off your hand! While you're here, you are a health professional and I'll thank you to act accordingly!" Emery waited for a respectful response. None came. "Tell the others they can't intimidate me. This clinic was here before any of you and it'll be here long after you're gone."

"Duly noted," Yancy monotoned.

Emery tightly crossed his arms. "You're a disgrace. All of you—a disgrace to your profession! Have you seen the postop infection rate? Do you know how high it is?"

After several protracted breaths, "Of course, you egotistical asshole! I knew about the rising infection rate while you were gallivanting off," taking another breath, "wherever the hell you—" She burped. "You've got something nasty floating around here."

"Now? You're telling me this *now?* You knew about this and didn't—"

"Shut your trap! I told tweedle-dee and tweedle-dum over there!" Yancy rasped, glancing at the residents and then massaged her eyes.

Emery turned on Collins and Putenkin.

"That's not true!" Collins protested.

"Check my notes," Yancy offered. She put her head between her legs.

Emery glared at Putenkin who immediately looked to Collins. The Russian resident nodded, barely. "Dr. Emery, we did not want to disturb you until we were certain."

"You're both finished here!" Emery yelled. "And Putenkin, you can tell Slatakov or whatever the hell your Russian uncle's name is—that he can go fuck himself!"

Yancy vomited.

Collins and Putenkin recoiled. Emery reached for her.

She vomited again. Violently. The effluvium on the floor was bloody.

Emery reached down and touched her forehead. "She's burning up! You two get her into isolation!"

Hurriedly, they collared an orderly, lifted Yancy onto a gurney, and rushed her down the hallway. Emery turned away, picked up a desk phone and punched in his pathologist's extension.

Baltimore-Washington Parkway, Southbound   3:02 P.M.

Stone's car sped south on the BW Parkway. Shards of sunlight broke through barren trees, a strobe-like staccato dancing across her eyes. Her head pounded. She coughed, deep and throaty. Cold air rushed along the back of her neck. It felt so strange having her long flowing hair tucked beneath her wig. She could feel cold air rush along the back of her neck as her car sped past a brown sign announcing the National Cryptologic Museum: only twenty-five miles to Washington. Her cellphone rang.

"Yes?" she answered. A tenuous, hushed voice responded. "I've been expecting your call." She rolled her eyes. "I understand your predicament and—" She grimaced. "Yes, but Salsbury's dead and, like it or not, Wheelan put you in charge." Her face contorted as she listened. "I understand your reluctance." The voice grew louder, panicked. "Perhaps you'd prefer giving me control over this matter?" Half a mile later, she smiled. "I think we can both live with that. What?" She looked in the rearview mirror: just coming over the top of a hill was the rest of her caravan. She shook her head. "Of course I've thought of that contingency. I think you'll feel better once I brief you."

In Transit   4:40 P.M.

Terrill hated helicopters: they were noisy, erratic, and most of all, vulnerable. True flying machines required wings, as nature had intended. As he surveyed the hills below, the vibration from the overhead rotor intruded on his thoughts, forcing him to concentrate harder.

His phone trilled. "It's about time, Julian," he answered. "What have you got?" He listened, trying to filter out the repetitive chopping whine of the overhead rotors. After ten miles, he said, "Did Novia mention the name Slatokhatov?"

"Negative," Agent Cicero said. "But she insists that Salsbury kept records in a safety deposit box at Henrico-James National. Those records might."

"I want the contents of that box."

"The bank closes in a couple minutes, and the vault's time-locked. I won't be able to get the order before it's sealed for the night. We'll have to wait till tomorrow."

"Put eyes on the bank. I don't want that box walking." Terrill disconnected.

He reflected back on Merritt's comments on Mongol tactics. With a little online reading from the Combined Arms Research Library, Terrill learned that the tactic was essentially a modified Cannae, named for the site of Hannibal's victory over the Roman Empire. A Cannae meant outflanking the enemy, preferably from two or three sides, in order to ultimate encircle and entrap it—one of warfare's most celebrated and difficult maneuvers. Executing a Cannae demanded more than exact knowledge of the enemy's location, strength, and maneuverability. It called for sacrifice by a frontal assault by one column on the enemy while neighboring columns marched silently beyond the enemy so that they could turn back against the enemy's flank and rear. But no matter how well planned, closing the circle to entrap the enemy was no certainty. And a failed Cannae meant disaster.

His wireless rang again four times before he noticed. "Go."

"Agent March here. We unscrambled something a few minutes ago from a tap on a previously inactive line."

"Merritt's?" Terrill asked.

"No, another line. One that's been inactive till now."

"Well, what've you got?"

The agent hesitated before answering. "Sir, I think it would be best if you hear this—straight from the source."

THIRTY-THREE

Grand Hyatt Hotel
H Street, Northwest
Washington, D.C.   5.35 P.M.

The wind whipped down the avenue between the Washington
Convention Center and the Grand Hyatt. Scott wrapped the
remnants of his tattered, frozen suit jacket around his neck.
Heat waves, rising from his exposed scalp, quickly dissipated. He looked up from the pavement and, without glasses,
tried to squint into focus the letters carved into the ornate
portico. *This has to be it.* Near blind, he could still feel the
doorman's condescending glare as he stumbled through the
hotel's glass and brass automatic revolving doors.

He entered a warm, brightly lit atrium. Silk trees centered
within aqua, circular, satiny-pillow benches lined the walkway to a white iron railing that overlooked a jigsaw fash-
ioned fountain. To his near right was a pink-script neon sign
at the entrance to a posh delicatessen. To his near left, a
square, dark mahogany bar set beneath a canopy of glasses
and goblets attracted patrons during happy hour. A marble

counter beneath platinum block lettering adjoining private offices stretched a quarter of the length of the courtyard's left side. *Claire de Lune* wafted through the air against the backdrop of guests' conversations. He shuffled to the railing and looked down at the restaurant, its tables nestled among fake trees. A pianist sat playing at a white baby grand on a circular island in a fountain filled with wishers' coins. Beneath the atrium's glass ceiling, guest room windows and cerulean and cream walkways overlooked the courtyard.

For Scott, it was all blurred: shapes and colors passed by him. A man in a business suit, a bellboy, a security guard—he felt disapproving eyes glare at him from walking blurs that slowly approached, then abruptly turned away, whispering.

He smelled a familiar scent—deep, primal, feminine. The same one as at the restaurant—his inquisitor! His teeth itched with anticipation. The feeling grew stronger, then receded, like a siren rushing off into the night—just as a blur passed him: a woman with long, blond hair wearing a black pants suit. He followed her.

She quickened her pace.

He lunged. Grabbed her elbow. Spun her around. "All right, Stone. Let's—."

The woman's arm trembled. "Please don't hurt me!"

It's not her! She must be wearing a similar scent. He released her. "I'm sorry. I thought you were—I'm sorry."

A husky man in a uniform stepped beside the woman. "Excuse me ma'am, is this man bothering you?"

She turned away from Scott. "Uh no, I think he just mistook me for someone else, that's all." She hurried away a few paces, quickly melting into the background blur.

"My mistake," Scott said to the guard. "I have to check in."

The guard placed a broad hand on Scott's neck. "I'm going to have to ask you to come with me, sir."

A second guard appeared beside the first. "I don't think that will be necessary."

Scott couldn't see their faces, their expressions. The guards whispered a moment, then the first grunted and walked away. "I'll escort you to registration, sir," the second guard said. Placing his palm firmly on Scott's shoulder blade, he led him through pedestrian traffic across the lobby to the registration desk. Two people stood in line in front of him. "Enjoy your stay, sir. I hope we'll have no further incidents," he said before disappearing.

"Scott?" shouted a gruff voice to his left. "Scott m'boy, is that you?"

An increasingly familiar blur sharpened into a man with a double-breasted gray suit carrying a laptop: Jack Gavin.

"Gees Scott, kind of a radical look! I could understand shaving off your beard, but your hair, too?" Putting his face uncomfortably close to Scott's, "You're a wreck!"

"I'm meeting someone, Jack."

"I thought we might get a drink, a steak, go over your testimony."

"Later, if you don't mind."

Gavin rubbed his ear, then said, "Let me at least get you checked in." Noting Scott's roving eyes, "Where're your glasses?"

"Broken."

"Why I'll bet you can't even see me clearly. Maybe we can get you to one of those one-hour optical places."

"It's under control."

"Have it your way." He shrugged. "You know, Scott, no one's heard from you since the meeting. We were getting a little nervous, especially after the break-in—and Vince's murder, of course. We're all very broken up about that." Gavin sighed. "Where's your luggage?"

Scott continued scanning the courtyard. "Coming."

"Here we go." Gavin led Scott up to an available desk clerk and slapped a corporate credit card on the counter. "This is Dr. Scott Merritt with the Verity Healthcare Consultants party. If possible, please upgrade him to a suite. And if his luggage doesn't arrive within an hour, please see to it that someone from Delcrest Custom Men's Outfitters comes to his room this evening."

"I'll notify the concierge, sir," the woman behind the counter replied.

"Looks like you had an," raising his eyebrows at Scott, "interesting weekend. By the way, how did the lunch go?"

Scott stopped scanning and gazed directly at Gavin. "Lunch?"

"Yes, lunch. At *Tout a Vous?*"

"Umm—fine, Jack. Fine."

"Did you guys do anything special after that?"

"Uh no, nothing special."

"Remember I promised you and the clan some time in the company condo in Sanibel? Well, I've arranged it to be at your disposal the last two weeks in March. And, I've thrown in three-day passes for everyone at Disney World."

Scott barely nodded.

Gavin squinted one eye. "You don't look very excited."

"All checked in, sir," the desk clerk announced, handing Scott an envelope with a key card and instructions. "You're in Suite 840. Your luggage will be sent up as soon as it arrives."

Gavin rubbed his ear. "So who're you meeting? A woman?"

Scott said nothing.

Gently nudging Scott's ribs, "Don't worry—won't say a thing. Where? The lobby? The restaurant?"

"Lobby I guess."

Gavin hesitated. "You know, without your glasses, you're blind. Why not have a drink with me at the restaurant downstairs? That way, anybody coming into the lobby can find us. When I see someone looking for you, I'll point 'em out."

"Dr. Merritt, I'm sorry to interrupt," the clerk began, "but we have something for—"

"Sounds reasonable," Scott answered Gavin, walking away from the clerk.

Gavin led him down a wide, winding staircase to the restaurant by the fountain. The hostess seated them at a table by the water's edge, clear of the silk trees, just as the piano player segued into a set of Andrew Lloyd Weber tunes. "My friend here drinks single malt scotch on the rocks. Glenfiddich, the ancient reserves, if you have it. I'll have an Absolut, with a twist," Gavin ordered from the waitress.

Scott took a quarter and a dime out of his rear pocket and tossed them into the fountain.

Gavin shrugged. "I suppose it's bad luck to ask what you just wished for."

F Street, Northwest
Washington, D.C.
Behind the wheel of the car and the safety of tinted glass, Hailey scanned F Street between Ninth and Tenth Streets. The pawnbroker shops, men's shoe stores, and lingerie outlets, decorated with red and white graffiti accentuated by drop shadow, were preparing to close. A panhandler, draped in a brown burlap bag riddled with holes and carrying half a dozen stuffed plastic bags tied together and balanced on his shoulders, rapped on the car, and pressed his scruffy beard against the driver's window. Hailey beeped his horn and waved the panhandler away. The man shouted, raised his right hand, then shuffled down the street.

"Hey, you hungry?" Buchanan asked from the back seat.

"I don't like this. Krysha's got us sitting in the skuzziest block in town," Hailey said.

"Hell, the President lives just a couple blocks away."

"See what I mean," he said. "Check the kids. I ain't heard nothing out of them since we drove down."

Buchanan looked at his feet. Brooke lay huddled on the car floor, her hands bound behind her shoulder blades, her hooded head wedged in the corner between the passenger seat and the bulge of the drive shaft. Beneath her, the idling engine hummed; on top, Andrew lay motionless. Buchanan jabbed the children with the lips of his rubber-soled shoes. Brooke contracted like an electrically shocked earthworm; Andrew lay quiet, unresponsive. "The boy's sleeping."

"He's been out the last couple days. See if he's still breathing."

Buchanan grabbed Andrew, shook him, and shouted in his face. The boy's head bounced like a dashboard decoration. When the shaking stopped, Andrew's jaw hung agape, his limbs heavy, pliant. A long, deep wheeze emerged, like air driven from a flat pillow. "He's alive." He dropped Andrew by the armrest. The boy crumbled against the door, his left arm folded behind his right ear.

"I got a bad feeling about this."

"There's a deli two stores down. What d'ya say I get us a couple of dogs while we wait?"

"Krysha told us to sit tight till he gives the signal. Then we either take the kids to the hotel or get rid of them."

"Don't that worry you? Krysha chooses this perfect location: two-way traffic, street parking on both sides through rush hour, not-so-hot block where cops'd stick out, and just a few blocks from the Fourteenth Street Bridge and National if we gotta take off. Then once we get here, the asshole pops out of the car and leaves us sitting with the kids so he can 'look out over the operation.'" Hailey pounded his fist against the wheel. "Look out, my ass! The only one Krysha's looking out for is himself. It's been twenty minutes, and I haven't seen him."

"I smell a set-up."

"So, what now?"

"Call Krysha."

"He told us not—"

"Fuck him."

Hailey shrugged, opened his cellphone, and punched up the instant connection to Krysha.

Buchanan felt a warm trickle run down his right pants cuff and pool in his thick, absorbent socks. He pulled his leg out from beneath Brooke. "Shit! I'm wet!"

Krysha's voice pierced Hailey's ear pressed against the wireless. "Yes?"

"It's me," Hailey started. "I—we haven't seen you."

"That is the idea," Krysha responded.

"Where are you?"

"What do you want?"

Behind the driver, Buchanan's burley hand yanked Brooke from beneath the seat. "You piss on me, kid?"

Brooke whimpered beneath her hood.

"Parents didn't potty train you?" Buchanan shouted.

". . . You break silence because you are frightened?" Krysha's voice came through Hailey's wireless. "Do you realize the damage you have just caused?"

"I don't like being expendable!" Hailey yelled into the wireless.

"Nor I being compromised. This conversation is pointless."

"First you trip me. Now you piss on me?" Buchanan yelled at Brooke. "You need one fucking hard spanking!"

"Krysha, you hang up and we're out of here. Who the hell do you . . ."

Behind him, Buchanan lifted his callused hand, formed a fist, and struck Brooke solidly on her buttocks. She screamed. The gag over her mouth collapsed. Buchanan raised his fist again.

". . . so Krysha, show yourself now or we cut loose," Hailey barked into the phone up front.

Krysha responded, "Three items. One, sitting exposed in that car, you have blind spots overhead and at relative positions five o'clock through seven o'clock. You may not see a trap forming. Two, you might remember that upon leaving the car, I stopped to tie my shoe. In point of fact, I placed a potent, remotely-controlled incendiary device next to the rear axle. If you so much as change gears, I'll detonate it."

"You're bluffing."

"You say that after Flight 841?" Krysha asked. "And three. After I hang up, you have five seconds to dissuade your partner in the back seat from beating that girl, or I will most certainly shoot off his hand." Click.

Hailey whirled around. Buchanan knelt behind the quivering girl, her pants down, her buttocks bleeding. He drew his automatic and whipped it against Buchanan's head. "Cut it out!' "

Buchanan touched his temple. A streak of blood stained his fingertips. "Why you—"

"I just saved your life, you dumb shit!"

The photoelectric cells in the street lamps signaled the oncoming night. Invisible to pedestrians, street vendors, and shopkeepers, the stooped panhandler shuffled along F Street Northwest toward a sedan parked in an illegal parking space alongside a fire hydrant. Pressing his nose against the glass, he wrapped on the passenger window. In the car, one of the men wearing a dark suit dismissed him. The panhandler stumbled backward and sprawled onto the sidewalk. Bracing himself against the sedan, he stumbled back onto his feet.

The man in the sedan's passenger seat lowered his window and glanced back just as the panhandler turned the corner onto Tenth Street. He did not notice the activated cellphone dangling from his sedan's tailpipe.

Grand Hyatt Hotel

Gavin sipped his vodka and waved the waitress away, promising to order dinner later. "Five after six," he said, checking his watch. "Looks like your party's late."

"Interesting table you've chosen, Jack," Scott said, jostling the cubes soaked in Scotch. "By the water. No tree cover."

Gavin looked up. "People like this sort of ambiance. Make's them feel like they're on a city sidewalk, except that it's safe."

"Sun Tzu instructs us not to make camp in a valley, especially with the enemy at hand."

"You're not on that military kick again, are you?" Gavin rubbed his ear. "Look, if whoever you're supposed to meet doesn't show soon, we can go upstairs and get you settled in. You can always leave a message for them at the front desk."

Scott finished his drink in a single gulp. "We both know that the party's here."

"Huh?"

"A good plan, Jack. Meet me at registration. Find out my room. Take me down for a drink. Distract me while your partners get inside my room. Then, when she doesn't show, I get a message that the exchange is delayed an hour or two, and you take me back up to my room and—" slamming his fist into an open palm, "isolate and entrap."

"What?"

"But the fallback position is almost as good. Here I sit, blind, vulnerable, probably with a clear line of sight at my head from any position in this courtyard."

"What the hell are you talking about?"

He glared at Gavin. "They were waiting for us at the restaurant."

"*They?* What they? What happened?"

"They almost killed us," Scott said slowly.

"Gees, I'm sorry to hear you got mugged. I certainly had nothing to do with it. If someone was waiting for you at the restaurant, they didn't hear it from me. I sure wasn't the only one at Verity who knew you were going out to lunch on Friday."

"But you were the only one who knew *where*."

"Oh come off—"

"You were the inside assist for the break-in. You, Tremayne, Ingenito—you three were the only ones with access to the employee identification pattern. And aside from Rogers, you three were the only ones really directly involved in the IRACT audit. It's counterintuitive to Tremayne's nature. Rogers is probably dead. Ingenito certainly is. That leaves you."

"You need a hot shower, some rest. Let's go upstairs and—"

"By the way, did you plan to have Vince killed, or was that just a lucky accident?"

Gavin knit his brows. Insidiously, a self-effacing smile replaced it. "Ingenito was assembling the mosaic. Remember the FYI copy of Todd's obituary he left you?"

"And Candice? Was she a threat to you, too?"

Averting Scott's glaring eyes, "You know I didn't want that."

Scott began nervously performing his pen trick. "When I get the chance, I will kill you."

Gavin folded his arms. "So ends the opening arguments. Let's proceed to the case. Give me the CD with the Institute's files and," holding up his index finger, "any files you've stored online."

"What about my children?"

He rubbed his ear, then said, "We'll leave them upstairs in the lobby, *after*."

"The kids first."

"Can't do that. You'll just have to trust us."

"That's not a deal." Scott gazed up at windows beyond his vision. "It's an ultimatum."

"From where I sit, it's all you have."

For the first time in decades, Scott felt cool beads of perspiration drip down his bare upper lip. Icy adrenalin shot through his chest, his arms. He stiffened his back. Deliberately, he placed his fists on the table. "No deal. We do it my way."

"Don't be an ass. You know Stone—"

"Is in the building? That she's been listening to every word we've said while barking instructions in your ear? That she probably has a rifle trained on my head?"

"This thing has been irritating the hell out of me—kind of like you," Gavin said, adjusted his previously well-hidden earphone. "She wants to know if you'd like to hear your children shot, just like your mother-in-law?"

"At ten A.M. tomorrow, copies of all IRACT's data and statistical files will appear on thirty-two select medical bulletin boards and in the e-mails of all the major news services. Phones at the Institute will begin ringing off the hook. Irate patients and families will assemble outside your doors. The

CDC will shut you down. The FDA will ban xenotransplantation and suspend Diabend and Tremulate. Executive and congressional investigative committees will convene. But," pushing his glass aside, "I wouldn't worry about that, Jack."

"Oh, and why not?"

"Because you'll already be long dead."

"You're no threat."

Scott smirked. "Two hours after the first wave, *Kompromat* will begin circulating the globe. Did you hear that, Stone?"

Gavin stared, mouth drooling. "You're bluffing!"

"Is that Gavin speaking? Or Stone?"

Gavin pressed his earpiece tightly. "You'd need someone working with you to get that information out."

"Emery watched while I set it up." Scott waited for Gavin to gulp the rest of his drink. "We've been here before, Stone. Raise or call."

Gavin looked up and scoured the atrium, as if seeking divine guidance. "She's listening."

"I give you the CD. Your man brings *both* my kids into the lobby, turns them *both* over to the concierge and immediately leaves the building. Then, and then only, I'll give you full access to the e-mail address. We all walk away, satisfied."

Gavin tapped on his earphone. "We'll turn the girl over after we get the CD. The boy, after we've checked the address."

"Before."

"After. It's not negotiable."

"Because he's dead, you bitch!"

"Simmer down, Scott. He's not dead."

"Let me see him in the lobby, alive, first."

Gavin held his breath. He listened, then nodded. "Okay. Produce the CD, now!"

Scott gave Gavin a long penetrating stare before answering. "I mailed it to myself." He pointed up and to his right. "It's at the registration desk."

"Like hell. I was with you the whole time."

"The clerk tried to tell me. You were standing right there." He pushed back his seat. "I'll get—"

Gavin grabbed his wrist. "Oh no you don't. Sit down. Give me your wallet!"

Scott hesitated.

"I said, give me your wallet!"

Reluctantly, Scott handed it to Gavin who rifled through the photographs before withdrawing an item from an inset plastic sleeve. He tossed the wallet back to Scott and held up a plastic card. "Your driver's license. What did you think, I was going to rob you?"

Scott exhaled silently.

Gavin turned in his seat, signaled the waitress, and said, "I'll have another vodka. Oh and could you do us a favor? Dr. Merritt, here, has a package waiting for him at registration. He's in Suite 840." Handing her a pair of $20s and Scott's ID, "Could you be a dear and get that package for us right away?"

Both waitress and currency disappeared.

Scott balled his hands. "It must've been through Barbieri. You're both sniveling and slimy. Tell me, what makes a deviant like you? Heredity or—oh yes. Momma!"

Gavin's Adam's apple jerked. "Let's keep this professional, shall we?"

"Professional? How does it feel being a mass murderer?"

"I had nothing to do with the bombing. I didn't plan it. I didn't plant it."

"But you know who did."

Gavin shook his head and smiled. "Look at him," motioning with his hand at the piano player. "Go on, take a good look at him."

Scott gazed at a blurry figure—a man with silvery hair and black tuxedo and tails who swayed as his hands caressed the white piano's keys. *Misty* drifted through the air.

"Look at him, Merritt, sitting there, on his own little island, pounding out his own little variation of a worn theme, convinced of his own importance. The sad truth is that no one hears, no one notices. You two have a lot in common."

That's Stone talking.

Gavin glanced up. "I see our waitress and—she has a package. Good." He turned back to Scott. "When I first chose you, I had no idea the road with you would be so arduous."

"Chose?"

"Aside from computer nerds, one doesn't find many experienced, intelligent people your age who are still so pathetically naïve." He rolled his wet cocktail napkin into a ball. "Verity was going to land the auditing contract. You were the perfect choice for auditor: a burned-out doctor, ranting about visions generated by psychosis or MS-induced mental impairment. Author of a report that danced on the edge of the lunatic fringe." Gavin rolled his napkin ball tighter. "The Institute's one and only chance to control all xeno data and give PTS time to solve the virus problem—tens of billions of dollars all precariously balancing on the result of a single audit."

"And whose epiphany was it to have me perform that audit? Yours?"

"Barbieri identified you as a candidate—but it was Stone's choice to have xenotransplantation's biggest critic perform the audit. She's been manipulating you for quite some time."

Scott gazed up at the glass ceiling. "Well done, Stone. If I'd followed your script, I'd've have simultaneously proven that IRACT was reputable, that the xeno solution was safe, and that my treatise for SEMA was just hot air. If I'd invalidated xeno, you'd've discredited me and my treatise, saying that I was biased by my mother's death. As Sun Tzu says, 'The victorious general only engages in battle after the battle is won.'"

Gavin cocked his head. "Dr. Stone thanks you. Our waitress will be here momentarily." Smiling, "It's ironic, Scott. If you hadn't seen that data set from Cruz, you and I would still be sitting here, right now, having a drink, but under entirely different circumstances."

Scott wiped sweat from his forehead. "Hasn't something been lost in all of this."

"What might that be?"

"The patients who've died, unnecessarily. The two billion innocents who may follow."

"George Bernard Shaw said that all professions are a conspiracy against the laity. Why should medicine be any different?"

"You're risking the future of the human race!"

"Science will find an answer. It always has, it always will. Till then, the risks are being scrupulously minimized."

"Have any trouble sleeping at night?"

"I have a seven-figure deal and the best bed money can buy. Besides, it's like I told you—do you want to be right, or do you want to be happy?"

The waitress appeared behind the vacant seat between them and handed Scott a sealed brown envelope and his license. "Your package, sir." Depositing a vodka to Gavin's right, "And your drink."

Gavin handed her cash. "We need a little more time before ordering."

When she left, Gavin yanked the envelope from Scott's hand, ripped away one edge, and turned it upside down. A CD clattered onto the table. "Show time." He placed his laptop onto the table, opened the lid, booted the system, and placed the CD in the slot. "I'm loading Merritt's files." He checked the laptop screen. "All Merritt files loaded. Eyeballing it, the file names appear the same. Let's check to see if we have the same number of files. And—we—do. Now checking for presence of *Kompromat* file—yes, it's there. Now running file comparison program."

Scott grabbed Gavin's drink and took a quick gulp. It was hot, tasteless, and left a trail of smoldering fire down his esophagus.

"You hate vodka," Gavin said, peering over the laptop lid. "Just a moment, Dr. Stone. There—all matching file names showing same file size. No mismatches in any sectors. I'm going to double check by comparing files with different names. If there aren't any, then we have all the files, intact." A moment later, "All verified." Gavin placed the CD in a case on the table.

"Now release my kids!"

F Street, Northwest

The vendors had packed their carts and the stores had lowered their steel curtains. An inexhaustible stream of cars crawled between the corner traffic lights. The glare from the line of vehicles behind the car reflected from the rearview mirror into Hailey's eyes. "I'm getting a headache."

"Switch the mirror to nighttime, dummy," Buchanan said from the back seat.

Hailey flicked the knob on the rearview mirror, dulling the glare, but reducing his view behind the car. His phone rang.

"I got a hundred that says it's Stone," Buchanan offered.

"I say it's Krysha," Hailey said, then answered the phone. He took out a $100 bill and slapped it in Buchanan's palm. "But I thought he was supposed to coordinate," he said into the receiver as he put his hand on the ignition key. He hesitated. "No, neither of us have seen Krysha since we parked." Hailey turned back to Buchanan. "He said that he planted a bomb under the car and—" pausing, "yeah, you're right, we don't know what his agenda is." He frowned. "Okay, we'll be there in a couple of minutes." He hung up.

Buchanan wiped his nose. "Don't tell me we're really going through with this."

Hailey removed his automatic from its holster. "I'm supposed to take both kids into the lobby and turn 'em over to the concierge."

"Boy's still sleeping. You'll have to lug him on your shoulder," Buchanan said. "What'd she say about me?"

Beckoning his partner to lean forward, "You're supposed to go into the lobby first, alone. When your phone rings, shoot the kids and anybody around 'em. Make it look random."

Buchanan slammed his forearm against the armrest. "That's just fucking beautiful! You know we're both just Goddamn diversions for Stone. Me especially."

"We'll see about that!" Daintily, Hailey turned the ignition key. The engine choked, sputtered, then roughly idled, blowing cold air through the vents. He checked his sideview mirror before pulling into traffic.

"I knew Krysha was bluffing," Buchanan boasted. "Hell, look on the bright side. After this job, we're gonna get some vaca—"

The car scraped—smashed into metal. The front end buckled, bent, and rode up onto the rear door of a crimson Nissan—advancing on it like a monster truck crushing a stock car. They slammed to a halt. Hailey's forehead smashed into the steering wheel. Buchanan's shoulder banged against the headrest atop the passenger seat.

Hailey wiped a trail of blood oozing down his forehead. "Some dumb fuck pulled right in front of me! Didn't even look!"

"Just back up and get us the hell out of here!"

Groggy, Hailey put the car in reverse. Metal clawed metal. The car rocked like an angry, shackled elephant, the left front wheel spun against air. The right wheel caught the edge of a newly formed rift on the Nissan's rear doorframe, launching them backward. They plowed into the car behind them, through its headlights, and came to rest embedded in its radiator. Horns blared from a line of cars stacked down the block.

"Told you it was a smart idea not to leave the kids in the trunk," Buchanan said.

Hailey gunned the engine. The car lurched. The tires screeched, burning the road. The steering wheel dragged left. He fought it, but the chassis dug into the street. The car, metal grinding against asphalt, sputtered, and spun perpendicular to the line of traffic. It died in the middle of the road. Hailey looked out the window at the front wheel bent outward from the car at a forty-five-degree angle. "The front tie rod's broken. The car's undriveable. We'll have to walk the two blocks."

"This just keeps getting better and better," Buchanan muttered as he unlocked the doors.

Hailey picked up his wireless. "I'll call Stone and let her know."

Traffic started pulling around the accident scene. Drivers honked as they passed.

"Will ya look at that!" Buchanan exclaimed.

Hailey looked up after initiating the call to Stone. A man stepped out of the disabled crimson Nissan in front. Six-foot-four inches, three hundred plus pounds, wearing a maroon Redskins jacket and cap, he approached, cradling a tire iron in his right arm like a nightstick. "Guess he's ticked about his car."

"My oh my, is he calling you out?"

Bam! The Redskins fan slammed his tire iron on the car, leaving a divot in the hood.

"Yep," Hailey muttered. "He's ticked about his car."

Bam! The tire iron slammed against the passenger door. Hailey felt the vibration through his ribs. He released the safety on his automatic and handed the phone back to Buchanan. "I'll deal with this asshole. You talk to Stone."

"Just shoot the fucker through the glass!"

Hailey lowered the window, unlocked the door, and stuck his head out of the window. "Hey! What do you say you put that thing down so we can talk this over?"

The man put his hands on his hips. "You gonna make me?"

"Buddy, I got a couple real sick kids in the back seat. I'm trying to get 'em to a doctor."

"They hurt?" the man asked, peering closer.

"Sure are."

The man curled his lower lip and dropped the tire iron.

Hailey opened his door. "Let me—"

A hand grabbed Hailey's wrist from a blind spot in the street behind him. Another seized his upper arm and swung him head first against the edge of the open door. Others whipped him from the car and launched him into midair. His right elbow snapped. His head smashed into the street. Skin ripped away from his cheek as his face slid on asphalt. More hands yanked his arms behind his back, driving him into the ground. Cuffs locked around his wrists.

A man burst into the vacated front seat, his gun locked on Buchanan's eyes.

Buchanan's hand tightened around his gun. The rear doors clicked.

"F—"

Buchanan's hand twitched. Simultaneously, both doors cracked open.

"—B—"

Buchanan's gun hand rotated.

The man's gun discharged.

Buchanan's face exploded. The rear window disintegrated. A blood-rich shock wave followed.

Both doors swung wide open.

Buchanan's body sat upright, one hand still brandishing the gun. But the head extended only to a sawed-off line at the top row of teeth—above, the bone had disintegrated. What remained of the face appeared to smile.

Another man poked his head in an open rear door and checked the children on the floor. "Get the EMTs!"

THIRTY-FOUR

Grand Hyatt Hotel

"They're still not here!" Scott rapped his fist on the table. "Five more minutes—then I walk!"

"You'll be dead before you reached the next table."

"My chances are better than yours."

Gavin patted his forehead with the napkin. "Nice try, but I'm too valuable to—"

"I once read that the real moment of death is when we become irrelevant."

"Divide and conquer? Not very original."

Scott glanced at the tables on either side. "Sometimes, even if outnumbered, it's better to fight one great battle than many smaller ones."

Gavin pressed on his earpiece. "What?" He frowned. "Come again?" He listened. "Yes, I'll tell him." To Scott, "Stone said to tell you, quote, 'not divide and conquer—rather, a Cannae,' unquote. What's that supposed to mean?"

* * *

"She knows we freed the hostages," a voice broke through the chatter in Terrill's earphone.

Terrill stepped away from the canopy of goblets in a secluded corner of the mahogany bar. "How?"

The voice answered, "Open line in the rear of the vehicle."

"Anyone spot the target?" Terrill asked into his transmitter. "No."

"I want a pair of eyes trained on every window, every balcony every access that looks down, up or sideways into the lobby. Guest rooms, bathrooms, conference rooms, ballrooms, dining rooms, exercise rooms, maintenance utility rooms—anything with walls. No one leaves without being checked by two teams, discretely."

The voice answered, "Sir, there's more than five hundred guest rooms—"

Terrill gazed across the courtyard at the lobby rear. "I see four sets of wide open doors. And a set of stairs beyond."

"They lead to the Metro station," the voice said.

"Electronically controlled?"

"Affirmative. The hotel seals the doors after nine P.M."

"Tell them it's nine. And have them lock out elevators from the underground garage." To Agent Kamen two paces behind and to his right, "That leaves three main entrances and two stairwells between lobby and garage, and four staircases from the upper floors opening onto the street."

"They're tied into the fire alarm system. Already covered," Kamen said. "Assuming Stone's still here."

"We locked onto her position from her accomplice's last call. She's inside this building." He scanned the courtyard and let out a long sigh. "I've missed something, Agent Kamen."

"Do we have teams posit—"

"Forget deployment patterns and logistics. Why would Stone still be here? She doesn't *need* to, not with Gavin here." Terrill's eyes narrowed as he scrutinized the exposed courtyard. More than four hundred people, dressed in black tie and tuxedos or evening gowns, milled around the multitier lobby. A cocktail party was set to commence at seven

P.M. around the fountain. *Unless she already knows!* "Start clearing those people out of the lobby. Now!"

Gavin pressed on his earpiece. "She says the charade is over, and not to deny it or she'll kill you where you sit."

Scott exhaled and then reached into his coat pocket.

"Careful!"

He took out a pair of black, bulky-framed glasses. "Mind if I use these?" He put them on. They promptly slid down his nose. "They're the best I could do on such short notice."

"Why didn't—" Gavin's face contorted as he listened to the voice in his ear. "You bastard! Police, FBI, there's a God-damn army here!" Craning around, "You've destroyed me!"

"And the downside?"

"If I had a gun I'd—"

"But Stone didn't let you have one, did she? What does that tell you?"

Gavin hesitated. "Remove your earpiece."

"Earpiece? What makes you think—"

"I said remove it!"

Scott pulled a small plug from his left ear and dropped it on the table.

"Transmitter, too."

"I'll have to strip."

"We don't care if it's strapped to your dick. Take it off and drop it on the floor!"

Scott reached under the table, put his hand in his pants, and yanked. "Owww!"

At the next table, a woman with long diamond earrings and upturned nose glanced at his hand fumbling between his legs. She cringed and slid her chair away. Scott put the transmitter on the floor. Gavin crushed it beneath his heel.

"What? Are you—but—" Gavin reached in his ear, pulled out his earpiece, and gave it to Scott. "She wants to talk to you, directly."

Scott wiped it on his stained shirt before inserting it in his ear. For a moment, he again smelled the choking black hood. "You underestimated me, Stone."

"You're still exposed, and now without a comforting voice in your ear." She coughed—a resonant, throaty sound chased by a high-pitched whine. "Give Gavin the e-mail address and password. He'll verify whether the info's there—and whether it's been forwarded. If you've kept your word, you're free. The FBI has doubtless informed you that they've recovered your children."

Scott drew in a long breath, swished the air around his mouth like fine brandy, then released a protracted, whistling sigh. "I don't think so. My life ends the instant you have that information. We both know that."

"There's always a chance—"

"When I was in practice, I balanced a therapy's risks against its benefits." Scott looked up at the glass roof. "When I walked into this place, I'd already committed to risking my life for my children. But to risk it on the chance that you might be magnanimous? That's not a balanced decision—that's stupidity. You want the information, Stone? You damn well come down here and get it yourself!"

"Look around you, Dr. Merritt."

Scott looked overhead at formally-dressed patrons lining the railing and glanced at a pair of children, a young girl in a satin and lace dress and boy with a clip-on Windsor knot, tossing pennies down into the fountain. An angular man with a black bow tie, tuxedo, and matching slicked-down hair passed behind them. Systematically, Scott continued scanning the formally-attired guests above him.

"Yes, the children on the balcony. They so remind me of yours, the way they—"

Something drew Scott's eyes back—back toward the children. Something was wrong with that snapshot in his mind. Something only noticeable through ingrained years of study—something clinical, subtle.

". . . So many lives are in your hands . . ."

The man who walked behind them, Scott thought.

". . . You fancy yourself an altruist, saving . . ."

His gait. Yes, the way he walked!

". . . envision yourself riding at the head of some army singing your praise . . ."

Keeping his head riveted on the children, Scott let his eyes rove. He caught a peripheral view of the man with the slicked-down hair, strolling, champagne glass in hand, on the promenade to his far right. He analyzed the man's gait. *Slightly excessive hip rotation. Effeminate—maybe, maybe not.* His eyes glanced down. *Lower extremities. Slight knock-knee. Heel strike, toe off—gait seems normal. Damn, can't tell if that's a man or a woman!*

". . . the only lives you can hope to save are those dining and dancing . . ."

Upper extremities. The arms. He studied the man's swinging left arm. Something *was* wrong with the way the elbow hung. He focused on the connection between upper arm and forearm.

". . . they'll never know your sacrifice . . ."

The carrying angle! The angle between forearm and upper arm. It's too large for a man. That has to be a woman!

The figure coughed.

He heard the cough in his earphone. *Stone!*

"Time's up! The address and the password!"

Scott wanted to stand and denounce her, but she was at the very edge of his vision—he'd be dead before her name left his lips. He opened his wallet, removed Ryan's scribbled paper wedged between portraits of Brooke and Andrew, and dropped it on the table. Gavin unfolded the paper, then gazed up at Scott who mock slit his throat. Eyes scouring the atrium, Gavin's fingers poised fearfully over the keyboard.

"What's he waiting for?" Stone demanded.

"What are you waiting for, Jack?" Scott repeated.

Gavin wiped the perspiration from his jowls with cool sweat from his vodka glass and then began industriously typing. "I'm in."

"Stone wants to know if the info's there?" Scott asked.

"Uh-huh. And what looks like Institute data files," Gavin rasped.

"She orders you to destroy them."

Gavin's hands shook. A bead of sweat dripped down the side of his face.

"What's the matter, Jack? You've already wiped all the IRACT files clean from the CD. And now, you're going to erase the last copies in cyberspace. Isn't this what you wanted?" Scott shoved his face inches from Gavin's nose. "Or is it that your usefulness for Stone ends when you click on those files?" Ignoring the rage in his ear, "Poor Jack, a brutal choice. Life in prison—or none at all."

Gavin looked at the pianist, surrounded by the fountain, and released a long, long sigh. Something appeared in the palm of Gavin's hand: silver, with a blue top, and the size a slender matchbox. Gently, Gavin passed his hand behind one of the laptop's USB ports—and stuck the palmed object into it, carefully shielding the attachment from view.

A tiny USB hard drive! Scott thought. *A.k.a. USB flash drive—a "stick!" He could probably store a couple Gigs of data on that.*

The USB hard drive attachment registered silently on the laptop as a new piece of hardware. Gavin put his hand over his mouth—and began copying the *Kompromat* file, then the hundreds of other data files he had just checked.

Scott watched silenty as the USB stick drive absorbed the wealth of IRACT's secretive files. *What's he doing?*

Gavin, seeing the confusion in Scott's eyes, typed '*MY BARGAINING CHIP*' in a small notepad window in the corner of the screen.

Scott's eyes narrowed. His head ever-so-slightly shook 'no.'

Gavin retyped '*OUR BARGAINING CHIP*'. In seconds, he finished, palmed teh USB stick drive and destroyed every remainng file on the laptop. "It's done."

Scott spied the disguised Stone poised by the railing overlooking the far end of the restaurant. She reached into her pocket. Planting both hands on Gavin's lapels, Scott hoisted him off his seat, and spun him directly into the line-of-sight with Stone. The table pitched over.

A bullet burst into the back of Gavin's neck.

The torso jerked. The head snapped back. The arms twitched. Gavin fell against Scott's chest. Eyes wide with shock, his hand released the tiny USB drive stick and the paper. Both fell into Scott's partially torn pocket.

A second shot slammed into Gavin's back. The body convulsed. Blood trickled from the mouth. Scott held Gavin firm, like a locked door holding off the onslaught of a mob. A third shot struck the abdomen. The body grew heavy, inert. The fourth bullet exploded through the front of the rib cage, slammed into Scott's left shoulder and hammered him into the floor. His arm radiated white-hot pain. Gavin's body crashed on top of him.

Stone retracted the silencer-tipped automatic into her coat like it was snapped back by a spring. Below, at the far end of the fountain-restaurant, Gavin and Scott lay strewn on the floor. Smiling, she lifted the glass of champagne to her lips before nonchalantly scanning the courtyard. No one rushed toward her. No eyes even met hers. Sipping her champagne, she meandered through the lobby crowd. If all went well, she'd make a quick stop to change her wardrobe and discard her piece, then walk right through the FBI checkpoints.

Scott heard a male voice: 'This one's dead.'

A man with a prominent square jaw pulled Gavin's body off of him. "He's alive."

Two men carried Scott to a secluded corner of the restaurant beside a trellis that had been trampled by terrified patrons. Scott sat up. The floor swayed as he tried to balance himself. Blood poured down his shoulder. His ears pounded from screaming guests clambering up the staircase.

A man with a double chin pressed a white linen napkin firmly against Scott's shoulder. "FBI. Special Agent Paine. Lay back and relax, Dr. Merritt. You've been shot."

"Orr here, sir," said his heavy-jowled partner into a transmitter. "Merritt's alive." He paused. "No, but the trajectory points to the north side of the building, lower floors, maybe the main lobby. I'm certain he saw the shooter."

"He's lost a lot of blood," Paine said.

Scott shook his head. The sound of waves breaking against a rocky shore reverberated painfully in his right ear. "Stop that!" Scott yelled, slapping his right ear.

"Stop what?" Agent Orr directed Scott's drooping face close to his own. "Dr. Merritt, did you see who shot you?"

"Stone. Oh man, my ear's killing me!"

Orr shook him. "Where did she go?"

"Water."

Paine looked at the fountain. "Nobody's been in there."

"Not the fountain! Running water and—and voices. I hear voices."

The agents scanned the restaurant. Diners and restaurant staff were being evacuated. Most guests in the lobby overhead were being herded into the bars, eateries, and lower levels with exit sites—all shielded from the exposed atrium.

"Evac him," Paine said.

"Voices," Scott continued. "Talking about the shooting. Three, no four, complaining about security. A scuffle, fight? It's over now. A door closing—hinge needs oiling. Oh!" He fell to his knees, reached into his right ear, and removed the earphone. "I know that sound." Jumping to his feet, he leaped past the surprised agents and bounded up the staircase. "C'mon, I know where she is!" The sound of a toilet being flushed still reverberated in his ears.

Scott stood behind the thirteen federal agents deployed between the southwestern elevator shaft and railing overlooking the fountain. Another ten stretched from the registration desk to the guardrail. Sharpshooters lay in wait from roof to lower lobby. An angular man in a gray suit walked out of the men's room. He twirled a key chain around his index finger.

"That's Stone!" Scott pointed from behind a row of agents.

Sixty guns locked on the man.

"FBI. Hands up. Now!" one voice demanded.

The man slowly raised his hands. "Is that you, Merritt, behind the human wall?" It was Stone's voice.

"Get those arms up! Up!"

"I knew I shouldn't have tried for a surgical strike," she said.

"Last chance. Hands up! Now!" the voice barked, the echo resounding across the vacated courtyard.

Stone surveyed the rows of agents. "I've planted a slew of bombs all over the hotel. Check out the north face, eighth floor, fourth window on the right." Her third finger twitched, glancing across a tiny button on her black key ring.

The window erupted. Pieces of furniture blasted out into the atrium. The boom reached their ears an instant later. Powerful echoes bounced across the enclosure as thick, black smoke poured out of the room. Glass shards rained onto the far end of the courtyard floor.

"Gavin's room," she stated. "And that was the baby of the bunch. Which of you is in charge?"

Terrill stepped away from the registration desk. "I'm Special—"

"I've planted devices with cubane-enhanced C4 throughout this building. I can easily detonate them all standing right here, right now."

"What do you want?"

"A four-, make that a six-hour head start." Before Terrill could answer, "My transmitter's powerful. I could detonate the lot if I were standing in Baltimore."

"Come now Dr. Stone, you can't—"

"You probably still have five hundred people in restaurants and bars. Another seven hundred in the upper floors. You can't possibly clear this place in less than fifteen minutes.

Now you can either kill me and hope that I don't turn this place into Hell or—do exactly as you're told."

"Where can you go? Why don't we—"

"No tails. No evac until I'm out of sight. And I want a shield—Merritt."

"Take me," Terrill offered.

"No substitutions, please!"

Scott lifted his head and rubbed his temples. "It's okay. It's okay."

Terrill said, "You know that—"

"We have no choice." Scott declared, staring at Stone. "She's not bluffing."

Terrill gazed around the courtyard. Faint sounds of piped dinner music from the mezzanine ballroom drifted across the hushed courtyard. "We can—"

"On the count of three. One . . ."

Terrill stared at her unflinching eyes. "What guarantee do I have that you won't—"

"Two . . ." The corner of her mouth upturned. Her eyes smiled. "Thr—"

"I agree!"

"Have your men fall back to the far end of the lobby."

Terrill nodded. The agents broke formation and retreated to the north side of the courtyard. Scott stood alone in front of the sealed doors. Blood dripping down his arm collected in a pool at his feet. Stone strode to him and seized his bloody left shoulder. Shouting to Terrill, "Open these doors!" The four sets of heavy doors simultaneously swung open. She dragged Scott out by his collar. "Oh, I also have goodies planted at the Convention Center across the street. I believe there're about five *thousand* people there. Now, close these damn doors behind us!"

The doors slammed closed, the sound crashing against Terrill's ears. They were gone.

"I want this building cleared within five minutes! Move it! Move it!" Terrill shouted. Then, into his receiver, "Bomb squad?"

"Grant here, sir."

"Deploy teams in here and the Convention Center. On the double. Eckert, evac the Convention Center. Alert perimeter units and District PD. Have them spot by foot or vehicle. But they are not—repeat, not—to move in until they get clearance from me. You coordinate." Then, "Donaldson, arrange for an 'accident' on the Fourteenth Street Bridge and the Teddy Roosevelt off Constitution. And don't forget Memorial Bridge behind the Lincoln. She could try going out the back door through Arlington National." Rubbing his forehead, "Agent Newman, you have a map of the Metro?"

"Just punched it up," the agent responded in Terrill's earpiece.

"I want every incoming train to Metro Center or Gallery Place cut off two stops on either side. Continuously monitor any movement within that radius."

Agent Kamen came out of Terrill's shadow. "Sir, your deployment is predicated that she's going to Virginia or taking the Metro."

"Not the Metro. Her transmitter probably won't work underground."

"But what if they head back through the city, northeast, northwest—"

"Restricted airspace, Kamen. We can't spot them from the air. It levels the playing field for her."

"So by blocking off the Fourteenth Street Bridge, traffic spills back into the Mall, and creates a gridlock that'll hamper their mobility?"

"Correct."

"What about Merritt?"

Stone gripped Scott's left arm as they stood on the corner of H and Eleventh Street, Northwest. The traffic light changed. She dragged him into the crosswalk, then turned and quickly appraised the Honda idling next to her. "Good." She walked to the driver's side and tapped on the window. The woman inside promptly checked her door locks. Stone stepped back, lifted her right foot, and drove it through the side window. Glass shattered. Stone's heel caught the woman's jaw and smashed her into the dashboard. Methodically, she opened the door, tossed the driver into the street, cleared the glass off the driver's seat, and slid across to the passenger side. "Get in. You drive."

Scott started toward the woman laying on the asphalt. Stone wagged a finger over the key chain. Reluctantly, he got into the car.

"Fourteenth Street Bridge," she ordered. "Go straight for two blocks to Thirteenth, then make a right."

"What's in Virginia?"

"You won't live long enough to find out."

Exhausted, cold, the road undulated in front of Scott. *I'm hemorrhaging—going into shock. Have to delay—*

"Make a right, idiot."

He sluggishly turned the car onto Thirteenth Street, nearly sideswiping a parked stationwagon, then stopped at the red light on New York Avenue.

"Watch what you're doing! Make a hard left when the light changes."

Prying his drooping eyes open, "And after all this—we're right back where we started." He turned the corner. "Gavin—Gavin deleted the files, but didn't overwrite them. They can be restored. He never—told you the address—did he?"

"You're reaching, Merritt."

He turned onto Fourteenth Street. "Made—backup copy right—under—your—ohhh!" Scott's eyes fluttered. He fell forward on the steering wheel. His foot jammed on the accelerator. The car shot forward.

Stone grappled with the wheel. The car swung into oncoming traffic. Columns of headlights swerved. Horns blared. Cars sped toward her, on and on, like a video game of never ending imminent collisions. She jabbed her elbow into Scott's ribs, knocking him against the door. She tried kicking his foot off the accelerator. Couldn't. Straining, she reached across with her left foot and slammed on the brake. The car skidded, glided, spun. The tires screeched. She looked up.

A lamppost appeared, dead on. Fifty feet. Closing. Twenty.

She exploded through the windshield. Glass stung her hands, her face like a swarm of enraged hornets. Her cheek struck the ground. Her head snapped back. Her spine burned as her body pitched and slammed on pavement and frozen grass.

A lamppost protruded through what had once been the carburetor, the front end of the car sliced in half.

An old, two-tone Chevrolet pulled behind the wreckage. A man in a worn jean jacket and engineer boots jumped out and ran toward them. "Help's on the way. I called an ambulance!"

The man poked his head in the remnants of the driver's window. Scott lay slumped on the deployed airbag. The man lifted Scott's head, touched the still pulsing carotid artery, then let it drop back. Stone lay strewn in the grass, her eyes fixed on the Washington Monument, a great white obelisk piercing the dark. The man appeared over her. "Only last week you lost a man like this."

"Krysha?"

"Where is it? Ahhh." He took the key ring laying beside her flaccid arm and dangled it over her face. "By the way, it is also an effective bug." He leaned over her, feigning CPR. "I heard—everything! Such a stupid woman!"

Stone scrunched her blood-soaked eyebrows and gazed far beyond him. "What did you say, Dad—dy?"

Krysha knelt over her, slid his right shoe by her head, positioned his heel over her neck, and crushed her throat.

Four Seasons Hotel at Georgetown   7.01 P.M.

"Do you want a divorce?" Hope cried from her bed.

Alexander sat in the lounge chair, one finger propping up his head. Heavy eyes stared at the carpet. "Now that you've tied us to a dead weight and thrown us overboard?"

She swatted the lamp from the nightstand. It crashed, igniting sparks. "You hypocritical bastard, how dare you look down your nose at me after the hell you've put me through! I'm the *only* one who supported you all those years you trampled on people who could least afford it."

"I manipulated numbers for my—our benefit, yes, but those were figures on a balance sheet." Still staring at the carpet, "That's a far cry from what you've done."

"Tell that to the two hundred suicides by employees in companies you've pillaged."

"You can't equate—"

The phone on the night stand trilled. They stared at each other as it continued to ring.

"Why don't you answer it?" Hope asked.

"Because it's probably for you."

She picked up the phone, listened impassively for a few moments, then rasped, "I understand." She let the receiver drop. "Salsbury kept a diary on my activities—very much like what I have on Slatokhatov. It's in a safety deposit box." She shivered. "The FBI's going to open that box in the morning."

"How bad?"

"Knowing Salsbury . . ." Her voice trailed off. She turned imploring eyes toward him.

"And Emery?"

"I'm fairly certain he kept records, too."

Alexander stood and walked to his wife shaking on the bed. "If it was just us, we could've fought it in the courts for years. But with Slatokhatov—what have you done to us?" He turned away, picked up a vase from a pedestal, and smashed it against the wall. His rigid frame relaxed, as if he'd purged the anger from his body like impurities in a sauna. "Where is that safety deposit box?"

"Henrico-James National Bank. Main office."

"And Emery's records?"

"He's not as careful as Salsbury is—was. Most likely, his are at home."

"Make yourself scarce. *I'll* deal with matters from this point forward."

Emery Residence
2322 Herbert Lane
Shaker Heights, Ohio

After smoothing a crease in her dress and adding a pin to shore up her hair bun, Grace Emery strolled through her colonial-style showpiece living room complete with eighteenth-century paintings. She stopped before the ornate oak doors to his study, and knocked. "Carl, dinner."

No reply.

"Carlton?" Slowly, she opened the door. Emery's study was dim, lit by a waning blaze in the fireplace that cast an eerie flicker across book-lined walls. Protruding from the side of Emery's favorite high-back chair, an arm held a high-ball glass. On the floor beneath the arm was a bottle of whiskey.

"Don't turn on the light," Emery whispered from his chair.

"Tim came in from the dorm special to be with us tonight." She approached him. "We're having *muscles fra diablo*."

The hand disappeared behind the chair. The glass tinkled. "Diablo, devil. Fitting."

She pulled a chair beside him. His face, three-quarters in shadow, turned away. "Jack Daniels instead of sherry before dinner? What happened in Washington?"

"Nothing."

"How was the boating?"

"Stormy."

She paused. "Clara Bender called the house this morning. She, uh, she gave notice." After he took a drink, "Clara said that she just couldn't continue working for a 'cyclops.' Then she hung up. Carl, she ran your office for ten years. Why would she say that?"

"Fuck her!"

"Carlton!" She breathed deeply. "Weren't you supposed to testify in Washington most of this week? You don't check in at your hotel. Suddenly you show up late in the afternoon, with no explanation where you've been, what you've been doing."

"I took an early flight. Spent most of the afternoon at the clinic."

"Why?"

He recessed deeper into shadows. "Barbieri thought it was better that I didn't testify."

"But you've been dying to testify!"

"Politics. You wouldn't understand."

Leaning forward, "Why wouldn't I?"

"Because you're not out there in the real world. Grace, we agreed before the children were born that I'd earn the living and handle the finances and you'd take care of the house and family." He took another gulp. "It's a little late to reverse roles."

She swatted the glass out of his hand. It struck the fireplace and shattered. "I accepted being relegated to that role because I knew you were a special man who needed his freedom to achieve greatness. And you did, beyond my wildest expectations. But don't forget that I sacrificed my needs for yours, so don't you dare—dare, throw *that* in my face!"

The last embers of the fire died. "Grace, what would you have done if Tim hadn't been a fine young boy. Suppose, he'd been a troublemaker. What would you have done?"

She shrugged. "If it was more than a phase, I'd have sought counseling. Or given him more love and discipline."

"Suppose his behavior had gotten worse, and he'd become a skillful liar?"

"I don't know." She grimaced. "It depends."

"Would you still love him?"

"He's my son."

"What if he was accused of rape, but swore his innocence?"

"I'd have to believe him, and support him—unless proven otherwise."

"What if you knew without doubt that he was a murderer? Would you still protect him?"

She gazed around the dark library. "I'd still have Christal."

He leaned out of the shadows. "What if Tim was all you had? What then?"

"Why all the hypotheticals?"

"My work is my child."

"I don't understand."

"Yes, Grace." He smiled. "Yes, you do."

She noticed a gun in his left hand. Instantly, she draped herself over him. "Carl! Please, put it down!"

The gun remained in his hand. He did not move.

"Carl, your children are in the other room! Please Carl, put—the—gun—down!"

He released a protracted sigh. "I'm—just terribly, terribly tired."

"We'll get past this, you and I." She kissed his hand. "Whatever's ahead, we'll face it, and win, together." The room grew cold.

The couple emerged from his study and ambled to the dining room. The table was formal, immaculate, replete with seven pieces of cutlery per setting. Christal, their daughter, wearing braces and French braids, sat at the far end of the table. Emery took his traditional seat at the head, his wife to his right. Their son, Tim, wearing a *Case Western Reserve* sweatshirt and sporting a blond patch beard and diamond-stud earrings, sauntered into the room.

"Daddy, have you been crying?" Christal asked.

Emery cleared his throat. "Go ahead, Grace. I know you need—want to."

Solemnly, she nodded. "Before dinner, I'd like to offer a small prayer. Will everybody please join hands?"

"Aw, come on Mom, do we have to—"

Emery pounded on the table. "Do as your mother asks!"

Grace bowed her head. "Dear Lord, we give thanks for this bounty that you—"

The doorbell rang.

". . . joy that you have given us by bringing this family together—"

It rang again, this time with an insistent knock.

Emery slammed down his napkin. "I'll get it." He strode to the foyer and opened the door.

Three large, grim-jawed men in overcoats stood poised before him. They immediately displayed their credentials in the dim yellow porch light.

"Dr. Carlton Emery, I'm Special Agent Johnson of the FBI," the lead man said. "You're under arrest." He grabbed Emery's right hand and twisted it behind his back. Cuffs quickly locked Emery's wrists together. Another man charged up the staircase behind Emery.

The family rushed into the foyer.

"What is this? What's the charge?" Emery yelled.

Another agent said, "Kidnapping. Attempted murder. Interstate flight." They started to lead him into the night. "Before you say anything else, you have the right to—"

Tim leaped at the lead agent. A second man stepped forward and raised his knee, knocking Tim to the ground like a master warding off an exuberant dog. "Son, do that again and you'll be charged with obstruction of justice."

An agent came down the stairs with Emery's laptop and a folder filled with papers tucked under his arms. He flashed a quick thumbs-up.

"Call the attorney!" Emery yelled to Grace as they led him away. "Sam Callahan!" An agent shoved Emery into a sedan with federal plates. "Call Callahan!"

Tim lay helpless on the ground as they drove his father into the night. By the time he picked himself up, his mother was already on the phone. Christal fiercely gripped her mother's hand.

"I don't know!" Grace screamed into the receiver. "They just came and—yes, yes, we'll wait here for your call! Where else would we go?"

THIRTY-FIVE

The pounding in his head and the fire in his shoulder roused Scott. He opened his eyes to a rose-colored blur. "Where am I?"

A flesh and white colored blur appeared over his face. "The ER at George Washington University Hospital. Do you know your name?"

He groaned as he tried to bring his right hand to his forehead. Something wiry restricted his arm movement. "Merritt. And you?"

"Dr. Dudikoff. Do you know what season this is?"

"We can dispense with the neurologic, doctor." Scott rolled his eyes around the featureless enclosure. "I can't see."

"Dr. Merritt, can you follow this?" Dudikoff asked, slowly moving a blurred finger laterally.

"Not without my glasses."

The doctor sheepishly smiled, reached over, and placed the black frames on Scott's nose. Above the face staring at him hung the white metal-encased head of the wall x-ray unit. A monitor beeped from behind him. He glanced at rose-colored walls, chipped and scuffed by gurneys, and lined with cabinets and gray trays containing Foleys, electrodes, intravenous supplies, tubing, emesis basins, non-rebreather masks, and blood culture and phlebotomy tubes. The familiar antiseptic odor sharpened his self-awareness. "My wife?"

"She'll be here in a moment," Dudikoff said.

Scott gripped his doctor's wrist. "My kids?"

"Came through here more than an hour ago. Your daughter is upstairs and, last I heard, stable. I don't know your son's status. Dr. Drake saw him."

Scott sat straight up, yanked the oxygen tubing from his nose. A metal stand with an intravenous drip shook. He traced the tubing into his right arm.

"Just rehydrating you. You're very lucky to be alive. I understand that the other occupant in the car did not survive."

Scott closed his eyes a moment and smiled.

"We've done a full work-up. Head, neck, spine, extremities—all negative. As for the gunshot, fortunately the bullet missed both brachial plexus and artery, and just nicked the deltoid. I closed the site with horizontal mattresses and steri-strips." He crossed his arms. "Now regarding your condition—"

"Thank you doctor for all you've done," Scott interrupted. He pulled back the sleeve of his gown. "I haven't had any attacks recently. And I sure as hell can't stay here. Not right now."

"Dr. Merritt, you are in no shape—"

"The matter's settled. I won't allow myself to be admitted."

"I don't suppose I could convince you otherwise." Seeing Scott's jaw tighten, "Well, at least finish the drip. I'll see to the paperwork."

"I'd like to see Dr. Drake."

"I'll have him stop by at his earliest opportunity," Dudikoff said before leaving.

Scott sat alone, his stomach churning, teeth burning, his

body chilled by a draft penetrating the open back of his gown. He began drifting off to sleep.

"Scott?" Arm in sling, black hair tousled, complexion pale, eyes drained, Candice appeared in the doorway, and approached him cautiously, like a four-year-old with a stranger. Scott heard himself sniffle. Fingers taut, his arm instinctively reached for her.

He watched many Candices advance: the one who had opened her blouse to him as they lay beneath a tree overlooking the upper Hudson River; the one who had posed beside him in a revealing red dress; the one who had sat on the floor playing solitaire while he read; the one who had curled her arms around him as he viewed his life in ruins. "Candice!"

Her brows furrowed, her eyes cringed. "Scott? Your hair, your face—"

"It's still me."

Her cheek touched his fingertips. He trembled. She moved toward him, as if drawn by a magnetism within his palm. His lips parted. They rocked together and kissed.

He whispered, "How's Brooke?"

Candice turned away. "She was pretty badly beaten. Her leg's broken, but she'll recover—physically."

Scott wanted to charge into the morgue and rip apart what was left of the animal who hurt his little girl. It didn't matter that the man was dead; being shot was too good for him. Same for Stone and Salsbury—they'd both died too easily, too mercifully. And the others who were responsible—they were beyond his grasp. With no outlet for his fury, all he could do was stomp his foot his foot in frustration. He whispered, "And Andy?"

Candice stifled a sob just as a a a rotund man with a stethoscope draped around his neck entered the room. "I'm Dr. Drake." He held up two charts. "Mr. and Mrs. Merritt?"

"*Doctor* Merritt."

"Medical doctor, eh?" Drake gruffly asked. His expression hardened. "I'll be candid. The good news is that your daughter has a non-displaced femoral shaft fracture—"

"At the neck?"

Drake checked his chart. "No, mid-shaft. She must have taken quite a blow. As you know, it takes a lot of force to snap a young strong leg bone like that. But the site didn't require open reduction and it's been immobilized."

Scott's fingertips bit into the mattress. "I have to see her."

"Of course, but she's heavily sedated."

He stared at the clinician. "The bad news?"

"Your son was admitted with severe head trauma. Subdural hematoma, confirmed by PET." Drake said. "Pupil dilation, incomprehensible sounds, withdrawal as best upper limb motor response—a seven on the Glasgow Coma scale. He needs intracranial decompression."

Scott took a long, hard, painful breath. "The prognosis?"

FBI Headquarters
Washington, D.C.

In the closet-sized visiting office, Terrill was working on his laptop when his wireless rang.

"Weisner here, sir. We've got a problem," the agent in Philadelphia started. "The data and stat files, the stat package, that file that I showed you earlier, everything that Merritt sent us—it's all been purged."

Terrill whistled. "You're certain?"

"Yes sir. Merritt's files are wiped clean, and relevant hard copies are missing. Must've been someone with high-level clearance who already knew the exact file locations, contents, and individual assignments."

"Did you contact central archive?"

"Yes, but we won't know what they have until noon tomorrow. That may not be much."

"It had to be," Terrill muttered. "Damn that Everett!"

Emery Residence   9:38 P.M.

Three glasses of sherry had done little to calm Grace Emery. She could wait no longer. She picked up the phone in the foyer and dialed the attorney at his home. The doorbell rang. "That's probably the attorney, now!"

Tim opened the door for her while Christal took the phone from her mother. Two men stood at attention on the front steps. A third prowled the grounds.

Tim scowled and held his fists in ready position. "Who are you?"

"Special Agent Johnson, FBI," the first stated, prominently displaying his identification and several papers. "We have a writ to search these premises and a warrant for the arrest of Dr. Carlton Emery."

"What are you talking about? You took him away an hour ago!"

The Federal agents looked at each other, perplexed.

*Hope is the only universal liar who never loses
the reputation for veracity.*
—ROBERT GREEN INGERSOLL

TUESDAY, FEBRUARY 8

THIRTY-SIX

Scott paced the perimeter of the curtained area around Andrew's bed, the sling around Scott's left shoulder skewing his stride. At the double door exit of the ICU, he stopped and checked his rear pocket: Gavin's small USB hard drive stick was still there beside his wallet. The ward's steady background of beeps and whirrs made him feel like he was encased in a perpetual motion machine. A prominent bronze placard from the women's auxiliary hung above the central station. The placard seemed very familiar, though this was his first time in George Washington University Hospital. All total, sixteen people were checking monitors, reading charts, discussing regimens, or finishing paperwork for the ward. In the far corner, a woman wrapped blood-work tubes in lab orders with a cold pack, put it all into a plastic container, and placed the contents in a pneumatic tube outlet built into the wall. After pressing a keypad, the container disappeared into the wall like a deposit at a drive-in bank. On the near side, a male orderly finished placing boxes of 18- and 25-gauge needles in an overhead cabinet, then proceeded past the first uniformed guard sitting outside Andrew's room and the backup unit by the double doors. Scott stared at the orderly shuffling by him, the man's right forefoot lightly brushing the floor just before the left heel struck.

"Would you please stop pacing?" Candice called from Andrew's bedside.

Scott poked his head past the officer seated outside Andrew's space. Candice sat beside the bed, her back to him. Head bandaged, ventilator taped to his face, Andrew's body lay encased in tubes and wires leading to monitors, an intravenous drip, and a catheter. The boy's chest rose and fell to rhythmic, mechanical sounds.

Scott drifted beside her, watching her stare at their son just in from postop recovery. "Andy's little, but you know how strong he is."

She took a shuddered breath. "In all our years together, I've never once asked of you—any hunch, dream, anything. But now, I just—I must know how strong I must be."

It doesn't work that way. It never works that way. He turned away. "I wish I had an answer."

"It's been a while since either of us have checked on Brooke." She wiped her eyes. "Go on. I'll be fine."

"Are you sure?"

She nodded. As he turned to leave, she said, "I'll need your help arranging Mother's funer—oh that's right, they haven't found her bod—." She straightened her shoulders, held up her head, and stood tall. "I want you to testify today."

"My place is with you and the kids."

"Your place is in front of that committee. I want you to tell the world what happened. I want you to make everyone suffer who did this to us!"

He kissed her forehead. "I will." Flashing her a subdued

smile, he headed towards the double doors, and stopped beside the guard. "Tell your boss that I intend to be at this morning's fireworks!"

Dulles International Airport

Hope Wheelan gazed through bulletproof windows at the blue runway lights as the limousine approached their private jet. Alexander, sitting beside her, pounded his fist on his knee. Hope touched her husband's hand, trying to ease his frustration at stealing away in the middle of the night under a banner of ignoble retreat. "It's just temporary," she whispered.

Alexander ignored her. He had talked with Slatokhatov a few hours ago, reassuring their investor that he would personally squelch any remaining problems. The Russian had been alarmed at first about the FBI's impending connection between them and the Institute, but had gradually accepted Alexander's assurances. Slatokhatov was accustomed to the vagaries of ventures. These were all difficulties that they could solve together.

Hope glanced at her husband. Alexander bared his teeth before looking away. He would miss the accolades, the notoriety, the thrill of the quest. Though it might be years before government investigators would find the weak spot she had exposed, first toppling PTS and then Cassandran Strategic, for now, the prudent choice was distance. Over the next few days, substantial monies would be transferred to newly created accounts well beyond America's grasp. Surreptitiously, he glanced at her. In time, he would forgive her. And time was what they now had in abundance.

The limousine stopped. A cadre of armed guards surrounded Alexander and Hope as they left the vehicle, then quickly escorted them to the jet. Slatokhatov was a businessman; Slatokhatov was also a barbarian. Such precautions were warranted. And if the Russian did try something untoward—well, Alexander had told him that he'd better succeed the first time around because, 'I've made more than a few unsavory contacts of my own over the years, and I can afford to pay them better.'

They strapped themselves in, Hope seated to Alexander's right. The next few weeks would be spent largely hopping around the South Pacific, inspecting suitable private islands for purchase.

The engines whined. The plane began taxiing forward. Hope's hand caressed his. 'It's a wireless web world. I could learn to make the beach my office,' he had said on the way to the airport. Alexander turned to her moist, imploring eyes. He smiled.

Perhaps there was hope.

From an observation window, Krysha watched the private jet's lights disappear into the night. He glanced down at his bag, the zipper partially open, exposing the maintenance worker's cap. It had been a rush job, but that didn't matter. The sea would cover his work.

Pediatric Wing
George Washington University Hospital   5:05 A.M.
Scott sat beside Brooke's bed while she faintly snored. Sweat-laden strands of golden hair framed her pained face. The sheets covering her fiberglass cast bulged. She winced. Her eyes opened slightly. Her fingers weakly squeezed his.

He saw his daughter: flying in jetes across the school stage; beaming as she rode on his shoulders; commanding him to kneel and transform into a bucking horse; singing alone on her own podium in front of her first grade glass; reading her story of a happy kingdom ruled by King Scott, Queen Candice, and Princess Brooke, that was threated by evil Prince Andy. Images of her face, from newborn to pre-teen, coalesced into a single composite—always smiling. He found himself stroking her hair.

Scott brushed back a lock of hair across her forehead. He

wanted to remember, to relive those happy moments with her. "It's all right, cutie. It's all right."

Quiet for the first time in days, Scott's mind drifted.

He saw himself floating in the familiar clinic. The standard-appearing ICU—the generic central nurses' station with its array of staffers and electronic equipment. But no nurses. Where were they? The frazzled woman in the worn blue coat wailing outside of Room Three-Something-Something, still there, as was the cadre of faceless white-coated doctors walking through the double doors at the far end. As the doctors approached, Scott honed on the bright red embroidery stitched on one coat. An orderly pushing a gurney passed in front of him and blocked his view. The orderly quickly passed by—but the angle was now wrong; Scott could not read the names on the doctor's coats.

Something gleaming appeared over the nurses' station— something new. A silver placard? Like the one in the ICU upstairs? He tried to focus. The letters sharpened:

Presented gratefully by the Women's Auxiliary to the Norlake Xenotransplant Center, Norlake Hospital for contributions to . . .

Could Emery's clinic really be ground zero—or am I just trying to get back at him? Scott paced, trying to separate his thoughts from his anger.

The phone by Brooke's bed double-rang, indicating a call from within the hospital. Scott picked it up. "Hi Candice. Brooke's sleeping but seems to be doing better. How's—"

"This isn't your wife, Dr. Merritt," interrupted a deep, masculine voice.

Scott's heart fluttered. His skin grew clammy. "Who are you?"

"We've met, but you were, forgive the cliché-pun, tied up at the time. We have—excuse me—*had* a mutual friend, Dr. Damara Stone?"

"It's over! Leave us alone!"

"Had I left your daughter alone, she'd have been beaten to death," the voice patiently answered.

"What do you want?"

"The USB flash drive and the e-mail address and password. Once I have that, I can be on my way."

"There's nothing left. Gavin erased it all."

"The stick's in a case in the rear pocket of your scrub suit, beside your wallet, which has the paper. I don't appreciate being lied to." The voice's pitch lowered. "If they both are not in my hands within ninety seconds, your son and everyone in that ward will be smattered across what's left of the walls. I will then finish off your daughter."

"I'll—yes, whatever you want."

"This hospital has a pneumatic tube system for transporting documents. There is an outlet across from the desk. Place the flash drive and information in a tube, then send it to Station 000. Your ninety seconds begins—now." Click.

He'll do it no matter what. He said 'tied up at the time.' Tied up—Stone—black hood. Couldn't see. He ripped apart his back pocket, grabbed the stick, opened his wallet, and dug between the photographs. *Heard sounds—sounds of shoes? Not Stone's.* He pulled out Ryan's worn paper stuffed in his wallet. *Scuffing gait. Heel strike with forefoot drop. Heard it with Stone. Heard it—recently. Where?* The answer came.

The orderly in ICU!

Scott flung open the door and charged, clipping the guard outside. The man careened head first into the wall. Scott stumbled past him to the pneumatic tube dispenser. He seized a plastic container from the inset shelf, dropped in the matchbox sized USB hard drive and paper, shoved it all in the slot, then pressed '000, SEND.' The container disappeared into the bowels of the wall as an LCD message flashed: *In Transit to Physical Plant.*

"What's going on here?" a nurse yelled at the sight of the guard sprawled on the floor.

I have three minutes, max! He burst through the stairwell

fire door, attacking the stairs three-at-a-time. *Two minutes for him to check the stick's contents. One to check the e-mail.*

Scott emerged by the upper floor elevator bank, ran down the corridor, and bowled over a pair of residents in white coats. The ICU double doors opened too slowly. He overtook one and slammed his forehead into its edge. Blood gushed into his left eye. The guard outside Andrew's door rushed beside him.

"The orderly! He was stocking needles!"

The man held his arm. "Hold on a—"

Scott shoved him aside, bounded to the ward's central area, and lunged at the overhead cabinet the orderly had been loading. He seized the cabinet handle and ripped the door off at the hinge: there was nothing but neatly stacked sealed boxes of 25-gauge needles. He tore into them, giving each a half-second glance before tossing them over his shoulder.

"Now see here!" a nurse barked as boxes plopped on the desk.

Powerful hands grasped Scott's arms from behind and shoved him into the desktop. "Dr. Merritt, why don't we all try and relax?"

The right side of his face pinned, Scott glanced up with his left eye at the cabinet. In the back row sat one unwrapped box of needles. He lifted his heel and slammed it back into the guard's shin. The man recoiled, grabbing his leg.

Scott snatched the unsealed box. It was heavy—unexpectedly heavy. Ripping away the top panel, he reached in and removed two thin layers of individually packaged needles. Beneath them was a compressed, mottled gray clay, impregnated with a domino-like object half the size of a matchbook. Indicator lights flashed at each pole.

* * *

Krysha withdrew the plastic container from the pneumatic tube dispenser, emptied the mini hard drive and paper into his hand, and then stepped over the maintenance worker whose lifeless eyes stared up at him. Two other hospital workers lay strewn on the other side of the office floor. After checking the laptop on the desk, Krysha placed the stick in the USB port. He whistled a delicate passage from Rachmaninoff's rhapsody on a theme of Pagonini, timing himself as he scanned the files Gavin had copied. A moment later, satisfied, he removed the USB flash drive, dropped it into a metal trashcan beside him, and ignited it. With Ryan's paper at his side, he thoroughly checked the e-mail address as he whistled the piece's final bars. "Grand."

He closed his laptop, placed it under his arm, walked to the doorway, turned out the light, and shut the wire-reinforced glass door. Orange flames peeked out of the trashcan where the mini hard drive was burning. In the hallway, he glanced down and squeezed his black key ring. Through a corner of the wire-reinforced glass window, he glimpsed the maintenance supervisor's office.

An opened box of 25-gauge needles appeared in the pneumatic tube dispenser.

"Oh—"

The door exploded off its hinge. Propelled him against the corridor wall. Mashed the lower half of his body into foundation concrete. A screaming, air-sucking gust of fire shot out. His remnants, a hot, gritty paste, dribbled down the shattered wall.

THIRTY-SEVEN

The Subcommittee Chairman, the Honorable Senator Stanford Bannerman, leaned forward on the center of the two-tier dais he shared with eleven other senators and their respective aides. "Please be seated, Ms. Lockhart."

The Senate hearing room was small with high windows that admitted outside light from the dreary overcast sky. Seating herself at the witness stand—a long, sturdy oak table with four microphones, each beside a laptop or fully-loaded PCs, all linked by a nest of cables to each other and a giant plasma wallscreen—Loretta Lockhart thrust out her jaw like a prizefighter with a mouth guard as she surveyed the row of male senators behind the mahogany-finished dais. In the front row to her right, Barbieri sat erect, proud. Two seats to his left sat M. Jessica Tremayne, Verity Healthcare's President, scouring the room for her missing entourage. Behind her, a low-rise, ornately carved oak balustrade separated the witnesses from the near three hundred onlookers populating the packed gallery. In the back row far aisle seat, sitting apart from the flock of medical science reporters, was Patrick Corliss, the *Wall Street Journal* investigative journalist. Spiral notebook in one hand, engraved pen inactive in the other, Corliss scrutinized the room, his eyes surreptitiously narrowing whenever Barbieri entered the center of his field of vision..

"Ms. Lockhart, the Senate Subcommittee on Labor, Health and Human Services, and Education thanks you for appearing today," Chairman Bannerman said. "Could you please identify yourself and your organization, for the record?"

"Loretta Lockhart, President and founder of Americans for Transplant Organ Progress, ATOP."

"Could you please describe the function of your organization?"

"ATOP's mission is to provide a clear, reliable source of information for patients undergoing xenotransplantation and their families. Patients have many sources of information, from online services to newsletters, but much is incomprehensible. At ATOP, we turn medical jargon into clear, intelligible language. Our staff reviews the world's leading xenotransplant and related journals, and translates the scientific articles published into language people can understand. We now have six thousand members and the support of the some of the world's most prestigious medical societies."

Senator Barry Morton, senior senator from Ohio and ranking minority member of the committee, leaned over and whispered to his aide. The young man beside him nodded respectfully as the Senator's stern, ruddy face grew increasingly animated.

Bannerman said, "Ms. Lockhart, the task set before this committee is to decide whether the Institute for the Research of Animal Compatible Transplantations is suitable to coordinate all xenotransplantation research data for this nation. As the primary administrative source for the National Xenotransplantation Registry, the Institute would be solely responsible for controlling data received from xenotransplant centers around the country." Bannerman glanced at the gallery. "We've already heard Dr. Barbieri's opening remarks. He is scheduled to give us a firsthand demonstration of the Institute's databases later this afternoon. But before that, this committee'd like to hear comments from your organization."

David Price, Bannerman's assistant, stepped from behind the chairman and distributed documents to the senators. Bannerman put on his reading glasses.

"I believe you all have our statement," Lockhart said, placing a letter on the desk. She read, "Americans for Transplant Organ Progress has enjoyed a warm and very receptive relationship with the Institute for the Research of Animal Compatible Transplantations since our inception. The Institute has always been candid, accurate, and willing to disseminate up-to-date information on innovations, successes, and even occasional setbacks in xenotransplant therapy. ATOP wholeheartedly recommends that the Institute be placed exclusively in charge of coordinating all xenotransplantation research and the information thereby contained and derived. It is time that America stop putting government bureaucracy first, and place that power back in the best, the most capable hands—the physicians who treat patients with organ failure diseases."

Gentle applause from a few onlookers drifted across the room.

Bannerman checked the dais flanks. "Questions from any of my esteemed colleagues?" After waiting for a response, "In that case—"

"Sir, ATOP was allotted fifteen minutes," Lockhart said. "Might I yield my remaining time to someone who has directly benefited from the Institute's activities?"

Bannerman glanced at the scribbling reporters. "We can allow that."

Lockhart turned around and waved to a woman in a well-worn dark blue suit in the second row. The woman, in her early thirties with a sallow face and bony arms, stood, placed one hand over her chest, and visibly gulped. Lockhart pressed the woman's hand, guiding her to the table. "Mr. Chairman, this is Mrs. Angelica Marshall. I believe she represents not only ATOP members, but our wives, our sons, our daughters, and our friends who are now fighting for their lives."

With a charming smile, Bannerman said, "I believe I speak for all of my colleagues when I say that we admire your courage, Mrs. Marshall."

After being sworn in, the woman read from note cards, "My name is Angelica Marshall. I live in Framingham, Massachusetts with my husband, Ronald, and our three children—Eric, seven, Christie, five, and Jessie, three. I worked as an executive secretary for the Myonar Corporation for three years—until I developed end-stage kidney disease." Her voice trembled. "I was on dialysis. I had to go to a clinic three times a week where they hooked me up to a machine that filtered my blood for four hours at a time. I kept getting muscle cramps. I felt weak, dizzy, and often very sick to my stomach. So they put me on peritoneal dialysis—a catheter in my belly hooked to a machine for ten to twelve hours every night. My kidneys still got worse. Twice the catheter got infected, the last time so bad I almost died." She sniffled. "They said I needed a new kidney, a transplant. Ronald offered me one of his, but the doctors said my body would reject it. They tested everyone in both our families. None would work. So they put me on a waiting list. One doctor privately told me that I'd probably die before I'd get one." She looked up. "We—Ronald's a wonderful man, but God love him, he's a disaster in the kitchen and he can't keep a schedule straight. And my children need their mother." She wiped her eyes. "I was referred to Dr. James Todd, God rest his soul. He removed my sick kidneys and replaced them with healthy pig kidneys. There are four reasons why I am alive today. One is because of Dr. Todd's skill. Another is because xenotransplantation works. A third is because the legislature of Massachusetts had the courage to demand that insurance companies pay for it. And the fourth is because Dr. Todd was able to know what was the best treatment for me because of records kept by the Institute for the Research of Animal Compatible Transplantations." She took a deep breath. "Mr. Chairman, distinguished members of this committee, people with kidney diseases are more than numbers on some government statistics sheet. We're people like you. Please, I beg you, let Dr. Todd's dream come true. Thank you."

Onlookers applauded. The ovation continued as Lockhart accompanied her to a seat by the window.

Bannerman banged his gavel. "Thank you, Mrs. Marshall. Our hearts and prayers go out to you." He looked at Tremayne. "The next item on the agenda is testimony by Verity Healthcare Consultants, specifically the audit of the Institute's database and protocols to verify whether it has been dispensing reliable and accurate information on the safety of xenotransplantation. Scheduled to speak is Scott Merritt, MD, Senior Consultant. Will Dr. Merritt please come forward?"

Tremayne stood, apprehensively. "Mr. Chairman, I'm Mary Jessica Tremayne, President of Verity Healthcare Consultants. Dr. Merritt is not present."

"Do you know where he is?"

"No sir."

"And just why not?"

"I don't have an explanation, sir."

"You do have someone who can testify in his place?"

"Yes sir, John Gavin, our Senior Vice President. But he also seems to have been delayed."

"Are you telling this committee that you have no one here to provide testimony?"

"I can attest to the accuracy of my firm's work, but I'm not qualified to answer specific questions pertaining to the audit itself. Sir, perhaps—"

"Our schedules are quite rigorous, Ms. Tremayne. And since all members of this subcommittee have your documentation in hand, I don't see any need for delay—"

Six U.S. Marshals and four FBI agents burst through the rear doors. Like a flying wedge, they bypassed the gallery and deposited a bald man with one arm in a sling into the front row.

Tremayne stared at the man. "Scott, is that you?"

Bannerman banged his gavel. "What is the meaning of this?"

A man at the back of the room held up identification, approached the dais, and said, "FBI. Special Agent in Charge George Terrill. Dr. Scott Merritt is under federal protection."

"Protection from whom?"

"I'm sorry sir, but answering that would compromise an ongoing investigation," Terrill said flatly.

Bannerman shook his gavel at the agent. "We'll sort this out later. I don't want to delay these proceedings any further."

"Yes sir." Terrill turned on his heel and strode to the back of the room, his subordinates trailing him.

Bannerman's eyes narrowed as he appraised the bald man. "Dr. Merritt, I presume. Are you injured, sir?"

Scott supported himself with his free arm. "I'm ready to testify."

"Raise your right hand. Do you swear before this subcommittee that what you are about to tell is the truth and the whole truth so help you God?"

"I do."

"Dr. Merritt, you are now under oath. Please, be seated."

Price handed the Chairman a thick, red-covered text. Bannerman promptly waved it in the air and said, "This is a copy of your company's evaluation of the Institute, the audit commissioned by this subcommittee. Dr. Merritt, were you the lead auditor?"

"Yes."

"I see you don't have a copy in front of you, doctor," chimed in Senator Morton from Ohio, glancing from Scott to Terrill.

"I don't need one."

Mortin's aide handed the aging senator a yellow-covered document.

Bannerman leafed through the red-covered audit. "I bring your attention to page 423, paragraph three, final conclusions. I quote, 'We find that the Institute for the Research of Animal Compatible Transplantations maintains an unbiased, comprehensive database of patients undergoing renal xenotransplantation,' unquote. Are those your words, Dr. Merritt?"

Scott gazed at Senator Morton rubbing his badly gnarled hands, trying to warm them. *Rheumatoid arthritis. A man who knows pain. Good, it'll help him understand.*

"Dr. Merritt, I ask you again. Are those your words?" the chairman repeated.

"Yes, Senator Bannerman." Eyes fixed on Morton, "but they contradict my findings for SEMA."

Bannerman removed his reading glasses. "I beg your pardon."

"The conclusions of my audit of IRACT completely disagree with my treatise evaluation performed while I worked for SEMA, the Society for Ethical Medical Advancements."

"I'm aware of your previous report. But never having read it—"

"That's not the impression you left me with last week."

Tremayne put her hands to her mouth.

Bannerman lifted his eyes. "Last week, last week, hmmm. I do remember taking a tour of your company. I don't remember seeing you, Dr. Merritt."

"I usually remember people who," glancing at Price behind the Senator, "use a hatchet man to browbeat me into submission."

"Doctor, you are under oath. Do not place yourself in peril of Contempt of Congress."

Scott focused on Morton. "Ironic, Mr. Chairman, that I could be held in contempt for *not* lying."

"Mr. Chairman, if I might," the senator from Ohio interjected. He held up the red-bound audit report with the yellow-bound treatise. "Dr. Merritt, did you work on both of these reports?"

"Yes, Senator Morton."

"Which of them are we to believe?" Morton asked.

Scott poured himself a glass of water from a pitcher on his right. "You know, Senator Morton, a good lie is like a fine cut of marbled beef. What makes the meat so savory is the unhealthy fat that's interwoven with the lean."

"Perhaps doctor, but this room is a crucible where we'll burn away that fat. Now, which report should this subcommittee believe?"

Scott replied slowly, "The audit report is, founded," glancing from Bannerman to Tremayne to Barbieri, "on lies."

Tremayne hung her head. Barbieri, smug, crossed his arms and whispered in Lockhart's ear.

"I don't understand your response, doctor," Bannerman said.

"I said, Senator Bannerman, that the audit is based on falsified data. IRACT keeps two sets of files on xenotransplant patients. One for showing the success of xenotransplantation to the world. The other, the real set, the one they don't show, which proves that xenotransplantation is a death sentence for some and the source of a potential catastrophy for the rest of us."

Terrill's wireless, on silent mode, vibrated against his hip. Eyes fixed on the dais, he back-stepped, pressed the phone to his ear, and whispered his name.

"Cicero here," the voice responded. "I'm in Henrico-James National Bank. I've been through Salsbury's box."

"What'd you find?"

"Nothing! Absolutely nothing!"

Terrill gnashed his teeth. "Was Novia lying?"

"I don't think so. She's convinced that Salsbury kept records implicating PTS investors."

"Julian, she electrocuted the man, then tried to commit suicide. Her grasp of reality might be somewhat skewed."

"She sure as hell was lucid when I interrogated her."

"Salsbury could have lied to her."

"Or someone else accessed that box before we did."

". . . extremely serious charges! You do have proof, don't you Dr. Merritt?" Bannerman growled.

Scott folded his hands. Slowly, impassively, "IRACT's database administrator had proof. Her house exploded. My research assistant had proof. His body is missing. My best friend had proof. He went down on Flight 841. My boss," turning to Tremayne, "erased the proof, and took four bullets for his trouble." Tremayne gasped. Scott turned back to the committee. "A professional assassin forced me to give him my proof. He and that proof were incinerated a few hours ago."

King asked, "Dr. Merritt, assuming your story is true, wouldn't the genuine files be on the Institute's computer system?"

Scott glanced at the computer on the table. "They've undoutedly long since been purged from the active system and buried somewhere deep and inaccessible in IRACT's archives."

"Then you have no proof," Bannerman declared.

Scott looked to the laptops on the table in front of him. "Mr. Chairman, are these linked to IRACT's database?"

"Yes. Dr. Barbieri already testified that these computers tie directly into the Institute's databases."

Scott swiveled one PC's mouse over the table, then looked up at an overhead screen on the wall to the right of the dais. "And those screens are linked to the monitor?"

"Dr. Barbieri assured us that the screen is synched to the monitor."

"Then could we please have the lights dimmed and the screen activated?"

A moment later, only dark blue light from the screen lit the room. White letters appeared on the screen: *ENTER PASSWORD.*

"We are now tied into IRACT's server," Scott said. "Just about everyone who's come into contact with the genuine patient data listing files has died. The files on my PC, on the Database Administrator's CD, on the backup CD that I mailed to myself, hidden online in my friend's e-mail address, on the bootleg copy made with a gun trained on my boss's head, even what I transmitted to the FBI—all destroyed. Except—before Ryan Knight, my friend who died on the airline bombing, planted a piece of computer code in IRACT's system—coding that copied all the fabricated and genuine patient data files, renamed them, placed them in a hidden, protected area of IRACT's server, and bundled them under a password only Ryan and I knew." Scott turned and grinned at Barbieri's widening eyes. "Didn't know about the files hidden in your own system, did you?"

"Dr. Merritt, kindly direct all statements to the committee," the Chairman said.

Scott typed: *ALYSSA.* "Ryan's daughter," he said as the screen exploded with file names. "She died a few years ago of fulminant liver failure." Two graphed curves, similar to those Scott had produced in his mother's apartment, appeared on-screen:

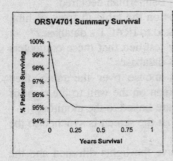

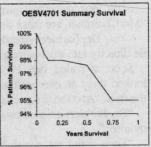

"Senator Morton, these are survival curves. The numbers on the horizontal lines under the curves represent survival in terms of fractions of a year. For example, 0.25 years represents a quarter of a year or three months, 0.5 years represents half a year or six months, and so on. The numbers on the vertical lines represent percentages of patients surviving. Could you please tell me what you see?"

"According to the curve on the top, 95% of the patients seem to live three months. From the one underneath, 98% do," Morton observed.

"And, Senator Morton, would you say that in there's a difference in these two curves? That they are not results from the same patients?"

"Obviously."

"Then sir, you'd be wrong. Both curves come from the same data from the same patients."

"Impossible."

Bannerman leaned against his desk mike. "Could this be some kind of, of—"

"Mistake? There's dozens of patients with false records in this one batch alone. And hundreds of files with the same discrepancies."

"Kindly explain then, doctor, how you, as chief auditor, didn't detect this alleged fraud."

Scott faced the Chairman. "They hid the real files extremely well. And because I was given a file containing one very key, very personal, very correct patient entry. The one they knew I'd check first. The one containing my mother's records. You see, she underwent xenotransplantation and died shortly thereafter."

"How did the Institute know to give you just one file with genuine data and hundreds of others with false information?"

"My boss, Jack Gavin, told them."

Tremayne slunk deep in her chair.

Scott slid the mouse. A series of numbers in blocks ap-

peared on the top half of the screen, alphanumeric codes in
the bottom half. "And they did it with 'AIMS', short for Allocation and Integrative Modeling System, a mathematical
modeling program that, quite simply, lets users rewrite
data." He clicked three boxes. The previous survival curves
appeared on the screen. An arrow pointed to the 0.25-year
threshold on the upper curve. "Not satisfied with 95% survival at three months? We can improve on that." He slid the
mouse and clicked. The curve on the top disappeared. And
reappeared—identical to the curve on the bottom. "Now,
98% of my patients live three months. See how easily I res-
urrect the dead?" His voice dropped. "This program was designed specifically to interact with the software IRACT uses
to compile its databases—for the expressed purpose of alter-
ing their patient files. It's readily available and easily adaptable for constant updating."

"Outrageous!" Morton declared.

"I hope you intend to prove that, doctor!" snapped Bannerman.

Scott converted the curve on the top back to its original
shape. "Behind every point in these curves is a person, a human being who touches someone." Graphs on the overhead
screens raced by. "Perhaps someone who touched us, personally." Focusing on the ranking minority committee member, "Your wife underwent kidney xenotransplantation,
didn't she?"

Senator Morton's eyes narrowed. "Yes, she did."

"And she had a bout with the Hanoi Flu, didn't she?"

"I believe so, yes."

"And she died shortly after undergoing the procedure,
didn't she?"

"Yes," Morton rasped.

"Are you certain, Senator?"

"What do you mean 'am I certain'? She died in my—."
Morton gaped at the overhead screen:

FILE: OESV4701-015   FILE: ORSV4701-015
Patient: Morton, Joyce S.   Patient: Morton, Joyce S.
ID: ORSV4701   ID: ORSV4701
Start Therapy: 1/2/13   Start Therapy: 4/2/13
Current Status: Ongoing   Current Status: Deceased
                         Date of Death: 5/1/13

"My wife!"

"Notice, sir, the second digit in the file name differs. The *R* file, ORSV, is the raw data, the actual patient listing. The *E* file, OESV, is the data that have been entered—that is, transformed by the AIMS subprogram. Unfortunately, your wife wasn't brought back to life. She was just transformed into adaptable bytes of data to bolster xenotransplantation success rates."

Morton turned to Barbieri. "You knew about this!"

IRACT's Chief Operating Officer sat placid, smiling.

Scott said, "To confirm that, you'll need to check hospital records of every patient in every IRACT patient listing data file—which this subcommittee did not commission due to time and budgetary restraints. The reason I suggest that you distinguished gentlemen examine hospital records is because they're under so much scrutiny by internal and external audits, utilization committees, and plaintiff's attorneys that it's difficult, if not impossible, to engage in widespread creative chart-keeping. Just compare the hospital record dates of individual patient onset and death with those reported in IRACT patient data files, and check patients history and physical admission work-up for confirmed or suspected history of Hanoi Flu. IRACT usually fabricated dates for start of treatment and/or death."

"With all due respect to my honorable colleague from Ohio, these are questionable numbers," Bannerman said. "Unfortunate, personally tragic in this case, but just data entry errors."

"Oh, they're much more than that, Senator Bannerman,"

Scott said. "With your permission, I'd like to access separate news websites to—"

"Dr. Merritt, perhaps you've forgotten that you're here to testify on the audit of—"

"Mr. Chairman, I *demand* that you give Dr. Merritt access to whatever he wants!" Morton bellowed, slamming his fist on the dais.

Bannerman gazed at both wings of his committee. Morton wasn't the only senator with a clenched fist. The objection crossed party lines. "Proceed."

Scott accessed and searched through CNN and MSNBC websites. Both presented live webcasts: armed national guards cordoning off a hospital with personnel scurrying about in orange bio-hazmat suits. Letters were supered over the live action: *Norlake Hospital, Cleveland, Ohio.* At the bottom of both screens, respective hyperlink banner headlines proclaimed: CDC SHUTS DOWN ANIMAL-TO-HUMAN TRANSPLANT CENTER AND DEADLY VIRUS FROM ANIMAL ORGANS DISCOVERED

Scott said, "Gentlemen, what you are witnessing is the Centers for Disease Control and Prevention sealing off Cleveland's Norlake Xenotransplant Center in Cleveland to try to stop a new, virulent, pig-human virus from erupting into a pandemic that could kill millions. This looming catastrophe is a direct result from xenotransplantation procedures, and supported by various medical specialists who, for years, knew of this threat, and worked in concert to conceal it." Turning to Barbieri, "Isn't that right, Eddie?"

A man in a gray wool suit tenuously opened the rear door. He spotted Terrill, tiptoed across the hearing room, and handed the senior agent a piece of paper. Terrill unfolded it, read it twice, and slapped his thigh. He handed the note to Agent Kamen. She read it, pursed her lips, then looked to Terrill. His eyes shifted from the paper in her hands to the witness.

* * *

"This committee has heard quite enough of your unsubstantiated conspiratorial delusions," Bannerman barked.

"I have proof, senators. Proof not only that PTS instigated this catastrophe, but that it's ultimately controlled by—"

Agent Kamen slipped behind Scott and handed him the piece of paper. Scott gazed at the note. His brows crinkled. He tilted his head, his eyes wide like a scolded puppy. The paper fluttered to the floor. He looked beyond Bannerman, beyond the dais.

His eyes fell. Focused on the tabletop.

The wooden table transformed into a polished wooden floor. A white ball, covered by white hexagons interspersed with black pentagons, rolled by. Four little boys in navy blue shirts and shin guards furiously kicked at each other, the ball rolling between them. Like a charging young bull, a boy in red broke through the disorganized pack. Arms pumping, face determined, he faked left, shifted right, and kicked the ball behind them. The goalie in blue, arms flailing, jumped forward. But the striker in red pulled back his leg and smashed the ball. It sailed, chest-high, past the goalie, between two orange cones into a makeshift net. The boy in red leaped through the air, his arms raised in victory. The image froze. The background behind the boy's face dissolved, faded to black. All that remained was the cherubic incarnation of his own face: Andrew.

Scott stood, quivering. "Bannerman, you bastard, you destroyed my son!"

"What?" the Senator blurted.

"You heard me, you fucking bastard! My son, Andrew, he's brain damaged! He's in a coma. They don't think he's ever coming out! And even if he does, he'll never be the same!"

"I don't know what you're talking about, but I will charge you with contempt if you utter another obscenity!"

Scott ripped away his sling. "*You* approved Stone's plan! *You* told her to kill my children after they got the CD! And for what? To fill your fucking war chest so you can run for the Goddamn presidency?"

Bannerman looked to his colleagues. "He's obviously delusional." To Terrill, "Have your men remove him at once!"

"They recorded your conversation with Stone, yesterday! I heard it myself!" Scott yelled.

"You are a madman!"

"Mad? Mad! You want to see mad? I'll show you mad!"

Scott shoved his free hand under the table and heaved. The computers slid off the top and crashed onto the floor. Sparks shot up. Arms outstretched, he jumped over the table, leaped over the dais, and seized Bannerman's throat in mid-flight. They tumbled over a chair and slammed into the back wall. Scott struggled on top. Sling undone, his thumbs closed in on the weak spot in Bannerman's throat. He felt Bannerman's tender flesh giving way, collapsing.

Four hands grappled with his wrists. Six hands, eight hands. Scott fought them. He felt his grip around Bannerman's throat slipping. A cadre of agents jerked him from Bannerman. Pinned him to the floor. Four attendants helped the gasping Bannerman to a chair.

"Let me go!"

"This won't help, doctor," Terrill whispered in Scott's ear.

"I don't care! Let me go!"

Terrill waited for him to take a few deep breaths. "Scott please, don't make me drag you out of here in shackles. Promise you'll sit quietly."

Reluctantly, Scott nodded. Three agents hoisted him into a chair. Blood gushed from his shoulder.

Wheezing, Bannerman pointed at Scott from a safe distance, "I want—*that* man—arrested!"

Terrill glanced at the rear of the room, and nodded.

"Didn't you—hear me? Assaulting—a United States Senator—is a federal crime!"

Senator Morton looked at the back of the room, then to Terrill. The ranking minority member picked up and banged Bannerman's gavel. "This hearing is adjourned. Clear the room."

"*You* can't do that! *I'm the Chairman!*"

The remaining federal agents and U.S. Marshalls from Terrill's entourage began quickly herding the witnesses and gallery out of the room. The senators and their aides abruptly slipped out the near invisible wood-paneled back entrance behind the dais. Within moments, the crowd's shuffling sounds disappeared. The hearing room grew ominously quiet.

Strutting footsteps began from the far side of the room, echoing from the high ceiling, approaching the dais. A shadow passed across Bannerman's face.

The Chairman looked up. "Kress?"

There stood William Kress, the Attorney General of the United States, half a foot shorter than his five assistants and wearing a red-striped tie that matched his sardonic smile. His entourage encircled Bannerman.

"What are you doing here?" Bannerman asked.

Kress adjusted his glasses and then nodded. One subordinate pulled Bannerman's arms back. Another cuffed him.

"Kress, have you lost your mind?"

The Attorney General's smile dissipated. "Senator Stanford Bannerman, you are hereby placed under arrest. Charges include but are not limited to kidnapping, attempted murder, and commission of crimes across interstate—"

"I am a United States Senator! You can't arrest—"

". . . you have the right to remain silent . . ."

"I am a U.S. Senator! Do you understand? A United Sta—"

". . . you have the right to . . ."

"Politics! It's all politics! I am a United States Senator! You can't—"

They ushered him out, his wailing protests fading down the corridor.

Scott eased his bloody arm onto the dais. Terrill removed a handkerchief from his pocket and applied pressure to

Scott's re-opened wound. Drained, Scott gazed across the hearing room: only Barbieri and a few agents remained. Silently, he watched as they cuffed IRACT's chief administrator and led him across the room.

Barbieri stopped in front of Scott. "You have accomplished *nothing*. We saw that much today before your little outburst: people value one heartbreaking testimonial more than ten thousand pages of statistical proof. They might lock us up today, put a moratorium on our work for a time, but ultimately, this technology will push forward. And in the meantime, while the ethicists and politicians haggle, people who would have otherwise lived with an animal organ are now going to die on a waiting list, courtesy of you. How does that make you feel, Merritt?"

"Barbieri, you—"

"And you know why xenotransplantation will go forward despite all of this? Because need inevitably outweighs risk. People don't want to know 'the truth.' All they want to know, all they ever want to know, is that things will be all right. You can't hope to stop that. You're a fool to try."

"Thank you, Dr. Barbieri!" a deep voice called from the back of the room.

Everyone turned to the empty gallery. Slowly, a man in a three-piece suit crouched behind the far back chair stood. Eyes on his notebook, he finished scribbling, then issued a final exclamation point with a flourish. Barbieri struggled to break lose. Agents on either side pulled back on his cuffs, forcing him down.

"The perfect closing quote to my story!" Corliss announced. "Dr. Barbieri, where should I address your reprints?" One of the agents headed toward Corliss, who immediately dashed to the door. The agent slowed. Corliss paused in the doorway, turned, and delivered a Cheshire cat smile. "Never mind. I'm sure they'll find their way to you wherever you go."

Terrill pointed at Barbieri. "Get him out of here, now!"

The remaining agents in the room led IRACT's director away. The door slammed behind him.

Scott blinked rapidly. His legs suddenly grew numb. He began to see double. A black curtain closed in from the edge of his vision. His left eye grew blind. *I'm having an attack!*

Terrill pressed against the saturated handkerchief on Scott's shoulder. Blood continued pouring from Scott's shirt, soaking his jacket, his pants. "I can't stop the bleeding. We've got to get you back to the hospital."

Scott's eyes grew watery. "I'm cold—so cold."

"Your warning about Norlake clinic, and what you've done here—a week ago I would have said it was as stupid a display as I've ever seen. But now, I believe it's the bravest." Terrill pressed harder against Scott's blood-stained shoulder. "The outbreak at Norlake Hospital is under CDC control, thanks to you. It looks like you've saved a lot of lives, Scott. A great many lives."

Scott brushed away his tears. He stared at a distant place—a distant time. "We can only hope."